At Any Cost

A D'Accio Investigations Novel

R. D. Chapman

Copyright © 2022 by Reneé D. Chapman
ISBN: 979-8-9906998-2-3

Editor: Ray Rhamey
Cover Design by SelfPubBookCovers.com and thrillerauthor

Shades of Fall Publishing
www.ShadesOfFall.com

At Any Cost

D'Accio Investigations #1

The *Depot*

We call ourselves *Despos*, a tattered tribute to our shelter from an uncaring world. In its youth the *Despondent Depot* had been a bar filled with gaiety and music and light. Now, its quiet is a soothing balm for ravaged lives. No games. No flickering TV. Muted conversations, broken by an occasional hollow laugh. Soft, soothing music played low for a shifter's acute hearing. Waitresses drift silently in the perpetual twilight, burned-out shadows serving other shadows.

It's a refuge and a haven. A bandage and a lifeline. A way station where we wait for whatever comes next, whether it's a second chance, redemption, inner peace…

Or in my case, death.

Chapter 1

I was enjoying the panoramic view of twilight through the three-paned window of my office when my neck hairs started quivering. I turned slowly, my left hand curling into a fist against my thigh. Finding a stranger studying me through the open doorway was…disconcerting. His stance and the look in his blue eyes even more so. If I was a shifter, my hackles would be standing at attention.

"I was in the area and noticed your lights were on," he said, moving forward with an unmistakable shifter glide.

Wolf, my instincts warned. I moved forward too, toward my desk and the gun in a drawer. "And you are?"

"Chandler. You were referred to me by a very satisfied client. I have a task for you."

His voice was smooth and polished, just like the rest of him. From his leather shoes up to his salon-styled blond hair, he was a monetary understatement, which usually meant the reverse. And he expected me to accommodate him here and now? Irritation shot clean down to my toes.

"I'm sorry, Mr. Chandler," I said politely while plucking my jacket from the back of my chair. "I don't do impromptu interviews with prospective clients this late in the evening and I have a dinner engagement. If you're still interested tomorrow, call my secretary and set up an appointment."

I kept him in front of me as I ushered him out and killed the lights.

"You're available?" he asked.

"For the appointment or the job?"

"Both."

"It depends on the first whether I'm available for the second."

I followed his stiff shoulders out into the night and watched him jerk open the door on a BMW convertible. The tag was visible in the streetlights as it shot away from the curb: C-Corp2. *Chandler Corp?*

I stopped in my tracks and glared at the car disappearing around the corner. One of Omaha's biggest CEOs was wanting to hire me? Really? Well, then, he should have fully identified himself instead of just *Chandler*. Not that it would have made any difference, but I'd probably have been less rude. Pissing off a powerful predator, especially one at the top of the social strata, could be hazardous to one's well-being.

***

I snagged the last available booth at *Chicago House*, one of Marge's favorite places. She had been gone for two weeks, sent by the Omaha-Herald to cover an Ameri-Tribe story up in the Dakota Territory. We'd been the best of friends—siblings in spirit if not blood—since she and her Aunt Jessie moved in two doors down from my family. She and my beer arrived at the same time.

She slipped into the seat across from me. "Just water, please," she told the waiter. "Sorry, Curt. Traffic on Dodge Street is terrible."

"It's been that way for years, Marge," I said dryly.

She laughed and patted my hand. "Yeah, but it makes for a nice excuse. Boy, the place is sure packed tonight. I had to park around back with the employees. How's work been?"

The waiter returned with her water and left with our orders for a pizza and a vegetarian calzone. Fifteen minutes of how-my-day-went and you-wouldn't-t-believe had us relaxed and laughing.

"Guess what?" I said airily. "I have two tickets to Saturday's Rick Stone concert at the Omaha Center. Want to go?"

"Saturday? Nah, I already have plans."

I leaned forward. "Yeah? What's his name? What's he do?"

"Wait just a bloody minute!" Her shoulders squared and her wolf glared at me behind her eyes. "I don't need you playing Big Brother."

"That's not what you said a couple of months ago," I retorted, grinning at her scowl.

"Hooking up my DVD player is one thing. Putting my dates through a 99-question Inquisition is another."

I tried out my offended look. "Is not, and it's only about forty questions."

"Not happening."

I laid my hand on hers and dropped the pretense. "I don't want to see you get hurt again." The devastation she'd experienced when a previous relationship imploded had rocked me almost as bad as the death of my parents.

Her fire died as quickly as it flared. Her left shoulder did the small shrug-and-roll movement I found amusing. "Live, learn and—"

"Survive," I finished for her. "Where's 'be happy' in that motto of yours?"

"Working on it. How about you?" she asked, flashing her high-wattage smile. "Got someone to go with that second ticket?"

"I will have. Plenty of fish still left in the sea."

"What happens when you run out of bait? Or it's all shriveled up?" she said, her eyebrows bobbing.

I laughed and was saved from answering by our food's arrival.

Chapter 2

To my surprise, Russell Chandler called the next day and made an appointment for late afternoon. I also fielded two morning appointments, but didn't commit to either job. I was curious as to what Chandler wanted.

Diana stepped into my office.

Discreet and efficient, Diana Kylman has been with me since I opened my firm four years ago. She handles everything from office work to hysterical clients in a professional and composed manner, including an incident last year with a client's knife-wielding husband who was furious with my "meddling." He unwisely turned his back on her. After calmly and expertly applying the baseball bat kept under her desk, she called my lawyer, police, and paramedics. In that order.

"I'm proofing Abigail Turner's report. I couldn't find a copy of Mr. Turner's birth certificate on file. You have it stuck somewhere?"

The bland voice was offset by the twinkle in her eyes. Suspicious, I asked, "Why would I have his birth certificate?"

"How do you propose to substantiate the multiple references to *bastard*?"

I swore. "Fine. Change them. Asshole, loser, son-of-a-pig, a—"

"I'll just use 'he,'" she said, letting a small grin escape as she turned back to her desk.

Diana was well aware that Mrs. Turner's soon-to-be-ex-husband had gotten under my skin. I'd been hired to find him and the money he'd disappeared with. He hadn't gone far, just across the river to Iowa where he was living the high life at one of the casinos and swiftly going broke. The money Asshole Turner had gambled away was the settlement awarded to the family to cover medical expenses from the accident that crippled their ten-year-old son.

I was still working on suitable adjective substitutions when Chandler arrived.

Scooping papers into folders, I made my desk present some semblance of order. Diana escorted him in and politely inquired if he would like coffee. He accepted with "just a little sugar." She was sliding his cup in front of him and refilling mine as we finished the customary handshake and polite greetings.

I studied him over the rim of my cup as we each took a polite sip.

The blue eyes were cool and unreadable, every strand of his dark blond hair in place. He appeared relaxed, but there was an undercurrent exuding from him that I couldn't quite put a finger on. Tense? Worried? Whatever. It had me on alert again.

A polite smile drifted across his lips as he briefly eyed the small stuffed owl sitting cross-legged on the edge of my desk, puffing on a pipe and looking through a magnifying glass.

"Excellent coffee, Mr. D'Accio. You wouldn't believe what some people have offered me."

"As a matter of fact, I would; I've been offered the same stuff." Maybe starting off with small talk would help diffuse whatever was zinging between us. Sipped. Waited. Then, maybe not.

"A past client referred you to me?"

He took another sip before saying in a patronizing tone, "Paul Solenski. He said you were professional, reliable, and discreet. However, he neglected to mention the prickly attitude. You didn't like me catching you unaware last night."

Was he trying for some kind of dominance? In *my* office?

"Did he also tell you I don't take cases I consider shady, crooked, or otherwise dishonest?" His fingers tightened briefly around his cup. I don't normally snap at prospective clients, but I couldn't help it. The man just plain irritated me. Besides, his smug arrogance had started it. "I also don't care to dig up dirt so someone can sling mud. If your business falls under any of those categories, you might as well leave now."

Chandler's shuttered gaze met mine. "What makes you think it might be?"

"Why aren't you using one of your company's well-paid in-house investigators?"

"I don't want my mother to know what I'm doing. Since she is president, majority stockholder, and authorizer-of-paychecks, everything gets reported to her."

Huh. Hadn't heard that one before. I couldn't tell whether or not that irritated him. His control was firmly in place. Leaning back in my chair, I bolted down a lid on my own emotions. This was a potentially lucrative job.

"What are you wanting me to do?"

"Find my sister."

"Kidnapping?"

"No. My sister travels extensively and often incognito."

"Does she *want* to be found?" I said, unable to resist asking it.

"Probably not." He paused for a beat, then added, "We only know where she is, or what she's doing, when we read about her in the gossip section of some newspaper. She doesn't have anything to do with us or the company, although that doesn't interfere with her spending her share of the profits."

Definitely irritation there. "Your sister is third heir and co-owner, I believe…and Chandler's natural daughter."

My hindbrain asked why I was trying to sabotage this meeting.

"I may have been adopted after their marriage," he said coldly, "but Father never treated me as anything other than a son. I've proven myself, as has my mother. She ran Chandler Corporation—now Import—by herself after his death until I graduated from college, which includes surviving several attempts by my uncles to manipulate it away from her. However, my *half*-sister has never shown the least bit interest in work. In fact, she left home before dawn on her nineteenth birthday and hasn't been back."

"She's made no attempt to contact you or your mother since?" That was hard to believe. "No letters or postcards? Nothing on holidays or birthdays?"

"No. We've only heard from her twice. Both times were to direct her trust fund distributions and company dividends to accounts she established. First in New Orleans, then to Nassau."

That was an interesting nugget. I pulled my notepad forward. "Her full name?"

"Tabitha Jean Chandler."

"Description?"

"She's tall, about five-ten. Hazel eyes. I have no idea what she weighs. It's been ten years, but she still appears slender in the photos I've seen. And, like you, she's a Zero," he added, his voiced edged with contempt.

I leaned back in my chair. Great. An elitist. "What was her father?"

"A First-Gen panther. At least he had claws and dark vision. Tabitha had zip."

"We don't get to pick our genes," I said flatly, not even attempting to hide my irritation. "You could have had *zip* too."

Zeros were humans before Mother Nature started to mix things up. Somewhere along our evolutionary history, children were born with abilities matching the predators around them. Claws, fangs, and increased senses. First Generation, the scientists of today labeled them. Then children that could shift fully into their animal form began appearing around twenty thousand years ago. The Second-Generation. The first recorded Third-Generation, a wolf and her Were-form, was slightly over six hundred years ago. The massive blending of human and animal was still rare.

I was even rarer.

I was a Zero-Plus. I couldn't shift a single finger, but I had inherited a number of my family's Gen traits. My parents and three grandparents were all Second-Gen wolf and cat shifters. My paternal grandmother was a First-Gen polar bear. While not fully at their level, my heightened abilities came in handy in my profession.

Russell Chandler and his mother were both Second-Gen wolves. Last night, his wolf had been riding close to the surface for some reason. That was what had prickled my neck hairs. He had better control of it today, but his attitude wasn't much better.

"Insults are not conducive to me taking your case," I continued. "Not being able to shift doesn't make me any less competent than you. Now, do you want to hire me or not?"

That scowl said he wasn't used to being slapped down.

"Yes," he finally said. "I need my sister found."

"And when I find her?"

"Tell her she's needed at home on company business and it involves her best interests. Convince her to return to Omaha—at least for a short while."

I kept my expression neutral as I added that to my notes. His pragmatic answer was on the same emotional level as pulling out a splinter. This was a chore to be done, however distasteful or painful.

"What else can you tell me about her? Likes, hobbies, friends?"

"You're for hire?" His lips lifted slightly in a parody of his wolf.

He made it sound as if he was buying me. I debated the benefits of a profitable case versus the pleasure of throwing him out of my office. Right now, the latter was winning. June was a week away and it was always a very profitable month for me.

"I've had several other inquiries from prospective clients. Your case sounds like I'd be doing some traveling, which would interfere with them. I'm afraid I can't—"

"Will ten thousand be enough to cover your undivided services?"

Chandler reached into the briefcase sitting next to his feet and pulled out two envelopes. He tossed the thickest one to me.

I found myself holding a large wad of cash. Well, hard to turn that down. "This would be…sufficient." Still, I hesitated for a moment before pulling a folder from the shelf behind me. I wrote Russell Chandler's name at the top and made an entry showing an advance of ten thousand dollars on the standard contract prepped inside it. I angled the paper around so he could read it, gave him my usual speech on expenses and terms, including the refund of any unused portion of his advance.

"Any questions?" I finished with.

"No, but I suppose I should warn you," he said while signing.

My eyes sharpened. I knew there was something hinky about this.

"My mother and sister did not part on the best of terms, Mr. D'Accio." Chandler made a small gesture. "In fact, they had a vicious argument the night before Tabitha left. Convincing her to return may prove to be difficult. Both equate reconciliation with 'giving in' and neither will make the first gesture."

Snotty attitudes must run in the family and explained the years of silence. "I'll be on my persuadable best."

"You'll need it." The small smile curving his lips didn't reach his eyes.

That did not make me feel any better.

My new client handed over the smaller envelope. "This is as much as I could get on my sister's interests and background without arousing Mother's suspicions. I've included several clippings from various U.S. newspapers that have featured her. I'm sure an internet search will give you more. My private cell number and an address for all correspondence and reports are also included. Do *not* contact me through the Company."

He stood. "While I doubt this will go quickly, I do expect it to be conducted quietly."

"I understand, Mr. Chandler." He didn't want Mama getting wind of it. I managed to see him out without having to shake his hand again. Returning to my desk, I stared at Chandler's two envelopes. For some reason, I felt like I'd fallen face-first into a pile of cow patties.

"What's wrong, Curt?" Diana sat down in the chair just vacated.

"Nothing."

"That's a wagon load of crap. You always flex your hand when you're bothered. One day you'll stretch your fingers clean out of their sockets."

"And you'll enjoy telling me 'I told you so' for the next year." I shrugged. "It appears to be a simple case, Diana. A brother wants to find a sister who doesn't want to be found—can't say I blame her, and without disapproving-Mama learning he's hunting her."

"Did he say why?"

"Said she was needed for company business. It appears to be an overall profitable and straightforward case, but… I don't know. I've got a feeling I should have passed on this one. Something about him has my guts out of whack."

I got up, stretched and wandered over to the window.

"If you ask me, I think he's planning a corporate takeover from his mother and needs his sister's support, not to mention her shares." Steven Chandler's will had left one-half of the company to the widow and one-fourth each to Russell and Tabitha.

I ran the interview through my head again. "What's your impression?" I asked, facing her. Fifty-plus years of experience had given Diana a normally dead-on evaluation of people.

"He's conservative and careful. He's the kind who plots out every possible reaction to his action before he makes a move. I bet he's one heck of a chess player. He hired you—despite the friction I'd have to be in my grave to miss—because he felt you were the best for the job."

My cheek twitched. "You mean he wouldn't risk pissing off his mother without an extremely good reason."

"That too."

I returned to my chair, stared at the fat envelope again. He had probably calculated on the physicality of that green wad to sway me. Well, I guess it had, getting that slightly dirty, just-bought feeling again.

"You've dealt with his type before, Curt. What's giving you indigestion this time?"

Brooding, I stretched the fingers of my left hand as far back as they'd go, then slowly rolled them closed into a fist, one finger at a time. Stretch, close. Stretch, close. She was right. I've dealt with arrogant, smug buffoons before and with a lot more finesse. What was it about him that fired my system?

I finally decided it was a valid case and my personal feelings toward the prick shouldn't influence me. Diana didn't bat an eyelash when I handed her the bulky envelope and told her to credit his account with ten thousand dollars. Cash. No check for his mother to trace.

"Call our two morning appointments and let them know I'll be unable to help them and recommend Mike's office." My old boss at Halligan Investigative Services and I were still on good terms and often referred would-be clients we couldn't take to each other. "Oh, send a thank you to Paul Solenski for the prick—Mr. Chandler's referral," I corrected when Diana's eyebrow winged upward.

I made a shooing gesture at her. Opening the second packet, I dumped its contents on my desk. The top sheet held Chandler's contact info, which I slid into his file. Next was a copy of Tabitha's birth certificate. *Hmmm.* She's going to hit the big 3-0 this October. I added that to the file, memories of hitting that same milestone four years ago unfurling briefly. Nate and Marge had taken me out to celebrate both my new decade and a new business license. I'd just incorporated D'Accio Investigations. I allowed myself a few more smiles before returning to the present.

I scanned her school records. Most were from local private schools, with one brief stint in Austria. Tabitha had been an average student during high school with no discipline problems or outstanding accomplishments. One of her counselors reported she was a natural linguist, another that she did well in sports.

I studied the black-and-white school picture of a thin, dark-haired girl about seventeen years old. She stared straight into the camera without a hint of a smile. The only other pieces of information were a dozen articles spanning the last seven years, spouting the "wealthy daughter and heiress seen here" routine common in all gossip columns. Other than fleshing out a bit, she hadn't changed much from her high school photo.

There was no list of friends, close or otherwise.

Switching to the internet, it wasn't surprising to find Tabitha was an international partier, but the low number of articles about her was. No scandals, no temper tantrums, no broken hearts—hers or someone else's. Those in her social class usually loved to see their antics on the front pages. Not this woman. I could see why her brother was having trouble finding her.

I studied the most recent article, dated almost three weeks ago in Cozumel.

The accompanying picture was a full-length shot, capturing her as she walked up the steps to some formal gala. The gown was a deep color— green?—with a gold-looking clasp at the neck. Tanned back and shoulders were exposed in one long dip to her waist. The photographer got a good facial shot as she half-turned and glanced over her shoulder. She was focused on someone off to the side, her lips curved upward in a small smile. She was…pretty. I wouldn't call her beautiful—her face was too thin. Too angular. Yet, something about it held my attention far longer than it should have.

I printed it.

The articles were mostly from seaside resorts and ports in the Gulf of Mexico or the Caribbean. The one I printed stated she'd set sail on a small yacht for destination unknown. Solo, which had me frowning. It meant she would be handling everything herself. That presented a different picture than the one offered by her brother. I re-read the article, got the same impression.

Diana had gone home for the night, so I left my notes on her desk. Fed the fish and watched twilight overtake the city. It didn't take long as it had been another drab rainy day. This whole month had been one rain system after another. Grabbing my jacket off the back of my chair, I paused to stare down at Tabitha Chandler's picture. Once again it drew me, held my attention. Who was she smiling at? Friend, acquaintance, or one of the paparazzi who'd gained her attention? What made this picture so different from the other ones?

I hit the lights, locked the office. My watch told me I still had time to join Nate at *Riley's*.

Halfway there I realized I wasn't in the mood for beer, dart games, or the bar scene in general. Maybe it was the light drizzle the windshield wipers were flicking away. Maybe I was restless because I hadn't gotten a date yet for Saturday night's concert. I made my excuses to Nate on my cell phone as I sped toward home and my address book.

Chapter 3

The stacks of paper waiting for me on my desk next morning told me Diana was working her way down the list I had left her. The biggest stack was the printouts of internet articles, some of which I hadn't seen yet. I slid them all into Chandler's file for reading later. The next stack revealed Tabitha's banking was done through a Nassau bank and her legal work by a Nassau firm. Guess it was safe to say she'd relocated to Nassau from New Orleans. Filed those too. The next slice of information had me shaking my head, completely baffled.

The yacht I'd read about was a forty-two-foot catamaran she'd bought five years ago and she had pretty much lived on it since. Never could get into the boating scene myself, but there were others—like one of my neighbors—who spent every spare minute on the Missouri River or out at Lake McConner. Maybe being on an ocean made a difference.

Yeah, the bottom's a lot farther down. A large cruise ship with lifeboats and emergency radios would be my personal preference.

"Curt!" Diana called through the open door. "I've got the manager for the Coz-Caribb Yacht Club in Cozumel."

My conversation with him was short and I waited until hanging up before swearing. Idiotic woman. Between barely disguised chuckles, he had assured me that Miss Chandler *never* filed a float plan. She came and went where and when she wanted to. I guess a boat wouldn't dare break down on Her Arrogance in the middle of nothing. How in God's name would anyone even know she was missing, much less which direction to start looking?

Where had she gone after leaving Cozumel? South toward Belize? North and west along the Yucatán Peninsula? I wouldn't put it past the idiot to strike out straight into the Caribbean for one of the islands. Yeah, it was going to be a simple case all right: simply brutal.

No wonder Russell Chandler threw it at someone else.

I'm going to throw it and his wad of money back at him. Didn't really want the case anyway. The Yucatán would be hot, muggy, buggy, and… My thoughts trailed off as my eyes fell on Tabitha's Cozumel picture.

I stomped out to the coffee maker and poured myself another cup. Ignoring Diana's speculative look, I gave myself another minute to swear silently before caving. "Diana, book me on a flight to Cozumel for Friday or Saturday."

"You'll miss the concert."

"Don't remind me."

"Couldn't get a date?"

"I'm craving sunshine that lasts more than a few hours at a time." To tell the truth, I'd flipped through my address book twice before tossing it back in the drawer. None of the names listed there had sparked my interest. Snapping at Diana wasn't going to help, either. I took a deep breath, releasing it and my aggravation. "You take them, go have a good time."

"Thanks, I will." She grinned slyly up at me. "You know, concert traffic can get real ugly. It'd be easier to handle if I was in something small and sleek, like a Sapphire Crossfire."

I rolled my eyes. She'd been trying to wheedle a drive with my sporty two-seater since I'd bought it last fall. Sitting on the edge of her desk, I watched her call up airline booking on her computer screen.

"Diana, what would make a young, rich girl leave home and never go back?"

"You want the whole list or just the top five? You know I'm a careful driver."

I laughed, shook my head. "No contact for ten years. If nothing else, she should want to make sure she's getting everything she's supposed to, now and when her mother passes on."

"That's what lawyers are for. Don't want the tires to go flat from sitting, do you?"

"Not worried."

"You want Friday night or Saturday morning? Seats for both."

"Friday. I'll sleep most of the flight."

"Not if I put you next to a snorer, the louder the better," she muttered.

I left Diana to finish my travel arrangements, confident airline data didn't include snorers and their decibel rating. I retrieved my passport from the middle desk drawer and tossed it along with Chandler's file into my briefcase. Keeping Tabitha's picture on top, I carefully folded the printout. Since it was the most recent and displayed her full face, it'd be perfect to show around. I rubbed my thumb over it gently.

What kind of woman would I find?

Tabitha Chandler liked the occasional social event, but didn't seem to need the glitz and luxuries of her peers. She sailed her own boat on open seas, ignoring prudent safety precautions. I had no doubt the woman lived her life as she wanted while telling the rest of us to go claw our throats. It was an intriguing mixture of confidence, independence, pride, and temper with a large dash of recklessness.

Not to mention that Chandler arrogance.

What other facets would I find when we finally met? And I did want to meet her. No idea as to why. I tucked the folded picture into my wallet.

Looking up, I saw Diana leaning against the doorjamb, arms folded.

"Your shots up-to-date?"

My expression was her answer.

"I'll add a stop at Dr. Gordon's office to your itinerary," she said, with a tad too much enthusiasm for my liking.

Chapter 4

Questions to Coz-Caribb dockworkers pointed me to Playa del Carmen on the mainland. Luckily, an old fisherman smoking a pipe under draped nets said he saw a boat like hers tacking north. I rented a car and was rewarded with a positive hit on her picture in Puerto Morelos. Okay, right direction. I continued to follow her wake north and west around Yucatán's bulge.

Cancun, Las Coloradas, San Felipe, Telchac Puerto, Campeche.

Every city, village, cluster of houses, and mosquito swarm in between blended into a muggy haze. Stretches of paved roads alternated with narrow dirt roads or goat paths. Three weeks of sliding in and out of the Jeep left worn, shiny edges on the cloth seat. The front tires also had worn shiny edges. Those frigging *topes* looked like they'd been there since the Mayans, although why they needed speed humps was lost somewhere in history. The least their descendants could do is post warning signs.

Tabitha's picture became worn, her catamaran better described in my improved Spanish. She dropped anchor for no more than a day or two, so I'd been steadily gaining on her. When I would casually ask what she'd done during her stay, people would get vague. Just visiting, just getting supplies, I was told. That was intriguing, especially after overhearing several interesting references to *Angel de Agua*.

Taking advantage of a paved road leading south from Campeche, I zipped down it to Champoton. I figured to catch up with the Water Angel by bypassing everything in between. Maybe even be waiting on the dock when she tied up. I should have known better. Nothing else about this job had been easy.

After waiting for two days, I backtracked up the coast. Given her previous pattern, we should have met somewhere north of Champoton. Nothing. Nada. Zilch. No one had seen her or her boat, the *Getaway,* since Campeche. I turned south again, thinking she might have simply bypassed Champoton.

In official cop-speak, the trail had gone cold.

Everything else went miserable.

For five sweat-drenched days I prowled the coast. My rental vehicle needed a tune-up, a clutch, and a new AC pump. My cell phone still worked— thank you, God—and Diana reported no sign of her on the internet either.

On the sixth day, things moved to the next level. Downward.

A nasty case of heat rash in the worse possible area was competing with my knotted left calf muscles for the Gold Medal in unpleasantness. The clutch gave out in a tiny map smudge somewhere between Champoton and Isla de Aguada. The girl at the rental office back in Playa del Carmen assured me they'd make arrangements to have it fixed or replaced, although it might take a few days, she apologized. Her suggestion—in bright, perky tones—to make myself comfortable had me muttering a number of suggestions after I hung up.

A local family took pity on me, offering a meal and a room.

Supper was a spicy, delicious mix of meat and vegetables with freshly made tortillas, washed down with a gut-clenching brew of some kind and endless questions from their six-year-old bouncing chatterbox. He and his dad also provided the post-supper entertainment on the living room rug, both shifting to full Jaguar and mock fighting. Grandmother offered me her homemade salve for my limp. The mildly pungent liquid soaked into my leg as fast as I rubbed it on and had me sighing with relief as the knots untied with surprising quickness.

God bless Grandma.

The bedroom was hot and oppressively small. The chair beside the bed barely fit between it and an interior wall. The slight breeze wafting in a small window directly above the bed did little to relieve the stuffy heat. A small chest sat at the bed's foot. No closet.

Stretched as comfortably as possible across a sturdy wrought-iron bed in my underwear, I debated my next move. It was obvious Tabitha had changed directions again. The ten-thousand-dollar question was, which way?

No. Question was, did I care?

I glanced over at the cell phone tossed on the chair with my clothes. My fingers itched. It was so tempting to leave instructions for Diana on my office machine, ordering her to arrange getting me home. Instead, I massage my temples and cheekbones. I had never just up and quit a job before, but this one—*No, Dice, you'd be giving up.*

Dammit. I could buy quitting, but not giving up. Professional pride, not ego, I told myself. Wiping sweat off my face with the sheet, I reached over to dig Chandler's file out of the briefcase.

Had she struck out across the Gulf or, knowing my luck, turned back eastward? That boat could be pointed anywhere from northeastern Mexico to Florida to the Caribbean. There had to be some other way of locating a crazy, mule-headed woman. Starting to flick away yet another bug, my finger froze as the description of that fancy party it sat on suddenly sunk in.

The bug went flying.

I hastily lined all the articles up across the bed. Ran through them again. *If I ignored the oldest as not relevant... Yes!* That was it. All those five years or younger were charity functions of some kind.

After a quick glance at my watch, I called my personal I-can-get-it expert who liked to watch late-night Sunday classics. By noon the next day I had a list of the upcoming regional charity events and Marge's recommendations on which Tabitha would be most likely to attend. I promised her a big hug and a night on the town in thanks. She said she'd rather have first dibs on interviewing the wandering heiress.

Marge had nixed the event two days from now in Mexico City in favor of the one coming up in Jamaica. My dog-eared travel guide showed Campeche had the nearest airport. I terminated my rental, grabbed my suitcase, and bought a ticket on the *combi*, a locally sponsored bus.

The ten-person bus was hot, crowded, and filled with conversations and laughter. We zigzagged back and forth across the countryside in what my grandfather would have called the milk run, delivering and picking up gossip, jokes, congratulations, and condolences as much as passengers. I wondered idly how long it would take a guy named Mateo to get out of the doghouse his new goat put him into after devouring his wife's just-planted flowers.

We finally got to Campeche well after suppertime, the driver kindly bypassing his regular stop to deliver me straight to the airport. I settled as comfortably as possible in one of the butt-numbing plastic seats all airport lobbies insist on using. I had a one-way ticket to Kingston, a warm soda, and a dried-up sandwich.

By the time of my morning flight, I was grumpy, stiff, and my clothes had developed a unique odor. Or was it me? And the day was just getting started. Thirteen hours and two connections later I disembarked in Kingston, more miserable and disgruntled than a cat caught in a rainstorm.

How fast could I get to the hotel?

The hotel and two-room suite I'd asked Marge to reserve for me were a bit more upscale than I normally frequented, but I'd earned the pampering. Maybe I'd also have a change in luck, as Tabitha had stayed there on previous visits. Plush carpet in intertwining shades of gray, white, and red complemented the subdued lighting reflected off polished, oak-grained wood paneling. Real plants provided a cool, regal welcome not even the snooty desk clerk could ruin.

An hour later, I was nursing a foul mood that had settled in somewhere between climbing out of a well-used shower stall and plunking my itchy butt onto a bar stool in the hotel's near-empty lounge. *Four frigging bloody weeks,* I thought sourly, scowling at myself in the mirror behind the bar. It wasn't the chasing that had me pissed. Patience and legwork were job requirements. Stupidity wasn't. Overlooking the obvious had wasted a month.

I could have waited for her to show up at one of those fancy gigs and then flown down. I could have taken those other jobs, enjoyed Rick Stone's concert and spent evenings and weekends with various friends or female acquaintances. I could have been—*God forbid!*—comfortable.

Noooo. I had to play Montana Jones in search of an elusive idiot.

I shifted slightly. The shower had helped mollify the rash, as did the loose-fitting, draw-stringed pair of cotton pants I'd purchased in the hotel's boutique. Comfortable as heck, the tan pants made sense in this neck of the world. I made a mental note to purchase a few more and save my jeans for the trip home.

I swirled my drink, sorting through all I needed to do before the Kingston Children's Charity Dinner on Saturday. I'd hit the yacht clubs and marinas first. There should still be plenty of workers around this early in the evening and hints of a large tip for spotting her boat might brighten up their night. Then I'd have to—

Screw that.

I was going to my room when I got off this stool. The job could hold for an evening. Downing my scotch, I motioned for a refill. Tonight I was going to luxuriate in man's two finest inventions: scotch and air-conditioning. I needed to work off some of this irritation. At me, at her, at this frigging heat rash. Tomorrow was soon enough to think about—

What the bloody hell did the woman have against people knowing where she was? Or headed? What if her lawyers needed something? What if her family needed—nope, scratch that. They weren't close. I scowled at the bottles lined up behind the bar. Right. I wasn't supposed to be thinking about Miss Chandler and her screwball behavior.

My refill arrived, one-third of it promptly disappeared. *Where was she?*

I frowned into my glass, refusing to let the small seed of worry take root. No storms reported recently, so the arrogant lady should be okay. I'd wait in this nice, comfy spot to see where she turns up. If not here, then she should make one of the next two events Marge had provided. Both of them were two weeks away, one in Nassau and the other in Port-au-Prince, meaning I'd have to work them in parallel. My guess would be her home base in Nassau, but the woman seemed to thrive on unpredictability.

I'll put out a few feelers at both and—*Marge scores again.*

Tabitha Chandler walked into the lounge. I didn't need to double check the picture in my pocket. That face had become imprinted on my brain over the past weeks. Disgusted annoyance hit hard again as she moved gracefully on long, browned legs to a table at the back of the room. *All those wasted weeks.*

A plain blue T-shirt hanging half-out of beige shorts accentuated her slender build. A tousled cap of sun-streaked brown hair fell just below her ears, framing a narrow face with wide-set eyes and full lips. An invisible wall, generated by an obviously self-contained aloofness, surrounded her and emitted a very firm message: stay far, far away.

 Happy to oblige, lady.

I needed to wind down from this black mood I was in. Tomorrow, after a good night's sleep, I'd approach her professionally, calmly and…and…*say what, Dice?* I swore softly. I'd been so focused on finding her I hadn't even thought about the other half of my task. Fine, I'll worry about that small detail tomorrow, too. I glanced over my shoulder again. *She* didn't appear to have any worries. In fact, she appeared cool, collected and not an itch in the world.

Screw that.

I grabbed my drink and headed for her table. "You ever heard of a float plan?" I snapped.

Her head tilted up as she leaned back. The eyes were indeed a rich hazel, currently holding surprise and a touch of wariness. A slight crease appeared between dense, dark brows as full lips twisted sideways into a pucker. Surprisingly, for someone with a tan like hers, the tip of her nose was slightly swollen and reddish. No sign of cosmetics.

"Excuse me?"

"Tabitha Jean Chandler, right?"

Her gaze traversed down and back up my frame without registering an opinion. "I don't particularly care for rude manners," she finally said.

"And I didn't particularly care for four frigging weeks in a mobile sweat box." I slid carefully onto the opposite chair. The dried stains on her shirt showed she'd been doing some sweating of her own.

"You weren't invited to sit," she said, giving me a first-class scowl.

I gave it right back. "Makes talking easier."

"You arrogant son-of-a-pig. If you—"

"*Annoyed* SOP. You've got the market on arrogance, lady."

She closed her mouth. Took a deep breath. "Listen, I'm in no mood to discuss float plans, sweat boxes or anything else. Why don't you—"

"What do you think you're doing, cruising around the ocean without any word where you're headed or when you'll get there?" Her eyes widened in disbelief. Hah! "Only idiots—arrogant or otherwise—think they will never have trouble or need help. The Coast Guard can't—"

"You obnoxious, conceited, moronic…jackass!" Leaning halfway across the table, she punctuated each coldly descriptive phrase with a finger-jab at my chest. "I can bloody well take care of myself. I'm not some helpless, *idiotic* bimbo whose goal in life is propping up some male's ego. Did it ever occur to your testosterone-handicapped brain I don't want people to know where I'm going?"

"This has nothing to do with chromosomes, but basic safety and something called consideration. Ever heard of it?" I took a quick drink. What was it about the Chandlers that lit me up? "And yeah, it occurred to me. Your boat's name, *Getaway*, is a big clue. It's a demand and a declaration of intent."

"Congratulations."

The transformation was shocking. Icy anger disappeared in a brilliant smile that melted every thought in my head. Breathtaking gorgeousness accompanied by a low, husky laugh sent my heart bouncing off my ribs. I was dazzled. Speechless.

"Not many people get it." She relaxed back against her chair. "And you are?"

I blinked, gave myself a hard mental shake. "Curt D'Accio." The waiter arriving to take her order for a white wine gave me a chance to regroup. "I'm a private investigator from Omaha. I was hired to find—"

"Good for you."

I was suddenly tempted to check myself for frostbite. Warmth was now glacial ice. Wow. Fascinating. The speed and intensity of those changes.

"Tell Mother you found me and give her a message. I don't need, want, wish, desire—get the picture?—her meddling in my life. Go piss up a rope."

"Uh-huh. Is that last sentence part of the message or for me?"

"Mother." A small grin cracked the mask. "For now."

"Actually, it was your brother who hired me." I nodded at her surprised look. "I'm to tell you it's in your best interests to return to Omaha on a matter of company business."

"Bullshit. His best interest."

I grinned. "Figured that much out myself." The waiter delivered her wine and moved on to a couple collapsing tiredly two tables away. "Probably needs your quarter interest for some power play."

She sipped her wine, then said thoughtfully, "No. No, he wouldn't go against Mother. Wonder what he's up to."

I doubted her low mutter had been directed toward me. "Why wouldn't he challenge your mother? At his age, I would think he'd be wanting the company reins himself." Something flashed in her eyes, too fast to decipher.

"Russell is…unobtrusive…patient and meticulous. He prefers Mother taking the limelight, giving him the freedom to maneuver in the background."

"He manipulates your mother?"

She gave a loud, full-bodied laugh. "No one manipulates Mother. I simply meant Russell works primarily the business end of things while Mother maintains the public and social relations. They're partners, two peas in a pod, each doing what they do best." She did another one of those sudden mood shifts, this one to bitterness. "Equal in every aspect."

"They didn't let you in the pod, did they?" I said quietly, watching her wine disappear. That's why she'd never smiled in those early pictures.

Her empty glass slapped the table. "You found me, delivered the message, and got your answer. Leave. Now."

"I've still to convince you to return to Omaha."

"What part of 'hell no' don't you understand?"

My gaze locked with hers. Moments—an eternity—passed before the spell cast by that hazel blaze broke. "Understanding is no problem. My job is to get you to change your mind."

My left eyebrow lifted. By the time my right brow followed its mate, the recently arrived couple had decided they had enough energy to take their drinks to a quieter area. It was amazing how many cuss words she'd picked up in her travels.

"Are you fluent in all those dialects or just with certain phrases?"

Giving me a final glare with some more advice—in English for my benefit—she stomped out of the lounge.

My breath released in a quick whoosh, taking very little of my internal turbulence with it. Chandler's warning had been an understatement. Considering Tabitha's boatload of animosity toward her family, convincing her to return to Nebraska might prove as big an ordeal as tracking her down had been.

On top of that, I now had an even bigger problem.

A PI's Number One Rule was no mixing of emotions and cases, as that was asking for trouble. Granted, there were always pokes under the skin like the Turner case, but my profession required clear-headed thinking induced by objectivity and emotional distance. But what had rocketed through my system had all the emotional punch of a hard-driven boot square into the gut. I rubbed my hands over my face.

And why didn't you stay on that stool? I asked myself, disgusted. I was constantly acting against my better judgment where that woman was concerned. Diminished capacity wasn't an excuse either since I hadn't even finished my second drink. After doing just that in two large gulps, I headed for my room.

Next morning, I left a message on Russell Chandler's voice mail letting him know I was in Jamaica. Informing him the ten-year family chasm hadn't gotten any narrower, I couldn't estimate how long it would take to complete the second half of my assignment. I managed to close my mouth before *if ever* popped out, but I sure was thinking it.

I left a written message for Tabitha at the desk. The clerk's promise to deliver it told me she hadn't checked out. I grabbed a magazine and settled into a burgundy leather chair in a discreet sitting area curtained from the main traffic flow by small trees in large pots. I tried to figure out the best approach. She wouldn't be pushed in to going back, and sweet-talking didn't have a snowball's chance. Bribery might work, I mused, assuming I found something she considered worth it.

It was mid-morning when Tabitha walked off the elevator and out the lobby door. I wandered behind her for the next several hours, not bothering to stay out of sight but keeping a reasonable distance between us. She alternated between ignoring me and demonstrating her linguistic skills in sign language.

It didn't take much effort to recognize the other guy skulking around with his camera and playing tourist as the paparazzi type. Unlike me, he was trying to stay unnoticed but doing a piss-poor job of it, professionally speaking. He watched our exchanges—her fluent hand, my amused grin—with interest.

By early afternoon she'd hit most of the shops in a three-block radius. Tabitha did buy a few items, but mostly browsed, poked, examined, and questioned. If I hadn't known better, I would have said she was hunting up new items for the family import business.

I was 99-percent certain she wouldn't leave Kingston until after the charity dinner. That gave me a couple of days to come up with a plan, so I decided to take a break and do some off-the-clock sightseeing. Silently wishing the paparazzi good luck, I headed straight for Port Royal. It drew me, irresistibly, as it had for countless other young boys who once dreamed of being a pirate.

I drifted through its Archaeological and Historical Museum, studying artifacts recovered from the old pirate city, sunk in an earthquake in 1692. I couldn't help wondering what it'd been like to see Captain Morgan swaggering down its streets, to feel the pulse of that heady, dangerous time. At Fort Charles I imagined the brooding presence of Lord Nelson standing on his quarterdeck, he and the silent cannons waiting patiently for recall to duty.

Taking the ferry back across the bay, I bypassed the art gallery on Ocean Boulevard my room's brochure recommended and took a cab to the zoo. As part of the Botanical Gardens complex, I wanted to see how it compared to our Denizens of the Wild Zoo in Omaha. The cityscape passing by the cab windows was interesting and full of contrasts. Architecture ranging from historical to modern snuggled side-by-side on wide streets, interspersed with narrow, crowded alleyways.

I noted the location of a pizza joint that I whizzed past.

***

Next morning, I decided to opt out of the hotel's complementary continental breakfast. Sitting in the dining room, I was about halfway through an excellent almost-everything omelet when Tabitha walked in. Her sleeveless yellow top and lopped off jeans with errant threads dangling over smooth thighs made my lips purse in appreciation. It also had a guy across the room divert his attention from the pool view outside the window.

Tapping her sunglasses against one of those lovely legs, her forward motion paused long enough for her to spot me and turn in my direction.

"I want to hire you."

"Huh?" No preamble, just straight to the point as soon as she reached me.

"I said, I want to hire you."

I motioned to the opposite chair. "Sit." She gave me an irritated look but complied. I scowled at the guy ogling her. He wisely went back to the pool view. "Why?"

"To keep that nuisance with a camera occupied and away from me."

"Why?" She should be used to them.

She blew out an annoyed puff of air and tossed her shades on the table. "I'm tired of being followed."

"Your sunburn looks better. Why don't you have some breakfast? I highly recommend the omelet." I took another bite, chewed. Her plan was ingenious, as it would keep us both from following her. Not that I'd planned to do so today.

"I don't do breakfast." She rubbed a finger across her nose. "Windburn."

Ah. "Maybe yesterday was enough for him."

"No, he's there. Across the street."

Her disgusted look was worth a chuckle. "Still haven't given me a good reason why." I saw the conflict in her eyes, watched it roll across her features. It was an expressive face when she didn't have it closed up. Arrogance, indecision, suspicion, anger, and embarrassment warred against each other. *Decisions, decisions,* I couldn't help thinking.

"I've something private I need to do," she finally admitted. "I'd like to keep it that way. I need—listen, D'Accio, will you do this for me or not?"

"You always this cranky in the morning? I'm thinking," I added, forestalling whatever she'd been about to say.

She closed her mouth, looked away.

I inserted another forkful of omelet and decided that sideways pucker was her standard irritated look. Studied her as I chewed. Whatever she needed to do, it was important enough to ask for my help despite her distrust and obvious dislike at having to do so.

"Since you've asked so nicely, we'll consider it part of your brother's package."

Her small nod was both thanks and acceptance. "I got your note. You could have apologized in person."

"Figured it was safer that way. I truly am sorry, Miss Chandler, as I don't normally do rude."

After a moment's debate, she visibly relaxed and returned my smile. "Maybe you're not so bad." She picked up my cup and took a swallow. Grimaced.

"Even though I'm an obnoxious, conceited, moronic jackass who likes black, sugarless coffee?" I let my smile tell her I wasn't offended. Mentally, I was congratulating myself at the first sign of progress.

She ran her finger around the cup rim. "I don't usually go off like that either. You *were* being obnoxious but," she scrunched her nose, "I think we'd both had a bad day."

"Got that right," I muttered. I finished off the last bite, took back my cup and drained it. "So, yesterday's hand signals?" I asked, tilting my head slightly.

She tilted her head. "I said usually, D'Accio."

"Call me Curt."

"You are that."

My grin matched hers, enjoying the easy-going moment. *Now, if I can keep her from doing one of those mood flips.*

"I apologize, too."

My cup froze above its saucer. Her apology was unexpected, as was the blush and lowering of eyes. This was not the coolly controlled, arrogant woman I'd come to know and be wary of. The waitress picked that moment to pop over to inquire how everything was. Tabitha requested coffee while I declined a refill.

Silence continued until after the waitress deposited a full cup in front of her.

"I was tired and out-of-sorts," Tabitha said, ripping two sugar packets open and emptying them into her cup. "I spent a week running long hours to get here. I'd just come in off the water and hadn't even had a shower." Several quick wrist flicks stirred them in. "Then there was this *other* obnoxious guy at the dock I had to deal with. So, when you pushed the wrong button, you just, sort of—you know—got both barrels."

"If you'll tell me who this other guy is, I'll be sure and give him his barrel's worth." Her answering smile caused my stomach to do a small flip-flop. "Now, in exchange for my assistance…" That delightfully hazel pair turned wary over her cup rim. "Dinner. Tonight. What you've got on will be fine."

She glanced down at her clothes, back at me. Wary. Hesitant. "Seven o'clock?"

I liked the nice mixture of suspicion and curiosity. "Works for me. I'll meet you at the leather shop three streets over to throw off the paparazzi. Remember the one selling purses and shoes you spent an hour in yesterday?" Even then, she'd come out with a single small bag. I'd only needed fifteen minutes in the place to pick out gifts for Marge and Diana.

"It wasn't more than thirty minutes. Tops."

I shook my head firmly. "An hour."

A loud clink sounded as she set her cup down sharply. "D'Accio—"

Uh-oh. Mood-shift coming.

Whatever eye-snapping remark she was about to make I short-circuited by standing. "Give me a minute, and it's Curt, remember?" Giving the tip of her nose a light tap, I strolled out the hotel doors and sauntered across to where her other personal pain-in-the-ass leaned against a street sign.

"Think we'll get any decent copy from her today?" he asked conversationally.

"Nope."

"You a freelancer?"

"Yep." I could see the wheels turning as he tried to figure out how serious a competition I was. "What'd you do to piss her off so bad yester—"

His sudden change in position alerted me and I grabbed him by the arm. A quick glance showed Tabitha and her shades moving rapidly down the sidewalk. "Sorry pal, but not today. Go chase someone else."

"Let go! I'll lose her."

"That's the idea. And, for the record, we're not in the same profession."

He almost broke free with a quick twist. I hauled him up until we were eyeball-to-eyeball, which meant his feet were about three inches off the pavement. I gave him my best glare, the one I'd practiced when I was fifteen and planned on being a cop. "Keep it up and you'll lose more than a picture."

For the second time in about as many days I got cussed out. However, compared to a linguistic pro, I considered his attempt weak and unimaginative. I let him rant, knowing she'd be well gone by the time I released him.

I spent the next couple of hours in my suite updating reports and converting notes and slips of paper into an expense sheet covering my Yucatán adventures. Diana would handle the peso-to-dollar conversions. Called the office to see how things were going and was told she enjoyed getting paid for doing next to nothing. I laughed, told her some busy work was winging her way across the internet. She quoted me my phone bill. Lord, international rates were a heart stopper. I told her I'd check in primarily via email now that I was back amid technology.

Then I made myself comfortable and waited, my thoughts wandering as the clock beside the bed crept toward seven. Where did she go? What was so important?

Tonight's invite had been an impulse. A quiet, no-strings, no-pressure evening that, hopefully, would start building a bridge between us. If I couldn't get Tabitha to trust me, at least a little bit, I'd never talk her back to Omaha. This morning had been a start. Now, can I get her to use my first name?

***

I had no trouble finding the pizza place, and a large-with-beer seduced us both into relaxing. We kept the conversation casual, running from general topics to my cases and her travel adventures. Her fury over Asshole Turner gambling away his son's medical settlement revealed a true soft spot for children and that the charities weren't just a tax write-off. That's where she'd gone this morning, to visit an orphanage. I also discovered a born storyteller. Her depiction of the pitched battle between three small boys, one stout fishing rod, and a very large fish was hilarious.

We were 'Curt and Tabitha' by the time we started wandering through a few late-night shops. Bought ice cream. Spotted the paparazzi glaring at us from his spot across the street as we climbed out of a cab. Turning to warn Tabitha, I found a wicked grin and a cocked eyebrow. My grin flashed acceptance of the unspoken challenge in those dancing eyes. Opening the hotel door, we paused, turned, and gave him a double dose of sign language he wouldn't have any trouble translating. We laughed all the way to her room. She pulled her key out of her pocket and turned.

I quit laughing. Swearing silently, I stuck my hands safely in my pockets. *This is not a date. You will not kiss the girl. You will not touch her. You will not—* "Sorry?"

"I asked if you are going to the charity dinner tomorrow night."

I shook my head. "I'm afraid that's too steep for me."

She gave me a smirk. "Not for my brother. Charge it as an expense in your campaign to entice me back to Omaha. The dinner charge goes to the charity. Ask the concierge about formal wear shops."

"I suppose so…and I do need to keep track of you," I said, trying for nonchalance. Pretty sure it failed. I swallowed. "Good night, Tabitha."

Turning, I headed for my room on not-so-steady legs. Lord, the woman packed a punch. I'd never had one hit me like this and was willing to bet the cold shower I needed that she bloody well knew it too.

Chapter 5

The room was big enough to host a soccer game and glittered with crystal glassware, faceted chandeliers, and expensive jewelry. Sequined white gauze fluttered gracefully around a bank of French doors opening onto a wide stone terrace soaking up the last rays of the day. Beyond it stretched an extensive garden, its numerous paths coaxing strollers to explore its softly lit pathways or lose themselves among the many hidden nooks. Servers in pastel shirts knotted sideways over black-framed hips moved through the guests, bearing trays with drinks and offerings from the buffet tables running full length along one wall.

Easels bearing photographs of dilapidated orphanages and bone-thin children in dirty rags lined the room's perimeter. While I assumed this was meant as a reminder of why we were here, I noticed that few of my fellow attendees paid any real attention to them. For some, this might have been a cause. For most, it was a ritzy party with an outrageous—but tax-deductible— cover charge.

I was beginning to wish I had sprung for that tux the concierge had recommended. There were others wearing a suit, but they probably considered mine a top-quality grease rag. One guy even went over and talked to the receptionist after staring down his aristocratic nose at me for a minute, undoubtedly checking to make sure the riff-raff hadn't crashed the party. I shrugged mentally. My suit might have cost less—okay, a lot less, but we all tucked our balls into our pants the same way.

Munching on something crunchy and spicy, I scanned the room from my strategic point between a large fern and a statue. Was the actual dinner itself held somewhere else? The few tables I saw were scattered around the room, and those would have to be removed soon to make more room. At the rate people were arriving, we were going to be packed tighter than a bar on half-price night. I studied the statue beside me again as I licked the last smears from my fingers.

Nope, still clueless.

From across the room, I had thought it was one of those modernistic collages of angles and protrusions. Up close, it looked like body parts being pulled through, I don't know, knotholes in a log? Maybe? Maybe it was the sculptured equivalent of those tell-me-what-you-see pictures shrinks use. I gave a soft snort. What inner revelations did my interpretation say?

Scanning the room again, I calculated the odds of making it to the buffet for some more of that spicy whatever-it-was without being snagged by someone. They weren't good. The conversations and clothing might be a bit more upscale, but they were disappointedly similar to ones I'd suffered through at countless other gatherings. The egoist still centered everything on the pronoun 'I', the gossiper reveled in detailing who did what where with whom, and—my personal horror—the sports addict doing a minute-by-minute replay of recent games complete with his 'expert' commentary on what should or shouldn't have been done.

So far, I'd managed to duck most of them in the hour-plus I'd been here. Sooner or later my luck was going to run out and I'd have to actually—I stumbled backward as a blond with two champagne flutes swooped in from the side and pinned me between the plant and the marble mystery.

A smoky-gray dress covered enough to keep her from getting arrested, but the way it clung to every curve she owned made no difference. I found smirking red lips and calculating brown eyes when my gaze finally managed to move upward. One of the glasses was shoved into my hand, miraculously not losing a drop.

"Incredibly good-looking men shouldn't be hiding in corners. At least, not by themselves," came a very throaty purr.

Uuh-ooohhh.

She moved closer, her perfume filling the air as subtly as she filled out that scrap of cloth. A finger slid leisurely up my arm as her gaze explored the contours of my black suit. "I haven't seen you around. I'm Charrise."

"I'm Curt. Ah, I've only been on the island a couple of days." I took a gulp of wine, instinctively flagging her as feline. "This is my first visit here."

Her smile was slow and predatory, her finger beginning a slide down my chest. She sipped her drink without taking her eyes off mine. "I'd be happy to show you around. I know all the right....spots."

I just bet she did. And the best position for them too, I thought, catching her wandering hand. Was her cat in heat?

A movement to the left caught my eye. *Now she shows.*

The rest of my thoughts simply petered out. Tabitha's dress was a silky waterfall of burnt gold, singed with edges of dark brown and tucked slightly at the waist. Flowing down across her breasts and leaving her left shoulder bare, it fell in graceful folds to her ankles and regally showcased her amber and tiger-eye jewelry. Dark combs, the color of my grandmother's walnut hutch, held her hair behind her ears.

Stunning didn't even begin to describe her impact. And I'd thought her just *pretty*?

"I see Miss Iceberg has made her grand entrance." Charrise pulled her hand out of mine.

"Excuse me?" If the blonde's tone had been sharp, her eyes were razors. She looked like she'd happily slice Tabitha to shreds. "Miss Iceberg?"

"Don't let the hot looks fool you, darling. She's as cold as ice. Anyone here will tell you she's a frigid, emotionless bitch who keeps to herself and bites your head off if you try to talk to her."

"She appears to be making an exception tonight," I murmured, turning back to see her absorbed into a conversational group. She accepted a glass from one of the waiters, our eyes briefly meeting across the room. Charrise might be right about the biting part, I reflected, but I certainly couldn't agree with her other evaluations. Not after last night.

"Probably needed to get off that boat of hers or, more likely, get herself off. Shouldn't take too long the way she's decked out tonight. That dress will easily slide up or down." Charrise proved to be a champion slider herself, leaving just enough space between us to run a hand up my chest. "Don't worry, handsome, I'll protect you from the big bad bitch."

What had I gotten myself into? *High society is right. They're all on something. This is the last—whoa!* I stepped backward, feeling like a fool when my shoulders rammed hard against the wall. She shifted forward, expertly keeping our bodies close. Cursing silently, I managed to block her hand from sliding south of my belt again.

"Um, Charrise, this isn't—I don't—"

"I do—in my purse." Her lips brushed my jaw, nipped my chin. "Why don't we go for a walk in the garden?"

How do I get out of this without making a scene? I flicked a quick glance around the room. "When do they serve dinner?"

"Serve dinner?" She laughed, gestured toward the buffet. "There's nothing formal, darling. People just…nibble."

She began to demonstrate on my ear lobe. My eyeballs tried to cross. Her hand escaped to revisit my crotch. My stomach muscles contracted as I grabbed her wrist and pushed her roughly away. Her temper flared.

"Look. I appreciate the offer, but I can't." Couldn't, wouldn't.

"What? I'm not your type?" she spat out. Claws flashed then quickly retracted around her glass. "Maybe I should send Paul over."

Good grief, was she actually going to throw a tantrum? A couple of curious looks were cast our way. Great. "You're going to get us both in trouble."

"Trouble?"

I stared blankly at her for several heartbeats, then arrowed back to that high society thought. "Listen, can you keep a secret?"

At her wary nod, I leaned forward. "I'm a Drug Enforcement agent," I whispered into her ear. The pulse in the wrist I held spiked.

"What, why are you here?"

"We got tipped there'd be more than food served here tonight." Her pulse spiked again. Interesting. What else besides condoms was in that tiny bag dangling off her shoulder? I flicked my eyes left and right as if watching for someone and dropped my voice to a conspirator level. "My boss is here, too, as one of the waiters. I can't just disappear." I tossed back the last of my drink

"Oh." She swallowed, smiled weakly, ran her tongue nervously across her lips. "But I don't—how could *I* cause trouble?"

"Because we're also lovers—off and on—and she's the jealous type. Very. Can you imagine what having a DEA flag against your records and passport can do?"

Her eyes grew large and round.

"I got cozy with a woman last year during an off time." I shrugged. "She still can't go through an airport without getting strip-searched and I got the assignment from hell's lower forty. I know, I know, it's not right, but who are you going to complain to?" Shaking my head sadly, I worked real hard to keep my tone and face serious.

"Oh. Okay. I think…I'll go get something from the buffet."

I squeezed her wrist, released it. "Remember, not a word to anyone."

I watched her heading toward the tables and, as fate would have it, was met halfway there by one of the female waiters. I was laughing into my hand as Charrise shook her head and backed away, practically bolting from the room, leaving a very puzzled waiter looking after her.

The chuckle died away when I spotted Tabitha. And the hand sliding down her hip. I followed it up to its owner to find a man old enough to be her father and certainly old enough to know better. She shifted sideways; his arm fell away. Good for her.

I exchanged my empty glass for a full one as I worked my way across the room. Halfway to Tabitha, my arm was gripped by a strong silver-haired, sixty-something tall matron. I was yanked into her circle with two other similarly aged companions.

Lips pursed, she surveyed me from hair to toes over her glasses. "I don't believe I know you, young man."

Please don't let this be Charrise's grandmother. "No ma'am."

"Polite and wears his suit well," a woman with short black hair said.

"I like his eyes, they're steady. Intelligent."

The third woman was short, squat and tilted her head like a bird, despite being a canid shifter of some kind.

"You taken?" asked the silver-haired woman who'd snagged me.

"Yes, ma'am. I wrote the check at the door."

The woman grinned and told me it was for a good cause while the black-haired one snickered and the auburn-haired pseudo-avian threw back her head and laughed loudly.

"He's got spunk," my abductor said.

The bird-woman snorted. "That was humor, Jan. I'm Mrs. Charles Stepherson. Call me Charlie. No, I didn't get absorbed by my husband," she added, seeing my expression. "It's for Charlotte."

Silver-hair introduced herself as Janice van Whitting. "…and this is Gloria Pettrick, the better half of Winston James Pettrick, the fourth."

"Please, Gloria, or just Glo."

"Looks like he's got a nice set of—"

"I should warn you, Charlie doesn't have a filter between her brain and her mouth," Janice commented. "She tries to live up to her foxy Gen reputation."

"Me? You're the one grabbing strange men," Charlie said chuckling.

I introduced myself, and found myself relaxing despite the polite inquisition over the next several minutes.

"So, what's a PI from Nebraska doing in Kingston at a charity dinner?" Miss Whitting finally asked.

"Ah, vacation?"

My jaw loosened at her acerbic reply. Not the expected response from a grandmotherly type. Well, she was a bear according to my inner radar. Probably a grizzly.

"It's obvious he's on a case and can't talk about it, Jan."

"So why's he here?" Jan poked her finger at Gloria.

"Jewel thief, what else? Easy to pick off someone out in that maze." Charlie waved her hand toward the garden. "Just shift out a claw and snag something in passing."

"Maybe it's one of the waiters from the caterer."

"Most likely. They're everywhere."

"I don't know. Everyone's pretty well screened. Maybe he's trailing a master criminal."

All three ladies scrutinized the room for a minute.

"If he's so great, how'd Curt trail him here?" Charlie asked.

I buried my face in my glass to hide my grin.

"How would I know? He's the investigator."

"No way. Probably snooping on someone for somebody. Most likely getting the skinny for a divorce. Anyone look nervous?"

"Just Curt here," Janice replied dryly.

This time I couldn't contain it and burst out laughing. The three women were a welcome relief and saved what had been an otherwise stuffy evening. "Ladies, please," I began, then flinched in surprise as a hand slid across my backside. The woman owning the hand continued on past me. I glanced over at a nearby couple holding a very close conversation. "Tell me, is everyone— present company excluded—always this, uh, affectionate?"

The women glanced over at the couple and gave a group snort. Janice's pithy reply didn't surprise me this time.

"A by-product of being raised with getting everything you want," added Gloria.

"No manners, no compunction, no bloody sense," was Charlie's contribution.

"Well, then, I'm glad I met three true ladies. I've enjoyed talking with you, but it wouldn't be fair to monopolize you all evening. Excuse me."

I headed for the men's room and managed to slow-leak about thirty minutes of privacy sitting on the porcelain throne. Returning to the dining room, I felt like a gladiator entering the arena and wished I had armor, preferably from the waist down. I spotted Tabitha outside one of the French doors. A blond hunk was whispering something in her ear, his arm pulling her against him. She gave a polite smile, patted his shoulder and stepped away.

She didn't make it five feet inside before someone else draped an arm around her.

For the next hour I drifted in and out the terrace doors, smiling, lifting my glass when someone caught my eye and not pausing. I did get sucked into a conversation twice more, one being with those delightful ladies again. My irritation grew to anger and moved viciously on toward fury as I watched Tabitha nonchalantly juggle numerous male versions of Charrise.

I was on the terrace half of my avoidance-drifting routine when she and a black-haired, golden-skinned Adonis came out. The creep was all but fondling her, and I could hear him, from my position some thirty feet away, urging her to go for a moonlit stroll in the garden.

What he obviously wanted was a moonlit *roll*.

My lips curled when Tabitha's eyes met mine over his shoulder. Turned away. Fed up, disgusted and no longer able to hide it, I knew I had to leave before I did something unprofessional, like put my fist through his perfect set of teeth. Dumping my drink, glass and all, into a large flowerpot, I followed the terrace around to the main entrance and down the steps. I bypassed the line of cabs, needing to walk off what was boiling inside of me.

I'd gone two blocks when a limo pulled up beside me. The window rolled down and Tabitha offered a ride to the hotel. I refused and kept walking. The limo pulled up ahead of me and stopped. Tabitha got out, waited as I approached.

"I'm glad you could make it."

"Just another hefty donation," I snapped.

"Can we talk?"

I shook my head and brushed past her. The limo pulled ahead and stopped again. Tabitha opened the door, saying nothing this time. I kept walking. We silently leapfrogged two more times before I finally gave in and climbed into the limo. I kept my gaze focused out the window.

"You didn't even say hello." Her voice was low, reserved.

"Didn't get much of a chance. It would've taken a crowbar to pry some of those guys off you."

"Yes, your disgust was quite eloquent."

I whipped my head around. "How could you let those men just—their hands were practically everywhere."

She shrugged. "It's all part of the dance. You had one with Charrise."

"Dance? Hah! It was a smorgasbord with appetizers on the table and the main menu selections circulating on the floor. 'Take a feel, take a nibble. See something you like?'" My hands balled into fists. I hadn't believed it possible to get any angrier. "You didn't even try to stop them. I guess you get real lonely living on that damn boat."

"You think I enjoyed it?" The fire she'd kept hidden broke free. "Making a scene would have done more harm than good. The press would've had a feeding frenzy and others would have viewed it as a challenge. My non-response, my disinterest, offered them nothing. *Nothing!*"

Rigid shoulders and an upward-thrust chin testified to the emotion vibrating through her. I stared, transfixed.

"I live on that damn boat to get away from them. Away from their games and their pretenses and their demands. I am, as you put it, an item on numerous menus: family mergers, business interests, a quick roll between the sheets. Donations. Money. Always money. You have no idea what it's like."

She whipped around, stared out her side of the limo.

We were both struggling for control.

"Iceberg."

"I beg your pardon?" She turned back.

"Charrise called you Miss Iceberg. She said you were frigid and unemotional." Resignation moved across her face. I heard the sigh.

"Yes, I've created that image," she murmured. "I suppose you think—"

I didn't stop to think. I pressed her against the back of the seat, my hand plunging deep into her hair and my mouth feeding hungrily on hers. Passion and desire, honed to a fine edge, sliced through me. Then she arched against me, her lips parted, and I stopped thinking altogether.

My hand locked around her neck, keeping her against me as we slid down onto the seat. My other hand streaked over her, touching and taking. Her hands were in my hair, her lips as demanding as my own. My tongue and lips caressed across her jaw, to a spot under her ear. She whimpered. That and the shudder I felt tear through her switched my brain back on.

My God, what was I doing?

I wrapped a chain around the maelstrom inside and throttled it back into first gear. Neutral was impossible. Pulling her up with me to a sitting position,

I slid away. Held up my hands. "Sorry. Sorry."

She straightened her dress and ran her fingers through her hair, smoothing it. I handed her one of her hair combs from off the floorboard, the other one nowhere to be seen. The light was too dim to make out what was in her eyes.

"Well, that should have melted a few ice caps," was her crisp response.

We rode the rest of the way to the hotel in silence. I helped her out of the limo, took her arm as I escorted her to the elevator. No one watching would have seen the emotions we had both carefully banked. Still silent, we walked to her suite. She inserted her key, gave the door a shove open, took a step inside, and turned abruptly into me. Her mouth closed on mine. My arms crushed her body against me as sensations exploded in a vortex of emotions.

I want. *You can't.*

I need. *You can't!*

Forcing my arms to release her, I grabbed the doorframe for support. Taking a deep breath, I pushed backwards and away from her. I left now or not at all.

It took forty-three torturous steps to reach the end of the corridor. My hand protested calling the elevator. Rebellious legs balked at entering the car when the doors finally—*finally*—opened. I jabbed the indicator for my floor. Only then, as the doors were sliding shut, did I allow myself to look back down the corridor where she still stood. Watching.

Two hours later I was still wide awake, pacing and berating myself. The quick foray into the world of wealth and privilege had provided some interesting conversations and fancy food. I'd also made a fool of myself and nearly took my client's sister in the back seat of her limo. The fact that she hadn't appeared to be objecting was immaterial. I ran my hands across my face.

God help me, I still wanted her. If I went back now…

I could still feel the heat where her eyes had bored into my back. I had walked away because the job demanded it, and now my pride insisted I stay away. Frustrated, flinging myself backwards across the bed, I stared up at the ceiling and replayed that briefest of instants our eyes met before the elevator doors snapped shut. They'd been stripped bare. Exposed. Vulnerable.

Vulnerable?

That's a laugh. Vulnerable women don't curse in—how many?—different languages. Vulnerable women don't calmly let men paw them. They don't—that wasn't fair of me. I had seen her shifting movements away from some of the more aggressive jerks. And she no sooner escaped from one leech than another would latch onto her. Wincing at my own experience with Charrise, I knew I shouldn't blame her for their actions, although I wished she hadn't insisted on being so passive.

A well-placed knee would have expressed her disinterest quietly and very plainly.

She certainly hadn't been disinterested in the limo or outside her suite. I couldn't help wondering how many other men hadn't walked away. So what? I'd had my share of relationships and weekend flings. Hers shouldn't matter. Irritated, I rolled over and glanced at the clock, which told me in bold red letters it was 1:17 AM.

But it did matter. She mattered.

I wanted to hear Tabitha's voice spinning another story. I wanted to feel her silky hair slipping through my fingers, the curve of her soft breast in my hand. I wanted to kiss her so hard and deep all thoughts of other men would be driven clean out of existence. A rich, beautiful, and unattached woman, she'd undoubtedly had—my thoughts screeched to a halt.

My eyes narrowed unseeing as the bedside clock flipped to *1:20*.

I could only remember one article linking her with a man, and that was over five years ago. A brief engagement. Most mentions were just that, a mention of being seen with so-and-so at some gala. If the party continued in private, if she'd had plenty of private parties, surely some sneaky paparazzi would have scooped a big paycheck. They couldn't *all* be kept under the sheets. Was that what the guy trailing her now hoped for? An exclusive?

I live on that damn boat to get away from them.

This time I heard the frustration under the anger. Dammit, I was missing something again. Reaching over to the nightstand, I slipped her picture out of my wallet. I'd studied that enigmatic smile countless times before, but this time I focused on her eyes. They were…wistful. In a momentary lapse, probably lasting no more than a few seconds, she'd dropped her guard as the photographer slipped in and took his shot.

Had he realized what he'd captured? Had she?

Who was Tabitha Jean Chandler?

Was she a tough, aloof, get-out-of-my-way loner? Was she the warm, vibrant storyteller who liked pizza with everything and orange sherbet? Was she a frozen simulation or the sensual volcano that had exploded in my arms? Tabitha had depths I hadn't bothered to look for. *Because I hadn't expected any*, I admitted guiltily. I'd arrived here with the pre-conceived belief Tabitha was a typically spoiled rich girl.

Rich, yes. Spoiled, maybe, but definitely not typical.

Linking my hands behind my head, I began to reassess what I knew of the woman. She'd had a lousy childhood, of that I was sure. As an adult…as an adult people saw only what she was, not who she was. I heard again the frustration in her voice. She'd been forced to sidestep—to escape as much as possible—the world that saw her only as a rich heiress to snag for a donation, a good time, or a convenient and lucrative marriage. Had anyone ever truly cared about *her*? How do people handle an empty life?

By filling it with lies and pretensions.

By hiding the hurt and the loneliness, convincing themselves it didn't matter and others they didn't care. They build walls to keep everything as far away as possible. Their heart is locked safely away in an unbreakable strongbox because if it shatters, just one more time, so will they.

Tabitha's wall was a lie, a façade of sarcastic toughness and coldness. She had created an image to control her life and now that image controlled her. The other evening, I'd gotten a glimpse of the warm, intelligent woman hiding beneath it. As for the woman I'd touched tonight?

I wanted more. I wanted the key to that strongbox.

Something spread through me. Starting somewhere deep inside, it seeped gently into the farthest reaches of my toes and fingers. The emotions that had flared so wildly before now burned as a steady flame.

I loved Tabitha Chandler.

The realization floored me. Where had it started? When? In Omaha, when I studied her picture? In the lounge, when she smiled at me that first time?

Where it started didn't matter. Where I went with it did.

Hours later, I watched the sun rise over the Blue Mountains from my hotel window. All the panic, all the reasons why it wouldn't work fostered by the darkness melted away in the strengthening light. Only one fact mattered: I loved her. And I'd stomp the next man who touched her into a bloody mess.

Okay, that was two facts.

I'd convince her to return to Nebraska for her brother. He could have her shares and her votes. Then I'd convince her to stay for me. With me. I'd do whatever was necessary to keep her from walking out of my life.

Now, how was I going to convince her of the first part?

I stripped out of the clothes I still wore from last night and pulled on jeans. Reminded myself to get more of those cotton pants. I grabbed an old, gray T-shirt. Sniffed it. Not too bad, I decided, and pulled it over my head. Started tucking it into my pants, my mind racing.

We'll create our own world. Together. Somewhere. If Omaha wasn't big enough for both Tabitha and her family, I'd relocate. PI business was pretty much universal. Maybe try my hand as an independent security specialist or troubleshooter. Yeah, that sounded good.

But I'm not living on a frigging boat.

Chapter 6

Stretching, I shifted the baseball cap shading my face to the top of my head and looked around groggily. I bolted to my feet, all trace of sleep disappearing. There was nothing but shades of blue above and—I swallowed hard—all around.

"Good, I was about to wake you."

I wheeled around as Tabitha emerged from the cabin.

"Where's the frigging land?"

She paused, eyes widening briefly. "About four, five miles to port."

"Port?"

"To the left…that-a-way." Her lips lifted, along with the hand waving in the general direction of more blue.

"There's nothing there! You can't—take this thing back now!"

"Why, Curt D'Accio," Tabitha chuckled, "if I didn't know better, I'd say you're afraid of a little water."

"This is more than a *little*," I blurted. Take a deep breath and stop panicking, I told myself. After all, Tabitha had been on this sea-going houseboat for five years and it hadn't sunk. *Yet,* my hindbrain snickered. I circled slowly, looking for something, anything, to break the emptiness.

"Why did you bring me out here?"

She gave me a puzzled look. "You weren't waiting for a ride?"

"No, just waiting." I'd gone straight to the dock after changing and evidently straight off into a deep sleep as soon as I'd gotten comfortable. I dropped back down into my seat. Glanced sideways. Was there a shark out there, circling, with my name on his dinner invitation?

A small smile touched her lips. "Afraid I might disappear again."

"That was one reason."

She sat opposite me, leaned back with arms crossed and feet stretched out. "You must not have gotten much sleep last night."

I shook my head. From the shadows under those somber eyes, neither had she. Realizing my hand was flexing, I forced it to relax. Clearing my throat, I said, "Mostly, I, uh, wanted to apologize for last night."

"For nearly taking me in the back seat of the limo or for walking away from me at the hotel?"

Her eyes mirrored the same matter-of-fact calm as her voice. There was no sign of the anger or embarrassment I'd expected. I didn't know whether to add relief or annoyance to my confusion. "For the limo." The other was a regret. "I don't normally—I haven't done anything like that before."

"Why did you?"

Her expression was so serious, I knew I had to tread carefully. She'd learned to hate insincerity and falseness, learned to expect it from everyone around her. If I wanted a chance with her, I'd have to win her trust first, which meant always giving her the truth.

"Watching the way those guys were all over you, and you seeming so, so indifferent..." I shifted my shoulders, heard a couple of small pops. "I guess I got wound up and…and guess I stopped thinking," I finished lamely.

"It's not me they really want."

Her wall dropped, exposing all the turbulent emotions she kept hidden. Her hand was in mine before I was even aware I'd leaned across the space between us. "Then they're just plain stupid," I told her firmly.

"Maybe."

There was a hint of puzzlement in her reply and the eyes studying me. My traitorous hand brushed strands of hair from her forehead before I could draw it back. Leaning back in my seat, I gave her what was hopefully a light-hearted smile. It was impossible to deny my attraction, but suicidal to reveal how much.

"You're an interesting person," I said.

"*I'm* interesting? You're the one that's—" She huffed out a breath. "I don't know what to expect from you from one moment to the next."

"Me? I could say the same for your lightning-fast mood shifts." Her confusion was a point in my favor. Studying the empty horizon, I said, "You *are* planning on going back to Kingston, right?"

She laughed and rose smoothly. "Eventually. Brunch should still be warm. I figured you missed breakfast."

The cabin was a couple of steps down and there was a lot more room than I expected. In fact, it resembled a small efficiency apartment. There was a compact kitchen on the left and a small table set for two on the right. My focus zeroed in on the platter of scrambled eggs and bacon slices, totally ignoring the fruit-laden one.

"Is that fresh coffee I smell?"

She motioned me toward the table and transferred a small coffee pot from the two-burner stove to a hot pad on the table before joining me.

I scraped a good-sized helping of eggs onto my plate along with a couple slices of bacon, minus the one that went straight into my mouth. I hadn't realized how famished I was until that pork hit my stomach.

"This is great," I impolitely said around a full mouth.

"When was the last time you ate?" she asked, watching me plow through my plate.

"Sometime yesterday. Oh, some of those spicy things last night." I reached for more, then noticed that all Tabitha had in front of her was fruit. As I started to bring my hand back, she shook her head.

"Told you I'm not a breakfast person. This is all I want."

"Don't you ever eat real food?" I swapped the platter with my plate.

"I believe I ate my share of pizza the other night and had ice cream afterward."

I wagged my fork at her. "Real food."

She wagged a grape back at me. "Pizza isn't just a major food group, it's all of them." She popped the green orb into her mouth, continued to talk around it. "You got bread, veggies, meat, and cheese all rolled into one bubbling, scrumptious sensation."

"You know, Omaha has practically exploded in the past decade. Restaurants especially. We got pizzerias all over the place. When you get tired of them you can try something different. You could probably experiment with a different type of cuisine every night for two weeks without repeating."

"Do you know how many different ways there are to cook a meal between Mexico City and Barbados? A lot more than two weeks' worth."

The warm, relaxed woman I had shared that pizza with had reemerged. Amusement danced in her eyes, her voice teased lightly. I fantasized about those softly smiling lips sucking in my tongue instead of fruit. My jeans suddenly went tight. I swallowed.

"I've got to start somewhere. Hell, Tabitha, isn't there *anything* in Omaha you miss?" My voice was level, unlike my blood pressure.

"Runza sandwiches."

The fork stopped halfway to my mouth. "You're kidding!"

She threw her head back and laughed. "Surprise." Two grapes disappeared between her lips. "Their Swiss Mushroom is unbeatable."

I squinted at her. If that's all she missed, I was ankle-deep in cow patties. The egg perched on my fork finished its journey.

"I like it simple, Curt."

I chewed, swallowed. "Simple? You live on a plush forty-two-foot catamaran and sail around the Gulf and Caribbean. You attend lavish parties draped in jewels."

"Simple can still be comfortable." A tangerine slice spurted as she bit into it. "And I'm very selective of which parties I attend. Which bothers you the most?" She wiped juice off her chin. "My having money or no shame?"

"I couldn't care less about your money."

"Ah, so I'm a shameless roll that enjoys public massages. You know, your eyes turn a lovely steel-gray when you're pissed." She leaned forward on her elbows, stared into the steel. "Very hard, very sharp. Like a knife. Fascinating."

"You explained yourself last night." I grabbed my cup and nearly choked on a large swallow.

She withdrew. Not physically, but there was this sudden void between us. "I'm trying to understand the man who walks away when it's obvious neither of us want him to." Her troubled eyes searched my face. "Why do you?"

"Because I have a job to do and, right now, you're the job. That's how I *have* to think of you." That hazel gaze latched on to something inside me, drawing more truth out than I had intended. "And when the job's over, I want to be more than just another roll between the sheets."

The cabin was suddenly too confining. I pushed away from the table and went back out on deck. I stared out over the water. Certainly wasn't anything else to look at. Behind me, dishes clinked as Tabitha cleared the table. Ironically, our positions had reversed. She'd dropped her wall and I'd just thrown up one of my own.

I swore silently. When we got back to Omaha, I'd give her plenty of chances to understand me. I turned as Tabitha came out and handed me my refilled cup.

"How did you get rid of Charrise so fast? I've never known her to leave a party that early or alone."

Grateful for the change in topic, I remembered she'd also mentioned the woman in the limo. "How'd you know?"

She shrugged. "I noticed."

Hummm was all I'd allow myself to think about that. Sipping coffee and relating my DEA fabrication eased the tension between us. Tabitha laughed for two straight minutes. Wiping tears from her eyes, she sat down at the wheel and started the engines. Throttling up, she turned the boat in what I hoped was the direction of Kingston.

"How do you know which way to go?"

"This magical device called a compass," she replied, tapping on a gauge. "We traveled out due south, so we go back due north. Next time, we'll use the sails."

Next time? I strained to see some sign of land. "Why are you staying at the hotel? Looks like you've got everything here."

"No tub." She turned her head and gave me a sheepish grin. "I can only go so long without a hot bubble-filled soak."

Finally. "Just think, Tabitha, of chowing down on a Swiss Mushroom Runza while soaking in a deep, frothy Omaha tub," I cajoled. The image of her body immersed in scented bubbles had my stomach muscles contracting sharply. Yep, that tub was going to get hot. Trying to head off another hard-on, I turned my attention to the horizon.

There. That dark line was definitely growing bigger.

"Hadn't thought about that. Besides, my lawyers needed a place to send my jewelry." She angled the boat slightly to the left.

Jewelry? I yanked my attention back to her, remembering the fabulous necklace and earrings she'd worn. "Tabitha! They're not here, on board?"

"Course not. They're in the safe back at the hotel."

I grabbed her arm. "You can't keep them on your boat. You'll be—"

"Sending them back by courier before I leave the island," she interrupted. She yanked her arm away, annoyed. "I'm not stupid. I only keep a few inexpensive pieces with me and the rest in a Nassau bank box. When I want something, I send for it."

I relaxed, massaged my neck. "And that knock-out dress you had on?"

A small smile tugged at the corners of her lips. "That's different. I had the aft bedroom converted into a closet. I…occasionally dress for dinner. Give Poseidon a treat."

I kept the anger hidden that shy confession sent pulsing through me. Anger that she'd been driven into such solitude, forced to hide away. *I'll never let anyone hurt her again,* I vowed.

We made it back without sinking, swamping, or whatever else they called a drowning situation. My high school baseball days came in handy as I threw the lines Tabitha indicated to the dockhand waiting to help us park. Dock. Whichever. He gave a thumbs-up and a wave before moving off.

I felt unashamedly relieved once my feet were on something solid. Tabitha leapt onto the dock. Swayed. My arms closed firmly around her.

"Tabitha?"

"It's nothing…just tired. I haven't had much sleep the last few days."

Her forehead was pressed against my chest, her hands caught between our bodies. I gently massaged the small of her back as she steadied, and I basked in the knowledge that she didn't push me away.

After a minute or so, her head raised. "Thanks."

"Any time."

I couldn't stop my fingers from tracing her lips. And the firm chin. Or the soft cheek. Surprise widened her eyes as something unreadable flashed in their depths. This time it was her pushing away, her hands going into her pockets.

I figured that was a good place for mine, too. "Sure you're all right?"

"Yeah. Sorry about the scare. With the boat, I mean. I wanted to spend some time—you know, just talk." She made a face. "Where you couldn't walk away."

I nodded. "You should go back to the hotel and lay down for a while."

"Maybe later, I have some things to do first."

We stood facing each other, mirror images of polite small talk with hands in our pockets. I saw her lips start twitching, felt mine start too. We burst out laughing simultaneously.

"This is ridiculous," I said, chuckling. "How about dinner tonight, in the hotel restaurant after you've rested? I'll go over Omaha's fine points and make my pitch about all the things you'll miss by not going back."

And that makes it a billable business dinner, I lied to myself.

***

I let out a string of oaths, irritated as the firm knock came yet again. And I ignored it yet again. I had less than an hour before meeting Tabitha for dinner and was about to step into the shower. Whoever was at the door—

Rap-rap-BAM!

The knuckle-fist combo was too aggressive to ignore. Pulling on a robe, I stomped to the door. Yanked it open. "What the fr-fr-fr…"

It was Tabitha, with unrestrained breasts outlined in sheer silk and holding up a wine bottle.

"Are you going to invite me in or stand there and gape?"

My mouth closed with an audible snap. I stepped back, fumbled the door closed behind her. The blouse was a deep, rich blue and, *oh God,* draped even lower in back on its two thin straps than the front. Her perfume as she passed was a soft, rain-fresh breeze that rammed my senses with a one-two punch. *Say something.*

"Umm, feeling better?" Ouch. Could I sound any dumber?

"Yes." Black shin-length pants slid smoothly over her legs as she walked to the small bar. They pulled snuggly across her hips, spiking my pulse as she bent over and placed the bottle in the small refrigerator.

"You're early." *Yep, dumber.*

"Yes." She slid her open-heeled sandals off.

I need some distance. I need some pants. I walked over to the TV, grabbed the control and muted the local channel's weatherman. "Looks like good weather again tomorrow."

"We'll go sailing. It's an incredible experience."

"Sure. Ah, can we keep the shoreline in sight?" Bedroom. Pants. That way. Move feet. But I was mesmerized by her steady gaze.

She sauntered over, took the remote from my limp fingers and flipped it into a chair. "You like new experiences?"

Her husky tone sent my pulse into overdrive. I took a step backward, shoving my hands into my robe pockets. "The wine. Why did you bring wine?" Cracks spidered across my defensive wall, spitting chips at my feet.

"Champagne. So we could celebrate."

"Celebrate?"

"The completion of your assignment. Job's over. Finished."

My brain went blank. What was she talking about?

"I'll need a few weeks to make arrangements, but I've decided to return to Omaha." She ran her hands up the front of my robe. "With you."

I swallowed, hard. "That's...that's great. I'm sure your brother will— with me?"

Her fingers were trailing down both of my arms. "Is that water I hear?"

"Water? The shower." I jammed a hand into my hair, grabbed a handful and pulled.

"How about I scrub your back for you?"

I snagged her hands before they made it under my robe. "Tabitha, please,

I can't—why are you doing this?"

"Because I'm no longer 'the job.' Because I want you, as I know you want me." She twisted her hands free, grabbed hold of my forearms and yanked me to her with surprising strength. The kiss was hard, hot, full of promise, and had my emotions spinning wildly by the time she released me.

Taking several steps backward, she turned and stripped off her blouse in a single fluid movement. Negligently tossed it…somewhere. I never knew a smooth, bare back could be so erotic or arousing, but hers blasted my remaining defenses into subatomic particles. She strolled across the room and, just as leisurely, began to slide her pants down her hips. Her head turned, her lips curved upward, and our eyes locked over her shoulder right before she vanished through the bedroom door.

I needed several deep breaths before trusting my legs enough to follow her trail. I stepped over the pants halfway across the bedroom. A small strip of lace dangled from the bathroom doorknob. I pushed it open.

The air was thick and steamy, condensation trails snaking down the sink's porcelain side. Above it…I stared at the short message she'd written in the fog blinding the mirror. The shower curtain parted. Tabitha stood with one hand on the curtain, the other one curled around the showerhead as water cascaded over her.

A sultry fire burned in her eyes, her lips parted. "Are you coming?"

My robe hit the floor.

Chapter 7

"Tabitha! I'd like to get to Omaha before dark."

A low laugh drifted out from the bathroom. "I'm almost ready."

I walked over to stare at the Kansas City skyline outside the hotel window. The drone of a hair dryer behind me punctuated just how drastically my life had changed over the past month. No dream could've turned out better.

I'd planned on being professional, waiting until we got back to Omaha before pursuing a relationship. There was no doubt we'd become lovers, but I had expected to have to work hard for the more permanent one I craved. Tabitha... Well, she had fallen just as hard and fast and hadn't even contemplated waiting.

I grinned. What was a man to do when a beautiful, sexy woman set out to seduce him? Writes *LOVE YOU* on a steamed-up mirror? The memory of Tabitha's body pressed firmly between mine and the shower tile, our bodies moving in joined rhythm, had my pulse doing a quick tap dance.

Whoa, boy, you need to think of something else.

Like being shanghaied. When the *Getaway* left Kingston—without a bloody float plan—three days later, I'd been on board as a very nervous first mate. No complaints, though, about the excellent fringe benefits that went with the position. Several positions, actually.

I owed her brother more than a refund.

Worry tightened my jaw, remembering the wall Tabitha flung up whenever talk turned to her family. Why should—*Cool it, Dice. She'll tell you when she's ready.* Or when I managed to sneak it out of her. She'd find that was one of the disadvantages of being involved with an expert investigator.

Warm arms encircled my waist.

"I don't know if I'm ready to go."

There it was again. I turned, wrapped my arms around her. "I don't see any reason for your mother to come into it since Russell handles all the business stuff. You can deal with your brother from nine to five in his office or wherever else is necessary. Other than that," I tapped her nose playfully, "put both of them on ignore and do whatever you want. Within reason."

She laughed, snuggled closer. "I'm looking forward to the luncheon date with your friend. I like her."

"Marge likes you, too. She's bouncing off the walls to meet you." We'd had several phone conversations over the past weeks, although Tabitha and I were holding off the best news until in person.

I stroked her hair, enjoying the quiet wonder of the moment. "And there's those specialists the Nassau doctors recommended. My secretary has set up your first appointment." I laughed at the face she made.

She pulled away, began fitting her toilet items into the suitcase on the second bed. After a moment, she said, "My hemochromatosis honestly doesn't bother you?"

"Course not." I glanced around the room, checking for anything left out. "Yours got caught before there was any major damage. It's something we'll need to be careful about to keep it under control."

"It's hereditary." The loud zipping sound as she closed her suitcase almost hid her soft reply.

I pulled her to me. Tilting her chin upward, I looked into those worried hazel depths. "If everyone with diabetes," I replied just as softly, "or migraines or ingrown toe nails didn't have children because they were afraid of passing it on, there wouldn't be a population problem. We know now what to watch for. The blood disorder you've developed, my love, requires getting the gene from both parents. Even if testing shows I do carry it, which is highly unlikely, yearly checkups will catch it early. For all of us." We both wanted children.

Hemochromatosis. We'd researched everything we could find on it since her shocking diagnosis ten days ago. I could now spell it and converse semi-lucidly about it with the doctor. "If I hadn't insisted you see a doctor, you'd still be ignoring the fatigue and aching joints."

Tabitha sighed. "I know. Russ and Mother will need to have tests, too." Her brow creased slightly. "I have no clue about Russ' biological father or Mother's parents. She rarely talked about any of them. I don't know much about Father's relatives, either."

"Stop worrying." I kissed her nose lightly. "Everything will be fine. If Omaha's medical system wasn't one of the best, I wouldn't trust you to them."

She smiled and kissed me back. I slid one hand up to her neck, the other down to her waist. Changing the angle and intensity of the kiss, I shifted her backwards.

"We're supposed to be leaving," she murmured from under my lips.

"This won't take long." My pulse was already pounding as we fell across the bed.

It didn't. A short time later, I was using my comb to straighten out her hair. Tabitha gave me one of her raised-eyebrow 'say what?' looks.

"Your after-sex sexy look is for private viewing only," I told her. I gave her forehead a kiss, tossed the comb into a side pocket of my suitcase, and zipped it shut. Giving the room a last glance, we headed down to the lobby. Five minutes after that, we were outside the hotel and I was asking the doorman to signal a cab.

The events that followed, in agonizing slow motion, were permanently seared into my brain.

…Images. I'm standing under a blazing hot sun. A gray Honda creeping down the inside lane pauses, catches my eye. I see a man, see the glint of blue steel in his hand. I turn to warn and protect, but her body is jerking backward with each impact. My shoulder explodes in pain, then my side. I follow her to the concrete.

…Sounds. Screaming tires, screaming people. Gunfire. Profanity from the doorman crouched behind a concrete flower urn. A whimper from the blood-soaked bundle beside me. I feel her shudders as I pull her close. Her eyes flicker open; her lips curve upward. The faintest touch of fingertips on my jaw. Her whisper brushes my ear, then she goes limp. I follow her into darkness.

Chapter 8

I was floundering in an ocean of darkness. *Up!* beat into my brain as another black wave swamped me.

"Damn it, Curt, wake *up!* Open your eyes."

The voice was a lifeline swirling out of the darkness, an anchor I grabbed in desperation. Darkness surged, then reluctantly receded when I refused to relinquish my hold. My eyelids lifted reluctantly, dropped back down. It took several tries before I could keep them open. A blurry, brown-haired woman leaned over me.

"Marge?" It was more an exhaled sigh than whisper.

Her head dropped, soft hair sweeping across my arm. I wanted to stroke it, but it took all my energy to whisper a simple question.

"You've had major surgery," Marge mumbled into my arm. Her head came back into view, her face steadying into focus. "Two bullet wounds. For three days you've—Oh God, Curt!" Her hand tightened, briefly, painfully, on my forearm. "I was so afraid you wouldn't make it either."

Either. Noooo!

I was unaware of my scream, of the machine's loud beeping, or the doctor running into the room. Memory was a searing agony as I spiraled back into darkness. I didn't struggle. I let it pull me back into the painless depths where Tabitha still smiled. Still lived.

***

Voices. Was that my name? I ignored it and floated away. Dreamed. Dreams didn't hurt.

***

After a brief struggle, I got my eyes open. Diana sitting in a chair and reading a magazine wavered into view.

She glanced over, put it aside. "Well, it's about time."

"Huh?" Was that croak me? My brain was groggy, my arms felt like fifty-pound sacks of concrete. My gaze drifted. Bed. I-V. *Hospital.* I latched onto the bed tray at my feet. A water bottle sitting there suddenly intensified my dry throat. Forget dry, it was sandpaper.

"You've been out of ICU for almost a week, Curt."

I licked my lips, unable to take my eyes off the bottle. Dimly-remembered lights and voices floated through my head. "They moved me to Omaha?"

"No." She got up and rolled the tray until it hung over my stomach. She lifted the water to my lips.

I sucked several deep draws of pure wet pleasure through the straw, spreading the wealth over parched lips with several sweeps of my tongue. "Thanks." I licked my lips again. "You didn't need to come here."

"I wasn't the first one."

My eyelids drifted downward. Remembered the feel of hair. "Marge. Marge was here."

"Yes. I sent her home yesterday."

A noise floated past me. *Bottle hitting tray hard,* my brain supplied.

"I watched her fall apart. She makes a lousy drunk."

I peeled my eyelids back up. "Marge never gets drunk." Not even when suicidal.

Diana folded her arms and stared at me. Somehow that expressionless face managed to convey extreme dissatisfaction. I picked at the blanket lying across me, did a couple of the corner-of-the-eye glances my mother always hated and finally avoided her gaze altogether by letting my eyelids drop again.

Marge got drunk…why?

I forced my eyes open to ask the question I knew she was waiting for, but she was gone. The room was in near darkness and the I-V wasn't in my arm. Talk about going out like a light. Then Diana walked back in, setting a fresh bottle of water on the tray and turning on the light above my bed.

"Why did she? Get drunk?" I asked, as if it'd been minutes instead of hours.

"She handled the shooting and the surgery. She dealt with ICU and the very real possibility of you dying. What Marge couldn't handle, what she couldn't deal with, was watching you will yourself into oblivion. Especially after beating everything else. The doctors are amazed at your rate of stabilization."

Stable? Medically, maybe.

"Ready to face the world?" Diana said, fluffing the pillow edges around my head.

"Not really," I muttered.

Diana hit the button on my bed control to angle it upward. Then she grabbed and fluffed a pillow from the other bed.

"How bad?" I asked, as she carefully positioned it behind me.

"Bad, Curt. You lost blood as fast as they pumped it in and had your heart jump-started twice. You've been flat on your back eating nothing but I-Vs for almost two weeks. A five-year-old could beat you in arm wrestling right now."

It was humiliating, but true. It was an effort just to hold my head up. I closed my eyes. "It hurts, Diana," I whispered. "She's gone."

"I know, Curt, I know. Treasure the time you had and the memories you made." She leaned forward, gripping my chin and holding my eyes with hers. "And live," she told me in a hard voice I'd never heard from her. "Live to spite them, live to look the bastards in the eyes when they're sent to rot in prison."

She dropped her hand to mine, squeezed it. "Rest now. I'll be back tomorrow."

I stared in surprise at the door closing behind her. Diana had never spoken to me—never touched me like that before. Shaking my head, I tried to find a comfortable position. There wasn't one. Didn't take much exploring to figure out where I'd been hit. The bandages were the second clue, the first being the dull throb radiating out from my right shoulder and left side.

The pain in my body was nothing compared to the one in my heart. *Live.* Apparently I was. *Look the bastards in the eyes.* Anger, hot and lethal, surged through me. Damn right I would, I swore.

The grogginess was gone by the next morning, although the effort it took to lift anything made me avoid it as much as possible. The two men entering my room shortly after a bland breakfast were easily identifiable as police detectives. The younger one positioned himself at the foot of my bed. Was he expecting me to get up and run?

"Mr. D'Accio, I'm Detective Caldwell. This is Detective Smith. Honest," he added, in response to my look. Smith gave me a friendly grin and flipped open his notebook. "We'd like to—"

"What have you found out?" I interrupted rudely.

Caldwell opened his notebook. "Curt Sebastian D'Accio. Age thirty-four, six feet even, eyes gray, hair dark brown. A southpaw Zero. No siblings. Pet dog named Swabby died when you were sixteen; you were devastated. You were severely injured in the vehicular accident at age eighteen that killed both your parents. Three years of surgeries and physical therapy. You spent almost two years trying to convince several state patrols, the U.S. military, and the Omaha Police Department to hire you. You were turned down by all due to before-mentioned injuries."

"I wasn't talking about me," I snapped, biting back a curse.

He spared me a glance then back to his notes. "You then worked various odd jobs, including bouncer, while getting an Associate in Criminal Justice. Then wasted another year trying for a law enforcement job again. Did a year apprenticeship with Halligan Investigative Services in Omaha before being licensed in Nebraska and Iowa as a private investigator seven years ago. You opened your own office four years ago. You like to play darts and pool at *Riley's Pub.* Never been in trouble with the law or a woman."

He snapped his book shut. "How'd I do?"

"Everything but my underwear size," I replied sourly.

"Thirty-four."

I'm not sure what my expression held, but Smith abruptly scratched his nose. There was probably a grin hid behind his hand.

Caldwell chuckled. "You look about the same size as me. Although I bet you've gone down a size or two now."

I let out a breath and made myself relax. "I didn't mean to be rude. Sorry."

"Truthfully, we don't have a whole lot on this case. The vehicle used was a gray Honda Roadster, stolen from the airport's long-term parking lot. The only thing witnesses can agree on," he waved his notebook, "is that there were two men inside it. No one paid attention until the passenger opened fire and then everybody was busy scrambling for cover. No one got a decent look. I'm hoping you can help us out. Up to it?"

The scene flashed before me. "The guy had a Glock…I'm pretty sure it was a Glock."

"That would match the forty-caliber bullets we retrieved," Caldwell confirmed. "Anything else?"

I stared at my water bottle, the image rearing up unbidden. "Ball cap...silver reflective sunglasses…I'm pretty sure the shooter was fair-skinned." Smith copied that information down, paused and waited for more. I'd give my left arm to have more. "I didn't see the driver. As soon as I saw the gun, I turned. Tabitha..."

Caldwell gave me a moment. "I'm sorry, Mr. D'Accio. I understand it's difficult to answer questions right now."

"Anything." I looked him square in the eye, my own gone hard. "Anything, anytime, if it'll help to catch the bastards." I was through moping.

"From the top then. You were hired in May to locate Miss Chandler by her brother in Omaha. You connected with her late June in Kingston. Literally."

"Yes." He could think whatever he wanted.

"You and Miss Chandler were together constantly for the next month in what, from all accounts, was a genuine close relationship. I am sorry for your loss." Smith's head bobbed in agreement.

I pressed my lips together and nodded my thanks.

"Motoring up the Mississippi and Missouri, you arrived in Kansas City the evening of August fifth aboard her private catamaran. You and Miss

Chandler stayed at a hotel, did some shopping and sightseeing. The shooting occurred on the morning of August seventh as you were leaving the hotel for the KC Marina, where her boat was berthed. Miss Chandler died on scene. The hotel doorman—an ex-Navy medic, by the way—kept you alive until the paramedics got there.

"Our first goal, Mr. D'Accio, was to determine the nature of the shooting. We have had three similar incidents over the past five months. According to Vice's Gang Unit, it's two gangs fighting over territory. Vehicles with multiple shooters roar in, gun-down pedestrians, shoot-up buildings, then peel out, leaving an entire block in chaos. At first glance, this case appears to be connected to them, with you and Miss Chandler getting the worst of it."

After studying me for several moments, he said, "It isn't."

I braced myself for the curve ball I could feel coming.

"One vehicle, one shooter. Property damage minimum. Only a few other injuries, mostly caused by panic. A sidewalk crowded with people, yet the shooter manages to graze just one more individual's arm *after* successfully nailing you and Miss Chandler? Twice each?" He shook his head. "The concentration and severity of the attack was deliberate, with the rest meant as a diversion. This was a professional job from square one."

Professional? There was a sudden thudding in my ears. Heartbeat, one corner of my brain identified.

"A street source tells me the driver was local, but the shooter came from out-of-town. We found the car, torched, and we're assuming the remains in it are the driver's. No prints, no scent, no ID, no leads. Now, who was the target?"

The sheet bunched in my fists.

"I haven't heard back from all of my inquiries, but it appears Miss Chandler was a wealthy recluse. No reports, so far, of her being in any trouble: legally, financially, or personally. She was estranged from her family and spent most of the past five years floating around the Caribbean and Gulf." Another pause, his face an unreadable mask. "With a lot of stops along Mexico and Central America."

I immediately knew what he was implying. "Tabitha didn't run drugs,"

I said, keeping my voice quiet but firm.

"A major pipeline has worked that region for over a decade. We've never gotten more than a whiff of it, even less on how they're bringing the stuff in. It's a tight, ruthless organization that doesn't hesitate to terminate problems. Existing or potential." Caldwell's shrug was negligent, his eyes weren't. "Like, say, someone with insider knowledge who has decided to walk away."

"Tabitha didn't run drugs," I repeated.

"A young, good-looking heiress sashaying through security with smiles, maybe a bit of flirting? Security is going to just give her a cursory check and VIP's don't get strip-searched."

My voice remained civil. "I'm sure you went over our belongings and the *Getaway* with a fine-tooth comb and a sharp-nosed shifter. Did you find any drug traces, Detective?"

"No," he admitted.

Tabitha had been a very private person. Having strangers rummaging through her things would have humiliated her.

"Hard to be somebody's delivery boy when you haven't set foot on U.S. soil in years. What Tabitha *did* do, Detective, was spread miracles." I flipped my hand up, indicating I needed a moment. I took a couple of deep breaths, pushing the anger down and away. They were only doing their job.

"*Angel de Agua.* Water Angel," I said quietly. "That's what the people along those coastlines called her. She'd stop somewhere and check out the area for how she could help. In one village it was a child with cataracts and a church with a leaky roof. In another it was a small medical clinic short on everything but compassion. The child and her parents took an all-expense paid trip to a specialist in Mexico City and the church got a new roof. The medical clinic now receives a generous monthly stipend from one of Tabitha's funds."

The room was quiet, even Smith's pen was stilled.

A flicker of something passed across Caldwell's face. "Then your loss is shared by all. I would have liked to have met her. So, who did you piss off in the last year or so? Professionally or personally?"

My mouth opened, closed. My blood iced, which melted in the hot wave of horror that followed close behind. *Because of me?*

We spent over an hour going over my past cases and people who might possibly bear me a grudge. Smith filled his notebook and part of Caldwell's too. They finally left, Caldwell saying the cop I hadn't known about would stay on the door a bit longer. Smith still hadn't said a word.

I must have dozed again, because I was awakened by a petite, smiling nurse who zipped in, plopped down a plate and told me I had to eat everything. She zipped back out before I could ask what the colored mounds on it were. On second thought, maybe it was better I didn't know.

Diana arrived while I was trying to figure out how to hide the stuff. My stomach was threatening to send back the two bites I'd tried.

"You want that?" she asked.

"Hell, no."

Diana reached into her purse and pulled out two cheeseburgers.

"You get a fat bonus if there's a pack of fries in there too."

She gave me an enigmatic look…and pulled them out.

Yes! I gave a victory fist-pump.

Diana gave me a brief outline of everything I'd missed out on while I ate. The Chandlers had claimed Tabitha's body as soon as it was released. Jackie, my favorite angelfish, had died. The Omaha Threshers were valiantly maintaining their losing streak. The *Getaway* had exploded and sank.

"What?" That last had a handful of fries freezing in mid-air. Detective Caldwell hadn't said anything about that.

"It's a variant of the obituary ghouls who break into homes left empty when people die," she said. "The boat was mentioned in the paper. The police had that awful tape around it but didn't post a guard—it wasn't the crime scene. Witnesses saw someone leaving with their hands full. A few minutes later, there was a *boom*, the inside lit up and it sank like a rock. The police figure it was deliberate to cover any physical or scent traces."

Bitterness swept through me. Didn't I have *anything* of Tabitha left? I didn't realize I'd spoken that aloud until Diana laid her hand on mine.

"Love never leaves, Curt, because it's a part of us. Memories. Their emotions and their warmth are its manifestation."

This new, unseen, side of her had reared again. "And the pain?"

"Their price. Would you rather have *not* known Tabitha?" she asked gently.

My head swung side-to-side slowly.

"I've kept your grandparents up-to-date. You can expect to be swarmed once you're home."

Quiet settled in until I told Diana she needed to return to Omaha. "I'm glad you came," I told her, cutting off her protests. "But the police need copies of my files. See Detective Caldwell, he'll tell you which ones he wants first. Be co-operative, but be sure they take copies, not the actual files."

"Fine. Anything else?" She dumped the stomach hazards into the burger wrappings and began rolling them up.

"Make a note of anything in particular the police ask, even if it appears casual. It might give me an idea of what they're thinking. I called Marge last night. She—we're both doing better. Thanks."

"Next time you get obstinate, I'm using my slugger." The toxic paper burrito disappeared into a plastic bag she'd found in a small drawer beside my bed. Diana promised to dispose of it discreetly and to call when she got back to Omaha.

I lay back, exhaustion sliding over me. My eyelids grew heavy, my thoughts drifted.

Tabitha was grinning, the breeze ruffling her hair while she loosened the lazy jacks. She was teaching me how to run up the main sail. I was all thumbs...mast lines...laughter...

Chapter 9

Four days later, I checked myself out of the hospital over the doctors' protests and my insurance agent's relief. Being limited to sleeping, thinking, and meal-dodging had been driving me not-so-slowly crazy, which I'd been more than happy to pass on. I spotted several happy good-riddance waves and one boogying ward nurse as I got on the elevator to leave.

Diana drove, with me dozing for most of the ride home. It felt good to be back. "Any word from the police?" I asked, adjusting my sling.

"None." Diana set a steaming cup of fresh coffee in front of me. "Of course, you don't think they'd tell me, the lowly secretary, do you?"

I inhaled deeply. Now that was how coffee should smell.

"The officer they sent to collect the copies I'd prepared had several others on his list and a crowbar up his butt."

I almost blew coffee out my nose.

"The twerp must have expected me to hand over the originals because he didn't like waiting while I made copies."

That was the closest thing to a rant I'd ever heard from her. The guy must have really got her goat. "Which files?"

She named three cases that had contributed to significant divorce settlements for my clients. I could see their point, as the exes—two male and one female—had been pretty pissed.

"Continue to only give copies if they ask for more. I might need them myself."

Diana studied me for a moment. "Curt, you've been flat on your back for three weeks. Go back to bed and let the police do their job."

One part of me knew she was right. I doubted if I could get out of my chair without a bad case of the shakes. I sighed, shook my head. She would know there was no way I was letting this go.

"I've requested a copy of your medical records from Kansas City mailed to Dr. Gordon. He's expecting you tomorrow morning at nine o'clock sharp." She collected her purse from the counter. "He says if you don't show he'll bill you anyway."

Annoyance flickered, even though I knew she was just looking out for me. "You sound like a wife."

"Is that a proposal?"

I grinned at her arched eyebrow. For a moment, the clock rolled backward. No worries, no pain, no shadows. "Only a fool or a very brave man would take you on."

Silence. "Don't worry, a wife isn't what you need right now."

"Oh? What would that be then?" I asked, curious.

"A friend. A strong shoulder. A dreamless night with a reason to see the morning."

Realization hit me. No wonder she'd known what to say. Four years and the woman had never said anything. "Who did you lose, Diana?" I asked softly.

"My fiancé and the child I was carrying. An on-coming truck was speeding. It hit ice, skidded across the center line, and slammed into us head on."

"Diana, I am so sorry." Especially about the proposal crack. "I didn't know."

"I didn't put it in my resume, Curt. Call one of us if you need anything. Preferably before you try doing it yourself." She paused, one hand on the doorknob and gave me a cool look. "My Edwin was no one's fool."

The door's soft click was worse than being slammed off it's hinges. I had some damage control to do there.

It was a struggle getting up out of the chair, and I may have wobbled more than slightly getting to the bedroom, but I made it. I conceded to my shaking legs and sat on the bed to zip open the suitcase Diana had to carry in.

The picture printed and framed before we left Nassau nestled snuggly among my clothes. I had snapped it as we sat in the catamaran's cockpit while she laughed at something I'd said. Or done. Couldn't remember which now.

It hadn't seemed important at the time.

My fingers slid over the frame as gently as Tabitha's last whisper had brushed my ear.

Remember me.

***

Nathanial Gordon had done his internship in the emergency rooms of several large cities before moving to Omaha. I seriously doubted there was an injury he hadn't seen or treated. I answered his questions mechanically while he examined my wounds. He was a bit surprised at how much they'd healed.

He finally closed my file and laid it on the counter. Sitting down, Nate rolled his stool in front of me, crossed his arms, and proceeded to study me for several moments. I figured a lecture on taking it easy was coming up.

"What did you have for breakfast?" he asked.

"Wasn't hungry."

"Get much sleep last night?"

I shrugged "Some."

"Curt..." His sigh bounced off the walls. "You've been hurt in just about every way imaginable, of which the physical wounds are the least damaging and the easiest to heal. The emotional and psychological ones will take a lot longer and could lead to physical degradation. Not good."

I didn't need to pay a deductible to know that.

"Anger, despair, revenge, guilt. These will all be natural, especially with the sudden and violent nature of her death and can affect you in unexpected ways. Trouble sleeping, lack of appetite, isolating yourself from others—especially friends—is normal. You need time to mourn. Time to heal and deal with everything. But don't let it go too far. Pay attention to yourself and stay tuned to your body. And be very, *very*, sure of your reasons behind any actions or decisions for the next while."

I snorted. "Afraid I'm going to commit suicide, Nate?"

68

"No, but you might be planning something just as stupid."

I saw compassion and understanding in his eyes. I saw the friend he'd become over the past five years.

"You will need to talk, Curt. Talking is good as it helps purge the system. I'm going to recommend a therapist, but I'm hoping you'll give me a call too. Office hours end at six but friendship calls are good 24/7." His mouth corners quirked upward. "I'll even treat you to a good drunk once you get off the meds."

The sadness that flared briefly in Nate's eyes said he was remembering when I'd made the same offer to him. I knew what had driven him to leave Emergency Care and open a small practice. "I'll hold you to that," I told him.

Then I got the lecture on taking it easy.

Afterward, I headed for the cemetery, laying flowers at the base of her elegant headstone. I must have stood there for half an hour, trying to say goodbye. The words wouldn't come. Finally, I turned to her father, lying beside her. "Tabitha's killers will pay for what they've done," I promised him.

It was midday before I finally got to my office. If the flowers surprised Diana, my kiss on her cheek downright shocked her. I did, indeed, have friends. The best.

It took a lot of fussing and cussing before I found I could type—kinda, sorta—with both hands if I set the keyboard in my lap. I was closing Russell Chandler's file and every line entered rippled with memories. Taking a deep breath, I typed the last line. *Client's sister killed in an attack in Kansas City before completing return to Omaha. Case closed.* I hit the save icon, set the keyboard back on the desk, and rested my head in my good hand.

I was still in my misery pose when I heard footsteps in the outer office. They weren't wearing high heels. The half-opened door moved slowly inward until I was looking at the man stepping through the doorway.

He found himself looking down the business end of a .357.

"Your license can be revoked for drawing against a police officer," he said.

"Prove it," I ordered, not daring to lose the advantage.

The man easily topped six-five and those shoulders didn't wear anything off a rack. He was a Gen of some kind. A big one, and undeterred by a weapon pointed at his chest. He hadn't stopped until halfway to my desk. At least he was smart enough to use two fingers to remove a thin wallet from his coat pocket.

He tossed it onto my desktop. I eyed his badge carefully before relaxing. "You should have announced yourself properly instead of just walking in here." I tossed it back as he approached and returned my Ruger to the drawer.

"The door wasn't locked, your secretary is out, and I'm here on official business," he replied. "I probably should have anticipated your reaction."

"Yeah, I always get a little uptight after someone tries to kill me. However, you'll notice you're not bleeding on my floor. Who are you?" *What are you?* My usually reliable Gen-dar was silent.

"Lieutenant Sinclair."

"Got that from your badge."

"Homicide. I'm looking into the attack on you and Miss Tabitha Chandler." He glanced at the file on my desk.

"Kansas City has jurisdiction." I flipped the folder closed.

"With obvious ties to Omaha. I'm conducting it on this end."

"Then why aren't you out there conducting, Lieutenant Sinclair? And why you? Did the Omaha Homicide Department run out of detectives?"

Normally I don't try to irritate the police but I was in no mood to be tactful. It also didn't help that my mouth had a tendency to outrun my brain when I'm rattled. My shifter identifying instinct had never failed before.

Twin chips of glacier-blue ice looked at me out of an impassive mask. "I have questions. You can answer them here or downtown. Do I get to choose?"

No way. "My chair is quite comfortable." I adjusted my sling and settled back.

I watched Sinclair warily as he settled across from me. I hadn't realized how much I depended on that inner assessment. It was like looking at him through a murky window. He filled my visitor chair so completely all I could see were the ends of the wooden arms jutting out on either side. I might need a new chair.

He opened a notebook. "Who do you place at the top of your suspect list?"

"That's the problem." My chair swiveled slightly. "There's two or three who'd love to rip out my throat if they found me alone on a dark street, but I can't see them arranging a hit in Kansas City." I still hadn't fully accepted it myself.

"Names."

I listed them. The questions he shot at me showed he'd read the prior cases I'd identified to Det. Caldwell, and that he was astute enough to have identified several weak or incomplete spots in some of my reports. I made a snide comment about not being police-perfect and got 'obviously' for a reply.

Okay, I slid into that one.

Would some of those gaps—things I'd deliberately left out because it didn't affect my case, now hide a killer? After about forty minutes, he closed his notes and rose to leave.

"I have a few questions of my own if you don't mind."

"I do. I don't answer questions concerning an open investigation. Keep that Ruger in your drawer and your nose out of my case."

Diana got caught in my glare, coming in as he was going out. She merely nodded knowingly and went on to her desk. It took almost an hour, but I finally wound down and ambled out to park my butt on her desk. My good arm massaged my bum one.

"Feel better?" Diana asked.

"For now. Unless I get another visit from Lieutenant Sinclair. I reserve the right to be as uptight as he is."

"He has a right to be. A friend in OPD Records told me he's facing a lot of animosity, and it's not just in his department. He transferred in about four months ago. Not an unusual occurrence. Having them come in and take over an important department like homicide is. Even some of the higher ups are questioning why a local wasn't promoted into the position."

Yeah, that would put a stick up someone's butt. "And now I get to deal with him. You'd think a detective would have drawn the case, especially if it's just running down information for KC."

"He *is* a detective. They didn't rescind his badge on promotion. Most likely it's political. The Commissioner's Office would want to assure the Chandler family that Miss Chandler's death was receiving maximum effort."

I grunted. Even more pressure. "Does your friend have any idea why Sinclair got the position?"

"Word is, he applied for it as soon as Lt. Olsen announced his retirement. The additional word," she added blandly, "was that it only took two weeks to transfer him here from Denver."

Uh-huh. We both knew better. He'd either made himself *persona non grata* in Denver or the Omaha Police Department needed an outsider due to internal issues. Maybe both, with one being the answer to the other. I chewed my lip thoughtfully for a moment. "What questions did he ask you?"

"How long I've worked for you. Any problems with clients or their wives."

My laugh was hollow. "Don't tell me he thinks some irate husband went after me in Kansas? That was a professional job. If he's grasping at that..." I shook my head.

"No." Diana tapped a nail thoughtfully on her desktop. "I think he's covering all bases."

Unfortunately, I had to agree with her. If he was facing internal scrutiny *and* political pressure, he couldn't afford to overlook anything.

I asked Diana to dig up several old files before heading back to my desk. Flipping open a new folder, I started a file on myself. Treating it like any other case should give me the objectivity I needed to—I snorted. No way could I distance myself from this. I'd just have to be careful and hope emotion doesn't blind me.

I paused. Had I already been blinded? Had I overlooked something important because I was too mired in anger and grief? Diana laid the requested files on my desk but didn't pull her hand away.

"You promised to rest for a few days."

"I'm only going to read for a while, then I'll go home." Her concerned face had me laying my hand on hers. "I have to find the answers to who and why. If the cops get the bastards first, great. But, sitting back and doing nothing? Just waiting?" I shook my head. "I *have* to join the hunt."

***

We'd given the cases and names with the most potential to the police. I now started working my way through all four years' worth of files. I studied each file, not just for what it contained, but also trying to remember anything I might have brushed off or left out of my notes. The sensitive or embarrassing personal data I felt had no bearing at the time, but could now be important. It was impossible, especially for the older records.

Lesson learned. My future clients' reports might not have everything, but my files sure would.

Three weeks later, I had survived the grandparent swarm, could pee standing without the shakes, and had a discouragingly small pile of what-ifs-and-maybe possibilities. I dug into the files.

There'd been several nasty custody and divorce battles in which my investigation had been pivotal and an extortion case that had rocked several prominent families in Omaha and across the river in Kanesville. Researching everyone involved in those cases over the next several days got me *zilch* toward the shooting. I did, however, get two ear benders—including one rather unique cursing I wished I could've recorded—and one sexual proposition.

Oddly enough, I also got a legal proposition for suing Kansas City. For what? Getting shot? Their hospital food?

I turned down both propositions.

Having nothing left, I turned my attention to a case I'd given the police. The large drug-ring bust almost two years ago had been my most vicious case. It'd been at the top of Det. Caldwell's list, even though it had been a homegrown enterprise with no indications of the ties or finances needed for his major pipeline. Probably Lt. Sinclair's too, not that he'd enlighten us non-official sources.

Two days later, I learned the single, major participant in the drug-ring not in prison was dead. I slammed the phone down, expressing my frustration with a few choice words. Rubbing my temples, I hoped the firm fingertip massage would dissuade the headache currently trying to throb itself into existence. There had to be something, somewhere. Maybe I needed to go back further, I thought, watching Diana walk in with the morning's mail.

"Thanks. Would you make an appointment for me with Mike over at HIS?" Maybe it was something from early in my career, perhaps all the way back when I'd been apprenticed at Halligan.

"Any particular time?"

"No. At his convenience." I started flipping through the mail. "I'd like at least an hour." Donation requests and personal went in a pile on my left. Bills went to the right, which Diana would take care of after I'd reviewed them.

"Your follow-up appointment with Dr. Gordon is at four-thirty this afternoon."

I slit open an orange envelope. "Reschedule for next week." The invitation to an ex-girlfriend's Halloween party joined the advertising fliers in the trashcan beside my desk. I wasn't ready for noisy gatherings filled with well-intentioned sympathy and nosy questions.

"I don't think you want to do that."

I shot Diana a look, something in her tone triggering wariness. "Why?"

"According to Dr. Gordon, if you miss another appointment he plans to pay *you* an office visit and personally administer a Penicillin G1 shot so he doesn't have to worry about infection."

I shrugged. Big deal. I'd had plenty of shots, what was one more.

"Impressive," she said. "Most people cringe at the thought of a miniature caulk gun inserting a thick white paste into their butt cheek through a thick needle."

I froze. "You're making that up."

"Bring a cushion to work. It takes a day or two for the body to absorb the golf-ball-sized knot. I hear it's nicknamed the Pipe Bender because—"

"Fine. I'll keep the frigging appointment. Just…give me a forty-five-minute heads up. Infection my ass," I muttered, watching the blackmailing duo's female half return to her desk. The anatomy reminder had me shifting uneasily in my chair, as did the shoulder ache beginning to reach an uncomfortable level.

I glared at my watch. *Not yet noon and I'm dragging.* Equal parts disgust and frustration roiled through me as I slipped my arm back into the sling dangling around my neck. I sure-as-crap wasn't giving anyone much of a fight, especially an ornery doctor and his smirking helper.

Screw this.

It was time I got pro-active, starting tomorrow at the gym.

Chapter 10

Limping out of the gym, I ignored the cold drizzle in favor of trying to find a muscle that didn't ache. The trainer I had 'leased' from the gym ten days ago had started me out slow. Tonight, he'd ramped it up. I was going to test my apartment building's hot water reserves as soon as I got home.

The hairs on my neck going stiff was the first warning. A shift in the shadows was the second. The black panther slammed into me, its claws sinking into my shoulders. I locked my hands together as we fell backward to the wet pavement. The hard landing punched air from lungs even as I rammed a double set of knuckles into his throat. Just as my cougar father had taught me

The cat staggered away, coughing, wheezing. I rolled painfully to my knees, sucking in air of my own.

A woman bolted toward me. "I've called 9," she yelled, shorthand for the emergency number, 999.

There was a rather pitiful attempt at a displeased squall, followed by several coughs. The panther staggered off into the bushes after giving me a baleful yellow glare. I'd damaged his windpipe. A smaller cat's would have been crushed.

"Thank you," I mumbled, recognizing her as one of the other trainers. She squatted beside me, her eyes on the bushes and her bear claws out. I swayed and collapsed flat. A police car followed closely by an ambulance roared into the parking lot.

Three hours later, I was unintentionally frustrating a detective from OPD's Assault Unit. Honestly, I was trying to answer his questions, but my mouth didn't seem to work right. Or maybe it was my brain. I shrugged when he asked if this could be related to the Kansas City attack. Who the bloody hell knows?

Did I say that out loud?

The detective heaved a sigh.

Yep. Did.

"I'm going to go talk with the female witness. Please call me, Mr. D'Accio, if you manage to think of anything that might be useful."

Starting to hand me a card, he switched and gave it to Nate instead. Wise decision. No telling where his card would end up.

Nate signed me out of the ER and gingerly stuffed me and my shiny new stitches into his car. He'd gotten a briefing from the doctor before even showing up at my bedside. There were stitches in my left thigh as well as both shoulders. I hadn't felt those three slashes until the ambulance's paramedic swabbed them.

"Gloria Dreyfuss," I mumbled. "Need flowers."

Nate was sliding under the steering wheel. "What?"

"Gloria. Flowers."

"She the brave witness?" The motor turned over.

"Yeah. Has claws like Grandma. You know Grandma's a bear, right? No one gives her any lip." I heard Nate laugh. "Need flowers."

"We'll get flowers tomorrow. I need to get you home and into bed, Curt. They pumped a pretty potent painkiller into you."

I smiled, leaned my head against the window. "Great stuff." Nothing hurt. Not stiches, not muscles, and not the new bruise down my back. Nate was saying something, but his voice kept drifting further and further away.

***

I jerked awake. Someone was in my bedroom. It was too dark to see them, but I could feel them. A hand touched my forehead and I grabbed it.

"It's me, Curt."

Nate's voice had me relaxing. Or I tried to. *Owwww.* "Nate? Tell me you have more of that drug."

He switched on a lamp and squinted at me. "We've been checking you for fever. The ER doctor cleaned your wounds, but those claws were dirty. So far, so good."

"Nate? Drugs?" Then added, "We?"

"Marge has day shift and I've got the nights. Diana is managing the office and said not to worry. I need to change your bandages," he said over the sound of water running in the bathroom. He came back out with a glass and a pill bottle.

Stunned, I asked how long I'd been out.

"Not long. This is the second night after your attack. You hadn't fully recovered from the KC attack, and losing more blood didn't help. Your body more-or-less shut down for repairs."

He lifted me enough to take the water without taking a bath. With a word of warning, he started changing my bandages. I locked my jaws, refusing to let the groans out.

"You know, I usually see that kind of repair shutdown in shifters," Nate said casually, taping a fresh bandage across my right shoulder. "I also heard about that move you did on the panther. Takes a lot of strength to damage a large cat's throat. Of course, it could have been adrenaline-powered."

I closed my eyes. Nate was putting together a few things he'd just been shrugging off.

Finished with my shoulders, he sat back, wearing a thoughtful expression. "Despite your *mental* sluggishness down in KC, your physical healing was exceptional. You're a Gen in everything except shifting, aren't you?"

No sense in denying it. "Our family doctor figured it out when I was twelve. He called me a Zero-Plus." I rubbed my neck, uncomfortable at talking about it. "Hearing, reflexes, and instincts are better than the average Zero. My strength is almost First-Gen. I can always tell if someone is a shifter—I call it my Gen-dar. You know, Gen *radar*?" Nate didn't even crack a smile. "I usually know their form, sometimes their actual species. Wolf really stands out. Probably due to their natural aggression."

Nate's brow furrowed. "I haven't heard of anything like that. And regular

Gens would know another shifter by scent."

In a small voice, I said, "We weren't aware of the rapid repair until I was eighteen." Memories flooded me. Pain. More pain. My legs twisted, blood flowing down my face. Calling for my parents. Knowing they were dead and thinking I was too as I blacked out. But I survived.

Rapid repair was Mother Nature's boon in a savage world.

The more serious a Gen's injury, the more likely it would kick in, repairing the worst of the cellular damage and replacing blood at an accelerated rate. The downside was vulnerability: the individual was often unconscious during it as the body redirected its energy. Then, at some undetermined milestone known only to itself, it switches off and regular healing takes over. It has limited effect on bones, although, depending on the shifter and where the break was, careful shifting over several days could repair them. I'd needed pins, casts, and patience.

"Quite a combination and why you don't splash it around," Nate said, nodding.

Uh-huh. Despite the vagaries of our DNA, I was an anomaly. People didn't like, didn't trust anomalies. As Nate started on my thigh bandages, I realized I was in my underwear. Convenient for bandage-changing, still, I felt my ears go warm. "Uh, did Marge change my bandages, too?"

Nate looked up, amusement in his eyes. "She offered but no. I've been doing it. Oh, Lieutenant Sinclair has been calling. He wants to, quote, 'follow up,' about the panther attack. I think he's getting a bit impatient."

I shrugged, froze, but things only ached a bit. That pill was worth its price. "I'm curious as to what the police have learned. Tomorrow is fine."

"I'll leave him a message, say…nine o'clock? I'll help you with your shower, dressing, and redo the bandages before I leave in the morning. Got a pot of chicken soup Diana sent over. Hungry?"

My stomach's growl answered for me.

***

By the time Nate arrived the next evening to tuck me in, I was as growly and ornery as a grizzly with a toothache. Marge had hovered over me all day like a mother-wolf. I'd forgone any painkiller so I'd have a clear head for my interview with Sinclair…which didn't happen until almost three o-clock. Neither of us had learned anything new from the other. There'd been no reports of a Second-Gen male seeking medical treatment for a damaged larynx.

"The lieutenant did have an interesting supposition," I told Nate, still a bit baffled that he'd mentioned it. Had he been fishing, hoping I knew something?

"Like what? This is your last happy pill. I'll leave a prescription for something milder tomorrow for one of your mother hens to pick up."

"That since Steven Chandler's family has a strong panther lineage—he was First-Gen himself—it might have been a reprisal for Tabitha's death. Everyone pretty much blames the attack on me."

"Not everyone," Nate objected. "And I think his theory is a bit far-fetched, considering she was estranged from the family."

He slid my shirt off my shoulders. "Hmmm. Good. Everything's scabbed over. The rapid repair cycle appears finished, so take it slow and easy for the next several days. You don't want to undo its work. You could go without bandages, but we'll keep them on for a few more days to avoid any possible infection."

And avoid speculation.

I nodded at Nate gratefully and sank down under the covers. As embarrassing as it was, it warmed me to have mother hens, one being of the male persuasion. *Mother rooster?* I was stiff, but feeling better. Tomorrow was Friday. I'd call Diana, see what my schedule was like and if there had been any inquiries. I'd be in the office on Monday and able to take on mild cases. Like background checks.

The gym trainer was definitely going on hold, though.

Chapter 11

The city was under siege.

We'd been held hostage for two days this time, as turbulent gray clouds spit icy projectiles in erratic gusts, battering stone and steel and flesh. The airport was closed. Again. The interstate was closed. Again. Even my favorite hangout, run by winter die-hards, was closed. Teachers and parents were grumbling because the schools' extended make-up days were already ruining June vacations.

"Thank God January is almost over," I grumbled, listening to the latest assault beat against the glass panes. I loathed winter in January. I was tired of gray skies and dirty snow. I was tired of frigid air freezing nose hairs stiff two steps outside of whatever warmth I was insane enough to leave. I wanted—

A warm breeze riffled my hair, hot sand shifted beneath my knees. I could feel the hot sun on my back and Tabitha beneath my hands.

Sighing, I gave myself a mental shake and banished the memories. Daydreaming about a secluded Caribbean beach resolved nothing and only made the ache worse.

Returning my attention to the computer screen, I scanned the report I was compiling. Another fluff job, like all the others as I'd gradually eased myself back into work. Nate and Marge might think it was at their insistence, but it had suited my needs by allowing time for my own personal research. *Not that it's done any good,* I groused. Every lead, every idea—every straw I'd grasped—had withered and died in dead ends. Even my panther attack last fall had gone unsolved.

Some son-of-a-pig was getting away with murder.

Documents rained down on the floor as I flung them across the room. A desk calendar, two pens, a notepad, and the miniature stuffed owl from Marge joined them before I buried my face in my hands.

The soft click of heels and rustle of paper had my shoulders hunching. Spreading my fingers slightly, I watched Diana stack everything back on my desk. Going to the outer office, she returned with two cups of hot caffeine. Settling opposite me, she blew the fragrant steam from her cup in my direction.

Ouch. Those double-arched eyebrows of hers gave a complete report of their own and I'd just received a blistering one. I quietly saved and closed the computer file before doing something else childish and apologized for my tantrum.

We drank in silence. I leaned back in my chair and did some arm rotations. Most of the stiffness was gone with only a little remaining soreness, thanks to the expertise of the personal trainer I'd used for a couple of months. He'd been a godsend, working around my various injuries as needed. Of course, that's not what I'd called the smug sadist as I sweated and ached at his instructions.

I checked the wall clock and the window. Four-forty and pitch black. The streets would be a nightmare. "Why don't you go on home, Diana? There's nothing more to be done that can't wait until tomorrow."

"I'll leave when you do."

"I—"

"—spend half your nights here, on top of your regular work. Have you *really* looked at yourself lately? You were putting on weight and color, at least up until Christmas. You look worse now than you did coming back from Kansas City."

I bit my lower lip as frustration swelled. Picking up the owl, I patted its bottom against the desktop a couple of times. "There's something I've missed, Diana, something I'm not seeing." It'd been gnawing at me for weeks.

"How many times are you going to pick those records apart? How many times before you realize that maybe, just maybe, there's nothing there to see? You ever consider it was a mistake? They confused you with someone else?"

I shook my head. "Professionals don't make mistakes like that. At least, not very often or they'd become a target themselves." I set the owl back in its normal place, ignored the rest of the stack Diana had rescued.

"But it could happen?" she persisted, pointing her cup at me.

I admitted it was possible, however remote. "Tell you what. I'll call Detective Caldwell tomorrow and ask him to check out everyone who stayed at the hotel about the same time we did. If there were any other sudden or violent deaths then maybe, *maybe*, you might be on to something."

"Excellent! Put on your coat, go home and get some sleep. I'll lock up."

"Yes, Mommy."

I flinched as another gust rattled the window. Nothing like getting your face needled at zero temps. I started bundling up, a process I'd gotten down to less than four minutes. Not counting boots. Rolled my shoulders. Maybe my coat was a little loose. So what? I had yet to regain my pre-KC weight.

***

Detective Caldwell returned my call promptly the next day. He didn't need me to tell him his job, as he had considered and investigated that angle months ago. The only other hotel guest during that time who had died since had been a ninety-plus old man of a heart attack. Hardly someone I'd be mistaken for.

"We've found nothing to warrant anyone making a specific hit against either you or Miss Chandler. Lieutenant Sinclair tells me you've had a bit of trouble up there. Has anything come of that?"

"Some additional stitches, otherwise, no. Not even sure it's connected."

The detective was quiet for several seconds. "Without motive or anything else to go on…"

The pause and sound of resignation told me where this was going.

"…the case is being moved to the freezer. The Gang Unit is busting balls—theirs and others—to tear down the two gangs I've mentioned. They're the most vicious we've seen in years. They'll keep a copy of it on file with the others in case it does somehow tie-in."

My hand clenched around the phone. "We know it doesn't."

"You find something to support that or for a specific hit, let me know.

Until then, I've plenty of cases, most of whom do have leads."

I thanked him for all he'd done and hung up. I had nowhere else to go, nowhere else to look, no other sources to call on. This last grasp, however slight, had become another dust cloud swirling around my ankles. I was right, though, professionals don't make—

The scene flashed before me in all its horror. A spasm rippled up my arms as the information my subconscious had been trying to tell me finally tore its way to the surface. I must've yelled because Diana came rushing in.

"I found it, Diana. I found it!" The keyboard bounced.

"Found what?"

"The missing piece." I rubbed my hand. Desktop was hard. "We're both right. Professionals don't make those kinds of mistakes and I wasn't the target. I was closer, wide open and in the direct line of fire, yet Tabitha was hit first. We've had it backwards, Diana. *Tabitha* was the target; I was secondary."

"But why?" The idea astonished her as much as it did me.

"I don't know." My guts were doing handstands—*about time* they were saying. "That's why we can't come up with a single lead for someone targeting me."

I sent Diana to copy all the contents in Russell Chandler's file and started a new one on Tabitha. The records I had spent months poring over became a haphazard pile dumped beside my desk. Too revved to sit still, I wandered around the office. Fed the fish, straightened a couple of books on the bookshelf. Stared out the window.

My God, was that a patch of blue showing through the clouds?

Motive. What was the motive?

I needed more information. Cops wouldn't talk about open cases, even those in the freezer. If Caldwell didn't have anything, then neither did Sinclair. I had, grudgingly, raised my opinion of Lt. Sinclair after the panther attack. He'd questioned the Chandlers, not letting their wealth or social standing impede his investigation. Diana's grapevine reported he'd gotten complaints from the affronted family.

Returning to my desk, I dialed a phone number I knew as well as my own.

"Hey, Marge. Want to do dinner this evening?"

***

Marge and Chinese arrived at the same time.

The delivery guy collected the large tip that kept my deliveries coming fast and hot as Marge peeled off her coat and boots. She tossed a folder on one end of the coffee table while I arranged the takeout cartons on the other. I reached for it only to have her push my hand away.

"Uh-uh. Eat first."

"I'm well adapted to eating and reading at the same time." This time my hand got slapped. Hard. "*Marge!*"

"Eat. And it leaves with me unless you promise not sit up all night reading it."

Annoyance morphed to pissed. "You've been talking to Diana."

"Bet your bloody butt I have." Her blue eyes smoldered. "When we had dinner last week, you should've left the cadaver look at home. She gave me an update on everything since Christmas, seeing as how you haven't been talking to me in months. And I mean more than just *blah, blah.*"

"I didn't have anything to tell you." I started to turn away.

"I don't want a report. I want to hear about you. Stop avoiding me."

I swung back, waved my hand toward our supper. "Does this look like I'm avoiding you?"

"Can't you see what you're doing to yourself, to your health?"

"I know what I'm doing," I snapped, fisting my hands on my hips.

She mirrored my stance and stepped toe-to-toe with me. "Stop acting like a spoiled child. If Tabitha was here right now, she'd jerk you up by the jock strap and tell you to get a grip on yourself."

"Well she's not, and I can take care of myself."

A claw poked me in the chest with wolf speed. "Then why aren't you?"

I opened my mouth. Shut it. Stomped into the kitchen, pulled two beers from the fridge, popped the top of one, and took two deep swallows before carrying them out to the living room. Shoving the unopened one at her, I grabbed a fork and attacked my broccoli and beef dinner, finishing well ahead of Marge and her fried rice. I got another beer for myself and resumed my stiff position on the couch. Stuffing the bottle between my legs, I grabbed the last chicken eggroll and ripped off a bite.

"Satisfied?"

"Eating, yes. Attitude, no." She reached over and laid a hand on mine. "Curt, take a good look at what you're doing to yourself."

"I can't stop. Won't." Not for anybody.

"I know. But exhaustion won't help you find the killer."

"Killers. The one who paid for it is as guilty as the one who pulled the trigger."

"Talk to me, Curt. Please."

I looked into eyes filled with concern and misery. Dammit, that wasn't fighting fair. I held out the half-eaten eggroll. "Want a bite?" I got the expected nose curl. "Fine, I've been an ass," I admitted. "Why haven't you whacked me upside the head?"

"Still an option," she said, poking me with her beer bottle. "Now, bray."

Bray? Oh. Unable to keep my lips from twitching, I stuffed the remainder in my mouth. Nate had been right once again. I'd pushed away the one person I'd normally talk to about everything and anything. I'd refused the same comforting strength that had helped a shattered teenager survive his parents' death. Pretending I could handle it.

Wasn't pretending a form of avoidance?

I sighed, picked up my beer. "Some days are okay, Marge, others …aren't. I was warned there'd be an emotional roller coaster and boy," I shook my head, "is it. Guilt. Lots of it. Believing Tabitha was dead because of me."

"No she wasn't," Marge protested. "We know that."

"*Now*. When I realized Tabitha had been the primary target all along, the relief was…overwhelming." I made a face. "Followed by more guilt at *being* relieved." I gave her a lopsided grin. "I'm dealing with it."

She gave a very unfeminine snort. "Try harder. So, the panther attack was about something else?"

"Pretty big coincidence if it is, as I don't know of anything that could have instigated it." I gave it a couple seconds of thought. "More likely it was a diversion. Everyone believed I was the primary target in KC. I'm willing to bet the killer grabbed that idea and hired someone to go after me."

"Which then keeps the focus on you and away from Tabitha," she said shrewdly.

I nodded, my thoughts turning inward. Leaning my head back, I took a deep breath and released it bit-by-bit as something inside me gradually loosened. For the first time in months, I felt…human, instead of like a coiled spring wound three turns past safety. My eyes drifted closed, and I let the memories come.

"We were going to get a place out in the country," I said, "close enough to commute but away from the congestion. Tabitha didn't want to be around crowds." Or her family.

"Did that come from living on the ocean for so long or as a natural—" She held up a hand. "Sorry. Ditching the reporter."

"We wanted something nice—not grandiose—but something a family could grow into." I rolled my head sideways and shot her a grin. "And if it didn't have a pool, we'd put one in."

"What was the mermaid going to do come winter?"

"Have it enclosed and heated." A large box in a corner drew my gaze. After a moment, Marge asked what it was.

"Tabitha's Christmas present. I commissioned it before we left Nassau." And hadn't had the courage to open it.

Silence. "May I see it?"

I nodded and watched as she carefully opened the box. Layers of padding piled around her until I heard the sharp inhale.

"Oh, Curt. It's beautiful. And huge." She twisted around to look at me. "It's the *Getaway*, isn't it?"

"A scaled-down model. I figured we'd watch it float in the pool and …remember."

"She'd have loved it."

I stared at the box bleakly. "I dream of her, Marge. She's teaching me to sail…or cooking in the galley…or making love with me. Then," I swallowed, "then she's dying in my arms. *Remember me,* she said. Tabitha's last words." Her last breath.

Marge came and sat down beside me. She rested her head on my shoulder. I leaned my head against hers. "What do I do, Marge?" I asked, miserable.

"Don't be afraid to remember," she replied, her tone crisp. "Don't relegate her to only nighttime dreams that slip pass your walls. And don't," she squeezed my arm, "be guilty about living or let it poison those memories, or you'll truly have nothing of her left."

I smiled into her hair. "Those are don'ts, not dos."

"Why, you *do* find the bastard who's responsible, of course."

A tired sigh escaped me, swamped by the reality of it. "You know I want that more than anything, but there's so many unknowns, so many blanks and too much world."

"So? You've already made a lot of progress. You started with a stack of questions, eliminating diversions and possibilities and determined the true target. Now you know where to focus." She patted my knee. "And you have me."

"Nothing to worry about then," I grumbled, yet gratified at her confidence. I reached around her to pick up the folder. "I guess we'd better get started."

Marge settled back against the couch with her beer. "Assuming the reason for the hit occurred in the past five years, I contacted my Caribbean counterparts. I told them the Omaha-Herald was thinking of doing a 'one-year later' article with an overall life review and asked for whatever they had. As you can see, it's not much, and most of it deals with society stuff. Except for the occasional charity function, the woman was practically a hermit for those years."

I thumbed through the printouts, many of which I had. The rest were regionally flavored articles that had evidently been deemed uninteresting or too low-key by the wire services for global distribution.

Marge took a swallow, tipped her bottle at the folder in my hands. "There are copies of all the official press releases from the KC and Omaha police departments. Neither will share much else because, even cold, they are still considered open cases."

Then why, I asked myself, *did Sinclair voluntarily tell me about his Chandler panther suspicion?* I couldn't see him making an *oops* of that nature. Wanting my reaction, maybe?

"I've included the background stuff that's easy to get," Marge continued. "Tabitha was born practically nine months to the day after the wedding. It was a difficult pregnancy for Mrs. Chandler, which might also explain early references about Tabitha being delicate. She grew up under an assortment of nannies, tutors and private schools, including one brief stint in Austria at age nine." She frowned. "That would have been after her father's death—when she was eight. She only stayed half a semester. I'm guessing she still wasn't dealing well and either the school or her mother sent her home."

She sent her daughter away while still grieving her father? To another country? The woman was so cold she'd give shivers to a polar bear.

"Anyway, Tabitha left home at nineteen and never returned. She spent several years on the southern coast, then shifted to the Caribbean. The rest you know better than me."

"Thanks, Marge. This stuff is great. You got more than I was hoping for. They're actually going to do the article?"

"If I have any say. It has all the right elements: money, high society, the exotic Caribbean, a mysterious woman, a violent death." She paused. "No telling what might get jogged or from whom."

I was surprised at the uncharacteristically hard turn of her voice.

She did her shoulder roll. "I liked her, okay? Even if all we had were a couple of phone calls. I was looking forward to meeting her and—*dammit!* They *hurt* you, Curt. No one messes with my family."

I couldn't hold back the grin. "Where've you been hiding all that hot blood?" She swatted my shoulder. "Have someone check out *Angel de Agua* along the Gulf-side of Mexico, the Caribbean, and Latin America," I said absently, flipping through the file. Tabitha had protected her secret from the world's jaded, cynical spotlight. There was no way her life was being recounted without this wonderful side of her finally revealed.

Marge's eyes grew moist and shiny as I explained. "You bet your skinny butt I will. I can guarantee my editor will definitely go for it now. 'The woman no one knew' just got depth. It'll be a great story. Now, you going to straighten up or do I get to break in my Christmas present from Diana?"

I winced. She'd received her own personal "good for muggers, assholes, and idiots" bat. I sincerely doubted it was coincidence Diana had been looking in my direction when she said it.

"Come to think of it, I ought to exercise my options and give you a few whacks for the worry you've put us though." Marge rose, laid a hand on my shoulder. "Sooner or later, Curt, you'll find your answers. Remember, long-distance runners pace themselves so they'll have something left at the end."

She was right. It would probably take years to find those answers. *If ever,* one part of me warned. I walked her to the door, helped her with her coat. "Thanks, Marge. For everything." My lips curved upward. "Can we hold off on the whacking if I promise to pace myself?"

"For now." Her eyes searched mine for several seconds before she finally smiled. "Welcome back," she said, then added in a worried tone. "Be very careful, Curt. I don't want to lose you to a diversion strike." A quick kiss on my cheek and she was gone.

I filled a garbage bag with our dinner trash and then gently repacked the ship model. I stared down at the top of the mast sticking up through the padding.

"Don't stand there like an idiot, we've got to reef the sails!"

"Do what?" I was clinging to the railing, my mouth hanging open as the world turned gray. Gray sea, gray sky—a gray wall bulging outward, topped with black clouds and blotting out everything as it boiled toward us.

Boiled. That was the only word for it. The clouds had heaved and tumbled upon themselves: a free-for-all street fight rapidly expanding to include us.

Tabitha was moving toward the mast, hair whipped around her face by the wind that had risen quickly and without warning. "We have to lower the main—shorten the jib, or we'll flip."

I could grin now, at how those words had made my heart jump out of my chest and sink into the ocean depths. I had wondered how soon the rest of me was going to follow.

"Turn us into the wind when I signal you," Tabitha yelled. *"That'll relieve the stress long enough for me to drop it."*

I hurried toward the controls, the lurching deck nearly pitching me overboard. I hadn't felt the bruise on my shin from banging into who-knows-what until much later. *Locking a white-knuckled grip on the steering wheel, I yelled "Ready!" over the wind's snarl. She waved her arm; I began the turn.*

God, at least I hadn't been totally useless. I'd fought the wind, keeping the boat positioned while she worked. She dropped the mainsail's three ribs faster than I could've dropped my pants in that heaving swell, then moved forward to crank in the jib. For my first storm at sea, I hadn't done too badly. I didn't even disgrace myself by puking on the deck. However, my best buddy for the next twelve-plus hours below deck had been a trashcan.

My lips twisted into a wry grin as I repacked and closed the box. Yep. Wonderful memories.

Chapter 12

A couple of days later, Marge slid into my visitor's chair. I held up a give-me-a-minute finger, finished my phone conversation, and added a few notes to the file in front of me before sighing. "My client is not going to be happy."

"Fidelity issues?" Marge said.

"Gambling." I eyed her. "What's got you practically bouncing in my chair?"

"We're doing it," she burst out enthusiastically. "Tabitha's life story. I got the go-ahead this morning. Full spread, all the hoots and hollers."

My face split in a grin. "That's great."

"My apartment toniii—you don't have stuff to do, do you?"

"Nope. Usual time?"

"Yep. Got stew in the crock pot." She bounced out of my office.

I shook my head. Marge was definitely in a good mood, and a home-cooked meal would soothe my evening. I grimaced at my notes. I was not looking forward to telling my client she might lose her home because of her husband's addiction.

Hours later, I was sitting on Marge's floor, propped against the couch and digesting a hearty meal. Her stews had a rich non-meaty broth and were stuffed full of thick-cut vegetables. Marge settled next to me on the couch.

Hiding a yawn, I patted her leg. "Nudge me if I start to doze off." Paper crinkled behind me.

"I'm starting with Tabitha's mother. I even went all the way back through courtships and marriages to build a strong foundation. I'll give you the highlights so as not to bore you."

"Appreciate it."

"To start off with, Cynthia Wilkes was born in Old Omaha, just this side of the Boondocks."

Ouch. That was almost as bad as being in it.

Both areas had started life together as part of the original settlement. The city had flourished from the trade going and coming via the docks south of it. But times changed. Modernization and larger barges had been the death knell for the old docks.

'Boondocks' became a misnomer. Then a sneer.

The area had gradually deteriorated until it was now at the bottom of the social and job strata. Many of its residents worked in the low-income hard and/or dirty jobs a city needed done that most people curled their nose at. The bad reputation wasn't totally undeserved, as many were also involved in various illegal activities.

Old Omaha had fared a bit better. While its residential areas ranged from okay to ragged, its commercial area had managed to maintain a genteel atmosphere. It was as big a tourist draw as Omaha's zoo. The narrow streets and sidewalks were laid with brick and the buildings had a tired, well-worn look. Considering most of them were over a hundred years old, they should. It was hard to believe the very modern Capitol building and State Senate Chambers were just a few blocks to the northwest.

"A Second-Gen wolf, she has no siblings and both her parents were alcoholic Zeros," Marge continued. "Both also had trouble keeping a job. The only reason they didn't end up *in* the Boondocks was because her father supposedly inherited the house from an uncle."

"Supposedly?"

"There appears to have been some disagreement among other family members. There were accusations that the will was either a forgery or the uncle was tricked into leaving it to Mr. Wilkes. Neither could be proved. Cynthia's home life was rough, which might be why she married Greg Greenbaum at seventeen after a very short courtship. He was twenty-three and had a very nice income from his construction work. According to police records and neighbors, problems started almost immediately."

"The parents expecting the new son-in-law to support their drinking?"

"Yep. Greenbaum called the police every time they set foot on his property, charging them with theft and/or harassment. The Wilkes charged him with threats, physical assault, and domestic abuse. That last was never substantiated, but—according to neighbors—Cynthia rarely left the house without her husband."

I snorted, leaned my head back. "Sounds to me like she had two good reasons not to."

"Agreed. And since Greenbaum was a Zero, I doubt he'd risk striking her. Anyway, that went on for over five months. Then both Wilkes died in a house fire. Cause was listed as two drunks and an unsupervised pan on the stove."

No surprise there. "I doubt either Cynthia or her husband mourned them."

"Me either. Russell was born fourteen months later and Cynthia was widowed two years after that when Greg was killed in a construction accident. She used the insurance settlement to re-invent herself and spent the next five years hanging on to steadily more affluent arms, then she met Steven Chandler at a party. They got married in a spectacular wedding ten months later. She was twenty-six to his forty-one."

I closed my eyes. "Not unusual in those circles. Was there a marriage contract?" There was no mistaking the mischievous grin in her voice when she replied "Yes."

Marriage contracts were an anachronism from previous centuries. While not unknown here in the States, it was mostly the European well-to-do that favored them nowadays.

"Among the usual," Marge said, "he would officially adopt Russell—who'd just turned eight—and she was bound to a fidelity clause. According to my source, he sprang it on her a few days before the wedding. She couldn't argue it without the obvious implication."

"Loses everything if she cheats?" Bet that ruined a few expectations.

"Phrase is 'ever found to be unfaithful,' which could be interpreted several ways."

Huh. Sounds as if he wasn't leaving anything to chance with a lovely young wife. I got whacked sharply on the head. "Marge!"

"You were dozing."

"Were not. I was resting my eyes. I'm listening, and I said *nudge*."

"Can't tell if you don't keep them open. Now, Steven Chandler," Marge continued. "A First-Generation panther and rogue son of Omaha's most snobbish family."

"Rogue?"

"The Chandlers have been at the top of Omaha's social ladder since his ancestor opened the city's first bank way back when. Their banking and financial empire currently stretches across five states. According to Ellen in our social news department, his family was mortified when he established Chandler Corporation at age twenty-four as a *retail* enterprise."

I rolled my eyes. "How horrible; a merchant in the family."

"Then he goes and marries a woman with Cynthia's background."

"Bet the snobs weren't happy about that."

"Scandalized. His first wife, socialite Cathy Everson, had died four years earlier from cancer and without producing any children. With Cynthia Greenbaum, he got a lovely young wife who had already birthed one child."

"And didn't take long to produce another one," I commented dryly.

"After Tabitha's birth, Mrs. Chandler became her husband's business partner and, as a matter of fact," Marge tap-tapped me on the head, "helped build the company to what it is today. The woman is a very shrewd and effective business manager. She's also extremely ruthless with a streak of vengeance according to a number of people I've spoken with. Personally, I wouldn't want to get on her bad side."

I angled my head to look up at her. "Is that your impression?"

"Yes," Marge replied. "She has the position, money, and temperament to be a very nasty enemy. And a very large possessive streak. She kept a close eye on Steven, accompanying him on both business and pleasure trips. He liked big game hunting and skiing."

"So, she didn't trust him either. Afraid of him 'hunting up' someone younger and prettier?"

Marge laughed. "Tit-for-tat. Anyway, Steven Chandler was killed on one of those skiing trips when Tabitha was eight. Both parents were caught in an avalanche. Mrs. Chandler shifted and dug herself out. She dug a few others out that were caught in it, too, but they didn't find her husband in time."

"She's never remarried?"

"No reason to. She dominates the social scene with her power, money, and looks. She can spend time with whomever she wants and then tell them to get lost when she tires of them. That apparently takes anywhere from two months to two years if you check the society pages. Currently, she's running solo."

"When did the name change to Chandler Import? I asked, curious.

Paper rattled. "Six years ago when they began adding foreign trade."

The top of my head got smacked again before she tossed the file aside.

"The rest is boring family info that will put us both to sleep. Most of it's the official bio spiel put out by their corporate publicist and, naturally, more society stuff. I'm going to follow up with interviews, both personal and business."

"How did you get all this in a few days?"

"If I were to tell you my sources, I wouldn't get any more free dinners," she said, laughing.

"I'm the one getting a free—and excellent—dinner. Those sources tell you anything else?"

She sobered instantly. "There's scuttlebutt with your name on it, Curt. Nothing concrete, nothing my street source can pin down. She's worried. I'm worried. You *are* being careful, right?"

I hugged her leg. "Yes," I replied, more assuredly than I felt. My nemesis was crafty.

Chapter 13

Exiting my Papillion apartment parking lot, I carefully navigated northward around winter's don't-forget-me kisses. Some of the crevasses and potholes were large enough to earn crater designation, like Big Bertha on Park Drive. So far, it had racked up five blowouts, two bent rims, one busted tie rod, and an untold number of frontend alignments. According to one of my neighbors, city hall might be sporting some black eyes if it didn't get filled in soon.

February had been a heartless tease. The blinding glare during its first week had been worth the crisp blue skies and the second week had followed with warmer temps. All but the largest snow dunes had practically melted overnight, leaving parked cars sitting a foot from muddy, sand-caked curbs. Halleluiah, winter was over.

Then *bam!* January all over again.

Every frigging four-legged February forecasting fur-ball should've been shot. Especially the news forecaster who announced the Canadian Clipper with smiles and jokes.

Hitting the interstate on-ramp, I melded easily into the shrouded eastbound traffic. The ceiling hung low this morning, wrapping everything in a gauzy, slightly out-of-focus look. The railroad trestle south of the sixtieth-street exit almost appeared to be floating. My hopes were pinned on March coming in next weekend with its winds and blowing this mess away.

Wasn't too long before my car was safely parked in the Woodworkers Union Tower garage and I was riding the elevator to the twenty-first floor for my ten o'clock meeting with Russell Chandler. Giving my shoulders a twist, I grinned at my reflection in the silvery doors just before they pinged opened.

This would be the reverse of our last meeting: his office, me the irritating visitor.

Chandler's office reflected the same quiet understatement as the man I'd come to question. The plush carpet was in mottled shades of black and brown, as was the couch and chairs in the small sitting area to the right of his desk. Oak wainscoting protected pale green walls adorned with tasteful art in two four-piece groupings. The pictures in the sitting area depicted Old Western cowboy themes.

The ones watching me over Chandler's shoulder as I settled into the straight-backed chair across from him looked Old World European. I studied them as his secretary placed steaming coffee in front of us. "Duncan and Fanning?" I asked, using my cup to indicate the two groupings.

"Rockwell and Russell," he said.

I'd have to check them out. "Thanks for seeing me on short notice. Coffee's great."

"You said this was about Tabitha."

Still no small talk. "Why did Tabitha leave home? Omaha?"

"She wanted to."

"Why did she and your mother fight the night before she left?"

"They wanted to."

"Why…" I paused, biting the inside of my lip to keep the question socially polite, "did you hire me?"

"I had to."

Had, not wanted. That terse admission explained his underlying friction and why his wolf had been restless that first meeting. He'd been forced to use resources outside his normal operations, which placed them—namely me—outside his control. My less-than-appreciative attitude undoubtedly hadn't helped either. "Why?"

"I explained why."

I took a healthy swallow of coffee. "You explained your mother. Why did you *need* to find Tabitha, or more accurately, her shares?"

"Being hired to perform a task does not necessitate knowing the reasons behind it. And it's not relevant," he added, leaning back.

The deep mahogany leather of his executive chair complimented the rest of the room's décor while making it, and the man sitting in it, the focal point. *Here sits the power,* it said. No way was that accidental. Nor was I going to let him keep stonewalling me.

"I guess her dying messed up whatever plans you had in work."

"Yes." He tipped his cup, studied me over the rim as he drank. "Why the questions?"

"I'm trying to find the who-what-why behind her murder."

"No secret there," he replied politely.

I pushed down the small flare of anger. Instead, I allowed one corner of my lips to lift slightly and sent him an amused look. "Ah, but there is." I caught the flash of wary surprise. My eyes wandered around the room, deliberately letting the silence drag out. They stopped on the cowboy pictures. Were they the Rockwell or the Russell?

"Do you plan to enlighten me or not?"

Is that irritation I hear? "Tabitha was the intended target in Kansas City," I said abruptly, wanting to gauge his response. All I saw was an amused eyebrow.

"Not likely."

It was my turn to raise an eyebrow, although I couldn't duplicate his arrogant sweep.

"Besides a very well defined *opinion* of right, wrong, and what she wanted," Chandler continued, "Tabitha preferred to avoid…entanglements."

Entanglements?

"That would require associating with people, which she avoided. Diligently," he added. "She did have a temper, but it rarely broke loose and never in public. Tabitha absolutely hated public scenes. A person was more likely to have body parts frozen off or scoured with that diamond-edged tongue of hers."

Oh, yeah. Remember that well.

I leaned forward for emphasis. "The Kansas City attack was a professional hit. On Tabitha. Disguised as a gang shooting."

His cheek twitched. "Aren't you being unrealistic?"

"The hit was unrealistic," I responded curtly. "It's too easy to make someone who lives on the ocean disappear into it. Quietly and untraceable. But she was constantly moving and never identified her destinations with float plans." I pushed myself back upright. "Until we returned to the States and gave someone the perfect opportunity. A public gang-style hit could be thrown together quickly and would serve to totally confuse and misdirect attention, especially since KC had been having problems with that. If the hit was recognized for what it was, everyone would then naturally assume—and did—I was the target."

Stubbornly he said, "Because you were."

Punching this moron would not get me what I wanted. I let out a small huff of air. *Easy, Dice. You need him.* "All possible scenarios and persons who might have a grudge against me, no matter how far-fetched, have been eliminated in triplicate: by Kansas City and Omaha police detectives and myself."

"Not finding an answer doesn't mean there isn't one."

Ah, ha! I pounced. "The same holds true for your sister. Just because there's no reason *that we know of* doesn't mean there isn't one."

That caught him off guard. I tapped my fingers against my leg, waiting, but he seemed to be temporarily out of comebacks. And—surprise, surprise— he seemed to be thinking.

"Consider this," I said, gesturing. "I was an open, easy target at the curb, as was an Ameri-Tribe couple standing a few feet away. Tabitha had stopped briefly to say something to the doorman and was coming up the sidewalk *behind* me. Yet she was hit first—two shots in quick succession—then a slight pause before I was hit in the same manner. A sequence confirmed by the ex-Navy doorman."

The desk intercom buzzed. He reached over. "Yes?"

"Your ten-thirty appointment is here, Mr. Chandler."

Our eyes locked and held: two dogs, one bone.

"Mr. Chandler?"

He told his secretary to extend his apologies and reschedule. "Continue," he said after closing the connection.

I settled back in my chair. "Those two sets of shots and the pause between them as the shooter redirected his aim were nowhere near the random and *steady* dispersal pattern typical of a drive-by. Also, despite the shooter's obvious accuracy and a sidewalk full of targets, only one other individual received a non-life-threatening shot in the arm."

Chandler's chair rocked gently as he considered all I'd told him. "Why?" he finally asked.

"That is the question, isn't it? I intend to find the answer." Determination coated my words.

"Have you informed the police of your theory? No? Could it be because they would be as skeptical as I am?"

"I don't care what they believe," I growled. "I will find the bastard because I'm good at what I do, and I have resources the police don't." I picked up my cup, took a swallow. I waited.

After a brief, fraught silence, Russell said, "All right, I'll play your game. Skipping over motive, what about opportunity?"

I met his gaze coolly. "Our itinerary wouldn't have been too hard to figure out. She had an appointment with the specialists here in Omaha, which her doctor's staff in Nassau was certainly aware of. Her legal and accounting firms had orders to forward everything to my home address, where she would be staying."

Chandler's eyebrows were going to molt if he kept that up.

"We had to file a float plan in New Orleans—it's mandatory for monitoring river traffic. Her boat was well-known and following us from the private dock in KC—the slip was reserved in advance—would have given them our hotel. Assuming they didn't already know where we'd be staying."

He cocked his head slightly. "And you had informed me."

"Did you tell anyone?"

"No."

"Could there have been a leak about your hiring me and why?"

"No."

I gave him my best scowl. "Work with me here."

"Why?" His chair creaked slightly. "What exactly is it you want from me?"

"Information."

"I know nothing about Tabitha's life after she left Omaha other than that provided in news articles or cocktail gossip."

"I want everything you have or can get on Tabitha. Not just what you scooted under mom's nose. As a family member, you can easily access all her records: medical, school—whatever." Marge and the internet could only provide what was public and I'd run out of things to research.

His face became impassive. "My mother—"

"Can go piss up a rope," I bit out, furious at the wimpy excuse. He wasn't a teenager. "She didn't give a bloody damn when Tabitha was alive and I seriously doubt that's changed. How bad did you need her shares?"

"I've already told you that's not—"

"How the *hell* do you know it's *not* relevant if you *don't* answer the damn question?" I said, leaning forward and glaring.

Russell's jaw muscles flexed. Flexed again. By the third flex it occurred to me, belatedly, he might be fighting to restrain his wolf. *Idiot. You're challenging him in his own territory.* Warily, I inched back in my seat. Decided to admire that very interesting grain-pattern on the front of his polished oak desk.

There was a barely audible huff across from me.

"The plans were…complicated," Russell said in a guttural voice. "They included purchasing the controlling interest in one company and buying another one outright. The Board was split and Mother didn't believe the potential profits outweighed the high level of risk. Tabitha's shares, with or without her personal support, would have shifted critical votes in my favor."

Russell's voice had regained its usual smoothness as he spoke. I felt it safe to look up. "Was it worth sabotaging to somebody?" I asked, keeping my tone non-aggressive.

His gaze sharpened. "Several people were trying to block me," he acknowledged, "but I doubt they'd go so far as murder. Especially since everyone believed Tabitha's death would have made my position stronger through inheritance of her shares."

"Now *there's* a motive." That got me a blank look. Oops.

"Hardly. Mother and I were aware of the terms in Tabitha's will. Her death put us in an extremely disadvantaged position and the timing couldn't have been worse. The resulting audit killed that specific project and delayed others we had in motion."

Her death had been an inconvenience.

True, negotiating company business with their new co-owner had to be a royal pain in their butts. Tabitha's will had funneled her twenty-five percent company ownership and stock into her foundation, which supported the two charity funds she had established to help those who needed it and any deserving petitioners. The Trustee Board's first action, chaired by the lawyer in Nassau who drafted it, had been a complete financial audit of Chandler Import.

"How did you learn the will's contents?"

"I didn't. Mother did, somehow."

I'll just bet. "Tabitha left after a heated argument with your mother?"

"I fail to see how that applies, but yes. Anything further on that subject you'll have to ask Mother. I wasn't there and she hasn't shared."

Bummer.

"You really believe she was the target?"

"I do."

Instinct stirred, and I realized both man and wolf were studying me. Scenting for deceit. Evaluating my commitment. I raised my chin, met them eye-to-eye.

He blinked and the wolf receded. "I'll get what I can of Tabitha's records."

I heaved a sigh and rose. "Thank you. You have my office address." Maybe, hidden under the familial antagonism, he had cared about his sister.

I brooded as the elevator took me down. I had let my emotions override both my professionalism and self-preservation. I had stomped all over Rule Number One and provoked a wolf in his den. This was not how I worked. This was not *me*. I either wrestled down my demons or stepped away from my investigation.

Good thing I'd done some wrangling on my grandparents' ranch.

Luckily for me, the Woodworkers's parking garage had security cameras. They caught the tiger attacking as I walked toward my car. I got new stitches in my right shoulder. The tiger got a bullet in his right eye. My weapon had been a permanent fixture of my attire since last fall.

My interview with the Assault Unit's detective pretty much went the same as the last one, although the lack of drugs made answering her questions go smoother. She was obviously trying to tie this attack to the KC attack. It could be but, as I'd told Sinclair after the panther attack, I did have enemies locally. I politely requested that if she could find a link, to be sure and let me and Lt. Sinclair know. He actually had the audacity to show up at my apartment for another 'follow-up' almost as soon as I got home. Tired, hurting, I told him to go read the AU detective's report and shut the door in his face.

The ruling a week later was justifiable defense.

I left the courthouse in a dark, contemplative mood. I was confident my theory about the KC attack was right, but was I wrong about these attacks? I could easily believe the panther attack was a diversionary attempt, but this one? After all these months?

Did I have a stalker out there for a totally unrelated reason? If so, for what? Would my adversary try again?

Chapter 14

Remember me.

I woke, my forehead beaded with sweat. Six AM, according to my bedside clock. Hell of a wake-up call. I let the nightmare of blood and death fade before finally getting up to shower and shave. Still, it was almost ten by the time I made it into the office. I'd only managed two cups of my four-scoop coffee to steady me, but my current case required footwork and I had an eleven o'clock appointment with one of my leads.

"There's a box that came by courier on your desk. It's from Russell Chandler," Diana said as I passed her desk.

A quick peek found it full of neatly labeled folders. Chandler had been a busy badger these past three weeks. As much as I wanted to tackle them, the Myres case came first. I reviewed my case notes, then spent most of the day following leads and asking questions. I made it back to my desk by late afternoon and began updating my notes.

I glanced at the clock when Diana stuck her head in to wish me good night. Five o'clock already? I waved, then finished my report. As my computer logged off, I eyed Russell's box. Bit my lip. Yes, I'd promised to ease back on my hours, but that top folder was on the skinny side and shouldn't take long.

Turned out it was a domestic dispute report filed by Houston police and the name inside pissed me off. Reginald Lawrence Coldbath, Junior. Tabitha's ex-fiancé had finally deigned to return my phone call last week. Our conversation had been short, his replies rude and condescending. He'd made no mention of any incidents, especially one with police involvement.

According to him, the reason *he* terminated the engagement was incompatibility issues.

Evidently his face wasn't compatible with her fist.

According to the police report, there were no major injuries and the individual with the bad nosebleed refused to press charges. Undoubtedly due to the names and money involved, it didn't go any further. Now, the asshole had some explaining to do. Closing the file, I felt a small smile tug at my lips. Russell Chandler had known about the police file. Finding it on top of the stack, meant he wanted me to know it too. The man's attitude toward his sister wasn't as callus as he pretended. He had kept a distant eye on her while she was still in the States.

Getting a look at the time, I called it quits for the night. I left a note on Diana's desk asking her to make a copy of the box's contents. That would allow me to work from both home and office as time allowed. Setting the security alarm, I headed for the stairwell.

***

The next morning, I visited Diana's desk before the coffee pot.

"The Lexson report is ready for review. I'll have the expense statements done shortly. The duplicates are on your desk," she said without looking up.

That was quick. "Thanks. See if you can get Coldbath Junior in Houston on the phone. Be persuasive." Then I got coffee.

I stuffed the duplicated stack of folders into my briefcase to take home. Closing the lid required a bit of coaxing, but it finally snapped tight. Setting it aside, I paused at the brief sense of déjà vu. It had also held files on Tabitha the last time I'd used it.

I added my digital signature to the Lexson report after a quick review. Since there was no telling how long it'd take to get hold of Coldbath, I pulled the folder marked 'Financial' from Russell's box. The statements inside left my mouth hanging open. I'd known she was rich, but seeing the actual numbers? Wow! Next in the stack was her legal documents. A quick skim of her will was all I could handle before closing it. Legalese gave me a headache. I'd review it and the other documents at home, with a dictionary and a glass of scotch at my elbow.

I started on her school records next. I'd gotten to that short semester at a prestigious Austrian private school when an expensively dressed woman breezed into my office.

"Mrs. Cynthia Chandler would like to speak with you, Mr. D'Accio," Diana informed me dryly from the doorway.

"I decided it was time we spoke." The tone was haughty, her carriage arrogant.

She decided. Well, that was mighty nice of her. My attention went back to the report in front of me. "According to you, via your secretary, we have nothing to discuss."

"Your persistence in certain matters has made it necessary."

Another day, another pompous Chandler. "Appointments, Diana?" I asked, raising my voice slightly and ignoring the seductive perfume wafting across my desk.

"Mr. Engle in forty-five minutes."

"May I sit down?" the woman huffed.

"Pick a chair," I told her, as Diana handed me several office expense statements.

My visitor was apparently unused to the cold shoulder treatment. Since there was no telling what an angry tongue might let slip, I took my time scanning them before initialing approval. Glancing over at my visitor, I told Diana to mark Mrs. Chandler down for thirty minutes. When she started to say something, I held my hand up, palm out and stopped her with an off-handed, 'you're not important' movement.

"Any luck with my phone call?" I asked Diana.

It was obvious who the template for Tabitha's ice-persona had been. I made a mental note to check the front of my desk for frost burns.

"Still tracking him down," she replied. Then Diana asked Mrs. Chandler if she'd like some coffee, getting a barely civil 'no' in response.

"Is this how you normally do business, Mr. D'Accio?"

"Only with people who barge uninvited into my office and behave like a rude, petulant teenager."

Her mouth dropped open. "How dare—I'll not be…" She rocketed up out of the chair.

I let her get halfway to the door.

"People normally kill for reasons that fall into one of two basic categories." She stopped mid-step. "To get something or to protect something. Either way, Tabitha posed a problem for someone."

She did a nice pivot. "Ridiculous."

I took several moments to study her and, hopefully, hide the jolt to my system. I had seen the resemblances between mother and daughter in pictures, but they paled against the impact of our first face-to-face. Except for coloring, it was as if I was looking at Tabitha. But where Tabitha had been warm and vibrant, her mother was one cold bitch.

Her shoulder-length blond hair was perfectly styled around a flawlessly carved face, the trim body expertly dressed to show off a still youthful figure. Icy blue-green daggers hurtled at me from beneath long, dark lashes. It was easy to see why Cynthia Chandler was still ranked as one of the world's most beautiful, despite being in her mid-fifties.

"Think so?" I finally said, using an amused-but-not-really-interested tone.

"Is this some kind of psychological avoidance to prevent believing you're responsible for my daughter's death?"

"Is there some kind of psychological reason you refuse to accept your daughter was a target?" I fired back. "Isn't that standard fare for the rich and famous?"

"Kidnapping and ransom, yes. Murder, no."

"Yeah, well—" Diana buzzed in on the intercom, letting me know Coldbath was on the phone. Mrs. Chandler's head tilted on hearing the name. "Excuse me, but I need to get this. Leave or sit," I ordered, not caring which she did.

"Mr. Coldbath, this is Curt D'Accio," I said, as she returned to the chair she'd vacated. "You remember me from our conversation last week? Great. Why didn't you mention the fight you two had prior to your breakup? …Would you like me to refresh your memory from a copy of the police report

I have? …Tabitha trashes your expensively decorated apartment, bloodies your nose, gets your name in a police blotter, and you *forgot* about it?"

My visitor's hairline joined mine going north.

"Well, I'm making it my business. In case you've forgotten, I'm investigating her murder. What was—" I rolled my eyes, listened to his rant. "I don't give a rat's tail who your family is, if you'll tell me what—" How had Tabitha even considered marrying this jackass? "Do that," I told him bluntly, cutting off his tirade. "My reporter will trump your lawyer any day." I hung up. *Let him stew on that,* I fumed.

"Such determination. I can see why Tabitha was attracted to you and how you were able to convince her to return home."

"Not home, to Omaha," I replied tartly. Then gave myself a mental smack. *Rein it back to professional, Dice.*

"Either way, does your *investigation* require pawing through her entire life?" She nodded toward the folders scattered on my desk.

I settled back into my chair. Explanation wouldn't hurt and might gain some cooperation. "Tabitha was, to put it mildly, reserved. I got to know her better and deeper than she let anyone else. I got to know and love the *person* she was. But…" I ran my gaze over the small snapshots of her life littering my desktop.

"It still takes time to learn all the whys and what-fors, to understand all the fears and hopes and events that shape a person into who they become. Time we didn't get," I said quietly. "Things I would have eventually learned about her, just as she would have learned why I don't like turkey anything."

For a moment, the sense of loss washed through me. The files wouldn't be enough. I'd need to contact anyone who'd known her, directly or indirectly. Not just for the case, but because I was greedy. I wanted to learn everything I could about the incredible woman who'd shared my life so briefly.

"So, yes," I said, looking up at my visitor, "this research gives me a better understanding of *who* she was and some of the whys. It will also help highlight something I find that doesn't seem right, that doesn't seem to fit, and might be a clue to her murder."

"If there's anything to find."

Her amused tone and the patronizing attitude it was delivered with irritated me. I took a deep breath before I inadvertently gave her the upper hand. "Unless the attack was a colossal mistake of planetary proportions, she was the target. Tabitha either had something someone else wanted very badly or she posed a threat to someone."

Her lip curled. "You must be joking. Tabitha wouldn't hurt anyone," she said, waving her hand.

From the veiled contempt, I bet Tabitha's mother would, could, and probably had. "Tell that to Coldbath," I said. "However, I agree in that I don't believe it was a physical threat. The issue at stake could've been something she knew, overheard or saw—whether or not she was aware of it. Isn't knowledge the ultimate power? Or threat?"

"Only if the knowledge is accurate and the persons involved let it matter."

Wasn't that the truth. Most people had at least one secret they'd rather the world didn't know. Whether it was a morality-thumping grandma who was a closet drunk or a relative serving ten-to-fifteen in the state pen…or not being a natural blond, I thought nastily, glancing at the woman sitting across from me. But this woman would flatten any exposé with a steamroller and double dare anyone to make anything of it.

I remembered the shadows that had sometimes flickered across Tabitha's face. She'd definitely had secrets and one of them may have killed her. "How did you learn the contents of your daughter's will?" Tabitha wouldn't have told them squat.

Mrs. Chandler smiled coyly and said, "I have my ways."

"Meaning you seduced or bribed someone in the lawyer's office." The smile became an icy glower. "Bet no one else knew the contents, though. Perhaps someone with long-term plans—like marriage—believed Russell inheriting Tabitha's shares would have made him powerful and wealthy. I hear he's currently dating the daughter of one of your Board members."

"Stanford Dawson and his daughter's reputations are both above reproach."

"But not above investigation."

Her voice went even colder. "I'm not used to having my word doubted."

"A good PI doubts everything, especially where money is concerned."

"The Dawsons are well situated financially."

"Some people can't seem to have enough."

"Personal experience, Mr. D'Accio?" Her tone would have gouged steel.

I couldn't help grinning. *Tit for tat, spit for spat.* I tossed my pen on the desktop and rested my crossed my arms on top of it. "You didn't come here to trade insults, Mrs. Chandler. What do you want?"

Control slid over her like a slip, smoothing and changing her body language from alley cat to feline seductress. I blinked. She was doing everything but purring. Impressive, considering she's a wolf. Tabitha evidently got her mood shifts from her mom, too.

"Curt—may I call you Curt?"

"No." That threw her off for a second.

"Tabitha's death was shocking and deeply affected our family. We don't want to dwell on it and would like to put it behind us. That's hard to do when you keep stirring things up. Your insinuations could even adversely affect our company's standing in the business world."

Put it behind us? Adversely affect our company's standing?

"I am not insinuating anything," I said, a clipped tone hiding my anger. "I am stating, for the record, Tabitha was murdered. She was deliberately targeted by an unknown party, for reasons yet unknown. You seem more worried about your precious company than justice for your daughter."

The woman gave an elegant shrug. "She's gone. We're not. Chandler Import is our livelihood. It's a matter of priorities."

I stared at her for several moments, unable to fully comprehend her words. I corrected my earlier stance. This woman was a mean, cold, *heartless* bitch. "News flash, lady: *my* priority is justice," I stated coldly. "I *will* find the why. I *will* find the bastards responsible. They *will* pay, the shooter and the one who hired him."

Uncertainty flicked in her eyes.

"When did you learn she was returning to the States?" I was done sparring, and she evidently recognized it from my tone.

"When I received a call from Dr. Cagle's office asking to set up appointments for myself and Russell and explaining why. I didn't know which surprised me most: her illness or her returning to Omaha."

"What did the two of you argue about the night before she left?"

A manicured nail tapped the chair arm several times, then was examined carefully for any damage. "We had a difference of opinion about her future. She was being foolish, insisting on taking up some silly profession."

I am, as you put it, a menu item on numerous menus...Money. Always money.

"And you wanted a nice, tidy, conveniently rich business merger." The memory of Tabitha's furious tirade added contempt to the frosty mixture.

"I expected her to behave as a Chandler and as my daughter. I told her in no uncertain terms that she would. She refused, claimed she wouldn't be 'sold to the highest bidder' I believe was her childish phrase. We argued. No one, *no one*, talks to me like that. Her desire to leave was no less than mine to see her gone."

Ten, eleven years and it still pissed her off. This woman knew how to hold a grudge. "When did you become aware your son had hired me and why?"

"Russell confessed when I wanted you investigated after stories began circulating about the two of you."

Paparazzi should be added to the shoot-all list. Once they scented romance, I didn't dare scratch my crotch in public. They were relentlessly sneaky and we never knew what would show up where and with what stupid caption.

She flipped the switch again, exchanging anger for sultry. She crossed her legs and slid her gaze down my arms. Across my chest. "I found myself intrigued and highly curious. I knew it would take an exceptional man to get her off the boat she'd been moldering on since her engagement broke up." She bit lightly on a corner of her lip as her eyes tracked across my shoulders and back down my chest. "And you are...quite so."

I felt like a slab of beef in a butcher shop window. Was she like this all the time, or did private investigators happen to be in season? "Time's up," I said abruptly, wanting her out of my office.

She pulled a card out of her purse and laid it on my desk as she rose. "I think your assertions are ludicrous. But, if it keeps you happy…" she waved a hand at the pile of documents. "We can continue this discussion another time, another place," she added, strolling across the room. Opening the door, she paused, looked back over her shoulder. "If I can be of any…" a delicate, feminine shrug lifted one shoulder "assistance, give me a call. Anytime. You have my number."

"Actually," came Diana's polite voice from around the corner. "I have all his numbers. Especially yours."

I was still laughing when the outer door closed with a loud bang.

Chapter 15

Didn't get much done on Tabitha's files after Mrs. Chandler stormed out. A short-notice job from a contact in Omaha Accidental and Death Insurance had me investigating a claimant. Janice Lopez had gotten an anonymous tip that Jake R. Saunders was taking a vacation at the Meridian Hotel in Missouri. Its main claim to tourism was its six golf courses. A strange choice for someone who was supposedly limited to a wheelchair or walker.

A three-hour drive was followed by one hour of discreetly following Saunders as he whacked that poor little white ball around a manicured pasture. Then another three-hour drive home. Diana would've already locked the office up for the night. I did call Janice to let her know the guy had no problem walking unassisted or getting in and out of golf carts. I'd email the pictures to her tomorrow after downloading them from my camera.

I'd no sooner settled gratefully into my comfortable recliner when Marge called. Yes, she could come over, as long as a bag of burgers and fries accompanied her. All three showed up about twenty minutes later.

Supper was a pleasing banter. Marge touted the advantages of vegetarianism as she whittled away her double helping of fries and how I was contributing to the demise of poor defenseless animals. I asked her if she'd ever seen anyone gored by a bull or chomped on by an alligator.

"Besides," I added, "vegetarian diets might pass for Zeros and First-Gen. But can you picture a Second or Third giving up the hunt and their meat?"

She pouted for a minute. "They could try."

"Face it, Marge. We evolved as a meat-eating predatory species. Fangs and claws weren't made for digging up and chewing on carrots. And with those slowly rising percentages you quoted the other day, all our descendants will one day be full shifters of some sort."

"Yeah, yeah," she said grumpily.

Tossing our wrappings into the trash, I retrieved my briefcase and started laying folders out on the table. "Russell Chandler came through. These are copies of the copies that arrived the other morning." I grimaced when she pulled over the folder on Tabitha's Foundation and Trust. "I'm skipping that one for now. If you find anything that might have a bearing, let me know."

There were three medical records. Two from local pediatricians and one from New Orleans. A note Diana had diligently copied said no records were available from Nassau because her doctor's office there was destroyed in a string of arson-robberies that had plagued the island late last year. Information on her last physicals, including her hemochromatosis diagnosis was gone. Not that it mattered now, I thought, feeling the familiar twinge.

I opened the oldest record. It wasn't very thick, only covering about four or five months. From what I could decipher, Tabitha had been sick those months. Marge had said something about Tabitha being delicate at birth. The last entries were a referral to the Delmarra Clinic in Kanesville and notice of transfer of the patient to another doctor.

At quick search found the Delmarra report clipped to the front cover under a bunch of lab tickets. The Summary paragraph had me fuming. I held up the single-page report. "Get this," I said to Marge. "Cynthia Chandler took Tabitha to a lab only to see what kind of shifter she'd be. At three months, no less."

Each child's birth was a roll of the dice. Shifter or non-shifter. Their Gen level. Favoring a parent or some multi-great-grandparent. Young shifters came into their form at about two or three years of age and often had trouble controlling their tempers and instincts. Genetic analysis was pretty straight-forward and accurate nowadays. Knowing ahead of time gave parents some idea of what to prepare for and help minimized lawsuits.

"That is a bit young. They usually wait until sometime after the first year." Marge's brow scrunched. "I'd have expected them to be looking for a reason why she was sickly."

"I'd have thought so, too, but the single test requested is for specie typing. Dr. Jonathan Delmarra's summary states, and I quote, 'While the parents have strong canid and feline genes, the child shows no shifting tendencies.' Bet Mrs. Chandler was upset to learn she had a Zero daughter." Was that one of the reasons for her coldness toward Tabitha?

I took one look at the rest of the report, shuddered, and dropped it back into the folder. Medicalese was an even bigger headache than legalese.

Marge looked up from her reading. "Have you read the report on the fire that killed Mrs. Chandler's parents?"

"Yeah. The fire started in the kitchen—a pan left unattended on the stove. According to the autopsy, they were both dead drunk. No pun intended." I caught her thoughtful expression. "Why?"

"They'd been on house arrest for almost three weeks. They couldn't leave and no one was bringing alcohol in. Can you see two, seriously alcoholic people having a three-week cache of *unopened* booze? So," Marge tapped the table, "where did the booze come from?"

Huh. "They probably paid someone to slip it in. The withdrawals by then wouldn't have been pretty."

With a pointed look, Marge said, "Paid with what? They were broke. Which is why they tried to pawn Greg Greenbaum's smoker."

My lips pursed. "Good question. Traded something from their home?"

"That's assuming they still had anything worth trading. They'd probably kept the house to stay off the streets. Nobody would take them in. I have a street source nosing around, looking for any information on the Wilkes."

"Marge. That was—what?—thirty-five years ago."

"My source is good. She knows how to get people to talk to her."

Studying the set of her jaw, I asked, "Where are you going with this, Marge?"

That chin lifted higher. "Because if we can't find a reason in Tabitha's life for her murder, maybe it was retribution based on something to do with her family. If so, it'd almost have to do with Mrs. Chandler."

I gaped at her in shock.

"You said Tabitha didn't like talking about her family. That you saw 'shadows' in her eyes when she did speak of them."

I nodded slowly, remembering her almost haunted look. "Shadows. Secrets. I believe she'd have told me what was troubling her, eventually, but we never got the time."

Marge's assertion did make some sense for an otherwise senseless crime. I licked dry lips. "That could explain why it happened as soon as she returned to the States. But what about her father?"

She shrugged. "Anything is possible. But everything I've found out about Steven Chandler says he was a straight arrow. His whole life is practically a public record in gossip, business, and finance columns. He built his company the hardworking, honest way and was respected by both peers and competitors. If he had a dirty secret, it's well hidden.

"As for Cynthia?" Her eyes narrowed. "Her public bio pretty much begins when she started courting society. There's very little information outside of the basics for her early years: birth, schooling, her first marriage, dead parents. But we know she grew up running the Boondock's streets. Associating with who-knows-who doing who-knows-what. And there's that 'ruthless with a streak of vengeance' people spoke of. Sure sounds like personal experience to me."

I stared unseeing, my brain trying to deal with the implication. Could Tabitha have really been murdered for someone else's misdeeds? For spite?

Marge reached over and laid her hand on mine. "Family secrets are just one of the possibilities, Curt. We'll keep looking at *all* of them till we find the right one." Giving my hand a squeeze, she added, "Now, tomorrow is the sixteenth. Where do you want to go for your birthday dinner?"

Chapter 16

The next two weeks passed in fits and starts. New cases started, clients having fits when they didn't like the results. The worst one? Having a Second-Gen cougar losing it in your office. A bit unnerving as well as embarrassing, since she'd been naked when she shifted back. I lent her my jacket until someone could bring her clothes.

Marge was bearing the brunt of my griping about yesterday's cougar fiasco at dinner and was nearly rolling out of her chair. "Really? I don't see the humor," I said sourly.

"Give it a couple of days," she said between snorts. "Just think, what if she'd been a bear or tiger?"

The look on my face sparked another round of boisterous laugher. My visitor's chair and her shredded clothes would have been the least of the damages in that scenario. "Anyway, I asked Diana to stock the office with a selection of sweatpants and T-shirts in various sizes to *cover* future embarrassments." She'd also added the cost of a new chair to the woman's bill.

Marge nodded, finally winding down. "How's the record search going?"

"Not well," I said, still a bit miffed at her. I'd been reading and rereading everything between cases and at home. "I think I've practically memorized most of it. A lot of Tabitha's information is intriguing or mind-boggling, but there's nothing I can point a claw at. Despite the parties and social scenes, she lived a very bland, normal life. If you can call living on that boat normal."

Marge was regaling me with the stats on the number of water-centric families when, surprisingly, her phone buzzed. She normally cut it off in restaurants. I was downright shocked when she answered it.

"Yes…I'll meet you there. I'll be bringing someone with me." Her eyes slid toward me. "Yes." She hung up. "Eat up. We've got an appointment."

I started to ask who with, but a shake of her head snapped my mouth shut.

***

By the time I'd found a parking spot in the warehouse district, all I'd learned was that we were meeting with Marge's street source who'd been nosing around in Cynthia Chandler's early life. Disgruntled, I sulked beside her until she started to turn into an alley between two humongous buildings. I grabbed her arm. There was nothing in that brick gorge. Not even a dumpster. So why was my neck hairs standing up?

"Just how well do you trust this person?" I asked, my gaze raking the area around us. My eyes shifted right, left, upward, searching for the hidden threat.

"I trust her completely. We meet here regularly and, yes, there is often someone hanging around if that's what's got your neck hairs up."

Where? I couldn't spot them.

Marge tugged her arm free and started down the alley. I followed close behind. We were almost at mid-point when an opening yawned to the left of us. With the onset of twilight, it was barely visible to my Zero eyes. Worse, there was no railing to keep the unwary from falling in. Reaching it, I saw unlit steps leading down into a pitch-black stairwell. I assumed there was a door down there.

I followed Marge warily, my hand pressed against the side to guide me as darkness enveloped me. "Marge, I can't see a frigging thing." Why couldn't dark vision have been one of my pluses?

She half-turned and put my free hand on her shoulder. "Can't take you anywhere without a flashlight," she said with a touch of humor.

"I'll be sure to keep one on me," I muttered as we continued to descend. "How far down does this go?"

"Just a few more steps. The *Depot* is completely underground."

119

Then shouldn't it be called the Cave?

Finally. We were at the bottom and I still couldn't see squat. Did they import darkness? I stretched my hand out in front of me. "I don't feel a door."

"A little bit farther," came Marge's amused voice beside me. She took my arm.

Five steps in, Marge pivoted me sharply to the right. Good thing, too, because my left shoulder brushed against hard wall. The dim outline of a recessed door was in front of us. I swallowed. I was about to enter what was probably a Gen-only bar.

Marge hauled me through the door into, yep, a dimly lit bar. Although, after the darkness of our passage, I had to squint while my sight adjusted. There were a lot of tables. Booths, too, although I noted they seemed to be placed randomly against two walls. I got a brief glance of a bar on my left as Marge continued pulling me along. I felt the stares and sensed a few discreet inhales as we crossed the room.

Yes, I'm a stranger. Get a snootful.

Marge slid into a booth along the back wall and pulled me down beside her. My first thought on seeing the shifter sitting across from us was, *she's a bit young for this.*

"You licensed?" I asked bluntly, as her makeup and wisp of blouse advertised her profession.

"Yep. You'll have to wait till I'm off my break."

That made her at least seventeen, even if she didn't look it.

Marge rolled her eyes. "Curt, this is my friend, Angie. Angie, Curt D'Accio, and he wasn't asking for service."

"You don't look like a PI," Angie said.

"How should I look?"

"Rough. Tough."

I leaned on my forearm and gave her my all-tooth smile. "I am as rough and as tough as a situation requires." She didn't appear impressed.

"Glad to see you two are bonding," Marge said dryly. "Where is she?"

Angie tossed her head. "She's watching—can't say whether or not she'll join us. You bringing a PI spooked her."

A waitress glided to a stop beside us.

"Two pitchers of White Top beer and three glasses," Angie said. She pointed to me. "He's buying."

I stared at the waitress's outstretched hand, glared at Angie, gave Marge a dirty look, and dug out my bank card. The waitress glided away.

"No sense getting uptight," Angie said, "Besides you being unknown, Frank is picky about running tabs. Very few of the regulars have earned it. For most of us, it's pay-before-you-drink."

"Frank?" I asked.

"The bartender," Angie said nodding in the bar's direction.

The bar ran almost the full length of the far wall. And I meant far. The room must run the full width of the warehouse above us. A man carrying what looked like three cases of beer emerged from a door next to the counter's open end. I squinted to better judge those arms against the cases. I doubted he got much argument. Frank was a bear of a man, probably literally as well as figuratively, although distance and dimness could be throwing my shifter-sense off.

My inspection continued on around the room.

The door we'd come in appeared to be the only one, unless there was one in that supply room. The lighting, what there was of it, was mostly along the walls and over the bar. A few of the room's support pilings also had softly lit scones, with sections of the room between them almost completely in shadow. I was struck by the quiet. I also didn't see the usual bar accoutrements of TV screen, dart board, or pool table.

"What is this place?"

"The *Despondent Depot*," Marge said.

"I never would've guessed," I said, leaning heavily on sarcasm.

"No joke," she said, laughing. "Renamed by a previous owner. No one's sure it if was for himself or his customers."

"Probably both." I watched as Frank set a beer down in front of a slouched figure on a stool. "Is it always this quiet?"

"Yep. Loud is frowned on and can get you evicted. Fighting will get you a three-month ban."

"So will shifting," Angie added. "Frank believes it's detrimental to the bar and customers alike."

Our order arrived. I signed the receipt and pocketed my card while Angie poured us all a glass. We sipped in silence for several minutes. Waiting. Finally, a woman emerged from the central shadows. Angie slid over so she could sit down.

The woman was at least sixty, with thin white hair and a heavily wrinkled face. But her eyes were sharp, her shoulders straight, her attitude stiff, and her glass empty. She remedied that last item by emptying the first pitcher into it. She gave me an up-and-down perusal while she sipped.

"We don't get many Zeros in here," she said.

"Can't say I'm surprised. I could have tumbled into that unmarked hole and broken my neck." She was a canid of some kind. Not wolf, though.

The woman gave a toothy grin. "Wouldn't be the first. We make sure they're found elsewhere at the bottom of steps or a fire escape or something."

My head rotated slowly toward Marge. Her beer was getting a lot of intense scrutiny.

"Call me Vic," she said. "And no one is to know I told you anything about the Wilkes."

"How's that going to work?" I asked. "We're in a bar full of shifter ears."

"Not a problem," Marge said. "All the booths have a noise generator that will either drown out or garble our conversation. It's below the audible range of most non-shifters."

I leaned over. There was a small metal grill in the booth's frame several inches below both our seats. Ear cocked and straining, I could just barely make out a staticky hum. "Okay, I'm impressed." Wouldn't have expected that technology here.

Vic had lived next door to the Wilkes, and the picture she painted of the family was appalling. Money was spent on booze before food or bills. She often saw young Cynthia slinking out of the house in her wolf coat and assumed she was off hunting dinner. Then, when the girl was sixteen, her father tried to bargain Cynthia's virginity for several cases of whisky.

Shocked, I asked how she knew that.

Vic stopped refilling her glass long enough to give me a cocky grin. "The whole neighborhood heard that screaming match. I think that's the first time the girl laid in to them. Rumor had it that her parents had been pressuring her for months to bring home money working the streets."

I flicked a quick glance at Angie. How did one get started in the sex-trade?

Marge leaned forward. "I imagine that was one of Cynthia's reasons for a quick marriage."

"Don't know where she met him, but it was a whirlwind courtship and marriage in less than two months," Vic said, sipping on her beer. She smacked her lips. "And Greenbaum was a good choice. Decent guy, decent job, decent home in a nice neighborhood. Unlike that other guy she'd been seeing."

"What other guy?" I asked, perking up.

She stared down in her glass for a moment. "All I ever heard him called was Ray. He was from the Boondocks. Word was, he was available for the right price."

"For what?"

"For whatever you wanted," she said grimly.

Interesting. "Were you surprised the Wilkes died in a fire while drunk?" I asked.

Vic shrugged. "I'm surprised it didn't happen sooner." She hesitated, looking between me and Marge for several seconds. She glanced sideways at Angie, who gave her an encouraging nod. Vic cleared her throat.

"About that fire. I remember overhearing the firemen say they'd been cooking fish. Well…thing is…neither of the Wilkes liked fish and I saw Ray across the street a day earlier. He was glaring at their house."

***

"Wondering what kind of place that was?" Marge asked as we walked back to my car.

"Other than being a shifter bar? It was a bit, uh, different."

"We call ourselves *Despos*." Her voice turned distant. "We're the desperate, the despondent, the disposable. It's a place for castoffs and the downtrodden."

I pulled her to a stop. "You are *not* any of that."

She gave me a sad smile. "But once upon a time, I was. Wasn't I?"

Her depression had lasted for months after losing the baby. If I could have gotten my hands on Donald Hanscombe, I'd have beaten him to a pulp then stomped him into the dirt.

Marge glanced back. "It's a safe haven to lick wounds, to rebuild oneself and find the courage to face tomorrow. It's also a refuge from the full-throttle world, a quiet place to simply relax and just let go. Some only come for the time they need it, others become regulars." She flicked me a quick sideways glance. "It's a place we could all occasionally use."

"How did you find it?" I asked, feeling a bit unsettled. Her voice had been an odd mixture: dreamy, wistfulness, contemplation. Until the final statement I knew was aimed at me.

"It seems to attract those who need it. Or, in my case, are led there. Angie brought me there one night. She had watched me walking the streets…just walking, going nowhere. Going to the *Depot*…talking with Angie and some of the others…it helped," Marge said, her voice somber.

That explained the times I couldn't get hold of her. And now she'd taken me there.

I felt a twinge of jealousy. Me, Nate, her co-workers…we'd all been so worried about her. We'd tried just about everything until, finally, she appeared to be coming out of it. Thanks to them. "Glad she and the *Depot* could help," I managed as we resumed our walk. My voice betrayed me.

This time it was Marge pulling me to a stop. "You *all* helped, Curt, with your support and just *being* there. But you and the others treated me as a fragile, don't-upset-the-invalid invalid. And you were always so wound up. I worried you'd go out and do something stupid."

"You were worried about *me*?"

"Especially after certain comments made the rounds," she said with a laugh, then took a deep breath. "At the *Depot* they listened. They sympathized. They grieved with me. Then, they patted me on the shoulder and said, 'you'll have one heck of a scar.' That's *Depot*-speak for 'wounds heal; move on.' So, I did."

"But you have the scar."

She touched me lightly on the breastbone. "So do you."

"Guess I owe the *Despo* regulars a round of beer," I said, giving her a hug.

Marge laughed and we started walking again. "I'm sure Hugh will appreciate it."

"Hugh?"

"The bartender. He probably gets a commission off of all sales."

"His name isn't Frank?"

"It is, and it isn't."

I rolled my eyes. "Marge, we didn't have that many beers," I said, as we neared my car. "Vic and Angie drank most of it."

Marge laughed again. I loved hearing it. "No one knows what his real name is. So, we each call him whatever feels right. To me he's *huge*, so Hugh."

That he was. "He looks like Boris the Bear to me," I said, opening the passenger door for her.

"That's safe," she said, her eyes twinkling. "While he doesn't seem to care what we call him most of the time, I do recommend avoiding anything with *mother* in it. I once saw him break the offender's jaw and both arms before slinging him—literally—up, out, and halfway across the alley."

That would be an impressive feat, considering the bar was fifteen steps below the alley. I settled under the steering wheel. "Think Ray killed them?"

"I'd lay odds on it," Marge said thoughtfully. "Get them passed-out drunk then set the stage. A hot, oily fish pan is a fire waiting to happen: no one would question it. The *real* question is, did he do it for himself or because Cynthia asked him to?"

I nodded. "Sounds as if they both had plenty of reasons to be pissed." Pulling away from the curb, I asked how her research was going.

"Slow. I'm getting bits and pieces. I'm going to interview Dr. Delmarra at his clinic and Mrs. Chandler, assuming I ever get past her secretary."

"Think she might regret not checking for genetic issues other than shifting?"

She snorted. "No. I'm sure she brushes Tabitha's hemochromatosis off as being the one-in-whatever-odds case. I'll let you know how my interview with her goes."

Chapter 17

I stood to greet the man Diana escorted into my office the next morning. I'd hesitated on the appointment, as I had several other cases ongoing. But she'd said he was adamant and, from the grim expression on his face, it was serious. Jason McFearson refused coffee and got straight to the point as soon as the door closed behind Diana.

"I'm being blackmailed."

Yep. That was serious and, boy, was he pissed about it.

"I paid the large amount demanded two months ago. Last week I got a second note for a smaller amount. It said that amount would be expected every two months. I left a note of my own instead of cash at the drop site. Yesterday, my fifteen-year-old son was beaten on his way to school. When we brought him home from the hospital, there was another note stuck in the door."

"Pay up or else?" I said, looking up from my note taking.

"Pay up or your lovely—underlined twice—daughter is next," he spit out. "Jolene is also fifteen, Jacob's twin."

No way was I not taking this case. McFearson slammed a fist on my desk hard enough to bounce a couple of items. The anger rolling off him was hot enough to boil water.

"Yes, I was a teenage hellion. Yes, I did some stupid things. I will *not* allow my past to endanger my family. I want the bastard found."

"Count on it."

Chapter 18

Dr. Delmarra had been droning on about the clinic for over thirty minutes. Marge's smile was still in place, but her brain had tuned out about ten minutes ago. He was the son of the original founder. The first Dr. Delmarra was killed when the clinic was bombed by a dissident thirty years ago. He and his mother had rebuilt it and resumed his work.

Which had turned this interview unproductive.

She rose to her feet when he paused to pull a pamphlet from a desk drawer. Thanking him for his time, information, and pamphlet, she exited as gracefully as she could. She stopped at the receptionist's desk. The woman appeared to be in her late fifties and had the air of a long-term employee. Could she be so lucky?

"Hi," Marge said, glancing at the desk plaque that read 'Marsha Calvert.' "Mind if I talk with you for a few minutes, Miss Calvert? Or is it Mrs.?"

"Mrs." The woman checked her computer monitor. "There's thirty minutes before the next client. What about?"

"I'm researching background for an article I'm working on," Marge said, flashing her warmest smile. "The Delmarra Clinic features indirectly in it but I like to be thorough. How long have you worked here?"

"Thirty-six years next month."

Yes! She set her recorder on the desk. "Then you knew the original Dr. Delmarra. I have a perspective of him from his son's point of view, who was a college student at the time of his death. Would you be willing to give me yours as an employee who actually knew and worked with him?"

Mrs. Calvert eyed the recorder. "He was a great person to work for.

Thoughtful, undemanding except for quality in our duties. He was very precise himself but very easy going. I rarely saw him lose his temper."

"My article is going to be about Tabitha Chandler's life. I realize all records were destroyed in a bombing, but would you, by chance, remember her mother bringing her in?" Afterall, the woman had been very prominent.

The woman snorted. "I'm not likely to forget. Dr. Delmarra's worse blowup was due to her. Mrs. Chandler, not the baby."

"Oh?"

"The woman was unbelievably arrogant," Mrs. Calvert said, shaking her head. "Even with the Doctor. As soon as the post-analysis consultation was finished, she demanded to leave with the baby's records. Dr. Delmarra explained they were property of the clinic. Mrs. Chandler said she'd paid for the work, therefore they were hers. It was embarrassing." She shook her head. "I remember there were two clients in the waiting room. We could all hear the argument through the door."

"Who won?" Marge asked, intrigued.

"Technically, she did. Mrs. Chandler walked out with the records, brazen as you please. Dr. Delmarra was furious, but with her money and connections he knew protesting wouldn't get anywhere and he couldn't afford a lawsuit. Fortunately, I had forwarded a copy of his report to the baby's pediatrician so he had me request a copy back for our records. Not that it mattered anyway," she said with a sigh. "He was dead and most of our records destroyed five weeks later."

"I, um, understand all of the clinic's staff was killed."

Mrs. Calvert gave a sad smile. "I wouldn't normally call my mother falling and breaking several ribs lucky. It certainly wasn't for the nice young man hired from a temp agency while I was on leave tending to her."

"Dr. Delmarra said they never caught the bomber. A dissident, I believe he said?"

"We never knew why, although that is the most likely reason since three other places were bombed over the next several weeks. There were never any complaints or demands or, or anything. Then it just stopped. I can still recall the tension, everyone waiting for the next one. Security was tightened and police patrols were doubled around medical facilities for weeks. I can't help but wonder," Mrs. Calvert said somberly, "if whoever it was will strike again some day."

Marge mulled over the interesting tidbits as she walked to her car. Learning Mrs. Chandler was one obnoxious, paranoid, controlling bitch was no surprise. The bombings were, though. And stopping with no demands or manifesto released? That didn't fit the usual extortionist or nutcase's pattern. Mrs. Calvert probably wasn't the only one giving the occasional look over her shoulder.

She drove to her office, checked her notes, then called Steinwood Pediatric Center. Dr. Joshua Kerfoot, who'd been Tabitha's pediatrician, had retired. She managed to snag a next day appointment with Dr. Martha Stoltenberg, his successor. In the meantime, she'd pay a visit to the newspaper archives.

***

Dr. Martha Stoltenberg was a fortyish matron Marge was sure the kids and their parents normally found comfortable. Right now, the doctor's stern expression was more scowl than frown.

"I realize Miss Chandler is no longer a patient, or even living, but I'm not asking for any, shall we say, *sensitive* information." Marge gave the doctor her best 'trust me' smile. It didn't work.

"There's no reason to request any information, Miss Lockewild. Medical histories are private. The fact that she is deceased is no excuse to—"

"Tabitha Chandler had hemochromatosis."

Dr. Stoltenberg's mouth snapped shut.

"The diagnosis was made shortly before her death. She had an appointment with a specialist scheduled for three days after her arrival in Omaha. Which, of course, never happened."

The doctor studied her for a moment, then requested Tabitha Chandler's file brought in from their Archived section. Hanging up the phone, she gave Marge a piercing look.

"Are you looking to see if the clinic mishandled Miss Chandler's medical

130

health?"

"No, ma'am. From what I've been told, it would not have been apparent on general tests. It would have taken special tests to find it and the genetic traces."

"Yes," the doctor stated firmly. "Even then, *if* such a test was run, and *if* the genetic markers for hemochromatosis were found, there is still no guarantee it would become active."

A nurse entered, handed a folder to the doctor and gave Marge a smile before exiting.

The doctor flipped the folder open. Marge kept her impatience firmly in rein as she flipped through and read several pages.

"It appears our records don't start on Tabitha Chandler until she's about four months old. Her earlier history was provided by her previous pediatrician, a Dr. Stanley Farr at the Nebraska Children's Hospital-Clinic. The child's first year, by their records and ours, show it was a rough one. Her lungs were underdeveloped at birth—let me check. Yes, everything was cleared up by her first birthday."

"Her older brother, Russell, also saw a pediatrician at NCHC. Wouldn't it be more logical to keep the same doctors for both?"

"Usually, yes," Dr. Stoltenberg agreed without glancing up. "It's quite possible the girl didn't acclimate to the doctor's personality. It does happen."

She read a few more pages, then closed the file and folded her hands on top of it. "You are correct. Routine tests by either of our offices would not, and did not, find any signs of a blood disorder. There is no indication Miss Chandler was other than a normal, healthy child after that first year."

"What about the referral to the Delmarra Clinic?"

Dr. Stoltenberg's gaze sharpened. "What referral? I saw no record of it."

"Tabitha was three months old. Her mother wanted to know her Gen status."

"That's early," Stoltenberg muttered, opening the folder again. Flipped more pages. "Are you certain about the referral?"

Marge nodded. "The Clinic sent a report of their results to Dr. Farr's office. It should have been included in the files you received."

Dr. Stoltenberg frowned down at the file, before straightening and flashing Marge a professional smile. "I'm afraid I can't help you. We obviously didn't get it, so you'll need to check with NCHC for any further information on that issue."

And therefore not your problem. Rising, Marge gave her a bland smile. "Administrative snafus do happen occasionally. Thank you for your time."

Dr. Stoltenberg had declined to be recorded. As soon as Marge got to her car she pulled out her recorder and proceeded to dictate what little she'd learned.

"Even if Mrs. Chandler had assumed the Delmarra report had been transferred with the rest of Dr. Farr's file," Marge mused thoughtfully into the microphone, "its absence would have become evident when Dr. Kerfoot mentioned the need for Gen-status testing. Why didn't she update Dr. Kerfoot's records? What reason did she give him? Surely, she wouldn't have destroyed her copy."

There was no way to get an answer. She'd stopped by the Administrator's office to get Dr. Kerfoot's contact information. Unfortunately, he'd passed on about four years ago.

***

Marge debated her next question as she sat on the penthouse terrace.

It had taken several days and a lot of persistent calls before she was *graciously* granted an interview by Mrs. Chandler in her sumptuous apartment. Graciousness had turned into quickly hidden displeasure and not-so-hidden condescension after learning the interview wasn't to discuss her or Chandler Import. She also got the impression the woman wouldn't have agreed to her use of a tape recorder if she'd known that beforehand.

Her questions about Tabitha's early life had been met with disinterest and what sounded like rote responses handed out to social busybodies. Or nosy reporters.

Tabitha was a quiet child. Good in school. Very athletic. Loved the water.

"Tabitha left Omaha at nineteen," Marge said, shifting to a slightly more aggressive tone. "Rumor says it was because of a family rift. Is that true?"

"I do not speculate on rumors."

My, could that nose go any higher? "Why else would she never have returned for so many years?" Marge got an arrogant glower in response. "Were you surprised to learn she was coming back to Omaha and why?"

"Yes. Both her return and the reason for it were unexpected."

That's all she had to say? "Were you hoping for a reconciliation between you and your daughter?"

Mrs. Chandler made a vague hand movement. "Of course. I contacted Tabitha privately before she left Nassau."

Not according to Curt. "When you took Tabitha to the Delmarra Clinic at age three months, were you shocked to learn your daughter was a Zero?"

Something changed.

Not the woman's posture. Not her voice. Nothing obvious, but Marge was suddenly certain Mrs. Chandler's wolf was lurking behind her eyes. Marge's wolf and reporter instincts both went on alert.

"How did you learn about that?" Mrs. Chandler asked.

"A copy of the clinic's report is in her pediatric records."

"No, it isn't. I was told all records were destroyed in that tragic bombing."

"Um, yes, it is. In Dr. Farr's files. Along with his referral. You transferred Tabitha to another pediatrician during that same timeframe. I guess whoever made copies of his file for Dr. Kerfoot's office missed it. Why didn't you provide them with a copy of yours?"

"My copy?" she asked, her tone neutral.

Tread softly, Marge's wolf warned. "According to the receptionist, you walked out of the clinic with Tabitha's records over Dr. Delmarra's vehement protest."

After a long, drawn-out moment, she said, "I had my reasons. You've seen the report in Tabitha's records, Miss Lockewild? It has all the medical analysis included?"

Why did that sound like a threat? "Well, yes, I'm assuming so. We could only read the summary paragraph. It'd take a doctor to interpret the rest."

They should have had Nate look at it.

"We?"

"Naturally, I've interviewed Curt D'Accio as part of my article."

"Ah, yes. Her lover."

Marge hid her unease. She could feel the wolf prowling behind the woman's eyes. "Back to my earlier question, were you surprised at your daughter's genetic results?"

"Yes, I was quite surprised, as we were expecting at least a First-Gen ability."

"Did you have any other DNA tests done? Perhaps somewhere else?"

"Such as?"

"Well, to learn why she was so sickly for one. Wouldn't they have found the hemochromatosis so that you, and she, could be watching for it?"

More silence. "There were no other tests," Mrs. Chandler stated, her gaze focused on Marge. "The doctors assured me that Tabitha's condition was undoubtedly due to complications of my pregnancy and that her weak lungs would be normal by her first birthday. Which they were. If you check, you'll find I was quite sickly myself during the last trimester."

"I have. You spent much of that time at the Loess Hills Sanitarium, a private hospital in Glenwood. You birthed Tabitha there." Marge realized her own wolf was becoming aggressive under the woman's intense stare.

"You seem to already know a great deal," Mrs. Chandler said coolly, rising from her seat. "No sense continuing this conversation."

Her aide must have been watching, as she hurriedly held the glass door open for Mrs. Chandler's regal exit and then escorted Marge out and into the foyer.

Marge studied the apartment's imposing double doors as she waited for the elevator. If her wolf was out, its ears would be cocked and its nose testing the air for secrets. Mrs. Chandler had been stiff and on guard as soon as the Delmarra Clinic was mentioned. Why?

Chapter 19

"I'm heading home, Curt."

Startled, I looked up. Diana stood in the doorway, and a quick glance at the clock showed it was past five o'clock. It'd only felt like a few minutes since I sat down around three.

"Don't forget, you have a dinner date with Marge at six-thirty," Diana said.

"Thanks," I called out, giving her a wave before she disappeared. I glanced at the clock again, then down at my notes. Would Marge mind if I called and canceled?

I'd been pouring over several days' worth of notes on McFearson's case. I was sure the blackmail-extortionist's identity was somewhere in them. I needed to find the one clue that made all the rest fall into place. I reached for the phone, then drew my hand back. Pinched the bridge of my nose.

No. A break would be good and might even help me spot that elusive sucker. Plus Marge was wanting to tell me what she'd found during her own days of sleuthing. I'd just do another half hour.

5:50.

I stretched, plopped the McFearson file in my Working basket, and turned off my office lights. I was moving toward the security panel in the outer office when I caught motion in the corner of my eye. My head caught something hard and heavy.

***

"Lay still, Curt. Police and paramedics are on their way."

I instantly knew three things. The muffled voice was Marge's, I probably had a concussion, and my office stank.

"Did they have to skunk my office?" I groaned.

Skunk bombs were favored by both criminals and pranksters. A few drops of skunk-oil added to smoke bombs made it impossible for a shifter to sniff out any scents. As bad as it smelled to me, it would be even worse for them.

I opened my eyes. Marge's face wavered into view with a rag held over her nose. Yep. Definitely a concussion. "Why don't you go wait in the hall," I managed to say, before squeezing my eyelids closed against the pounding pain.

"I've got several windows open. It's starting to air out."

Right. We both knew the scent would linger for days. Several heavy footsteps came through the door, followed by sneezing and cussing. Police or paramedics?

I'm pretty sure Marge rode with me in the ambulance, but I was floating in and out. The ER doctor let her into my curtained cubby after they were done poking, prodding, and x-raying. I squinted at the two police officers he'd also let in. It looked like—

"Detective Chizek, I don't suppose you'd wait until tomorrow?" Marge said.

I let out a groan that had nothing to do with my head. The patrol supervisor had called for a detective and the Robbery Unit's senior detective had grabbed it. Detective Chizek was dedicated, smart, and meticulous. She was also as tenacious and stubborn as a wolverine. Had the personality of one, too, despite being a First-Gen feline.

"Miss Lockewild, you were the one to call the police. What led you to Mr. D'Accio's office at," Chizek checked her notebook, "seven-fifteen this evening?"

"Curt and I were supposed to meet for dinner at six-thirty. When he didn't show and never responded to a call, I went to his office. I expected to find him working on case notes. I found him unconscious on the floor, his office in a mess, and called 9. I only touched Curt, a door handle, and several window sashes." She gave the detective a bright smile. "You and the other responders can thank me for that last item."

"Mr. D'Accio, what do you remember?"

"Pain." The junior officer taking notes behind her rolled his eyes.

"You know darn well a concussed victim has trouble remembering what gave it to them," Marge said tartly.

"Considering how hard-headed Mr. D'Accio has proven to be, I figured he might be an exception."

The officer smothered a snicker.

"We won't know what's missing until you or your secretary can furnish a list. However," her lips pursed, "the responding officer's report indicates hard drives on both computers are gone and paper files strewn all over. What are you working on?"

"I have several at the moment, but my primary case is a blackmail-turned-to-nasty-extortion. I'm getting close to solving it." My notes had probably disappeared with my attacker.

"Who and what?" Det. Chizek demanded.

I shook my head, then had to wait for the room to stabilize. "Client confidentiality."

"Which my case overrides."

"Your case is about who attacked me and trashed my office," I retorted. That earned me a glare. "If they targeted my case files, this could very well center on any one of them, current or past. No telling whose hide I've pricked."

Eyes narrowed, Chizek said, "Could this be related to the two—maybe three?—previous attacks on you?"

"How would I know," I said, testily, "since none of them has been solved. I've been—" A horrible thought suddenly hit me.

"Marge," I gasped. "My gun? They take it?"

I breathed a sigh of relief when she shook her head. It had been my sixteenth birthday present from my father and we'd spent hours honing my skill. All in preparation for the law career I was never to achieve. Losing it would hurt worse than my head.

"A lawyer from next door showed up in the middle of all that. He'd come back from his dinner for last-minute work on a brief and offered to lock your weapon in his safe." Marge slid a sideways look at the detective. "To keep the police from impounding it."

Thank God. It could have taken months to get it back.

"Call if you do think of something you can tell me or my office," Det. Chizek snapped, flipping her notebook closed with a twist of her wrist.

"I'll have my secretary forward a list as soon as we're able," I called out as she marched off. Her junior shadow gave a wave, showing he'd heard.

A nurse whisked the curtain aside. "Mr. D'Accio? All tests are clear and there's no sign of a skull fracture. The doctor will release you if someone can stay—excellent," she said when Marge held up a hand. "I'll have the paperwork for release and prescriptions at the desk ready for you and have an orderly bring a wheelchair." She zipped back out.

I gave Marge a wobbly smile. "Got a car?"

<h1 style="text-align:center;"><u>Chapter 20</u></h1>

"Well, what do you think?" Marge whispered.

We lay stretched out on the floor in Marge's apartment, toasting our feet in front of a gas fireplace. I held up a finger and finished reading the final paragraphs on Tabitha's early life. "It's excellent," I told her.

I handed the pages back and stretched my toes toward the flames. Happy, content, and pain free. I'd told Diana to start taking appointments again this morning. D'Accio Investigations was reopening.

I still had an occasional headache, but after three weeks they'd migrated down to minor. The office was finally odor-free and the paper files had been pieced back together. The last of my open cases had been closed a week ago, thanks to my old mentor and partner from Halligan popping in for several days to help.

I'd forgotten how smoothly Thomas Tall Elk and I worked together. I worked the phone and computer, he ran down leads and did on-site interviews, and we collaborated on the reports. In the evenings, he'd regaled Nate and Marge with tales from my early days at HIS, including the time *I* had been skunked. By the real thing when, uh, reconnoitering a suspect's home.

If I ever decided to branch out, Thomas would be the one I'd call.

"Have you heard anything more about Jason McFearson?"

My McFearson notes hadn't disappeared, and the link I'd been looking for had practically assaulted me for stupidity as I rebuilt his file out of that mess. He had taken the name straight to the police station. He not only turned himself in for the old arson case Mark Carrioc was blackmailing him for, he also provided evidence on another old case. It seems Carrico was unaware

McFearson had witnessed his killing of a drug peddler and then rifling through his pockets for cash and a very distinctive knife afterwards. Which the idiot still carried.

"Willing to take his lumps is in his favor. He's getting probation for the old arson charge in exchange for being the DA's primary witness against Mark Carrioc. Turns out, that's what made him realize exactly what kind of crowd he was involved with and walked away."

"What about the attack on you in your office? Did Carrico admit to that?"

I shook my head. "It wasn't Carrico; he was gambling at the Moonlight Casino in Kanesville until well after midnight. Unless we can figure out what files went missing, or something else breaks, it will probably never be resolved." Thomas and I had spent several evenings speculating on what my attacker had been after.

"I hope they got whatever it was they wanted," Marge grumbled, "and don't do a repeat."

"You and me both. I'm also getting a bell installed. I'm tired of people sneaking up on me. Do you have the next part of your article worked out?"

"Yep. That's going to be the spicy part." She stuck that recorder extension of herself in my face. "Care to give a statement, Mr. D'Accio?"

"No. Do your own legwork." Twisting it out of her hold, I tossed it on the end table.

"As I'm spending a couple of weeks in the Caribbean and the Gulf, starting this Saturday, I will be." Marge stretched, stood. "I'll be getting the skinny on her life there."

"Be glad it's mid-April instead of June." I shuddered, remembering that rash.

She flashed a smile a tad short of wicked. "I'll be getting the skinny on you, too."

"Hah. Just read last year's tabloids." I rolled to my feet.

Marge smirked. "Like the one revealing your 'abusive' treatment of Tabitha?"

I shot her an annoyed glare. That frigging picture was going to haunt me to my grave. Shot from a distance with a telescopic lens, it looked like I was in the process of slapping Tabitha. Naturally, a bold-faced caption about me shooing away flying pests wouldn't have generated as many sales. "Maybe I should take my Moscato and go."

"Maybe I'll pour us a glass. Any leads yet on Tabitha's murder?" she said over her shoulder.

"No," I replied, listening to glasses clink in the kitchen. "None, nada, *zilch*." Things had dried up even before I had my brain rattled three weeks ago.

"Humph. Don't be so wishy-washy," she said, coming back into the living room. Handing me my wine, she sat back down on the floor. "Don't worry, as a good investigator you know how—"

"Good?" I collapsed on the couch, wine held to my chest and mortification plastered on my face. "Please. Try fantastic, excellent, unbeatable, first-rate or even tip top. Anything, my dear, but not just *good*."

Marge hugged her knees, laughing. "You are so full of crapola. Talk about ego."

I put a hurt look on my face. "Ego? I have no ego. I have *confidence*."

"Yeah, lots of it. Lots and lots and—"

"Okay, okay," I said, finally breaking down into laughter, "I got it."

"You betcha." She sipped her wine. "Now, as I was saying before being so rudely interrupted, you know how to get from point A to point C by extrapolating point B."

I winced. "Now you sound like my tenth-grade math teacher."

"You had trouble with math."

"Tell me about it."

"However, you are *exceptionally* good," she rolled her eyes, "when it comes to people and real life. You see connections and patterns. You, my dear Holmes, are a master de-puzzler." She toasted me with her glass.

I grinned. "De-puzzler. I like it." My grin faded. "Unfortunately, there's a lot of pieces missing to this puzzle. I've gone over everything Russell Chandler sent me, even had a CPA go over her finances looking for any unexplained large cash transfers or withdrawals."

Marge kicked off her slippers and stretched her legs out toward the fire.

"Thinking embezzlement?"

"Or blackmail. Maybe things were fixing to bust out into the open." That'd not only be potentially dangerous for whoever the blackmail subject was, but exposure for the blackmailer. As my recent case had led me to thinking. "I still think the key is her return to the States." I swirled my wine thoughtfully. "Maybe there's more than one reason she isolated herself on the water and didn't file float plans. I'm going to be looking at things here, too…and I still don't know why Tabitha belted Coldbath."

"He's a bastard."

I threw her a startled look. "What did you learn from his interview?" She'd flown to Texas and New Orleans for personal interviews with several of Tabitha's old acquaintances.

"That he's a bastard."

"*Marrrge!*"

"Selfish, condescending, egotistical, hedonistic ignoramus with a Zeus complex."

"What," my hand tightened around my glass, "did he do?"

"Besides pissing me off?" She snorted. "He's a walking erection. He not only ogled my chest for the entire interview, but I'm also pretty sure he was stroking himself under the desk. Then he showed up at my hotel room later that evening expecting a more in-depth *interview*. He was a tad bit irked when I threw him and his penis out."

Definitely a bastard. If he'd stepped out of line—scratch that. *When* he stepped out on Tabitha, she would've been highly pissed when she caught him. Enough to enflame her to the point of throwing a punch? Of course, not being in public, she might've figured it was worth it. I wouldn't mind taking him down a notch myself.

"Oh, before I forget it." Marge held up a finger. "We ought to have Nate interpret the Delmarra report for us. Mrs. Chandler seemed a bit, I don't know, touchy about it. She most certainly didn't like me asking about Tabitha's hemochromatosis."

"I'll bring it up. Now, there's a couple of places you should visit. In Kingston you should…"

Chapter 21

The phone's shrill ring dragged me awake. It took two more rings before I finally collected myself enough to check the caller ID and answer it.

"Morning, Marge. Isn't this a bit early on a Sunday for you?" I yawned. "I heard you'd gotten back. How'd the Caribbean trip go?"

"Breakfast at Claude's. Thirty minutes." She disconnected.

Her clipped tone put me on an immediate alert. I threw on a relatively clean pair of jeans and yanked a shirt off its hanger. Grabbed my jacket on the way out.

Marge and a steaming pot of coffee were waiting in a back booth when I arrived. I took a sip and let Claude's famously strong brew work its magic. The waitress came over to take our order: ham-steak and egg platter for me, a three-cheese omelet with homemade hash browns for Marge. I sipped warily, watching as Marge topped off her coffee from her water glass. The stiff set of her jaw did not bode well.

I sat my cup down. "Okay, Marge, spit it out."

"Cat Island. Ring a bell?"

I blinked.

"As in wedding bell?"

A quick visual sweep showed no one close enough to have heard her.

She leaned forward. "You and Tabitha got married and you never. Frigging. *Told* me."

"We didn't—"

"Don't lie to me! I found the marriage certificate. I found the pastor and his wife you took sailing one afternoon to a secluded beach. Does Diana know?"

"No." We'd gotten married on one of Bahama's Outer Islands, wanting to avoid the publicity hoopla. Not finding the license in Chandler's stack of documents had made me think we'd succeeded.

"Why keep it secret?"

"It's no longer relevant," I said, a hitch in my voice. "I'm no longer married."

"The will. Why didn't you challenge it?"

My back stiffened. "I don't want or need her money. Her trust funds her foundation and all the good they provide. That had meant everything to Tabitha. That's where her money *should* be."

"But—"

"No." My cup *thunked* against the tabletop. "Leave it alone, Marge."

Our meal arrived and we dug in silently. "Have you turned your story in yet?" I finally asked.

"No." She speared a bite of omelet with her fork. "I wanted to review my notes and finalize a few details."

My gaze met hers, and I was suddenly chewing on cardboard eggs at the realization I was sitting across from a reporter, not a friend.

"So, whose idea was it to get married?" She took another bite, her eyes on me.

"Both of us." I managed to swallow the cardboard.

"Whose idea to have it on Cat Island?"

"Hers." My guts twisted.

"You could at least say 'please.'"

"Huh?"

"It's the least you can do when asking someone to give up a journalistic scoop." A small smile lifted the corners of her lips. In the blink of a shutter, the reporter was gone.

It took several seconds before I remembered to close my mouth. Her eyes had warmed up, although there was still a residue of anger and hurt swirling around their edges. My heart rate dropped back to normal. "Will a very big thank you suffice?"

"And buying breakfast."

I nodded and breathed a heartfelt sigh. "We were going to tell you, Marge. The luncheon that never happened?" I jabbed the last bite with my fork. "Tabitha was going to ask you to help her plan the dinner party here in Omaha. We intended to make a formal announcement during it."

Emotions warred across Marge's face. Reality slipped. I was sitting at another breakfast table, watching turbulence play across another woman's features. Marge's hand clasping mine pulled me back.

"God, Curt, I'm so sorry. I shouldn't have gotten so worked up. I couldn't believe you would get married and not tell me. It's just, crap, I don't know. I'm sorry," she repeated.

"Forget it." I gave her hand a quick squeeze before pulling mine free. "I'd probably feel the same if you got married without telling me." I raised my cup to my lips, pretending not to see the quick swipe at a tear she made across her cheek. "Learn anything else while you were there?"

She made a face, leaned back. "Yeah. Lord, that woman covered a lot of territory on that boat."

"Warned you."

"At least I knew where to go, thank you very much. There's not a whole lot that's new." Marge did one of her shoulder-rolls. "She pretty much kept to herself on the water. Interviewed her lawyer in Nassau. I got some good info on her foundation work and the Water Angel, even visited a few of the sites. Her foundation *is* doing a lot of good work. Besides maintaining Tabitha's trust and foundation, did you know Mr. Olineo was also the will's executor?"

"Guess that makes sense. She didn't have anyone else."

"That was about to change," Marge said, studying me. "Tabitha called him right before you left Nassau. Told him she was planning on getting married and would be making changes."

I had not known that.

"With no public announcement and you not coming forward, he assumed the marriage hadn't taken place yet and the will in his files was still valid. Your secret is still safe, Curt. Nosing around later is when I found out about

Cat Island and I did not update him."

"Thank you. I wouldn't know the first thing about managing trusts or foundations. He's the best one for the job. I'm surprised Mrs. Chandler and her son didn't try to break the will."

"They did. However, Mr. Olineo knows his legalese and the attempt failed. Mrs. Chandler also tried to void the section on Tabitha's burial."

"What?"

"Tabitha specified she wanted to be buried next to her father. Mrs. Chandler had Tabitha cremated before Mr. Olineo was aware of it."

I stared at her nonplussed. I'd read her burial preference in the stack of legal documents Russell provided and cremation wasn't it.

"She said that since her daughter didn't want to live in Nebraska, Tabitha probably didn't want to be buried here either. That she believed Tabitha would have preferred her ashes consigned to the waters she did prefer."

"*Bullshit*. She and Russell were both aware of the will's contents."

"Really? Well, Mr. Olineo's threat of a very public lawsuit did get Tabitha's ashes interred next to her father. Maybe Mrs. Chandler expected that to be her plot."

Had she hated her own daughter that much? I fumed. Enough to spite Tabitha even in death? Unbelievable. "How are they going to do Tabitha's story?"

She tossed her hair back. "It's going to be in three parts, all Sunday editions—starting July seventeenth—and ending the week before the anniversary of her death in August. Which also happens to be on a Sunday this year."

"One year," I reflected. A lifetime. So many changes I could hardly grasp them all. "A year ago, I was cursing the Chandler name and wondering why I was chasing after some spoiled rich girl."

"And then you found her."

"We found each other," I corrected.

"And then you lost her," Marge said, looking away.

The bleak tone caught me off guard. "What's wrong, Marge?"

"Just tired, Curt. These past few weeks have been hectic. I still have some additional research to do. My editor wants my final copy by the first week of June."

I watched her fiddle with her glass stem. Why was that a problem? It was only the first week of—*crap*. I resisted the urge to curse when I realized why she was acting off.

May. The month that'd seen her world come crashing down. I'd sat beside her, holding her hand while her heart bled out in more tears than any one body should be able to hold. For the first time in three years, I hadn't even given it a thought. Too bad the jackass had the good sense to relocate.

I settled back. "Tell you what," I said casually. "Why don't you come by this evening. I'll regale you with mine and Tabitha's first days. I'll fix spaghetti."

"Deal. I'll bring a salad."

***

The spaghetti and salad were excellent. Afterwards, I recounted mine and Tabitha's first, tumultuous meetings. The charity ball with Charrise and the spry Cocktail Ladies sent her into near hysterical fits. I surprised myself by laughing along with her. The retelling of our time together was bittersweet. I promised her another dinner when her articles were finished.

<h1 style="text-align:center"><u>Chapter 22</u></h1>

Marge came by my apartment the first week in June and spent several hours going through Tabitha's records. When I asked about the notes she was making, her vague reply of 'needing to verify a few things' had me curious. She'd turned in her articles on Tabitha, so what was she checking on? The way she was going through them seemed as if she was searching for something in particular.

I called Marge several times over the next couple of weeks to suggest taking an evening out to unwind. She said she was working on something and would get back with me later. I let it go, busy myself. June was always a lucrative month for me. Kids graduating from high school or college and applying for jobs or getting the love-bite. Background checks for either personal or business didn't take long and I could usually get one or two done in one day.

When my last call went to voicemail, my curiosity tripled. As focused as Marge could get when chasing a story, I still rarely got brushed off. Whatever it was, it must be big. I was looking forward to hearing about it.

*****

The phone rang several times before it was answered.

"Cho's Chow. May I take your order?"

"Hi. This is Marge Lockewild. I'd like to place a delivery order." Her phone was set on speaker.

"Certainly. What would you like?"

Marge looked into the barrel of the gun aimed at her forehead and swallowed. "Order of broccoli beef, please."

Would you like a couple of eggrolls to go with it?"

"No, thank you. I'm not real hungry tonight."

The employee gave her the price, then added, *"We're kind of busy, so it'll be about forty-five minutes."*

"Thanks." Marge disconnected.

The killer reached over, a gloved hand taking her phone. The cold smile didn't reach the even colder eyes. "That should give you plenty of time to write your suicide note."

Chapter 23

June eighteenth. A day as black as August seventh, although it took two days to know it.

Diana's grim look told me something was seriously wrong as soon as I arrived at the office Monday morning. I couldn't believe what she told me.

Refused to believe it.

Didn't want to believe it.

Forced to believe it as I stood beside the lifeless body stretched out on a cold steel slab.

Marge was dead.

It was late evening before the worst of the shock wore off. Diana had accompanied me to the morgue, so I guess she shepherded me home. I was too numb to notice. She was puttering around in the kitchen, the scent of fresh coffee wafting through the room. I walked over to the window and stared at the lights dotting the buildings around me.

"Marge liked to watch the lights at night. She'd make up stories of what was going on behind the windows. Some were pretty funny."

"I'll make something if you promise to eat."

I shook my head, continued to stare out into the night. The doorbell sounded, followed by low voices.

"It's Lieutenant Sinclair," Diana announced.

I turned wearily from the window. A Q&A session was inevitable, but I'd hoped for some more time to…adjust.

"I'm sorry to intrude at a time like this, but I have something for you concerning Miss Lockewild."

"Would you care for some coffee?" Diana asked him.

"Thank you. Black, plain."

Diana brought us all a cup. We sat in the living room, Diana and Sinclair on each end of the couch with me facing them in a chair. Sinclair sipped, winced, then set his cup down. My smile was fleeting, knowing Diana had made it to my taste. That she hadn't watered his down along with hers expressed her annoyance with him.

"You have something for me," I prompted, eyeing the brown manila envelope in his lap.

Sinclair carefully removed a sheet of paper enclosed in a transparent document protector. "The suicide note she left was addressed to you. We'll need to keep it until the case is closed, but I thought you might at least like a chance to read it. Privately." He saw my hesitation. "Handwriting and fingerprints have been authenticated," he added.

I didn't need an expert's opinion to tell me it was Marge's. The graceful curvature of her letters was as familiar as my own scribble.

Kurt,

My life is too empty. The scar keeps breaking open and I can't handle it any longer. Give Sherwood a big squeeze and think of me. Forgive me. Remember me.

Marge

The words blurred: *Remember me.* Those words had been precious, now they were priceless. I looked up, blinking fast. "Why do you have her letter?"

"You should be aware that any sudden or unnatural death is investigated as a potential homicide until proven otherwise. I was notified after the responding team found the letter in her apartment."

"Why?" I said dully, handing the letter back.

"There's a number of open cases with your name attached. I've requested to be notified anytime it pops up."

I'd process his interest in me later.

"He's the one who called to tell me," Diana said.

"I understand you two were close. I'm sorry for your loss."

"We were the siblings neither one had," I said, watching him tuck the paper back into the envelope. "We watched out for each other. I was Big Brother."

"Who's this Sherwood?"

"Congratulations, Curt." Marge gave me a big hug. "This is perfect."

"You should know since you helped pick it out." I couldn't stop grinning. It was bare walls. It was my office. My dream.

Marge reached into her purse and thrust what she pulled out into my hands. "For luck, not that you actually need any."

It was a small stuffed owl made up to look like Sherwood Holmes, complete with pipe. I returned her hug. "I'll keep Sherwood on my desk. Soon as I get one."

I snapped back to the present. "A stuffed owl Marge gave me for good luck when I first opened my office."

"Why did Miss Lockewild consider her life empty?" Sinclair asked. "Everyone I've spoken with seems to disagree."

"Marge liked her career, but she wanted a home and a family. She wanted a child as badly as Hanscombe didn't." What she'd wanted was to love and to be loved. Until Tabitha, I hadn't fully understood how deep that need could go.

"Hanscombe?"

"Donald Hanscombe," I said coldly. Right, Sinclair wasn't here then. "Four years ago, they were the quintessential professional couple, until Marge came up pregnant. Hanscombe didn't hit the roof, he went through it. His accusations ranged from 'not mine' to 'deliberate entrapment.' Marge went into an emotional tailspin: shock, hurt, disbelief, anger. A lot of anger. He not only didn't want the child—any child for that matter—he wanted her to abort it. Said he wasn't paying the next seventeen years for *her* mistake."

"What an asshole."

I snorted at Diana's disgusted comment. Sinclair's expression had gone stony. "That and a lot of other things. Anyway, Marge made it quite clear that the pregnancy wasn't planned and the only mistake in the picture was him."

I can't believe how blind I was, Curt. There's no way I want that cold-hearted, soul-shriveled, self-serving bastard in my or my child's life.

"Marge told him she was having a lawyer draw up papers to terminate his paternal rights and, of course, any responsibilities. He didn't believe her. Said she'd come back later and dig her claws into him." I sank back in my chair, needing several deep breaths before continuing.

"He called Marge one night, asked her to come to his place. To talk." My knuckles went white. Her story had come out, slowly, disjointed, between bouts of soul shattering sobs. "He offered her a large one-time monetary payment conditional on—you guessed it—an abortion. She refused. He was furious." I gave Sinclair a hard look. "I'm pretty sure he pushed her down that staircase instead of the 'trip and fall' he claimed."

The Lieutenant's eyes narrowed. "Was he ever charged?"

"No proof and no reason to, according to the police, as Marge had informed him she was legally assuming all responsibility for the child. They also discounted the 'emotional ramblings' of a 'traumatized woman.'"

Diana pushed up out of her seat and took my cup into the kitchen. This was all new for her, too. I'd never shared the details.

"Marge had a concussion on top of shock from losing the baby. Her memories were disjointed. She didn't remember anything between them arguing and waking up in the hospital. Then," I said stiffly, "a month later the nightmares started. They'd begin with them arguing and then she's falling backwards…and all she sees is a big smile on the bastard's face."

Diana handed me back my cup. From the scent, it was coffee-laced whisky.

I took a large swallow. "When she finally told me about the nightmares—she wouldn't leave. Spent the night at my apartment. She was afraid that if left to myself, I'd have gone out and killed the bastard." I huffed out a breath. She was probably right and probably not something I should be saying to a policeman. "I was semi-rational by morning. However, pounding him into a bloody pulp is still high on my to-do list."

Something loud and punk started up in the hall.

"May is—was—a bad month for her, but she'd gotten over it. Mostly."

Sinclair studied me for a moment, his head tilted slightly. "You haven't. Why should she? The roots of suicide can sometimes run deep into the past.

Is there anything else that could have contributed? Her co-workers mentioned her taking several weeks off when the woman who raised her died two years ago."

"Aunt Jessie. Her parents died when she was a toddler. Yes, Marge took it hard, but she accepted her death as part of the natural life cycle." I stared into my cup. "Marge seemed fine last time we had dinner—June first. I had taken her out for a congratulatory dinner after turning in her articles. I called a couple of more times after that, but she kept declining to go out. I didn't think anything of it at the time," I admitted, regret burning a hole in me. "Marge could be very focused on her work."

"According to Miss Lockewild's co-workers, for the past several weeks she'd been distracted and out a lot—she used up most of her vacation hours. She also started getting edgy and short-tempered. Even snapped at a co-worker named Merle Smith."

She snapped at Marshmallow Merle?

"Everything appears normal—more or less—until Friday afternoon. Miss Lockewild left work early—claimed she wasn't feeling well. Saturday afternoon she ordered delivery from *Cho's Chow*. After finishing it, she washed down a large bottle of sleeping pills—recently prescribed by her physician—with a bottle of whisky that was also on hand. The food would have kept her from getting nauseous and losing it. It's assumed she wrote the note during that time due to some obvious unsteadiness."

Is that why she spelled my name wrong?

"She came by the office Friday afternoon," Diana said, giving me a guilty look. "You were at the firing range. Marge didn't stay long and, other than appearing tired, her behavior was normal. She said she'd call you this weekend—I'm sorry, Curt. I didn't think to say anything when you came back."

I gave her a small nod, letting her know it was all right. Marge was good at appearing normal when she wasn't. Too good, evidently.

"I'll add her office visit to my file," Sinclair said. "A coworker from the paper and the apartment manager found her this morning. She had failed to show for an important early breakfast interview. We're waiting for the coroner's final report and follow-up work on some details." He rose. "You're listed as next of kin and executor, Mr. D'Accio. I'll see Miss Lockewild's items are returned when we're done."

Diana saw him to the door. I dimly heard him saying he'd make a stop across the hall. Was there some clue I missed that could have prevented this?

"I called. Yesterday," I managed around a tight chest. "I should have gone over when all I got was voicemail."

The noise across the hallway stopped.

"It wouldn't have mattered," Diana told me gently.

No. it wouldn't. Marge was already gone, stretched out on her couch. She'd drifted away silently. Painlessly. Alone. *Why, Marge, why?*

I stared down into my cup and swirled its contents. No answers rose to the top.

***

Three days later, at Marge's funeral, I still didn't have any answers. I made it through the service, numb and adrift. The condolences from everyone only pounded my loss deeper. Nate and Diana sat beside me, then accompanied me to the private graveside service. Marge's will requested burial beside her Aunt Jessie, as she hadn't really known her parents. Afterwards, Nate clasped my shoulder and offered to spend the afternoon with me.

I declined and escaped to my apartment. I needed to be alone.

I was in Sinclair's office early the next day to pick up her things. The case was closed. Verdict: suicide. He placed a medium-sized box in front of me.

"These are the items we removed from Miss Lockewild's apartment and office. I need for you to go over this itemized list and verify everything is accounted for."

I sifted through the items. A woman of vitality in life, reduced to a box of memorabilia in death. Her purse. The day planner and mini-recorder she was never without. Some crinkled receipts. Scribbled note pads, a thumb drive—evidently they'd been looking for anything else she might have written or recorded. Two cassettes were in a bag marked "office," a single cassette in a baggie marked "purse." I held the single up.

"Blank. One from the office held a brief interview with Fire Chief Anderson about an old arson string and the other was blank. There were no rambling thoughts or confessions."

I dropped it back into the box. "Marge believed in keeping ready so she bought them by the pack. She said you never knew when something would splat right in front of you. She also liked to dictate her reports—saying it out loud helped to clarify her thoughts. Her editor then had them transcribed."

Sinclair nodded slowly. I got the feeling he was turning something over in his mind. He opened Marge's case file and removed the protected note. He stared at it for several seconds before handing it to me. Almost reluctantly. Was he unhappy with the ruling?

"We have a copy."

I placed the letter with the rest of her things and signed the accountability form.

"Sometimes," Sinclair said quietly, "the people we think we know the best surprise us the most. We think we know everything about them. Then they pull something from a deep, dark corner and we're stunned. Maybe even feel a bit betrayed because they did keep it from us. It's the people we don't know very well we can believe anything of."

Sinclair the philosopher surprised me. It also sounded like personal experience. Perhaps the reason why he left Denver?

"I have other cases to work on."

That was a dismissal if I ever heard one.

Naturally, my cell phone rings when my hands are full while simultaneously trying to open my car door. Sliding Marge's box on top, I grabbed it, the readout indicating it was from the office. "Diana? What are you—*what*?" I froze. "I'm on my way." I tossed my phone into the box and shoved it on the passenger seat. I slammed my door shut and fired the engine.

Smoking tires out of the police parking lot probably wasn't the smartest thing to do.

I arrived at the office to find Diana hadn't exaggerated: it was in shambles. File cabinets hung open, their contents dumped on the floor. The drawers to Diana's desk were upended on top of it instead of neatly slotted in their tracks. This time, her entire computer was missing. At least the coffee counter appeared untouched.

"Young man, how can I possibly know what else is missing if I can't touch anything?"

I let Diana handle the young officer and went straight into my office.

A second officer was poking through the mess. The contents of my bookcase had been flung around the room. Everything that had been on my desk was now somewhere else: floor, chair, even on top of the curtain rod. The visitor's chair looked as if it'd been stomped on. My computer was also missing, and the pile beside my desk appeared to be everything from its drawers. I dug frenetically.

"I hope you have a license for this," the officer said.

Hurrying over, I followed her finger to the fish tank. There was Gerty, swimming serenely around my Ruger. Relief washed through me. It had been locked in my desk drawer since Monday. Diana had recommended removing it before heading to the morgue and I hadn't given it much thought since. I certainly wouldn't have worn it to the funeral or into the police department.

"Unlike computers, it's too easy to track. License?"

I pulled out my wallet. "I'm a private investigator…Officer Hanns," I said, glancing at her nametag as I handed over my card.

"So it says on the door." She read my license, made a couple of squiggles in her notebook. "Lotta power for tracking cheating spouses."

A reply would have been wasted, so I went back to the pile on the floor and dug around until I found my passport. The drawer that'd held my gun and ammo was on its side, warped from being wrenched open. I made a cursory pass through the room, shifting more pieces of debris. "Looks like they took the ammo, though. I had nearly a full box of .357 cartridges and a handful of .38s."

"What's a handful?"

"A dozen, maybe less."

She made a couple more notations. "Anything else you can determine missing at this point, besides the computers?

"No. My passport and gun are accounted for, so the only other important items are my files." Good thing I'd contracted with Alliance Storage Service after the last break in. They had backups of all our digital files, updated every Saturday night. Since I hadn't worked this week, I hadn't lost anything. Digitally, at least.

"My written notes should be around here." Somewhere, I hoped. Once again, we'd have to put the hard files back together. At least all but my first year's files had a digital copy. I made a mental note to rectify that as soon as possible.

I spotted the box that'd held Tabitha's files tossed in a corner.

"What are your current cases?" Was Officer Hanns being official or nosy?

"One hit-and-run, two possible insurance frauds, one vandalism—the cheating spouse was last month," I said absently, hurrying over to the box. I recognized several pages scattered around it.

"Any problems with them?" the officer persisted.

"Not so far." I started shoving the loose papers back into the box. I paused to ask if either she or her partner had gotten any scents off of things. I hadn't been skunked this time.

She flipped her notebook closed. "Nothing fresh, except for you and your secretary. Someone's coming to take prints."

The print guys showed up ten minutes later. Their forty minutes added to the mess but yielded very few prints. Mine and Diana's most likely. The culprits had undoubtedly worn gloves.

"If anything important comes up missing, let us know," Officer Hanns said, taking another glance around before collecting her partner and following the print team out.

"Why'd you come in?" I asked Diana. We'd closed the office for the whole week.

"I wanted to check the mail and water Charrise."

My small grin partnered with a fresh pang of grief. Marge had presented me with the large potted ivy—boldly labeled and twined around two posts. The ransackers hadn't bothered it.

"They also got the law firm next door."

Nice of the police officer to let me know. "Let's lock the door and go home."

Diana gave me a look. "I don't think the office fairy is going to pop in and take care of this."

I looked around and back through the connecting door into my office. "Monday's soon enough to deal with this." What a mess. This was getting bloody old.

"I'll let you know if I find anything missing." She moved to her desk and started fitting the drawers back into place.

"Dammit, go home, Diana."

"Unlike you, I don't have anything planned this weekend."

"I don't have anything planned," I retorted.

"Sure you do. A guilt trip and a pity party." She flicked print dust off her desk with her scarf and started putting things back in their places.

I stuck my hands in my pockets and stared at her. Suddenly, for the first time in days, I laughed. Really laughed. "Diana. What would I do without you? All right. I'll make—you make the coffee," I amended, catching the look on her face.

I guess it did beat sitting around thinking about all the ways I could've screwed up. Going back into my office, I fished out my gun. A quick check showed the only load it was carrying was water. I took it into the bathroom and set it into the sink to drain. I stared at my reflection in the mirror. At the baggy eyes, gaunt cheeks, and wispy beard.

Had it really been less than a week?

When did my hair acquire those silver sprinkles?

If Tabitha was here right now, she'd jerk you up by the jock strap and tell you to get a grip on yourself.

Marge would be yanking right along with her now.

<h1 style="text-align:center"><u>Chapter 24</u></h1>

We spent the weekend getting the office cleaned and back in order, something we were getting really good at. Files and loose pages were stacked in piles around our desks. New computers were delivered on Monday, an hour before the ASS guy arrived with a box of disks to install our most recent files and any others we wanted recovered. I shoved papers belonging to Tabitha's files back in the box as I found them. I had my home set to work with.

According to the police, a power transformer behind us had blown out. It'd had help, according to the debris analysis. The entire building's security was down for the four hours it took Omaha Utilities and Power to replace it. More than enough time for the thieves to trash the two offices. My lawyer neighbors were semi-regular clients. It was assumed the perpetrators had been searching for something tied to one of their cases in both our offices, then they made a mess to hide whatever they were interested in.

Which meant I didn't get one of Lieutenant Sinclair's lovely follow-ups.

We spent the rest of the week getting the files straightened out. I also did a few quick background checks but passed the missing runaway teenager to my old partner at Halligan. My excuse was getting the office situated as well as dealing with Marge's estate. While true, I wasn't ready to commit to the level a case like that would require.

Friday rolled around and Nate insisted on going to *Riley's Pub*. It had been our general unwind night for a couple of years now. Whichever of our small group showed up played pool or darts, drank beer, flirted, and just chatted. Tonight, it was Theresa and Dan. They took their beers into the adjoining room, giving me an understanding nod when I declined to join them.

I couldn't unwind. The music and overlapping conversations were jarring. After about twenty minutes of stop-and-go conversation, Nate stretched and suggested we call it an early evening. We finished our drinks and dropped a decent tip on the table before leaving. It had to be the shortest Friday outing on record for both of us. It wasn't even dark yet.

We walked around the building toward the parking lot in back. Letting out a gusty sigh as we stopped beside his Lexus, I kept my apology simple. "Sorry, Nate. I'm lousy company tonight."

"Didn't notice."

My lips twitched. "Meaning I'm normally a bore?"

Nate tipped back on his heels, pursed his lips in thought. "Well, now that you mention it…" He grinned, lightly tapped me on the shoulder. "Next week?"

"Next week," I agreed with a weak smile.

Instead of heading home, I found myself driving east. A short time later, I was standing at the entrance to an alley between two forbidding buildings. Not giving myself time to rethink this, or lose what little light remained, I hurried to the nearly hidden stairwell and descended, trailing my hand along the wall to stay oriented.

Once inside the *Depot*, I threaded my way through the shadowed tables to the bar. Boris moved toward me as I slid on a stool. "Scotch. Large. MacEverson if you have it," I said. He stared at me. Oh, right. I laid a twenty in front of me. The bill disappeared and a minute later a glass and my change replaced it. I rolled the first golden sip around with my tongue, alerting my tastebuds. Then I passed the message down my throat. It landed in my stomach with a pleasing warmth.

Time slowed, and I lost track of it completely. I sipped my drink to the soft clink of glasses and low-murmured conversations. Soft instrumental music faded in and out of my hearing. I wished I had a full dose of Gen-ears to hear it all.

My mind wandered from when Marge and I first met, through our teenage years and adult ambitions to now. By the time I reached the bottom of my glass, the restlessness that had driven me here was gone. The *Depot* had worked its magic. Marge was gone. It was a grudging acceptance of what had happened. One day, I might even accept the how.

I didn't glance over when someone took the stool next to me until she said, "Buy you a refill?" It was Angie. I hadn't seen her since Marge's funeral. I had intended to have her join us at the gravesite, but she'd vanished in the well-wishing throng.

"A White Top beer and a refill," Angie said pointing at my empty glass.

I don't know how she pulled cash out of those tight jeans. Her flannel shirt hung open over a low cut something too skimpy to be qualify as a blouse.

"Taking a break?" I asked.

She squinted at the change Boris left with our glasses. "One dollar? That's it? What the hell are you drinking?"

"MacEverson scotch. Thanks."

She made a face. "That's what I get for not asking first. Didn't expect to see you here." She took a long sip.

"I needed a place to think," I mumbled.

"To brood?"

"No…yes…I don't know." She raised an eyebrow over her glass rim. "Marge's death bothers me. It just doesn't seem like her. I guess…I don't understand *why*."

Angie licked suds from her top lip. "Let's go sit elsewhere."

I winced. Right. I was soul-baring in a room full of shifter ears. We settled in one of the privacy booths, halfway between two light sconces.

"Someone told me that it's the people we think we know the best that can surprise us the most," I said, continuing my grouse. "But Marge? Surprise isn't even close to covering it adequately."

"Did you see her in the weeks before it?"

I shook my head. "I tried a couple of times, but she always brushed me off. Said she was busy on a story. I know how focused she can get, so I didn't push." Guilt assailed me briefly.

"Yeah, she was busy on something. Digging like a badger." Angie wrapped a hand around her glass. Her gaze locked with mine. "Hearing she'd suicided was…more than odd."

My brows drew together as I realized what she was, and wasn't, saying. The uncertainty I'd been feeling crystalized. Anger flooded me as I said it aloud: "Marge was murdered."

"Pretty sure," Angie agreed.

I battled the rising fury. *Down, Dice, down. You need to think clearly.* Still, it took a couple of minutes and several swallows of scotch. "You said she was digging hard. Do you know on what?" *What did you get into, Marge?*

"Not exactly. I know it was something she ran across during her research on the Chandler family."

Still seething, I asked, "Any guesses?" The girl was shrewd and observant.

"Something to do with the mother, Cynthia Chandler. Marge had me hunting what I could find on the street, while she hit all the social and other things. She never gave me a hint on what *she* was finding or how it might tie together."

Marge hadn't liked the woman, but she wasn't spiteful. She wouldn't dig up dirt to destroy a reputation for no reason. I leaned forward. "What did you find?"

"Not a whole lot," she grumped. "Ray, the guy Vic didn't like? His name is Raynor Chester Silverstone. According to various sources, he and widow-Cynthia got together occasionally, up until she married Chandler. In fact, this was one of the places they'd frequent."

So, Cynthia Chandler dated a man with an unsavory reputation in her youth, then resumed the relationship after she was widowed. That wouldn't go over well with the snooty crowd or her business contacts. And not like anyone from her social scene would see them here.

"Anything else?" I asked, disappointed at her head shake. "Can you keep your ears open? Let me know if you hear anything interesting on either Chandler or Silverstone." I started to pull out my wallet. "I can pay you—" Angie's scowl stopped me.

"Yes, I'll keep my ears open. No, I don't want your cash. I'm doing it for my friend," she said fiercely. "Marge didn't look down on me, push or preach. Sometimes she'd show up at my place with a take-out bag of some kind and we'd talk. Just talk. Laugh." She shot me a small grin. "I liked the one about you and Charrise."

I sighed. Another debacle. At this rate, my casket was going to be crowded. "When was the last time you saw her?"

"That Thursday. We met here, as that's my off-night. I rest up for the weekend."

Uh-huh. I kept my face blank and my eyes above the cleavage line. "She was okay? Everything normal?"

"No. She pretended it was, but she was distracted. Wound up. When I finally called her on it, she admitted she didn't know what to do with what she had. She had no hard proof, just a theory."

My non-existent shifter ears sharpened. "Of what?"

"Stubborn woman wouldn't say." Angie's fist smacked the table and she gave vent to her frustration.

"Hard-headed," I agreed after the cussing stopped.

"You're going after whoever did this. I want to help. I *need* to help. And before you start with the macho thing about danger, remember what I do and where I do it." The hand curled around her glass morphed. "My cougar claws aren't virgins."

"Think they know about you? That you were one source of Marge's information?"

"Maybe." Claws turned back into fingers. "Which means I'm already involved. Partners?"

I hesitated then nodded. "Partners. Be careful, okay? You need help, give me a call."

"Sure, Dice. Goes ditto for you. By the way, that beard of yours?"

"I know, I know, it's scruffy." My face produced hair very grudgingly. "I'll need to shave it off before next week." My background jobs this week had all been by phone.

She shook her head "Don't. It'll look good on you once it fills in."

"Um, thanks?"

We finished our drinks, exchanged phone numbers, and Angie safely navigated me out of the dark alley. I was buying a pocket-sized flashlight from the first convenience store I passed.

Sitting in my car, I stared out the windshield and went back over everything Angie and I had discussed. I thought back to the suicide note and the now obvious clues. The misspelling of my name. The reference to a dead, murdered woman. She had flagged 'something wrong here' as much as possible under her killer's nose.

Had she snuck anything else by him?

***

I let myself into Marge's apartment early the next morning. The building manager had graciously offered to release her estate from the lease but I'd just as graciously declined. It would mean packing up and getting rid of all her things. I wasn't ready to do that. Maybe in three months when the lease ran out I could handle it. For now, I kept my eyes off of the couch as I passed through the living room to her second-bedroom office.

I went through her computer. And, like the police who'd already done so, I didn't find any answers or reasons for her suicide. I snorted; because it wasn't. I gathered up all her personal finance records and placed them in the box I'd brought. It was time to knuckle down and begin settling her estate. I ignored the gut-twist that caused.

Next, I went methodically through her file cabinet and her desk drawers. There were files on older articles, investigations, and various research. It was what I didn't find that was telling.

There was nothing in the cabinet's front section or in the top right desk drawer, the places she normally kept her in-work projects. No computer printouts. No tapes, despite a couple of wadded up four-pack wrappings in the trashcan beside the printer. There was nothing to indicate she was working on anything. Lt. Sinclair had said the blank tape was found in her purse. The man was precise, *soooo*…the recorder was empty? Marge would just as soon have had an unprepped recorder as walk down the street naked.

Since Angie's story of Marge working on something corroborated what Marge had brushed me off with, it meant someone had cleaned out all traces of it. Just to be sure, I'd verify with her editor that Marge hadn't submitted, or left for safe keeping, any tapes or files lately.

Interestingly enough, Marge had split out the original Chandler Family file between Mrs. Chandler and Russell Chandler. Their files each held a small baggy with a couple of tapes, neatly labeled with names and dates. All three Chandler files went in the box. Hopefully I could spot and then follow whatever it was Marge had found.

After that, I searched the entire apartment. A few mementos—pictures mostly—went into the box. Then, puzzled, I plucked Sherwood off a bookshelf. How did he get here? *Give Sherwood a big squeeze and think of me.* Marge must have taken him when she came to my office that Friday. That explained the reference in her note. With everything happening, I hadn't even noticed he was gone. But why? Comfort, maybe, as she'd been upset? I laid him gently in the box.

The living room couch I left to last, even though it was the most likely spot for any flagging Marge might have managed. Methodically, I worked my way around the seams and crevasses. Unsurprisingly, I didn't find anything. The forensic teams were very thorough.

Standing in the middle of the living room, I took a good look around. Despite all the furniture and knickknacks, it was empty. A hollow shell devoid of the warmth Marge had infused the place with. I picked up my box and left.

***

It was late afternoon before I pulled Tabitha's folder I'd brought from Marge's apartment and Tabitha's folder from my briefcase. Laying them side-by-side on the kitchen table, I ran my hand across the file I'd been compiling since Tabitha's murder. I hadn't even thought about her case since Marge's death. Flipping it open, I smiled at her picture clipped to the inside. The memories washing over me tugged gently, which wrung a sigh that was both relief and regret. Still so much unknown. I'd run out of ideas, tracked down every possible lead I could find.

Maybe there was something in Marge's file that would provide new ones. Her file on Tabitha held all her notes and research from birth to death, not just what she'd used to build her articles. I stacked the two files off to the side. I'd go through them later.

I pulled Marge's depressingly thin file out next. I'd started it last night, entering a summation of Angie's comments, the salient points I remembered from the police, and anything else I could think of. I needed to talk to Marge's co-workers and neighbors. 'Just trying to find closure' would be a good excuse. They could have seen or heard something that, looking at it from a murder context, would give me a different meaning.

Hmmm. What else?

I rifled through the items the police had returned. Her tape recorder…I'll need that. Set aside the cassettes. I'd double check those to make sure there was nothing I could use. Receipts that looked rescued from a trash can. A couple of grocery items from Food Saver. Gas. Take out from—my brain froze. My eyes jerked to the date at the top. June eighteenth. I inhaled sharply. Sinclair had said she'd ordered take out. Did she eat it or did the killer? I had to find out. At the very least, it would prove someone else had been there that day.

Chapter 25

Monday morning found me sitting in Lieutenant Sinclair's office. He'd found me waiting for him in the station's public room. My fingers tapped the side of my thighs restlessly. According to the smiley cat-face clock hanging on the wall behind Sinclair's desk, he'd been gone for over twenty minutes. Had to have been a gift, as I couldn't image him buying it.

Sinclair closed the door behind him and returned to his desk. Marge Lockewild's file, that I had very politely asked to see, lay in front of him.

"Why?" Sinclair asked.

"Still looking for answers."

After a few more seconds of study, Sinclair slide the file over to me. His chair squeaked in protest as he leaned back and crossed his arms.

Steeling myself, I opened the folder. His report was concise and factual. *...female body on couch...empty pill bottle...whisky...suicide note... coworkers report recent personality change...* The words were running together by the time I reached the end. I cleared my throat. "Concise report."

"Thanks. Find any answers?"

I glanced up. Despite the lack of expression, I had the feeling the lieutenant was watching me closely. I shrugged and skimmed the next item, which was the itemized list of her effects. I skipped that and got to the part I'd come for. The autopsy report.

Bracing myself, I started to read. Two thirds of the way down I had my answer. I read the paragraph twice. After skimming the remaining paragraphs, I flipped to the front and read the copy of the fake suicide note and its clues. I closed and carefully laid the folder in the center of Sinclair's desk.

Way to go, Marge. Your message is loud and clear. Sorry it took so long.

"What did you see in that file?" Sinclair said curtly.

Rising, I opened his door and observed the activity in the large open room. Did they look for answers or just fill squares? Did they really care about the lives they shoved into filing cabinets or were they just names, case numbers, and a step on that ladder upward? I looked back at the folder, then met Sinclair's sharp gaze.

He knew something was off, but not what. Whoever killed Marge was dangerous. And powerful. And like her, I had no proof. But I threw him a bone.

"Sometimes," I said, "it's the little things that trip people up."

Like someone unaware a staunch vegetarian was ordering a meal with meat. That had been the biggest flag of all and exploded any remaining doubt about it being murder. I closed the door gently behind me.

***

The week was, for all intents and appearances, normal. I took on a couple of cases, much to Diana and Nate's relief. I also quietly pursued my personal case in between them and in the evenings. I hadn't told them about Marge. It wasn't safe. I already had one killer stalking me.

By Friday I had good a lead on the Fletcher case and had resolved the Brown one. Mrs. Brown had not been happy to hear the personal aide she'd suspected wasn't the one embezzling from her accounts. It was her daughter. I'd also added some interesting information from several of Marge's co-workers to Marge's file.

I waved good-night to Diana and headed home. Coffee dripped into a glass carafe while I changed into comfortable sweats. Taking a cup of the thick, steaming liquid into the living room, I reviewed my notes in Marge's file, then leaned back and pondered.

As far as I could tell, things changed after May, after she turned in her three-part report on Tabitha. Taking time off from work. Skipping her Tuesday lunches with Janet Twinsomm. Nothing erratic enough to get people worried who knew how focused she could become.

I certainly hadn't been.

Thursday, June sixteenth, she was wound up, distracted but not worried, according to Angie. According to co-workers Merle Smith and Randy Longtooth, Friday was normal until early afternoon. They said she was doing follow-up work on her Tabitha Chandler articles when they left for lunch. They'd come back to find her pale, flustered. Merle claimed she was disoriented, too. They encouraged her to go home. Other than her brief stop by my office, that was the last anyone saw her. Alive.

Something happened that Friday. Marge heard or saw something that, from the sound of it, scared her. Like what? No one noticed anything different at the office. No visitors were cleared from the first-floor receptionist. A phone call? Something on the internet? An 'oh, crap' realization?

I ran a hand across my face. I could use one of those myself right now. And why in all the Gods' names hadn't she called me? I had no idea where to start. Whatever trail Marge had followed had been erased. No notes. No tapes. Nothing left with her editor.

Alrighty then, I'll do like you did, Marge. I'll start at the beginning.

***

The following Thursday, I had a pitcher of beer waiting for Angie at the *Depot*. She gave me an appreciative grin as she slid in opposite me. "Think they think we're having an affair?" I asked, returning her grin.

"Nah," she said, filling her glass. "You're not my type."

It took me a moment. Oh. *Ummm…*

"No, I never hit on Marge," Angie said. "I knew I wasn't hers either, but I loved her."

"Did Marge know?"

"No. It would have made her uncomfortable and I valued her friendship."

It also explained why she insisted on helping find the killer. I updated her with everything I'd learned. "It looks as if Friday was the trigger day. Something alerted her. Scared her. She was working on Tabitha's articles that morning, which ties—sort of—back to something she found previously. How about you?"

170

"I've confirmed that Ray Silverstone would meet up with Cynthia Greenbaum whenever he was in town after she was widowed. Word is he wasn't happy that she broke things off permanently when she remarried. One of the *Despo* regulars said that Silverstone still shows up here every once in a while."

I swallowed a mouthful of beer. "Steven Chandler inserted a fidelity clause in their marriage contract. She cheats, she's gone and with no settlement."

"Figures. Anyway, it appears Silverstone went from 'available' to 'professional' sometime after she married Greenbaum." She leaned forward, her voice turning serious. "The individual who admitted that was drunk at the time. Later, he tried to assure me he had been talking through his whisky. But I'll tell you this much, the guy was *scared*. Armpit-sweat scared. I could smell it."

"Is Ray Silverstone a shifter?"

Angie nodded. "Second-Gen lynx."

Ouch. Those over-sized claws would be formidable. I finished what was in my glass. "Want to meet again next week?"

"Nope. It's Independence Week."

That's right. The third week of July, when America won its war with England. Personally, I always figured they were tired of fighting and decided to save face by *magnanimously* granting us our independence.

"Lots of celebrations and parties," Angie continued, eyebrows waggling. "I'll be pretty busy."

Uh-huh. I wondered how that worked for her clients but wasn't sure how to ask.

"Ask, whatever it is."

Women. Frigging mind readers. "Just wondering…how does it work for customers who have a Gen partner? I mean…won't they smell another on them?"

"Why, Dice, are you blushing?" She laughed. "Showers, of course. The high-end brothels have one in each room. Lower ranking ones provide shower rooms for customers. Those visiting street workers, like me, will have to utilize a public shower somewhere. Or borrow a friend's."

Which would make them a co-cheater. And since we were on the subject… "Have you ever thought of doing something else?"

"Sure. Me and Marge talked about it occasionally. I'd like to open a shop some day. Don't know what kind, though. I know how to deal with people and I like being my own boss, which is why I'm an Independent. For now, I keep my license and monthly medical checks up-to-date and save what I can. Need me to walk you out?"

Standing, I pulled a mini-light from my pocket. "I came prepared. Two weeks, then? Great. Oh! Don't forget to check this Sunday's paper. The first part of Tabitha's story will be in it."

Chapter 26

Marge's story of Tabitha Chandler's early life was a gentle one. She was portrayed as a quiet girl with linguistic talents and a love of water, cocooned in her family's wealth and position. Marge ended it when Tabitha was nineteen, only saying that Tabitha had left home due to a 'disagreement in life-direction' with her family. Nor did Marge say it was on her birthday.

My own life-direction—finding two killers—was going nowhere.

After my second read-through of my compiled file, I pulled out Marge's file on Tabitha. She had a few additional names and places I didn't, but none of them looked promising. I'd check them out, eventually, just to be thorough. Then, flipping through a bunch of internet social articles, I found a copy of our marriage certificate. *Marge, you sneak.* Did she have it in case I tried to lie to her? For some future news-scooping article?

Gently, I tugged it free from the clip. I gazed at it, remembering the hopes and dreams and plans Tabitha and I had envisioned when we signed it. A flash of pain arrowed through my chest. Carefully, I laid it back in her file. It belonged there, although I didn't put it back in the clip. Marge probably grouped them together during her Caribbean trip and never got around to separating them.

Resigned, I closed the file and laid it with my file on Tabitha. I placed both of them in the box holding my copies of everything Russell Chandler had acquired for me. Closed the lid. As much as I hated it, my hunt for Tabitha's killer would have to rest for now. Marge's murder had become my priority.

I took off Tuesday afternoon to visit the Delmarra Clinic. I'd seen the gleam in Marge's eyes when she spoke about Mrs. Calvert and the clinic. She only gleamed on things that had her reporter instincts firing. Not finding any notes on their interview, I wanted to talk with her. Hopefully, figure out what had sparked Marge's interest.

After politely listening to over ten minutes of enthusiastic discourse about the clinic, I impolitely interrupted him and asked about Mrs. Calvert. The youngish secretary out front certainly wasn't her. Had she retired?

No, the doctor related sadly. Mrs. Calvert, a widow, had been killed during a recent home burglary. I expressed my condolences and admitted she was the actual reason I was here. I had wanted to verify a few things she'd told an associate of mine. Annoyed, Dr. Delmarra said he was aware of the conversation but not its contents. Mrs. Calvert had simply assured him she hadn't provided any confidential information. He also informed me that their conversation had been recorded before ushering me out of his office.

I spent the evening going through Marge's notes and finally found one that indicated Mrs. Calvert's interview was on the same tape as Mrs. Chandler's. Unfortunately, it was among the missing. Whatever Mrs. Calvert had told Marge was gone.

Scanning Cynthia Chandler's file, I found a lot less information than I'd expected. If Marge had been looking into her life, as Angie claimed, there should have been research notes. There was nothing dated after April, written or on tape. Not. A. Frigging. Thing.

I checked Russell's file. There were a couple of May entries, including last year's hiring of me to find his sister. And a written entry in Marge's handwriting for Tuesday, June fourteenth. He'd come to her office and requested a 'preview' of her upcoming articles on Tabitha. She'd declined but assured him there was nothing detrimental to his family's image. He'd left in a bit of a huff.

I grinned at the note. He'd gotten 'huffed' by both of us.

It was almost midnight before I turned out the bedroom lights. I'd gone carefully through both Chandler files. Hands behind my head, I stared up at the dark ceiling and lined up my facts.

Russell Chandler's file appears to be complete with nothing

questionable.

Mrs. Chandler's file has several gaps, with the two missing interviews the most obvious.

Marge ran across something that flagged her interest while building her articles on Tabitha's life and began investigating/researching it starting the first of June.

Marge had Angie gathering everything she could on Cynthia's early life.

Marge had been revisiting her article notes that Friday when something upset her.

All of Marge's post-May research and notes have vanished.

 I could only draw one conclusion.

Marge had been right. There was something in Cynthia Chandler's background that someone didn't want exposed. Remembering the shadows in Tabitha's eyes, I was certain now that her death had been the price of that secret. They hadn't wanted to chance her revealing whatever it was she knew.

Once again, the path I'd followed had been futile, clueless. The attack had nothing to do with me or Tabitha. The real reason lay elsewhere. And Marge had paid a price, too, when she found it.

My two cases had just merged into one.

***

The rest of the week passed in a blur. I worked on cases during the day and on a things-to-check list well into the night. Angie's help would be essential for some of it.

Merle Smith had interviewed me in my office on Wednesday. There was going to be a special report on Marge presented on television following the release of her third installment. I gave Merle a few reminisces from our growing up, then the questions turned to more recent events.

Yes, Marge helped me deal with Tabitha Chandler's death. Yes, I'm sure Tabitha's killer will be found.

When Merle broached Marge's suicide, I said it was private and declined to answer. Turns out, Marshmallow Merle has a firm center. She tried to get an indirect response with other questions. She grudgingly admitted defeat after the fifth attempt.

And then it was Sunday.

In Sunday's second installment, the social butterfly had emerged from her cocoon. Tabitha spread her wings all around the Southern states, Gulf of Mexico, and the Caribbean. I couldn't help wondering if people noted where she hadn't fluttered. Her engagement had lasted approximately as long as the whirlwind courtship: about three months each. Shortly after the breakup, she'd purchased her boat, shifted everything to Nassau, and all but dropped out of the headlines.

Was it disillusionment, Marge postulated in her article, *that led Tabitha into the next phase of her life?*

A different person emerged in the details Marge then revealed. The flighty socialite had matured into a woman of compassion and generosity that she spread throughout the region. The charities everyone knew about. The good deeds few knew about.

Angel de Agua. Water Angel.

That revelation alone kept my phone ringing all afternoon. I even got a call from one of the Cocktail Ladies—Janice van Whitting. When I expressed my surprise, she admitted to having been intrigued by me. I didn't know whether to be flattered or worried about that. She'd kept an eye on the news. Mrs. Whitting and her friends had been appalled about the Kansas City attack, and she said in no uncertain terms they believed I'd find my answers.

I was both heartened and touched by her confidence in me.

Mrs. Whitting—*call me Jan*—also expressed her astonishment to learn Tabitha Chandler had been the mysterious Water Angel she'd heard rumors about. Now, she and her two friends wanted to support and continue her good deeds. I thanked her and gave her Mr. Olineo's personal phone number. I figured the substantial influx of support and cash would override any irritation at my presumption.

This segment of Tabitha's story had ended with her arrival in Kingston. I stared at Tabitha's picture. Was I ready to relive the next part through the eyes of the world?

***

I kept my 'date' with Angie on Thursday. We drank beer and went over my list in one of the *Depot's* booths. I would investigate the Chandlers' public and social rise. She would take on Cynthia Chandler's early life. It would be a repeat of how Marge had worked, as Angie would be able to learn more on the underside of town from Vic and others than I could.

I expanded her area of research to include Raynor Silverstone and *his* early life. Hanging around him, there was no telling what Mrs. Chandler could have seen, heard, or done. Did anyone know where he was now? Would he kill the daughter of an old flame out of spite? Especially when she didn't restart their relationship after the death of her second husband?

When I asked Angie that, she said 'no.' Hired by someone for another reason? She'd shrugged and said 'fifty/fifty.' That it would depend on the reason and the pay. Well, assassins usually were sociopaths. I had no doubt he'd remove anyone he felt was a danger to him.

We left the *Depot* separately. We both knew the danger we were taking on. Being seen together might draw someone's attention we'd rather not. When I commented about the *Depot's* patrons knowing, Angie told me it was a neutral ground. *What happens in the Depot, stays in the Depot*, she told me. I gave that a 'fifty/fifty' and for the same reasons.

Driving home, I decided to recheck everything in her apartment this weekend. If Marge had any warning at all, she'd have found some way to leave clues her killer wouldn't find. Or understood, as her fake-note and last meal were.

This weekend was also the last segment on Tabitha's life. I hadn't seen it. Marge must have believed it'd be too uncomfortable for me. Uncomfortable? I still saw it. Still relived it in my nightmares.

My thorough search of Marge's apartment gained me nothing. I'd even checked the carpets looking for loose segments. Nothing. Nada. Zilch. Frustrating.

Now, I sat in front of my television, waiting. I had the three Sunday editions in front of me, all folded to display Tabitha's stories. This morning's edition had been…poignant. Wrenching. It'd taken me several tries to make it all the way through to the conclusion. To the funeral I had missed. And, unlike the last two Sundays, my phone had been quiet. No one called to discuss it.

I appreciated their silent sympathy.

Good evening, folks. Welcome to Channel Three's Sunday Special Presentation. This evening's edition is on one of our very own that we recently lost: Miss Margret Lockewild.

<h1 style="text-align:center"><u>Chapter 27</u></h1>

Diana took one look as I stomped in and pointed toward my office.

"Go. Sit. I'll bring coffee."

I was glowering at the bookcase across the room when she brought a cup and the morning stack of mail. She handed me the cup and set the mail in the center of my desk.

"I'm going to assume last night's Channel Three Special is behind this morning's grumpiness. Don't blame you," she said, before wisely going back to her desk.

I glowered at the not-dark-enough liquid before taking a sip. Should have brought a thermos of my own brew from home.

The hour-long special had been to honor Marge. "One of their own," the reporter had said during her introduction. Didn't know the Omaha-Herald owned the channel. I'd been looking forward to their broadcast. That changed halfway through it. The forty-five-minute interview I'd given two weeks ago had been pared down to a seven-minute 'childhood friends, I'll miss her' salute. No problem. It was the *fifteen* frigging minutes with the frigging asshole in frigging Chicago that had my blood boiling.

I'd listened in slack-jaw disbelief as Donald Hanscombe recounted their "perfect" relationship, how he had been heartbroken when she "fell apart" after the loss of "their" baby. How she'd "rebuffed" his attempts to console her. How "upset" he was that she hadn't reached out to him if she had been that troubled.

Wasn't a built-in bullshit meter a professional requirement? I still couldn't believe anyone, especially a supposedly seasoned reporter, would be taken in by his obvious insincerity.

The top letter on the pile didn't improve my temperament any. It was from the State Licensing Board, notifying me of a complaint filed against me. Seems Coldbath Senior didn't like my "aggressive and intimidating tactics" concerning his son and assisting in the smearing of his son's name.

Whoop-de-poop.

Tabitha's ex-asshole and their short engagement were barely mentioned in the second installment. She'd even glossed over the ending of it, including the—*hah*! That was it. The family had managed to keep word of the police file suppressed and now he's embarrassed? If Junior can't handle a few smirks, he won't be taking over daddy's CEO chair.

Diana came in with papers and laid them in front of me. "The Dewitt information you requested and Mrs. Samuel Acosto's file—she's due at nine-thirty. The afternoon appointment has cancelled."

I handed the State's letter to Diana.

She did a quick scan. "At least you didn't punch Junior."

No, but I probably would have if our conversation hadn't been by phone. That was still an option if we ever met. Hanscombe, too. The mental image of applying that particular satisfying response to Hanscombe's lies, repeatedly, helped to settle my mood.

I checked my watch. Twenty minutes until Acosto's appointment. I called Miss Pinkerton. Surprising me, she agreed to my request for copies of all Marge's expense reports since January. Correlating them with whatever I could find should let me backtrack most of her movements. If I could deduce where she'd been going, who'd she talked to, maybe I'd be closer to figuring out the why, which would lead to other answers. Hopefully. Now that my afternoon was open, I could pay a visit to a name I'd found in Marge's list of all of Tabitha's support team: nannies, private tutors, a swim coach, counselors, and teachers.

She'd spent more time with them than her mother and brother combined.

***

My destination was an address in a nice, quiet suburban area down in

Bellview. It took several minutes of doorstep explaining before Mrs. Everett would let me in. I was soon perched in an old-fashioned wingback chair in an immaculate living room, a cup of hot tea in my hand. The alert, knowing brown eyes studied me for a few seconds.

"Now, young man, how can reminiscing about my days with the Chandlers help you?"

"I'm trying to resolve Tabitha's death. For that, I'm trying to get an understanding of the family dynamics."

Reviewing Marge's information had reminded me of how uncomfortable Tabitha was at any mention of her family. Since that aspect, and her leaving home, could have set other things in motion, I had decided to take a closer look. As Tabitha's first nanny, Mrs. Everett could provide insight to the family's early years.

Her right eyebrow scrunched down. "I fail to see how that would help. You're the detective who was with her when it happened, aren't you?"

"I'm flattered. Not too many people would remember."

"I kept track of Tabitha after I left her mother's employment. I always felt sorry for her. Her mother didn't give her much in the way of maternal love."

"She was neglected?'

"No, and yes. Her mother saw she got everything she needed. Materially, that is. Oh, she put on a good act whenever there was company. But that was all it was, an act." The woman shook her head. "I never saw any real warmth from Mrs. Chandler toward her daughter."

"Any idea why that might have been?"

"No."

"What about her son?"

She looked thoughtful for a moment. "She definitely favored Russell over his sister. She spent more time with him, did more things with him and such. There was an unmistakable fondness there and, in her own way, I believe she did love him. But I believe she always thought of herself and her needs first, if you know what I mean."

I did. "You were there for about five years. Was there any friction between the kids? Did Russell resent his younger half-sister?"

"No. The boy paid about as much attention to the girl as his mother."

"What was he like as a child?"

"Deliberate."

"Deliberate?" That was an unusual description for a child.

"He was never spontaneous, or impulsive, like most children. Ask him if he'd like to go to the park and play, and he'd spend a minute thinking about it. And most young boys throw on anything, not caring what they wore. Not Russell. Everything had to be just so."

Huh. Diana's description had been accurate. "What was Tabitha like?"

"A delicate child, at first. Mrs. Chandler didn't bring her home until she was about a month old, and even then she was just skin stretched over bones. She was sickly, too—had trouble putting on weight. Chilled easy and caught colds all the time. I always kept my pockets full of tissue. By the time she was two, though, you'd never have known she'd had such a rough start. Always did stay skinny, though." Mrs. Everett's smile was one of fond remembrance. "You should have seen her in the pool or at the beach. I had to have an extra helper to keep track of her. She loved water so."

Suddenly I was elsewhere, watching Tabitha walk along a beach, waves splashing around her bare ankles. I shook it off. "Yes, she did. How was Mr. Chandler with the children?"

"A bit formal with Russell, but he treated him as a true son. Tabitha? He adored her. She was his light and life, which annoyed Mrs. Chandler." She laughed. "Natural enough, though, if you ask me. Their marriage had very little love."

No surprise there. "It was a business arrangement?"

"Business and social, I'd say. She wanted the benefits of his position and financial status, he wanted a young, beautiful wife hanging on his arm and children."

Hoping for gossip, I asked, "Any instances where you think she might have cheated?"

"No."

The crisp, emphatic tone was surprising. "How can you be so positive?

After all, she was a rich, good looking woman whose marriage was evidently for convenience, not love."

She showed the first sign of hesitation since I arrived. No, make that nervousness. "What?" I asked.

"I...I overheard something one night." She hesitated again, then appeared to make up her mind. "I'd gotten up to check on Tabitha, to make sure she hadn't wandered down to the kitchen—her parents were giving a party. As I passed one of the rooms on the second floor, I heard Mrs. Chandler inside quite clearly. Her voice was...well…unlike anything I've ever heard."

Marge's wolf would be pricking its ears forward on that.

Mrs. Everett paused. "I know it's ridiculous. But, even now, remembering her voice, I get shivers up my spine. I truly feel she'd have done what she threatened. I tenured my resignation shortly afterwards. I was just too uncomfortable around her."

I leaned forward. "Can you remember what it was about?"

"I can tell you exactly. Mrs. Chandler said, 'Do you think I'd risk everything for a nothing like you? Wave it in my direction again, subject me to speculation again, and I'll see it's cut off and shoved up *your* ass.'"

I'm not sure what my expression held, but Mrs. Everett nodded in confirmation.

Wow. It had made quite an impression for her to remember it so precisely after all these years. Mrs. Chandler had taken that fidelity contract clause to heart. "Did you see who she was talking too?"

She shook her head. "I went on to Tabitha's room rather hurriedly, I'm afraid. I waited until they went back downstairs—his footsteps sounded rushed—before returning to my room. I didn't want to meet her in the hallway."

What could have made Mrs. Everett so frightened, she didn't even want to pass her employer in the hall? The question must have been on my face.

"If you'd heard it, you'd understand," she said. "It was as if her wolf was speaking. All humanity had been stripped from it. It gave me quite a shock. I'd known since the first day I was hired that the woman could be cold, but this went beyond that. Far beyond it."

I studied her for several moments. "Do you think Mrs. Chandler or her son have changed since you worked for them?"

She gave that several seconds of thought. "I've followed them in the news. Russell still appears to be as careful and ponderous as ever. I can't say about Mrs. Chandler. There's never been anything negative written about her. Even her 'ruthless business drive' is discussed in a positive manner. However, I don't think people like her ever really change. They simply adjust their mask as needed."

I left Mrs. Everett's warm home for the cold streets. She'd seen something in Mrs. Chandler that bothered her so badly she'd resigned her well-paid position. Did a similar episode drive Tabitha away from home? And why, more than a decade later, she'd still been wary?

The rest of the week passed in a grouchy whirl. While I managed to keep from alienating any clients, I was short-tempered and brusque with everyone else. Hanscombe's lies. Marge's murder. Tabitha's murder. No clues. No leads. Dead ends. Unanswered questions. It all festered inside me. And this coming Sunday was the anniversary of Tabitha's death.

Friday afternoon, I was scowling at a report when Diana came back from her lunch. She marched into my office and plopped a bag down on my desk.

"Go home. Your calendar is clear from now through next Tuesday. I expect nothing but your normal gruff behavior when you show up. You need to lance that boil on your butt this weekend." She pivoted on her heel and went to her desk.

I found two bottles of MacEverson in the bag. Diana was due a raise.

Chapter 28

Relaxing against an old-fashioned lamppost on the corner of Tenth and Jackson, I people-watched. Wasn't hard, as everyone walked inside Old Omaha's commercial boundaries. Only specially modified emergency vehicles were allowed in the area and only when needed. Everyone else parked at one of the northern lots or nearby at someone's house. Then they either walked, biked, or took one of the horse-drawn cabs. Security patrolled the area on foot and with old-fashioned English Bobby hats and nightsticks as their badges.

Those nightsticks weren't just for show, either.

The weathered shops carried local and Ameri-Tribe crafts from woven tapestries and blankets to hand-turned furniture. The shop behind me was a recent addition with hand-blown glassware. Various themed restaurants provided menus from Omaha's diverse cultures, with many of the staffs dressed to match and enhance the dining experience.

A couple of tourists window-arguing drew my attention. She wanted to browse longer, he wanted to go eat. My stomach growled in sympathy with him. Great. Now it wanted food. My system had been a bit, uh, sensitive since my Scottish weekend. But it had burned off all the excess emotion from last week and gotten me past the anniversary.

I'd dragged myself into the office Tuesday morning with a thermos of my own coffee, double strength. Diana had closed the door between us when the first whiff drifted her way. Whether by luck or Diana-redirects, background checks were all I had to do until this morning.

"Looking for a good time?"

Angie's familiar purr had me grinning, although I said, "Not funny." I'd asked her to meet me here as a couple would draw less attention than a loitering single male. Besides, Thursdays were our normal meet-day anyway.

"What are we doing?" Angie asked, leaning her chin on my arm.

"Staking out a mystery spouse."

"Somebody doesn't know who they're married to?"

A lot of people could say that. "No. His wife has suddenly started shopping every Thursday afternoon, but rarely comes home with anything. She brushes off questions and he can't follow her. Mr. Blakely is in a wheelchair. Learned anything new on your end?"

"Just that Cynthia Chandler had been very determined to leave the Boondocks and its environs far behind and move uptown. Several did tell me she had a mean streak."

"Only way to survive with drunks for parents," I said. Plus it supported what Mrs. Everett had heard that night. "What about Ray Silverstone?"

I straightened. The woman matching the picture in my pocket was coming down Tenth Street. She turned into *The Tenth Street Bistro*, the place her husband had found a receipt for. Their large plate glass windows made it easy to see her step up to the cashier.

"Father's dead, brother's dead, mom's a lifer in prison, and nobody likes talking about him. It's as if they're afraid he'll come back and rip out their throats."

We contemplated the woman now paying for her drink.

"Well, as a professional assassin, he would want to make sure nothing can be used to track him. Although someone has to know how to contact him for jobs," I said thoughtfully.

Mrs. Blakely exited the *Bistro*, carrying a large coffee cup. She continued on down Tenth. I took Angie's hand in mine and we strolled along behind her on our side of the brick street. A horse carriage rolled past.

"Well, the squirrel didn't bury that acorn very far from its tree. Mom is in prison for killing his father, the Zero he was humping, and two cops before they could get her tranquilized. Second-Gen grizzly."

I winced. "Was the father a lynx?" Besides being an idiot.

Mrs. Blakely crossed to our side of the street. Convenient. When she turned down Stuart Avenue, we were only about two dozen or so feet behind her. Being a non-shifter, Mrs. Blakely probably couldn't hear us. Still, we kept our voices low and casual.

"Nope. He was a First-Gen wolf. Lynx came from a paternal grandfather."

Idiot, squared. And dead. Probably dismembered.

"One other thing," Angie said, leaning toward me. "Know what Wolfbane is?"

"A highly lethal poison," I replied absently, my attention on my quarry.

"According to whispers from I-didn't-tell-you-squat sources, it's also the name of a highly lethal assassin. No description, no other name. Nothing definite, except the smell of rancid fear."

I'd stumbled but managed to keep walking as she spoke. Glancing at Angie, I saw the same awareness in her eyes. "We need to tread very carefully," I said, sotto voce. Her eyes rolled. Yeah, that was a Class One *duh* remark.

Mrs. Blakely went up two steps, opened a door, and disappeared from view. I noted the business name blazed across the door as we sauntered past. We went a couple of more steps then stopped. I stared back, puzzled. "What's so secretive about going to a gym?"

"Maybe it's the *why* that's secretive," Angie said, lips pursed. "Murdoch's Gym teaches self-defense two nights a week. Thursday is the women's night."

I gave her a sharp look. Was that based on street knowledge or memories?

"I'll wander in, strike up a conversation. Say I'm thinking of attending. I'll meet you back at the *Bistro*."

"Angie," I called out as she opened the door. "Be careful, and thanks."

***

Marge hadn't been kidding about Angie's ability to get people to talk to her.

I arrived the next morning at my client's house with Angie's report,

Marge's miniature tape recorder, and a cassette four-pack. His wife, a Zero, was taking self-defense lessons because a new First-Gen wolf neighbor was hassling her and making unwanted advances. She was afraid of the day he wouldn't take *no*. My client was ready to wheel out the door with his shotgun, blast the wolf, and then run his chair over the carcass a couple of times. Which was why his wife hadn't told him. While Mr. Blakely's attitude was understandable, the outcome of such a confrontation probably wouldn't go well for him.

"He's got wolf vision, Mrs. Blakely, so you'll need to turn it on before leaving the house or getting out of the car. If you can wear something with pockets for the next while to hide—uh, yeah, that works too," I sputtered as the recorder disappeared inside her blouse. Bet that cleavage was what drew the wolf's attention. "Once you have two or three tapes-worth of your interactions, take them to the police. Hopefully, it will be enough for a stalking charge. If not, he'll at least get a talking-to and made aware the police are watching."

As I headed to my office, I realized I felt good with myself and my world. Problems? Yes. Mysteries to solve? Yes. But the emotionally charged thunderhead I'd been working under was gone. That boil had indeed been lanced. Diana would get her raise and I'd take the weekend to unwind. Leave everything at the office. Recoup. Recharge. No problems.

Chapter 29

My Sundays didn't usually start with a pounding on my door. Or being arrested for murder.

I listened in disbelief as the two cops read me my rights, handcuffed and stuffed me into the back of their car. Disbelief had long given way to anger by the time I was unceremoniously dumped in front of Sinclair's desk.

"This is bullshit. Who did I supposedly kill?"

"Donald Hanscombe."

"The bastard's dead?"

"Yes."

I laughed. "Give someone a cigar. Let me out of here, I've got to book a trip to Chicago." Seeing Sinclair's head tilt, I added, "I want spit on his corpse."

"I don't believe the Douglas County coroner would appreciate that."

I stared at Sinclair blankly for a moment. "He's here?"

"Yes."

"Dead?"

"Very dead. Ballistics matched the fatal bullet to your Ruger."

My gun killed Hanscombe?

Sinclair picked up the large baggie the arresting cop had plunked down in front of him. "Where was this found?"

"In a side holster in his bedroom. Fully loaded."

He handed it back. "Take it down to ballistics. Have them test it."

"Why? We already have a match."

"I want it reverified."

"That's a stupid waste of time."

"Have it reverified, *Detective* Brinkman," Sinclair said, each word enunciated clearly, coldly.

Brinkman's neck thickened.

Sinclair shifted forward in his chair.

My heart started hammering. I was stuck in a small room with Brinkman's bear and Sinclair's whatever about to erupt into a claws-out brawl. Even the floor wouldn't be safe. Could I make the door in time?

Then, with barely concealed menace, Brinkman growled out, "Yes, *sir*." He wheeled around and stomped out.

Thank God. I licked dry lips as the tension level dropped. "I'd heard there was some, uh, resentment toward you. Would he have really attacked? Here, in the station?"

The lieutenant leaned back in his chair and crossed his arms. "Departmental issues will be dealt with, internally and through proper channels. I do not recommend following—or starting—gossip. How long have you had the Ruger?"

Back to business. "Since I was sixteen. You've matched the bullet to my gun?"

He gave me an enigmatic look. "That's why you've been arrested. Your gun's ballistic pattern is on file, Mr. D'Accio. A case several years ago when you apprehended a suspected drug runner and the more recent attack on yourself."

Both instances had involved tigers.

"I carry the Ruger because I'm a Zero. Remember? You might be able to wrestle down a Siberian tiger aiming for your throat, but most of us can't." The slight narrowing of his eyes told me I'd guessed right, even though my Gen-dar was still being stubbornly silent.

Okay, Dice, put brain in gear, stop reacting like an idiot and start thinking. "Even if I had killed Hanscombe, why would I use my own gun, which I *knew* was registered?"

"Because you didn't expect us to find the bullet."

I snorted. "That'd be stupid. Where'd it happen?"

"Did you get lost in last night's fog? Death occurred in an alley off Thirteenth Street, but the body was dumped behind a restaurant two blocks away. Two winos found it when they were dumpster-dipping for food scraps. Officers were able to trace back to the fresh blood pool and we recovered the bullet from a wall a short distance away."

This was getting worse. "When?"

After a short pause, he said, "Last night. The call came in at five-seventeen."

Finally. Relief had me relaxing back into the chair. "Hate to spoil your celebration, but it definitely wasn't me."

"Alibi?" was his clipped response.

"I spent most of the weekend at my apartment. You know, unwinding from everything? The delivery boy from *Cho's Chow* can testify I was there at ten. Later, ah," I rubbed the back of my neck, "a half hour or so, me and the teenager across the hallway got into it about his music. You've heard it—same kid, same volume. I decided to go down the street and unwind at Lotte's Brew and Games. Got to Lotte's…must have been shortly before eleven and I was there till closing. Two o'clock." I shrugged. "I was there actually a little bit longer. I waited until the bartender—Jim Swantz—finished up and could leave."

"Why?"

"He followed me home."

"You drove while intoxicated?"

"No. I only had water. Jim's thinking of moving and he wanted to see what the apartments at my complex looked like. We got there sometime after two-thirty—I wasn't paying attention to the time. We talked; he checked out the apartment then left. Probably around three."

Sinclair gave me a long, hard stare. "You sat at a bar for three hours and only drank water?"

"Yep." Jim had offered me a scotch on the house. My stomach had politely declined. He was still watching me with that same hard look. I could almost choreograph his next words.

"So, you made your presence known at home, at a bar where you *didn't* drink. Had someone follow you home. One would think you were expecting to need an alibi and be sober.”

Yep, nailed it. “Well, I wasn’t,” I growled, although it wasn’t nearly as deep as Brinkman’s had been. Starting to run a hand through my hair, its manacled partner smacked my jaw. I dropped both hands back into my lap and tamped down the frustration.

“Look. The kid ramped his portable player up to jet-level. So, yeah, I went to Lotte’s to keep from mopping the hallway with the foul-mouthed kid. Especially with a lot of eyes—I haven’t a clue what was going on but the hallway was full of teenagers. I sat at Lotte’s counter and me and Jim talked between orders. Including about apartments.”

“Still plenty of time. The coroner’s report will narrow it.” He glanced at his watch. “Anytime now.”

I gave a grunt and collapsed back in my chair. He didn’t believe me. Despite his recent empathy concerning Marge, he was not my friend. He was a cop, first and foremost.

The drone of voices, the ringing of phones and some talented cursing from outside Sinclair's office filled the silence inside it. I studied the large dent in the center panel of his desk, A size seventeen or eighteen was my guess. Big guy. The smiley-face clock hanging behind him quietly tracked the passing minutes. I wondered who’d given it to him and why he kept it in his office. Maybe Sinclair actually had a sense of humor. Somewhere.

My slight jolt when the desk phone rang showed how tightly I was wound. The smooth stretch of Sinclair’s arm as he calmly picked up the receiver didn’t help.

“Sinclair.” He listened intently, then his eyes flickered. “Would you repeat that last statement, Doctor? No doubt whatsoever? Thank you. Yes, I’d like a written report emailed as soon as possible.” He held the phone for several moments before hanging it up.

Sinclair studied me. Was he aware his finger was lightly tapping the desktop? “Well?” I finally asked.

“Mr. Hanscombe's death occurred between midnight and four AM.”

The rush of relief almost made me giddy. God bless modern forensics.

"Something went wrong with the ballistic test or the records have somehow been screwed. Re-testing will clear me."

On the heels of that confident statement the door opened and Brinkman stalked in. "Fatal bullet came from this gun," he said, sneering at Sinclair as he slapped the bag down in front him.

My brain temporarily disconnected.

"Fingerprints?" Sinclair said, his voice cold enough to shatter an iceberg.

"Just his and it's been fired recently."

"I go to the firing range Friday afternoons," I muttered, looking down at my restraints. It wasn't possible. How could my gun been used to commit a murder clear across town? I'd kept it with—

My head shot up. "I didn't take it with me to Lotte's."

Brinkman grabbed my arm and yanked me sideways out of my chair. "I'll take him to booking."

"You'll take Mr. D'Accio to holding."

"We've got cause and evidence for charges."

"He goes to holding."

"You're kidding!"

"You're close to insubordination."

I winced as Brinkman's grip tightened. I held up a finger. "I want my phone call."

***

Five hours later I was back in front of Sinclair's desk. This time without handcuffs and my attorney present. Sinclair came in with the gun baggie and three folders. He carefully arranged the items on his desk, clasped his hands together on top of the folders, and contemplated me for several seconds.

"We have three positive matches for the ballistics of your Ruger .357. An older shootout with drug-dealers, a recent parking garage attack, and the death of Mr. Hanscombe."

"The first two were deemed justifiable. The last one my client is not responsible for."

"Mr...?"

"Jetter. I'm assuming the reason we're here and not in booking, is that you've verified his alibi. However much it pains you."

"It is, unquestionably, the same gun in all three incidents."

"But not the same shooter." Jetter held up a finger. "Did you, or did you not, confirm my client was at his apartment, at Lotte's Brew and Games at Eightieth and Park, or otherwise in the presence of others from approximately ten PM last night until approximately three AM this morning? With no gaps that would have allowed for a quick trip to Thirteenth Street for mayhem and murder?"

Sinclair's attention shifted back to me. "Yes, but there's still an hour unaccounted for."

Jetter leaned forward. "An hour. For a timeframe that is itself a cautious, *outside* estimate time of death. You do not know who fired the gun that killed Mr. Hanscombe. We have proven it couldn't have been Mr. D'Accio. Therefore, you have no grounds to hold my client or file charges. He is to be released immediately."

"He has the motive, the weapon, and the guts."

"And the brains not to use his own personal weapon to commit a felony, even if he'd had the opportunity instead of being across town and in his home."

"There's this thing called accomplice."

Jetter snorted. "Would you risk a murder one charge for someone?" Silence. "Would you *trust* anyone with that knowledge?" More silence. "And not only is hiring it out—assuming he knew how—even riskier, he certainly wouldn't have provided his own gun to do it with. It's obvious someone managed to access his weapon and is trying to frame my client."

"How? How did the gun in D'Accio's apartment on Seventy-Eighth Street kill Hanscombe on Thirteenth?"

"That's your problem," Jetter retorted.

I could almost hear Sinclair's teeth grinding. "I didn't even know Hanscombe was in town."

"His picture was in the Omaha-Herald. Front page."

I swallowed the cuss word on my tongue. "Think about it, Lieutenant.

Smart would be to do it in Chicago and *not*," my chin angled toward my gun, "have the finger pointing straight at me." His signature carved-marble look wasn't helpful. "I honestly don't have a clue how—check on who had access to the bullet and could have made a substitution."

Sinclair gave a small negative shake of his head. "A picture was taken as soon as an officer dug it free of the wall. Verified by the attending detective—Brinkman's partner. It had a very distinctive blunted nose, as does the one in the lab. I was flagged as soon as they ran ballistics."

Where my name popped up. Why such an interest in me? Before I could ask, Sinclair said I was free to leave. No question was worth staying another minute.

"Don't leave town," Sinclair added as we stood.

"Wasn't planning to," I all but snarled.

***

I took the stairs up to the third floor after Mr. Jetter dropped me off. Normally this was for both exercise and expediency, as the stairwell was right outside my corner office while the elevator was at the other end of the hallway. However, I didn't usually pound up them two at a time.

Stalking into the office, I didn't even have time to growl before a steaming cup of coffee was thrust into my hand. God, it tasted good. The single stingy cup I'd been granted at the police station had been about as bad as the stuff in the Kansas City hospital. Maybe worse. I inhaled more of the rich aroma and felt some of the tension drain out of my shoulders.

"Thanks, Diana. You timed that well."

"Stairwell acoustics."

I felt myself blushing, remembering some of what I'd been flinging out. "Ah….thanks. Thanks for taking care of everything. And for staying." She'd been my one phone call from the police station, as I knew she would co-ordinate everything needing done. She had also opened the office, on a Sunday no less, without arguing.

I nodded and headed into my office. I propped my feet on my desktop, wrapped my hands around my coffee, and let my head fall back. Closed my eyes and concentrated on the warmth seeping into me from the cup. The phone rang in the outer office. Police? Lawyer? A reporter that'd gotten a tip about my arrest? I heard Diana's skirt rustle as she set down in the visitor's chair.

"Mr. Jetter has scheduled an appointment for Monday afternoon to review today's events," she said briskly.

"It was a set-up, Diana," I said without opening my eyes. "By a miracle…by a foul-mouthed, loud-punk fluke, I'm not sitting in jail right now on a murder charge."

Seconds stretched into silent minutes after I finished telling her everything that had happened today. Finally, "I know how it looks, Diana. I know what the police think, but I swear, I didn't do it and I didn't hire someone do it for me, either."

"Of course not. You wouldn't have been caught if you had."

She ignored the amused look I shot her.

"And only idiots use their own gun. While Lieutenant Sinclair may consider you to be a number of things, I don't believe that particular descriptor is one of them. He is bound by procedure, and right now all the dots connect to you." She tapped a nail against her cup and considered me thoughtfully. "Why would someone expend the effort required to craft such an elaborate frame?"

To stop me from investigating two murders? My enemy had indeed changed tactics. I resumed the closed-eyes head-back position to hide the lie. "Haven't a clue."

<h1 style="text-align:center"><u>Chapter 30</u></h1>

Mr. Jetter had obtained a copy of the police report on Donald Hanscombe's murder by the time of our afternoon appointment. According to it, Hanscombe and an associate had flown to Omaha Thursday night to attend a three-day financial management seminar held in a mid-town hotel conference center. It was accompanied by the usual evening socializing. According to his fellow financier, Charles Browning, Hanscombe left Saturday night's party shortly after one o'clock after being paged by the hotel desk clerk.

When Mr. Jetter read me Browning's statement that Hanscombe told him he was meeting Martina Sullivan 'for business,' we both rolled our eyes. Browning probably had, too, especially after adding that his associate's attitude had suddenly turned 'jaunty.'

That information had tightened the murder window even further.

After our meeting, I'd come to the park side of Thirteenth Street's alley. Scowling past the police tape wasn't making things any clearer. Police markings were still evident, including a large circle drawn around the hole in the wall where the bullet had entered it. After the police shifters had sniffed out the fresh blood, they'd matched it to the body, matched the bullet to my gun, and then came banging on my door. Open and shut case, right?

I turned and eyed the park.

Jenson Park was over one hundred and twenty acres, and it was the biggest natural area inside the city. Besides the usual recreational activities, it was meant to give shifters a place to run and stretch their limbs. It had been a risk, killing him here, as there could have been a four-footed, late-night roamer. But the park and its immediate environs provided the advantage of no nighttime lighting, unlike the rest of the city.

The police theory was that my female accomplice lured Hanscombe to the park for wild sex. I shot him as he was undressing prior to shifting into his coyote, then we tossed body, shoes, and pants in the dumpster. Perfect frame.

Except for that kick-in-the-fang thing called fate.

The body was found fresh enough to determine the time of death accurately enough to clear me. Unfortunately, the odors and trash in the dumpster had ruined any chance of getting the killer's scent off the body, and an early fog had rolled in and diffused the alley scents.

It was a win/lose situation for both of us. I hope he was as exasperated as I was.

***

By Wednesday evening I needed someone to talk to and called Nate. He offered to brood with me at *Riley's*.

"Not a clue," I told Nate honestly. After all, he'd asked the 'how' not the 'why' question after getting a quick summary of my weekend. Nor did I want to voice unproven theories. He'd been completely unaware of my problem, as the particulars of Hanscombe's murder hadn't been released. I took a double swig of beer. "There's no trace someone got into my place—twice. Once to get my gun and then return it."

"Normally you keep it with you." Nate's brow scrunched. "How did someone know you'd left it behind?"

"Yeah. That's another *how* without an answer." I hadn't had any sense of being watched when I left. And even if I had been, the teenage-filled hall would have been an unexpected complication. This whole debacle reeked of a hastily thrown-together, impulsive action. Which could also describe the attack in Kansas City.

"Pretty slick," Nate said, slouching back in his chair.

"Very slick," I agreed sourly. "Better be glad you were busy Saturday night."

"Why?"

"Since *I* didn't do it, I must have a very good *friend*. Someone I could trust to help me and lent them my Ruger."

"Oh. *Oh!*" Startlement widened Nate's eyes. "Think Mrs. Herman would understand getting a thank you card for having a *grand mal* seizure?" He tipped his bottle up, took a large swallow.

We spent the next couple of minutes brooding.

"They ever find this Sullivan person who called Hanscombe?" Nate asked.

I shook my head. "The only Martina Sullivan in the metro area is a spry seventy-four-year-old living in the Red Rose Retirement Home in Bellview. While having no idea what they were talking about, she was more than happy to assist the police with their inquiries."

Nate blinked, grinned. "Assist with inquiries?"

"Transplanted English lawyer. It's either coincidence her name matches the fake one or the killer grabbed it from a phonebook when she called Hanscombe. The hotel's phone records show the call came from one of those cash-and-carry phones." Another dead end.

Silence. For a whole two minutes. Then Nate straightened suddenly.

"Maybe she's just pretending to be clueless," Nate said.

"Huh?"

"Maybe she's part of the Night Wacker Club."

"The what?"

"Who'd suspect a bunch of white-hair CWGs of taking out the human trash?"

"CWGs?"

"Cane Wielding Gramps. Or grannies. Most people tend to overlook or ignore them. *Huge* mistake. Never. Ever. Trifle with a CWG of either sex."

"You're kidding!"

"Nope. Especially the grannies. Trust me."

My mouth was hanging open. "Uh, Nate?"

"Think about how much varied knowledge and experience exists in any given retirement home. People that have survived everything from war to teenagers."

"I'm thinking you've had several too many."

"Farmers. Academics. Medical. Military and law enforcement. Maybe they even scored an agent or Special Forces. For all you know, that transplanted lawyer could've been a lethal participant in one of the European Wars."

I made a grab for the bottle he was waving at me. He swung it out of my reach.

"I—oops." Nate muttered an apology to the guy he smacked in the butt and quickly tucked both beer and hand against his chest. "I'm always recommending my senior patients take up some kind of hobby or activity. Helps keep the brain from going to mush."

"I think yours is already there," I told him, laughing. "I doubt a secret nightlife knocking off people would be considered a hobby." I paused. "You *are* kidding, right?"

Nate roared with laughter.

I shook my head, relaxing as the knots in my muscles smoothed out. Which probably had been Nate's intention. That or he was developing some serious paranoia issues.

We spent a couple of minutes laughing about all the different skill sets a group of senior citizens could utilize to take out people they felt deserved it. Shifters were strong, and there were probably several among them that still had the strength to physically carry 170 pounds to an alley a block or two away and then toss it into a dumpster. It was a ridiculous idea but, in a way, Nate was right. No telling what the Red Rose inhabitants had done in their younger days. Our chuckles gradually petered off into silence.

Nate sighed. "It doesn't make sense."

My response was a grumpy scowl, along with "Name me one thing about this that does." However, Nate's idea of meeting here was working. While his harebrained idea was in the weeds well past the barn—*Red Rose Night Wacker Club, indeed*—he had gotten me out of my brood.

Nate leaned across the table. "Reverse it." He pointed his empty bottle at me. "What if Hanscombe was killed here, using the history between the two of you to keep attention pointed away from Chicago?"

The beer halfway to my lips drifted back to the table. "*My* frame was the diversion to get rid of *Hanscombe*? That's good," I murmured. Very good. Being a scapegoat made as much sense as being targeted for nosing around. "He certainly managed to piss off people here in Omaha."

"Maybe he pissed off the wrong people in Chicago. They do have a reputation." Nate held up his bottle and two fingers at the black-haired waitress. "It wouldn't take too much effort to find out the history between him, Marge, and you. I still remember that quote: 'When I get my hands on the son-of-a-pig I'll rip all five limbs off.'"

"I meant it, too." I finished off the last couple of swallows.

"Which is probably the reason behind his overnight express move to Chicago," Nate commented dryly. "Everyone knew his head wasn't the fifth extremity being referred to. Besides, you didn't know he was back."

I grimaced. "The conference was getting a lot of publicity. Hanscombe— a born egotist—made sure he was front and center of one of the pictures splayed across the paper's front page." I waited until the waitress left with our empties. "Their theory is that I saw him in the picture and reacted. That, on top of everything else lately, pushed me over a line."

"Another useful and well-documented fact—her suicide, not your mental condition," Nate said, nodding thoughtfully.

What else was going to be used against me? "I probably ought to warn Angie. The police might have her on my accomplice list as the fake Martina."

"Misdirection, confusion, just plain muddy-the-water—it fits," Nate continued. "It also wouldn't take much effort to learn about your other problems. You've been attacked, twice, and both were in the news. Three, if you count when your office was trashed the first time. And all that's *after* Kansas City." He shot me a sharp look. "Someone is determined to take you out, Curt. Any sociopaths in your history?"

"Two. Drug-dealer and his brother. Both dead." I'd shot one and the other died in a prison fight.

"At least those police officers didn't blow off the two winos," he said, his frustration plain. "If they'd hauled them off to the tank instead of checking their story out, you'd really be strapped. I still can't believe they think you'd be so idiotic as to use your own weapon."

While I appreciated everyone's support, the term was getting annoying. "Ego. Not expecting the bullet to be found. Whatever." I shrugged. "They can always work up a scenario that will put me exactly where they want me, which is behind bars. The only reason I figure I've not been arrested yet is because they're still trying to figure out who my accomplice is."

"No, it's not," said a voice behind me.

Sinclair? That was a surprise. I was even more surprised when he settled into a chair between us.

"Nothing yet, thanks," he told the waitress materializing beside him. He swung his head back to me. "I have a couple of questions."

I groaned. "Don't you ever go off duty?"

"When I go in my front door. What did you do with your gun after Mr. Swantz left?"

"I put it in the nightstand next to my bed, where your people found it."

"Did you visually check to make sure it was your gun in the holster?"

"No." I eyed Sinclair warily, realizing he was thinking about a decoy gun. "But I think I'd have noticed any difference, especially in the grip's feel."

"You took a shower the next morning?"

"Yes."

"The Ruger shower with you?"

Say what? The quick flash of amusement in those blue pieces of marble showed the bastard did have a sense of humor, albeit slightly warped. "What kind of question is that?"

"A legitimate one. Assuming no one could come into your bedroom without you waking up," he paused, waited for my nodded confirmation, "the only time that weapon was unattended for the hours in question was while you were at Lotte's and while you scrubbed."

"You think it was taken while I was at Lotte's then returned while I showered?" I thought it over. Finally shook my head. "That would require some fantastical luck with exceptionally good timing, unless you think someone was hiding in my apartment and waiting for me to climb into the shower."

"Wouldn't necessarily have to be hiding." Sinclair glanced casually at

Nate.

"I did *not* have anyone, much less a friend, kill the bastard for me," I said indignantly.

"Regardless of when it was returned, the real issue is when it was *removed* from your residence. *That* is the reason neither of you have been arrested, either as primary or as an accomplice. It's not just you we can't place at the crime scene. We can't—"

"My friends are *not* murderers." My back molars were grinding. How many times did I need to say it?

Nate tipped his bottle at me. "And speaking as one of those non-murderous friends," Nate angled himself around to face Sinclair, "I can swear that neither is Dice—D'Accio."

"He once threatened extensive bodily harm toward the victim."

"So? Extensive bodily harm can be survived. I'm a doctor, I should know. Dice might have felt justified in administering a legally incorrect beating—"

"But well deserved," I inserted.

"—for which Hanscombe would gleefully have filed assault charges, but it's still a far cry from committing a carefully orchestrated murder. And speaking as Mr. D'Accio's personal physician of several years, I will also swear his mental state is not in question." Nate switched from serious to scowling. "So don't think he's gone loopy either."

I grinned at Nate. "Thanks." It was good to have friends. I shot Sinclair a smug grin. "Any more questions, official or otherwise?"

He studied me for a moment. "I don't think you realize the problem here."

"The problem is you can't prove I did it," I taunted.

"The problem is we can't prove *anyone* did it." Sinclair got a stereophonic "Huh?" from both sides. He rolled his wrist over and checked his watch. "Now I'm off duty."

"You want to explain that last statement?" I said, puzzled.

"Your theory is that someone entered your apartment, took your weapon, killed Hanscombe and returned it, thereby framing you for the act."

"Fact, not theory," I told him firmly.

"When?"

"Between ten-thirty and two-thirty. While I was gone," I said. Tight, but doable, especially with a fast car.

Sinclair gave me a veiled look. "Your gun was seen physically by the delivery boy from *Cho's Chow* at approximately ten PM. It was laid out next to a cleaning kit."

"I'd been at the firing range the day before, as I told you. I was planning to clean it and then the punk music started up. I left instead and it was too late when I got back. Which is why it still smelled when the police examined it the following morning."

I eyed the lieutenant suspiciously. An off-duty discussion, in an almost friendly manner about an ongoing case with unofficial sources—not to mention with the chief suspect? What was going on here? Could the good-cop-bad-cop routine be pulled off simultaneously by the same cop?

"Mr. Swantz noticed the holstered gun, which he's ready to swear was your Ruger, when he accompanied you to your apartment around two-thirty. He also swears it was a little after three AM when he left. You then moved it your bedroom. All of which collaborates your statements. The Ruger's next verified presence was when my men took possession."

I leaned forward. He was leading up to something.

"You noticed the kids in the hallway when you returned?"

I nodded. There weren't as many as when I left, and the music had been toned down.

"They were the leftovers from a hall party. That's why it was crowded earlier when you confronted the evening's DJ—the foul-mouthed punk—at approximately ten-thirty."

And we were back to the carved-marble look.

"After said confrontation you went back to your apartment, started to clean your gun, but evidently changed your mind after the music started back up and only at a slightly lower volume. You shoved the gun in its holster and tossed it in a chair where Mr. Swantz saw it later. Your cleaning kit went under the coffee table. Grabbed your wallet, keys and left. No jacket. Took about fifteen minutes."

I blinked. He was good. That, or there was a camera in my apartment.

"None of the hallway occupants you stomped past saw a weapon or anything remotely resembling a weapon bulge—the three who think you have hot buns checked out all your bulges."

I gave Nate and his snicker a dirty look.

Sinclair made a fist and held up a finger, "The gun was verified to be in your apartment prior to you leaving shortly before eleven PM and there's no evidence it left with you." Another finger went up. "No one entered your apartment until your return at approximately two-thirty with a friend or after said friend left, also with no bulges. This was verified by a continuously occupied hallway of partiers and their chaperones until *after* four AM, which included a number of Gen noses that would have smelled the gun's presence even if you had managed to hide it somehow. Third. You're on the third floor of a seven-story building, with no balcony allowing outside access from top, bottom or sideways."

I looked at the three fingers sticking up and realized exactly what the problem was even before Sinclair spelled it out.

"The evidence clearly indicates your gun could *not* have been removed, replaced and/or returned last Saturday between the hours of ten PM and four AM. Donald Hanscombe could *not* have been shot with a .357 bullet from your Ruger in a Thirteenth Street alley during that same timeframe. My ballistics and forensic experts—with a total experience of thirty-six years, three months and eighteen days—tell me that's exactly what *did* happen."

Sinclair sprawled back in his seat, tucked his hands under his armpits, and the marble cracked. Frustration. Aggravation. And it was in his voice when he said, "Forget about who pulled the trigger. I want to know how the bloody hell it was done."

Chapter 31

Nate whistled softly. "Some problem. That puts Dice free and clear, right?"

I shook my head. "I wish."

"But the evidence—"

"Conflicts itself," I interrupted. "Which means all the data becomes questionable because something, somewhere, is wrong."

"Or there's a vital piece missing," Sinclair added. "Regardless, we're back to square one."

Nate drained the last of his drink. "Okay, you're back to square one," he said, shooting Sinclair a bad-tempered look. "So? That means Dice didn't, couldn't have done it."

My bottle joined Nate's empty one and I leaned back in my chair. Nate's obstinate expression had me sighing. "Nate, if the time of death is wrong, my alibi—and yours—is no good. If the ballistics are wrong, it could have been done with a different gun by anyone, including me or an accomplice."

The emotions flashing across Nate's face probably equated to some fancy cursing. I turned to Sinclair and asked bluntly "Do you believe I did it?"

"If a witness suddenly comes forward saying they saw you—physically and recognizably—either pulling the trigger or dumping the body, I'll be arresting you."

"You expect one to?"

"Wouldn't be surprised."

My pulse sped up. "You know it's a frame."

Sinclair took several silent seconds to study us, visibly debating what and how much to say. He then did a slow, casual scan of the room. The bar was in full Wednesday mid-week swing: lots of bodies and noise. It was the perfect setting for a private conversation, even for shifters.

"Off the record and I'll deny I ever said it."

We nodded and leaned inward to keep the conversation low. Frustration. That had to driving Sinclair's unexpected behavior. Not that I was complaining.

"At first glance, it appears to be an emotion-fueled, impromptu crime. But everything was too well planned and thought out to be anything other than a two-pronged hit. Everything, that is, but the confrontation that drove you from your apartment. Even then, it might have succeeded if it hadn't been for the two winos."

My lightbulb went off. "It moved the discovery of the body forward."

He nodded. "That dumpster is used by two businesses, both of which are closed by eleven PM on Saturday and all day on Sunday. Since most people toss trash without glancing inside, odds are—and I bet counted on—the body wouldn't have been discovered before Monday at the earliest, or during the scheduled pickup on Tuesday at the latest. Even a shifter wouldn't have smelled anything over the normal August stench. By the time we got involved and the body to forensics, the time of death couldn't have been narrowed to anything less than a twelve-to-fourteen-hour window."

"Which would've sucked big time for Dice."

"Big time," I agreed.

"Big time," Sinclair echoed. "All evidence is being reviewed and triple-checked. With everything pretty well screwed up, no arrests can be made. D'Accio is still at the top of the list but, for now, other avenues will have to be pursued."

"By two-pronged you mean?" I asked, mulling over his information.

"Hanscombe dead, you framed. Theories?"

"Well, Nate came up with a couple of theories."

"And?" Sinclair prompted after a couple of seconds.

"First one involves CWGs from the Red Rose NWC," I said, managing to keep a straight face.

"The what, from what?" Sinclair's eyebrows bunched together.

"Cane Welding Gramps—"

"Or Grannies," Nate insisted with a two-finger point.

I made a mental note to ask Nate later about whatever harrowing event he'd evidently had with one. "—of the Night Wacker Club." I finished. Miracle of miracles, I still wasn't laughing. But it was hard.

"And they are?" Sinclair asked cautiously.

"Red Rose Retirement Home residents who have banded together to utilize their many varied and extensive skills and years of experience to rid the world of undesirables and themselves of boredom. Sullivan is their point woman."

Comically, Sinclair's pupils slid sideways in Nate's direction. "I see."

Nate flashed him an all-teeth smile. "Hobbies are good. Everyone needs a hobby. What's yours?"

Unable to hold it in any longer, I burst out laughing. Sinclair twisted around, snagged a waitress' attention and held up a finger. Looking over his shoulder at the laughing idiots, he held up two more.

Our chuckles had died off by the time the waitress dropped off three cold ones. Even Sinclair's lips were turned up at the corners. "I think you'll understand when I put that at the bottom of my list. Should I even bother asking about the other one?"

He listened attentively as Nate outlined his second theory. He pulled quietly on his beer after Nate finished. "While your first idea is," he coughed, "intriguing, I'll check with Chicago. See what they have on him there." He switched his attention to me. "What's your theory?"

"I've pissed someone off."

"For the overt attacks, obviously. But this would be a little extreme, don't you think?"

"Sure. But it makes Nate's second theory more realistic."

Sinclair's nostrils flexed, then his expression hardened. "You're hedging."

Crap. Shifter plus cop instincts. Or maybe he smelled my nervousness.

Nate met Sinclair's gaze, nodded and swung around toward me. "Give."

"Honest. I don't know who would or could do this." I tried dodging one last time.

"How about the why, Dice?" Nate said, leaning on his arm.

I bounced an uncertain look between the two of them. Nate's shifted downward. Following, I found my fingers flexing. I balled my hand into a fist, kept it there. They remained silent, watchful. I sighed, realizing I'd run out of options.

"I've been working on something personal," I admitted.

"Tabitha?" Nate shot a quick frown at Sinclair. "I know you've been trying to find the reason behind her murder."

"Not Miss Chandler. Margret Lockewild," Sinclair said, studying me. "He's been looking into her murder."

"Murder?" Nate gasped. "Not suicide?"

"I knew it. You sensed something wasn't right, didn't you?" I said.

He tapped his finger against his bottle. "Based on interviews, I personally believed her behavior change appeared to be more of one deeply occupied than depressed."

"Then why did you close it as suicide?" I demanded.

"Not counting the pressure coming down from the top? I had nothing concrete to take to my superiors."

"What about instinct? What about gut feelings?"

"All of which require something *solid* to back it up." Exasperation flashed across his face. "Everything supported suicide, especially a note written in her own handwriting. Yes, something didn't feel right, but there was nothing, absolutely nothing, I could point at. I didn't know the woman. You did, and you saw something in Miss Lockewild's file. What was it?"

My opinion of Sinclair shifted higher. "Her last meal."

"The broccoli beef?"

"Not hardly," Nate snorted.

I flashed him a wry smile. "You tell him."

Nate rolled his eyes toward Sinclair. "Marge was a vegetarian. Confirmed, committed, and downright obsessive at times. Remember her lectures about all those helpless, extorted critters, Dice? She wouldn't have voluntarily eaten meat if her life depended on it." He winced. "Uh, feel free to ignore that last comment."

I dropped my voice. "A street source has verified Marge was working on something she ran across while researching the Chandler family. Marge also once said that if we couldn't find something in Tabitha's life that led to her murder, then maybe she paid the penalty for something in her family's. I believe Marge found it. I have *one* case involving two murders.

Nate sucked in a breath.

"You're sure about this?" Sinclair asked sharply.

"I know Marge was working hard on a story—you know how focused she gets, Nate? Marge was fanatical about recording her information, either on tape or written notes. Often both. There were tape wrappers in her home's trashcan. But there was nothing new in her home office. *Nothing* from the first of June on. No notes or tapes, other than the ones you found in her office and inside her purse. Her recorder was empty?"

I'd been assuming it was, but it was good to get his confirming head-nod.

Nate rubbed his chin. "That doesn't sound like Marge."

"Someone cleaned out her home office. They went through her files on the Chandlers, removing anything that might provide a lead. Her phone records for the last three months are missing, too." I'd discovered the missing statements when going through her personal records.

"I agree, it sounds suspicious," Sinclair said. "But it doesn't mean that whatever it is has to do with the Chandler family itself."

I gave him a feral grin. "Then why did Marge have a street source sniffing out information on Mrs. Chandler's early life and associates? One of whom is a professional assassin."

The lieutenant frowned. "We just don't have enough information. It could be anything." Sinclair rubbed his chin. "What else did the informant tell you?"

"That Marge didn't appear worried until that last week. No, sorry— distracted was what she said. Marge had no hard proof of whatever she'd found and didn't know what to do with it."

"And didn't tell anyone what it was?" Nate said.

"Not a peep, to me or Angie. She'd kept everything secret up to that point."

Thoughtfully, Sinclair said, "But something changed that Friday."

"Whatever it was, she came by my office that afternoon, evidently to finally talk with me, but I wasn't there. I tried to call over the weekend, but it went straight to voicemail. Figured I'd catch her the next week." My hand tightened around my drink. "Marge had pretty good instincts and she was careful, so she must have been caught off-guard."

She would have felt her life slipping away, helpless to stop it. Helpless. God, I hated that emotion. "She couldn't stop it, so she did what she could to alert me," I said, hearing the hitch in my voice. "Little things she could slip past the killer. How she worded the note. The meal."

"I remember your name was misspelled. What else?"

"A private reference in the note," I told him.

He shot me a hard look. "She had to have left you something else."

"Not a damn thing. It's all gone."

"You're holding back."

"You went through her home office. You had me sign for the box. Did you see anything in it?"

"She left something when she came by your office that day. *That's* why it was turned upside down."

"Then explain the legal office next door getting hit, too."

"You're—"

A beer bottle slammed down between us. "Children! That's enough." Nate grinned at our glares. "No wonder the two of you can't get along." He waved his hand between us. "You're too much alike."

Looking over, I saw the near identical shoulder-stiff, armpit-tucked slouch as me.

"We're not alike."

Sinclair's mutter had my lips twitching, which spread into a grin. After a moment his body language relaxed, but he refused to return my grin. "Truce?" I said.

He nodded. "Truce. I'll see about reopening Miss Lockewild's case."

"No. Be better if you don't. There's power and probably a lot of money involved. I have a feeling someone on the State Licensing Committee had a 'suggestion' planted in their ear. As of this morning, my PI license is under review."

"What?" Nate exclaimed.

I nodded glumly. "The letter listed a previous Coldbath complaint and the current investigation into my suspicion of premediated murder."

Sinclair's eyes narrowed. "That information has not been officially released."

"Well, someone told them. And if I'm right, if we're right," I corrected, "this someone has killed and/or paid for it at least twice. Might be best if they thought they'd gotten away with it so no one else dies. Like Marge's street source."

"You said she didn't know anything." Worry wrinkles etched Nate's forehead.

"About what Marge found on her own? No, but she is a connection and has provided other information. The killer can't be sure what she does or doesn't know. Currently, she's also helping me hunt for Marge's killer. Angie was more than Marge's source, they were friends." Seeing Sinclair's questioning look, I added, "Non-intimate friends. We've been meeting, sharing what information we find. I'm trying to follow Marge's path, rebuilding her notes and hoping to see whatever it was she did."

Nate's lips pursed. "Blacken your name enough and, even if you did find something, you might not be believed."

"Especially if he's lost his license. I'll do what checks I can, but we're still blind on where to focus. We're still trying to figure out how Hanscombe was killed."

"I thought it was a bullet through the heart," Nate said blandly.

I laughed; the lieutenant glared. Nate was on a roll tonight.

Standing, Sinclair said, "Want me to get Lockewild's phone records?"

I shook my head. "I put the request in. As Executor, I tap-danced a reason for needing copies."

Chapter 32

"Curt D'Accio! Was it the death of your good friend, Margret Lockewild, on top of the anniversary of your lover's death that had you lashing out at Donald Hanscombe?"

What? I straightened up. On the other side of my car stood a medium-sized man with a large smirk. "Who the hell are you?"

"Dave Thompson with *Today's StoryLine*. Who helped you lure Hanscombe out to his death?"

Great. Just what I needed. I climbed into my car, ignoring the barrage of questions. Omaha was in my rearview mirror before I stopped fuming. Thompson was going to be a problem. The reporters for that trash paper lived for sensationalism and were more than happy to stretch, ad-lib, and just plain fabricate an article's contents. They even knew how to misconstrue 'No comment.'

Considering the case details, including my name, had not yet been released, someone had fed them to the jackass. I made a mental note to call Sinclair when I got back and warn him his case was about to go public in a trashy way.

I was on my way for a Saturday afternoon visit with Greg Greenbaum's parents. They lived in Lincoln, a quiet college town about an hour away. Well, it was, five nights a week. On Fridays and Saturdays, the youngsters turn it into a high-spirited party town. 'Stress relief from our studies,' one graduate had told me with a straight face.

Henry and Althea Greenbaum were retired university professors. Their home phone number was one of the numbers on the duplicated phone statements I'd received yesterday. Marge had only spoken to them by phone, but I'd called and arranged to meet with them. Face-to-face was my personal preference since body language was often more revealing than words.

Another number I'd found was both surprising and worrisome. Dialing it, I'd found myself talking to the arson section of Nassau's Police Department. The helpful officer said that if Miss Lockewild had been looking for information on a case, she probably talked to Inspector Balcer. She offered to leave a message for a return call on the Inspector's desk. He was currently on vacation.

There had been that string of robbery-arsons last year, which Tabitha's doctor's clinic had fallen victim to. Was that it? Some other case? What had she been hunting for? Questions and possibilities kept me entertained on the long drive.

***

The Greenbaum home was in a nice suburb on the southwest side of Lincoln. Directly behind it the land lay open, perfect for activities and shifter running. Mrs. Greenbaum welcomed me warmly and had a glass of iced tea in my hand three seconds after I sat down. Mr. Greenbaum had his hands folded on his cane and was watching me with a pursed-lip speculative look his students had probably found unnerving. I had the feeling the reason I'd given them for this visit had flunked.

I listened closely as they told me about their son's whirlwind courtship. Their first year of marriage and the problems caused by Cyntha's parents. Mrs. Greenbaum said it was a miracle they hadn't burned the house down earlier, when Cynthia might have been too young to escape.

Mr. Greenbaum thumped his cane. "Life was a lot happier for everyone after those two drunks were gone."

"Henry," his wife chided gently.

"You felt the same, Althea."

"Well, yes. But you could be more tactful."

I grinned. From his expression, tactful wasn't in his syllabus. "I understand. So, there were no other, uh, issues in their marriage?" I asked, trying for tact myself.

"Why don't you tell us the real reason you're here, Mr. Private Investigator?" Mr. Greenbaum said.

Mrs. Greenbaum's smile was polite but a bit pointy. Right. She was a First-Gen fox. I threw my supposed follow-up to Tabitha's story out the window and went for blunt honesty.

"You're aware of Marge Lockewild's recent three-part report on Tabitha Chandler's life and death? Well, she filed her report on Tabitha at the end of May. Then she immediately switched to investigative mode on something she'd come across during the course of that research. What, we don't know. All her notes since the first of June have disappeared, as have a few other documents since her unexpected death."

They stared at me, at each other, then back at me.

"Miss Lockewild's death wasn't suicide and you're trying to retrace her steps."

"Yes, sir. Her list of phone calls is one of the few avenues I have."

Their expressions turned contemplative.

"We didn't know very much about Cynthia's life before she married our son. Our conversation with Miss Lockewild was about their married life, and I don't believe..." Mrs. Greenbaum paused, then shook her head. "I can't think of anything we discussed that would fit what you're looking for. Cynthia may have married Greg partly to get away from home, but she cared for him. We were all ecstatic when Cynthia announced her pregnancy."

"Did she have any trouble with the pregnancy? She had a difficult one with Tabitha."

"No, none at all. I'd never seen the girl smile so much and she was practically bouncing all over the place. She was disappointed at having to give up working with Greg, but they didn't want to risk losing the baby."

"She worked at construction sites with her husband?"

"Oh, yes. Up until she was about four months along." Mr. Greenbaum chucked. "She said blowing things up was very cathartic."

"Excuse me?"

"We've confused him, dear. Greg was a demolition expert, Mr. D'Accio.

One of the best, I'm proud to say. Cynthia proved to be very adept at it. I can tell by your expression that you're having a hard time reconciling that image with her current high-class one."

I nodded. That was something I'd have to process later, along with the bouncy, smiley image. "What happened the day Greg died?"

"Carelessness," Mr. Greenbaum said, his wife's face turning sad. "Two support beams hadn't been shored up properly and a wall collapsed, crushing Greg and one other. Cynthia and the other guy's family received large settlements."

Which she'd used to propel herself upward and away from everything in her life at that point. I was trying to figure out how to word my next question when they beat me to it.

"Were we upset when Cynthia left us behind, so to speak?" Mr. Greenbaum said. He shared another look with his wife. "Yes, and no. Cynthia was always ambitious, a directive undoubtedly entrenched by her early childhood and the desire to escape its conditions. She and Greg had started laying the framework for their own construction company. After his death, no one would talk to her or even consider giving her a start-up loan. Nor would any company hire her for demo work, including those she'd worked for previously. It turned her bitter."

"We offered to help," Mrs. Greenbaum said, "but she knew it would strain our resources. Professors aren't exactly in the best income brackets. Cynthia's pride had also taken a hit. I believe, truly believe, it was the additional 'I'll show them' attitude that drove her after that. We weren't surprised when she married into society, but it did hurt when Russell was adopted by her new husband and took his name."

The room fell quiet. They were reliving the past and I was adjusting to this new facet of the woman. For the first time, I felt sympathy for her. Cynthia Chandler had escaped a horrible childhood, found a happy marriage and motherhood, and was building a future. A future that was brutally and callously yanked away. Maybe she did have some basis for her attitude.

"Do you ever get to see Russell?" I asked. Both their faces broke into a smile.

"He visits us occasionally," Mrs. Greenbaum said happily. "No ostentatious display, no arrogance, and no patronizing. He likes my green pepper casserole."

We talked for a little while longer, mostly them relating stories about Russell. Both agreed they'd never seen such a well-behaved young wolf. Both also felt he would have ended up in an academic career of some kind if things had been different.

I left the Greenbaum home in a mixed mood and with their promise to remain silent about my suspicions. My opinion of Cynthia Chandler hadn't changed, but I viewed her in a different light now. I understood what drove her. Russell's unassuming and unknown visits to his biological grandparents had also caught me off-guard. Like Tabitha, he'd managed to keep some things private. A remarkable feat, in our modern, technology-driven culture.

As evidenced by that reporter outside my apartment this morning.

But I was still left with the unknown *what* that Marge had found. Cynthia Chandler's life during her first marriage appeared open and happy. No problems, apparently, outside of it either. Both her in-laws were astute enough to have noticed if there were. Mrs. Greenbaum's fox senses, especially, would have noticed worry or nervousness.

Wondering if Thompson was still stalking my apartment, I decided to swing by Nate's place. If he wasn't on call, we could go do darts and beer. Nate had recently started volunteering as a substitute at Papillion Mercy Hospital. In their ER, no less. Guess part of him missed it, although I was surprised to hear it. I never expected him to go back.

He was indeed on call, so I headed for home, coffee, and my files.

Chapter 33

Angie slid into the booth opposite Curt cautiously. The one-third empty pitcher of beer wasn't nearly as worrisome as the dark look on his face. What had happened since last week?

She'd added Curt to her short list of friends and looked forward to their Thursday nights. He was friendly, pragmatic, and treated her as a regular person, same as Marge had. Most people viewed sex workers as those too lazy to get a 'real' job. She'd shut down one snooty woman, explaining the principle of supply and demand, the various wages depending on service, then finished with the statistics on the number of brothels and street workers the city had to meet its demand. She could still picture the woman's horrified expression.

She poured beer into the waiting glass and sipped quietly. Waited.

"My parents died when I was eighteen," Curt said, his voice wooden. "Car wreck. We'd spent the weekend with Dad's parents in Thedford. Got caught up in one of those out-of-nowhere blizzards on our way back. Dad was going to pull off the interstate at the next exit but…"

Angie took another sip, letting him tell the story at his own rate.

"The pileup started somewhere ahead of us. Even with Dad's reflexes…our car was crushed between a tractor-trailer rig and a concrete truck. It took three years of surgeries and physical therapy to get me back on my feet. Another year of psych therapy to feel normal. Hah! What's normal?"

Angie watched him refill his glass. She had assumed the pain she'd sensed inside him had been from the loss of Tabitha and then Marge. Apparently, its roots were older.

"As far back as I can remember, I always wanted a law enforcement career," Curt said, brooding into his beer. "I was fully healed, but no one would hire me. Anywhere. Not state patrols, not city or county police departments…not even the U.S. Territorial Marshalls."

Another hard blow. Angie wanted to reach over and give him a hug.

"I worked my butt off to get an Associate in Criminal Justice: day classes, night jobs. Then I revisited those same offices. I couldn't even get an interview, Angie. They all cited possible long-term *issues* from my injuries."

Her heart cracked a little bit at the anguish in his voice. She understood the pain of broken dreams. "So you went the private investigator route," she said, keeping her voice even.

"I interned with Halligan Investigative Services for a year. Got my PI license, worked for them another three years and then opened my own office. Worked hard to build my reputation. A year ago I fell in love and we planned a future. Now…Tabitha is dead. Marge is dead. And my PI license has been suspended."

The beer went down the wrong way. Angie managed a "What?" between coughs.

"This morning's letter—a whopping two paragraphs—cited a complaint from a rich buffoon in Texas, the recent suspicion of murder, and a couple of well-written, B-S articles that leaves the impression I'm unstable, unpredictable, and possibly dangerous."

"They took those articles in *StoryLine* seriously?" No wonder the guy was in a black mood. The article supposedly citing several *anonymous* street workers' claim of him roughing them up for information had pissed her off. If it had really happened, she'd have heard about it.

Curt nodded and downed half his beer.

Angie shoved her glass aside and leaned forward. "Don't they have to do a review or something first?"

"There'll be a review, yes, in a couple of weeks. That'll decide whether to re-instate or revoke it completely. Until then…" he shrugged, and his eyes lost focus. "Where do you go when there's nowhere else?"

Not where her mother had gone, that was for bloody sure. Angie kicked him.

"*Yeooow!*" Curt yelped, jerking his legs sideways.

"You've had some bad knocks. I understand and empathize. You're entitled to a black mood and maudlin thoughts, but you're not allowed to spiral down into drunken suicide."

He straightened and shot her a dirty look. "I'm not."

"I read those articles. That asinine reporter—Thompson?—did nothing but dance with speculation and innuendo and his own imagination. I can't believe the State Board would have taken anything in that lying rag seriously or moved that fast. They *shouldn't* have."

It took a couple of seconds for his alcohol-fuzzed brain to get it.

He loosed a short stream of curses. "You're right. Someone is pushing them. We theorized that if I was discredited enough, no one would believe anything I found on the murders."

We? Probably his inner-circle friends. The small chest-pang that thought caused surprised her. "Whoever it is, they're probably the one that aimed the reporter at you."

His lips peeled back in a feral grin that would do a shifter proud.

"I'm being watched. I thought it was the reporter following me, or the cops keeping an eye on me. Maybe it's not. How good an actress are you?"

Angie leaned back, crossed her arms, and cocked an eyebrow. "I'm a prostitute."

***

"This is your car?" Angie said, not needing to pretend surprise. It was her first time seeing it.

"Yeah, yeah," Curt slurred out. "From another life." He was practically draped over her.

Angie managed to get the passenger door open and shoved him down into the seat. Straightening back up, she admired the car for a minute. "Some life. Driving this is going to be a bonus."

"Sssssaid I'd pay you."

"Yeah, you are, and only for getting you home. This is my night off.

Where's home?"

Curt's arm came up and he managed to vaguely wave before flopping it back down. "That way."

"You're not much help." She leaned forward, pushed him onto his side, and came up with his wallet.

"*Hey*. Pay you at home."

"I doubt you'll be conscious by then." She pulled out his license, holding it up toward a streetlight. "Apartment 305? Third floor? If there's no elevators, I'm dumping you in the stairwell." She pulled out some bills and tucked them in her bra before putting the wallet back in his pants.

Angie fired the engine up and revved the motor a couple of times. "Very nice," she said, grinning into the sideview mirror before pulling smoothly away from the curb.

They passed through two intersections.

"Anyone following?" Curt asked quietly, his head propped against the window.

"Not sure," Angie replied, checking the rearview mirror. "Nothing's close."

"Did you feel it?"

"My neck hairs are still curled," she replied. "Your watcher is definitely the unfriendly type."

<u>Chapter 34</u>

I waited until almost noon before slouching into my office. Diana pursed her lips but refrained from any remarks while I poured coffee into our largest cup. I propped my feet on my desk and stared morosely into my coffee. She followed me in.

"Mike has agreed to take over your two current cases and wants you to call him when you get in. I've canceled today's appointment, referring them also to HIS."

It hurt. Years of hard work blown out the window. "Glad to help Mike's business." I didn't have to pretend bitterness as I wadded up the State letter. It sailed across the room and made a two-point splash into Gertie's fish tank.

"Good thing that's a copy, although I was expecting more along the lines of confetti."

I shot her a sharp glance. "Where's the original?"

"In your general business file, where it stays. You'll need it in fighting this nonsense." She turned to leave.

"Diana," I said on a sigh. "Thank you. You've got a couple of paid weeks of vacation coming. Take them. Maybe by then…" I couldn't finish.

She came back and sat in my visitor chair. "I can't believe they suspended your license on something so vague and unproven. Daniel Marchard didn't lose his license until *after* he was convicted of fraud."

I stared down into my cup. "Guess they don't want to wait this time."

"Curt—" The office phone ringing interrupted her. She leaned over my desk to answer it.

"D'Accio Investigations… Yes, please hold." Placing it on hold, she held the receiver out. "Inspector Dominic Balcer from the Nassau Police Department returning your call."

I yanked my feet down, my cup's contents nearly sloshing out from being set down so fast. Taking it, I waited until Diana had exited before punching the call button.

"Inspector Balcer, thank you for calling. I hope you had a pleasant vacation."

"It was. We took one of those cruises. My wife enjoyed having someone else do the cooking and cleaning. Now, which case of mine are you interested in?"

"Do you remember talking with Marge Lockewild a couple of months ago?"

"I do. She wanted information about a string of robbery-arson cases that occurred a year ago. They hit several medical offices and labs. Still unsolved, by the way."

My pulse sped up. "Did she say why she was interested?"

There was a pause. "Why don't you ask her?" The tone held a trace of suspicion.

"Miss Lockewild died recently. I'm following up on her work but her notes are, uh, scanty."

"How scanty?" Definitely suspicious.

"As in non-existent," I said bluntly. I wasn't going to fool him. "I got your number from her phone records." Seconds ticked by silently.

"Miss Lockewild wanted to know if I could share anything about those events that wasn't released publicly in the news articles at the time. I couldn't give her much more. As I said, it's still an open case. She believed they were related to another string of arsons she was investigating there in the States."

"Did she give any idea of which ones?"

"You have a lot?" Balcer said dryly, before his voice returned to serious. "Just that it was some years ago—she didn't specify how long. Just that they resulted in multiple fatalities. How did Miss Lockewild die?"

"Suicide, according to the official report," I said tersely. When the silence stretched out a full minute, I knew he was drawing his own conclusions.

"You're a PI?" he finally asked.

"Yes. Marge was my sister." She always would be, blood be damned.

"I'll send you a copy of my confidential notes by email," he said abruptly. "I'll also re-examine everything. If I find anything new, I'll let you know."

I gave him my personal email address, not the office one. We ended the call, me promising to let him know if I turned up anything linked to his case, and him telling me to be careful. No, he hadn't been fooled.

My pondering was derailed by Diana's march to my visitor chair. Uh-oh. That was her don't-give-me-crap face.

"You going to tell me what's going on?" Diana said.

"Going on?" I parroted weakly.

"After five years, I consider you a friend as well as an employer. You're in trouble, Curt. Several troubles. I can't help if I don't know how or what."

I sighed inwardly. Truth was, Diana needed to know and to be more cautious. She worked in my office, privy to my files and information. My son-of-a-pig nemesis might already have her on his to-do list.

I told her everything: all my facts and all my suspicions. I finished, drained. Diana took my cup, returning with it filled and one for her. A companionable silence stretched for several minutes.

I sneaked a quick peek at Diana's face. Her expression had gone from distressed at Marge's non-suicide to contemplative. I had no clue what she was thinking, but this past year had shown how much I'd underestimated her.

"It was a mistake killing Hanscombe," she finally said.

Before I could open my mouth and agree, she finished with "It should have been you." I blinked. Did I hear that right?

"Despondent over their deaths, you take your own life. No one would give it a second thought. Now? Too many questions, too many deaths, all tying back to Kansas City. Your death would be examined hard, as well as those questions, since most still believe you were the target there. Which is why they switched to framing you when last year's attacks didn't succeed."

"Which is also failing, so now he's gone for discrediting me. So far," I said sourly, "it's working."

She gave me a hard look. "Except he knows you won't ever give up on Tabitha or Marge. Clues exist. Marge found them, or she wouldn't be dead."

My jaw set. True, but I hadn't found them.

"You're in danger, Curt. You're being followed. Watched. Two physical attacks. At least one of those break-ins here has to be related."

"Whoever was watching my apartment building last night had a more benign stare than whoever was watching me earlier. Most likely the reporter. If nothing else, he might serve as a deterrent. I doubt my enemy wants a witness."

"I doubt the reporter is there 24/7. And if he is, this psycho wouldn't fret about bashing his head in."

"What do you want me to do, Diana?" I said, exasperated. "You know I won't give up. Putting myself in the crosshairs is my only chance to solve this. My nemesis has two choices. Kill me or walk away, hoping I don't find those clues. If he tries for me? I really, really hope he does," I said with feeling. I didn't have claws, but a good face-pounding would be just as cathartic.

"Go on, Diana, take your vacation. I want you safely off somewhere else. I have a feeling this will be decided soon, one way or the other."

"Then I don't need to be gone, she said, rising. "I'll come in to check the mail. Fish will need to be fed and Charrise watered while we're closed."

Arguing would be wasted breath. I listened to the sounds of things being closed up or put away. Diana reappeared in my doorway.

"I left the coffeemaker on. Be sure and turn it off when you leave." She hesitated. "Good-by, Curt. Call me when you're ready to reopen the office or if you need something."

Her footsteps receded. The outer door closed with a tingle and sharp snap. We'd installed a bell over it over a month ago. Unless I could solve my own case, no one would be coming in.

***

"So…you're *pretending* to be despondent?" Nate asked.

We were at *Riley's*, the bar's Friday night in full swing. Tables were full, some with couples and others with the unattached eyeing each other. Clinking glasses, babbling voices and laughter surrounded us. Yells or groans accompanied the crack of pool balls and the *thunk* of darts from the adjoining room. There was music, too, blaring loud enough to drive any and all shifters elsewhere.

"Yep," I replied, wincing. Had the music always been this loud?

"You're doing it exceedingly well."

I squinted at him. "I'm bummed, Nate, but not despondent," I assured him, seeing his concerned expression. "Otherwise I'd be at the *Depot*."

"The what?"

"It's a shifter place Marge took me to. That's where Angie and I meet. Anyway, I want whoever's behind this to be overconfident. Off guard. I intend to go to my review with facts and questions of my own."

Nate nodded. "Might keep them from hatching anything else."

"That too. In the meantime, I can now concentrate on my personal case. Inspector Balcer's information should come in this weekend. I'm hoping it will provide a major clue. Something had Marge looking at it."

"I'm hoping it doesn't lead to another *suicide*," Nate said tersely. "She died less than two weeks after that phone call. If they know you've done the same, if they're somehow tracking your calls as well as your movements, then you are inviting the same response."

I gave him my best toothy grin. "Can't wait for the bastard to try it." More cheers drifted from the game room. "Have you seen any of the guys?" I asked, realizing I hadn't seen them in a couple of weeks.

Nate looked away for a moment, then back. "They switched to Saturdays," he said neutrally.

Surprise turned to hurt, knowing why Nate knew and I didn't. Dan was a cop. I could see why he would suddenly avoid me after *StoryLine* started printing Thompson's garbage. But Harold and Theresa were friends from high school and college, respectively. Surely they didn't believe… Evidently they did.

"Sure you want to be seen with me?" I said, my voice harsh.

"I got no problem with it. And if others do, there's a ton of stiff-necked doctors in the city they can switch to. Now, finish your beer. I'm going to beat your butt at pool."

My shoulders relaxed. "I might even let you," I told my best friend.

We played two games of pool and one of darts. The pool was a tie and I won the darts. Then we called it a night as Nate was substituting tomorrow. Overall, I was in a good mood. That lasted until I pulled into my apartment's parking lot.

Resignation became my predominant emotion when I spotted the patrol car. I pulled into an open spot and got out to meet them. If my "Now, what?" sounded a bit surly, I had good reason.

"We'd like for you to come down to police headquarters," the older cop said.

"It's late. What for and how about tomorrow morning?"

"How about now?" the younger one replied, taking a step forward aggressively.

"Your partner needs better control of his cat," I said warily.

The older cop's gaze flicked to the younger man, who was wearing a surprised look.

Yeah, yeah, I pegged you. I might as well get whatever it was over with. "I'll follow you there."

Both cops eyed my car. Wondering if they could catch me if I ran?

"That won't be necessary. We'll take you there," the older one replied.

I climbed into their back seat. At least I wasn't wearing cuffs.

The next five hours were boring, irritating, and highly resented. Hard-nosed grilling by two detectives were interspaced with periods of isolation, where I presumed they expected me to 'sweat.' It seems Dave Thompson had gotten himself assaulted behind a store one street away from my apartment and, timewise, shortly before I left to meet Nate at *Riley's*. While I felt the guy deserved it, my unknown adversary undoubtedly did it as another stab at my credibility.

I suppose laughing when I heard about it didn't help. The stolen wallet, watch, and pinky ring were deemed cover for the real objective: namely an old-fashioned ass-whooping. Motive: his very uncomplimentary articles about me—especially his focus on my status as "person of interest" in Donald Hanscombe's murder which had led to my license suspension.

It was dawn before I was abruptly told to go home after getting the requisite *don't leave town*.

"Great. Who's driving me home?" I asked.

The desk sergeant pointed at the door. "Bus stop is two blocks over."

Nate was on ER duty this morning and I didn't feel like calling a cab. So I called Diana. "You did tell me to call if I needed something," I said, laughing when she complained about the time.

I watched the sun rise as I waited at the curb, a sense of anticipation also rising in me. I had my nemesis worried. Why else try shoveling more crap my way?

Chapter 35

Lieutenant Sinclair pushed open the door to the hospital room. His nose wrinkled. It was still offensive, even though the doctors had managed to scrub most of the odor off of him.

Dave Thompson's bed was angled up and he was holding a bottle of water precariously between his bandaged hands. According to the doctor, they'd protected his head. His ribs and legs hadn't been so fortunate.

Thompson carefully maneuvered his cup down on the small tray in front of him. "You look like a cop."

"Lieutenant Sinclair, Homicide."

"Yeah? Well, I'm not dead, no thanks to you. If you'd done your job right with D'Accio, I wouldn't be in this shape." He raised his hands. "I have a hell of a story and I can't even type."

"About that," Sinclair said, letting the comments slide past him. "In your article on Wednesday, you mentioned two facts that were not publicly released. Where did you get them?"

"I have my sources."

Sinclair kept his irritation at the guy's smug tone and expression hidden. "What alerted you about D'Accio in the first place? You normally work out of the Southeastern states."

"I go wherever there's an interesting story. Having an inept police force letting a PI get away with murder? My readers find that *very* interesting."

The report he'd received from the Augustine PD was right. The arrogant bastard liked to piss off people. "Mr. Hanscombe's unsolved murder is not national news. You were pointed here. Anonymously, I presume?"

Thompson's face went blank.

That's what he'd thought. "Let me lay it out for you, Mr. Thompson. Both Mr. D'Accio and his closest friend have unshakeable alibis for Hanscombe's murder. You are being used—and set up—to discredit Mr. D'Accio by the *real* murderer he is after. Your assault was intended as another spike in his coffin. You probably *would* be dead if not for a delivery truck pulling in; I'm pretty sure the intent was to beat you to death."

"D'Accio did this and you're protecting him. What's he got on you?"

Sinclair gave himself a couple of seconds before responding. "You're a First-Gen jackal. How did a Zero sneak up on you?"

"Because he's a Zero-Plus," Thompson said slyly.

"Zero-Plus?"

"His family has a lot of shifters. He might not be able to shift himself, but he's inherited many of their traits and instincts. Like the strength to nearly take down that panther last year. He knew I was watching him. Following him. He knew where to find me."

That would explain a few things. "Who told you about his status? The same anonymous *source?* Sounds as if I have grounds to arrest you for stalking and invasion of privacy, as well as obstruction and accessory after the fact."

Thompson's chin jutted out. "I'm a reporter. I have a right to observe people. And accessory to *what*?"

"Murder." Thompson's mouth fell open.

"Not only do you have confidential information concerning my case," Sinclair's voice hardened, "but you released information we *didn't* have. We've been hunting the cab we assumed Hanscombe took to Thirteenth Street. We canvassed the area twice, interviewed all the night people, checked all the security cameras. Nothing. Yet someone's come forth—to you, way down in Florida instead of the police here. Someone who knows he was picked up by private car a block-and-a-half away from the conference center."

Thompson mimicked a fish, his mouth opening and closing several times.

"According to you, your assailant's initial strike was from behind and to your right side. D'Accio is left-handed. The delivery driver saving your hide states your assailant disappeared too fast down an alley to be other than a Gen, even while throwing skunk-bombs."

Two besides the one on Thompson, which had eliminated any scent tracking.

"Yet he used a chunk of wood from a nearby construction site instead of claws, further implicating a Zero. Do you need any more proof you're being used? I strongly suggest you dump whatever story you've got written in your head. In fact, I recommend you don't write anything more about the situation here in Nebraska. Because if you do, if you negatively impact my case any more than you already have, I'll see you are held legally liable."

"Are you threatening me, Lieutenant?" Thompson blustered.

"No. I'm promising you."

Chapter 36

It was mid-afternoon before I stumbled into the kitchen and started a pot of coffee. My brain needed to be fully functional before tackling Inspector Balcer's file. It'd been sitting in my email when I got home this morning. I spent the wait waking my muscles with stretches.

Aaaaah! That first cup of the day was always blissful.

I poured a second cup and headed for my computer. Two hours later, I took my printouts to the kitchen table, grabbed another cup of coffee, and leaned back in my chair to think. He'd included a few brief paragraphs on what he could remember from Marge's phone call and his own follow-up. The Inspector had done a quick check for similar cases based on her comment, but not having a timeframe or even a specific area, he'd come up empty.

I stared at the wall, mulling over Angie's and the Inspector's words. *Digging like a badger…something she ran across during her research on Tabitha Chandler…related to another string of arsons in the States.*

So, something in the last thirty or so years and somewhere within a reasonable distance of Omaha that must have somehow touched the Chandler family, even if only peripherally. I'd pretty much memorized my Chandler files. The single fire referenced was the one killing Mrs. Chandler's parents. A single occurrence blamed on stupidity wouldn't count.

Something nudged at my brain. Nudged again. I snapped my fingers. The tapes. Lieutenant Sinclair had said one recovered from Marge's office held an interview with Fire Chief Anderson about an old arson string.

Crap. Mrs. Blakely still had Marge's tape reorder.

I grabbed my files. Found what I was looking for in Marge's notes. An old article about the Delmarra Clinic with a sticky note that said 'see Chief Anderson' attached. The clinic was being rebuilt by the Director's widow after being destroyed by a massive explosion. It had been one of several attacked in a three-week spree by still unknown bomber or bombers. That would count as an arson string. It was also the one with the most fatalities, the entire staff killed.

No, not all. I felt a prickling down my spine. The receptionist, Mrs. Calvert. She'd survived, until killed recently in a home-burglary. Also unsolved.

Suddenly, it wasn't just my vertebrae tingling. This was it. I'd found my clue and Marge's path. What had Mrs. Calvert said that triggered her instincts? Was I wrong about her killer and Tabitha's being the same? Was that why Marge had been so focused, so busy? She was working on *two* stories that, coincidently, intersected?

I checked the time. I could only think of one person to call and I only had her Omaha-Herald number. Did she work Saturdays? She did and, fortunately, was still at her desk.

"You want copies of *all* our articles dealing with a *thirty*-year-old bombing string from Archives?"

I heard both curiosity and suspicion in Merle Smith's voice. "Yes."

"Is this dealing with a case you're investigating?"

"Yes. I can't give you any details." A loud snort came over the line.

"Do you have something that might solve it?"

I hesitated. "Not sure."

"Do I get your info later if—no, *when* you close your case? Whether or not you solve it?"

"When and if I'm able."

"Deal. I'll bring them to your apartment—"

"No," I interrupted firmly. "Let me know when you have them and I'll meet you somewhere."

Miss Smith processed that for several seconds then agreed and we hung up. I wasn't going to endanger anyone else if my shadow was still hanging around. I spent the rest of the evening going back through everything, hunting for any similarities between the two strings of events or that could be connected, regardless of how remotely or absurdly possible.

***

I walked into Marge's apartment building the next afternoon with a box as if I intended to do more work there. I couldn't feel eyes on me, but I wasn't taking any chances. Merle Smith was waiting for me in the hallway and I let us in. Miss Smith halted, staring at the couch.

"Yeah," I said quietly, "I do that, too." I went on toward the kitchen, setting the box on the island bar. "Water? Sorry, there's nothing else."

"No, thanks." She joined me at the kitchen table. "Everything is so clean."

"I kept Marge's cleaning service. They come in once a week. The lease is up at the end of next month, and I'll release them then. Copies?"

Merle handed me the fat manila envelope she'd been clutching.

"I read over them," she said. "There were four attacks: the Delmarra Clinic in Kanesville, the Loess Hill Lab in Glenwood, the Steinbridge Clinic in West Omaha, and the Lancaster University Lab in Lincoln. There were deaths and injuries at all but the University Lab."

"After hours?" I asked, pulling the manila contents out.

"No. It was a teaching lab. Students and instructors were there at all hours. Someone pulled the fire alarm and the building was empty when it exploded twelve minutes later. That led the investigators at the time to postulate the bomber was connected to the University in some manner, either as student or staff."

"But they never found out who?" I made a mental note to call the Greenbaums. They might remember any suspicions floating around the university's campus during that time.

She shook her head. "For either the bombing or pulling the alarm. It was also the last one. The Delmarra Clinic was the first and the worst. The entire staff was killed."

"Uh-uh. The regular receptionist was out tending to her injured mother. Her temporary replacement was killed."

"What does she say?"

"Unfortunately," I replied carefully, keeping my eyes on the article in front of me," she died several weeks ago." Despite my attempt at nonchalance, Merle pounced.

"How did she die?"

"A home-robbery gone bad."

"Is that what you're investigating? Is she connected to the bombings? Did she know something about them? Is the bomber still active? About to strike again?"

I held my hand up to stop her questions. "I told you I couldn't give you any details. At this time," I added when her mouth popped open.

"This is big, D'Accio. Big. National-scoop big. You need research—heck, anything, call me. Anytime, day or night. I want your word that I get exclusive access to your information. Scratch that. I want in on the investigation."

I shook my head. "I can't do that. It's too dangerous."

"I don't give a flying frog. My cousin's father was killed at the Steinbridge Clinic. It tore the family up bad."

She met me stare for stare. How in the world did this woman get saddled with Marshmallow? I let my gaze drift toward the couch. It only took a moment before I heard a sharp intake of breath.

"Marge? That's what Marge was working on? It wasn't suicide. She was *murdered*."

"You still sure you want in, Miss Smith?" Was I sure I wanted to let her?

She pulled a notepad and pen out from her satchel. "Call me Merle," she said, clicking the pen. "You can tell me or I'll start digging on my own."

Nate. Angie. Sinclair. Diana. Now Merle. My circle was growing. I now had resources covering medical, the street, law enforcement, and journalism. Maybe this is what was needed. Marge had kept us on the periphery, not wanting to endanger us and had stubbornly searched on her own. In trying to go it alone—as I had been—had we inadvertently let the killer slip free? Free to kill again?

Would Marge still be alive?

I recognized the sudden stab for what it was: anger. Anger that she hadn't let me help. The same anger I now saw on Merle's face. If others were willing, why should I refuse their help? It was their choice, as it should have been mine. I took a deep breath, let it out slowly.

"Marge ran across something that snared her curiosity about the lab bombings…"

Merle left about an hour later with everything I knew about the bombings. She was a bit miffed at not getting all of Inspector Balcer's information, but I wouldn't forward his confidential notes without his permission. I packed a few more things in my box and paused at the door. The lease would be up soon, and I needed to make decisions about Marge's things. Umm, later.

Coward, one part of my brain snipped. Yep. Maybe I could get Diana to deal with it.

I'd barely gotten home when Merle called with information about Mrs. Calvert.

"Do NOT do anything out of the ordinary," I all but shouted.

"Sunday research *is* ordinary for me," she retorted. "Now, do you want to hear it or not?"

"Yes," I said, grumbling.

"Mrs. Calvert was killed the night of Thursday, June Sixteenth. Her obituary would have been submitted by noon to make the next day's evening edition. When we told you Marge was doing follow-up that Friday on Tabitha's articles, we *assumed* that because we were unaware of anything else. But if it was actually about the bombings and she tried to contact Mrs. Calvert…"

"Marge either saw the obit or was told what happened when she called the clinic. She wouldn't have believed it was coincidental. *That* caused the sudden change in her behavior that Friday afternoon." And explained why she had come to my office. Rattled. Scared.

If only I'd been there… If only she'd talked to me… All the different ways that weekend could have gone. I shook the melancholy off, realizing Merle was talking about Mrs. Calvert.

"…piece of information that, unbeknownst to her, provided a clue to the bombing. Maybe even to the bomber himself."

"I'll take that bet. Marge's killer grabbed anything that might provide a clue to her investigation. All her post-May notes and tapes, as well as Mrs. Calvert's interview." Which, unfortunately, had also removed all her research on Mrs. Chandler, too. "All I had to go on was her phone records."

"Now we have a lot more. Need anything else researched?"

"Is there a way to find out if any of those first labs had any incidents—medical, personnel, or otherwise—prior to the bombings? Someone who might have caused a previous ruckus. The Nassau cases appear to be more greed oriented. Drugs, money, or both."

"Any previous ruckus. Any links to Nassau. I'll let you know. By the way, you should be getting an email from Inspector Balcer. I told him we were working together."

I shook my head at the disconnect tone.

After pouring myself a glass of scotch, I turned the television on to give myself a break. Soccer playoffs started last weekend. Today, it was the Chicago Lakers versus the Kansas City Trailblazers. Watching a bunch of hefty Gens aggressively kick a ball around—or each other—usually provided snort-worthy entertainment. I managed to keep my brain from drifting away from it too often.

***

I crawled out of bed the next morning with a pounding headache. No, wait. That was the door. I stumbled twice on my way to it. I squinted bleary-eyed at Nate.

"Curt. You alive?"

"Yeah. Think so. Come on in." I shuffled toward the couch, letting Nate close the door. My toes smacked something. *Owww*. Hopping, I fell onto the couch, both ends of me hurting. Nate reached down, set an empty bottle of scotch on the coffee table.

"Well, that explains a few things," he said, amused.

"Don't talk so loud. Why are you here?"

"I've been trying to get hold of you since last night. When I couldn't, or this morning, I thought I had better check on you."

"Wondering if I'd suicided, too?"

"I was worried," he said, his tone a bit sharper than usual. "Predators only play with their prey for so long—"

"Then go for the kill," I finished, completing the old saying. "Why were you—who's dead?" My stomach clenched.

"No one we know. I have vacation time coming and I figured, since you had free time now, we could go fishing. A guy I work with in ER will loan us his cabin down in Missouri at Lake Grandview. It's a couple miles south of KC."

Fishing? Oh. He was attempting to get me out of town. "Thanks, Nate. I appreciate it. But going to Missouri won't solve my problems."

"No, but it might help you survive them," he retorted, plopping into a chair.

Before I could reply, there was a muffled ringing.

"Your ass is calling you," Nate said, his tense expression relaxing into amusement.

"Ha, ha." I reached under the cushion and pulled out my phone. Winced at the next loud ring. "Hello?...Yes... Yes, and I have new information, too…seven-ish tonight?... Good. Could you get information on a woman who was killed in Kanesville back in mid-June? ...That's part of my news. Her name was Mrs. Marsha Calvert... Thanks." I tossed it aside.

"I take it that was Lieutenant Sinclair?"

I nodded, then wished I hadn't. "He's got new info on our Kansas City attack." Then added, "Want to join us, around seven here?"

"I'll be here. I'll even bring food." He stood. Halfway to the door, he did a half-turn at the waist. Looked at the bottle, looked at me, and said, "Now is not the time to be stupid."

He was right. "Won't happen again." Letting my guard down last night had been idiotic. If my nemesis had stopped playing—ugh. I locked the door, then started a pot of coffee on my way to the bedroom. Aspirin, shower, and coffee. In that order.

Chapter 37

Nate showed up with a bag of Runza sandwiches and fries. Sinclair showed up with an attitude. After five minutes of listening to him fuming about the 'stiff-necked asshole detective' in a Kanesville precinct he'd had to deal with, I had to laugh.

"Reminds me of you, back at the start," I said.

"I am not an asshole," Sinclair said, glaring at me.

"But you can be stiff-necked," Nate said, handing him a sandwich.

"I'm having re-location issues."

"The local cops resented someone new coming in and taking over the homicide department," I clarified for Nate, accepting my own sandwich. "Fries?" I asked, aware of the lieutenant's sharp glance. "By the way, how's Brinkman?"

Even without knowing what Sinclair's Gen-form was, some instinct told me the detective would be the loser if they ever settled their differences the old-fashioned way. Since Brinkman was some version of bear, what did that imply about Sinclair?

"Detective Brinkman is on vacation."

"At who's request?" popped out before I could throttle it.

Sinclair bit into his Runza without comment. At Nate's questioning look, I mouthed *later*.

A combination of hunger and desire to get to the meeting's main course had us finishing our food in ten minutes. Cleanup took a whopping ninety seconds and Nate poured three coffees while Sinclair and I spread my files out on the table.

Sinclair gave the cup Nate handed him with a wary eye.

"Don't worry. I diluted ours."

"Wimps," I said.

"No, just considerate of our stomach linings." Nate sat. "As your doctor, I'm advising you to start. You left twenty behind years ago."

I scowled. "Not decrepit yet, either."

"Keep drinking this sludge and it won't be long."

"I got a call from Detective Caldwell in Kansas City this morning," Sinclair said loudly, gaining our full attention. "They arrested a slimeball on several murder charges over the weekend. To avoid the death penalty, he's been cooperating, providing information on several unsolved murders. One of them was the attack on you and Miss Chandler."

Nate sucked in a breath. "He knew who did it?"

"No, but he gave a not-very helpful description of her."

"Her?" Nate and I chorused together.

"Average height, reflective sunglasses and a ball cap that hid most of her face and hair. Add in the shirt and a closed jacket, and all the shooting witnesses thought it was a man."

So had I. "A woman? He's sure?"

Sinclair nodded. "She was from out of town and had made arrangements for a local driver and car with his boss. Our slimeball was the one who stole the car, so he got a quick glimpse when she met the driver at the rendezvous. Car and driver were found burned later. He says his boss—who was violently replaced several months ago—was a bit irritated. He'd have sent someone expendable and charged her more if he'd known she intended to kill the driver before disappearing."

"That was inconsiderate of her," Nate deadpanned. "So, nothing helpful."

"He swears she's a canid-Gen of some kind, so that helps," Sinclair said with a straight face.

Nate rolled his eyes. "So we only need to look for a wolf, coyote, fox, or mastiff of any Gen-level. Do you know what percentage of the shifter population they comprise?"

"Uh-huh," Sinclair said.

"He couldn't narrow it down further?" I asked on a sigh.

Sinclair shook his head. "Interestingly enough, the case you asked me to check on in Kanesville? The ME is ninety-six percent certain it was wolf claws that ripped her up. Considering that wolf-population percentage, it's most likely pure coincidence. Unless you do have something that connects the two events."

"My previous assumption about a single killer appears to be wrong." I pulled out the pages with information on the two series of arsons and gave them a quick summary. "I have no clue what caused her to link the old cases to the more recent Nassau arsons. Marge must have been working the two investigations simultaneously and it was the bomber who murdered her."

"Then cleaned out her research to protect himself," Nate said absently. He appeared focused on the paper he'd picked up.

"Unfortunately, yes, as it also removed her Chandler research. Mrs. Calvert died on a Thursday night and her obituary was filed with the Omaha-Herald the next day. That Friday." I emphasized the last two words with a tabletop finger-tap.

"She saw the obit." Sinclair nodded. "That's why her demeanor changed that afternoon."

"Not only for knowing the woman was dead, but also that she made have inadvertently caused it. Nate, what are you so engrossed in?"

"Hmmm? Oh, it's the Delmarra Clinic's report on Tabitha's DNA tests."

"Oh, yeah. I forgot. Marge suggested having you read it for us. We couldn't make it past the summary. They did the Gen-testing which identified her as a Zero," I said for Sinclair's benefit. "Find anything different, like maybe traces of hemochromatosis?"

Nate stared at me for a moment. "You only read the summary?" He flipped the paper to the front section. "It identifies her parents only as strong canid and feline," he said, studying the print. "Mr. Chandler was a panther, right?"

"First Generation, yeah. Why?" I asked, exchanging a curious glance with the lieutenant.

Nate flipped the paper back over. "According to the detailed medicalese you didn't read, her DNA parents are specifically identified as a wolf," he looked up, "and a lynx."

Everything came crashing in. The depth…the horrible scope of it… Felt hands on my shoulders.

"Dice, breathe," Nate ordered.

"He looks about to pass out."

I held up a hand. "Give…give me a moment."

The lieutenant asked Nate about any available alcohol. A cabinet opened. A glass materialized in front of me with dark red contents. Port. Right. I'd drunk all the scotch. My hand shook as I reached for the wine.

Silence. More silence as they waited.

"I know," I finally whispered as all the bits and pieces coalesced into a horrible whole.

"I take it the epiphany is a nasty one," Sinclair said, quiet sympathy in his voice.

My laugh rang hollow.

"Obviously, Steven Chandler wasn't Tabitha's biological father," Nate said. "He probably didn't read past the Summary either and wouldn't have known. Since Tabitha was born about nine months after the wedding, it means…." He trailed off with a grimace.

"Tabitha's mother had an on-and-off relationship for years with a questionable character from her younger days," I said. "A Second-Gen lynx that went the professional assassin route."

"Strange way to prep for a wedding to someone else," Sinclair commented.

"Considering her upcoming marriage was more-or-less a business arrangement, she probably planned on keeping him on the side. Then she was surprised with a marriage contract several days before the wedding that had a fidelity clause that would strip her of everything if invoked."

I pointed to the report laying in front of Nate.

"Mrs. Chandler was undoubtedly shocked by the results. What were the odds when her lover hadn't gotten her pregnant over the years?"

Both my listeners' lips pursed.

"Well, technically, they weren't married, yet, on that last visit," Nate said.

"The phrase is 'ever found to be unfaithful.'"

"*Oooookay*. That could be problematic."

I made a strangled noise. "Problematic? Try life-destroying in Cynthia Chandler's mind. Which is why she has destroyed anything and anyone that could reveal it."

The silence lasted about three seconds.

"Wait a minute," Nate sputtered. "You're implying what I think you are?"

"Yes." I tossed back the last of my drink. Whisky would have been preferrable, but my hand was steady when I set the glass down. Determination was fast overhauling the shock.

"That," Sinclair said firmly, "is heavy on circumstantial conjecture *and* belief. Yes, she stood to lose her financial and social standing. That does not automatically lead to your supposition, especially if you are insinuating she had her own daughter killed. Maybe even by her old lover?"

"According to a former nanny, Mrs. Chandler was obsessed with retaining her social position." *It was as if her wolf was speaking. All humanity had been stripped from it.* "She didn't need anyone. She did it herself."

Even Sinclair was staring open-mouthed at me.

"Mrs. Chandler removed the initial threat of exposure—not only the Delmarra Clinic's results, but the staff that might remember it. That's why it had the most fatalities. The Loess lab was undoubtedly hit because Tabitha was born there. Private hospitals are not as constrained as the public ones. The lab techs there might have run additional and/or more extensive tests than usual on a newborn's blood under the heading of research. The other labs were meant as distractions and to keep the authorities from looking too deeply at Delmarra's clientele.

"And, yes," I held up a hand when Sinclair started to say something, "she knew explosives. She did demolition work with her first husband for over a year. Years passed, and she thought she was safe. Then she received word

Tabitha was coming back for medical treatment."

"Duel-gene hemochromatosis," Nate said, still wearing a dazed look. "Her doctor would have run a battery of tests. Steven Chandler's family would have run tests."

"Which she couldn't allow," I burst out in a bitter-angry voice. I looked away, needing a moment to settle. "Our float plan filed in New Orleans and the KC marina reservation gave her our schedule. Mrs. Chandler knew how to contact the right sort in Kansas City from her assassin ex-lover. She knew how to shoot from the hunting trips she took with Steven Chandler. Kansas City is, at most, a three-hour drive," I said matter-of-factly. "She would have been back home before receiving the tragic call about her daughter. Then another quick trip later to blow up the *Getaway*."

"Then," Sinclair scoffed, "it would have been easier and less risky to just blow you up with the boat."

"You'd think so," I agreed, stumped. That would have been more logical.

"Not feasible, given what you're suggesting," Nate said. "They would have to do genetic analysis on the pieces," we both winced, "to verify identity and which parts went together."

Quiet. So quiet. I could hear my pulse beating in my ears.

"Mrs. Chandler had Tabitha's body cremated before anyone could object, which left only one possible source for Tabitha's DNA," I said quietly. "The Nassau arsons—disguised as robberies—eliminated Tabitha's records and lab work there, although that job she did have to hire out. Mrs. Chandler didn't do Caribbean vacations, so coming up with an excuse to be in the same area would have been difficult. It also kept curious busybodies from spotting any similarities or connections to the earlier ones."

Their expressions had changed as I laid out my points, from skepticism to acceptance. Now, Sinclair appeared thoughtful and Nate looked resigned. I had a feeling he was remembering what had originally drove him from ER work after years of repairing the damage one person could do to another. I took a deep breath, brought in the last pieces.

"Again, Cynthia Chandler thought she was in the clear. Until her interview with Marge. Marge mentioned the Delmarra report in Tabitha's pediatrician records when questioning her about Tabitha's hemochromatosis. It undoubtedly was a shock to the woman to realize that a copy existed."

I snapped my fingers. "*She* was the one that ransacked and skunked my office. I'm willing to bet that Russell's copy of the report has been missing since then."

"Mrs. Chandler didn't know how much you knew," Nate said, worry lacing his voice. "And you both kept on investigating."

"Marge had to have suspected what was going on and why—hence the call to Nassau. Did she know if Mrs. Chandler was the culprit or just funding the hits?" I think my sigh came up from my toes. "We'll probably never know how she put it all together. Marge didn't have any proof…didn't have all the details we do, but Cynthia Chandler was worried enough about her poking around that she once again took action against a perceived threat."

"Mrs. Calvert," Sinclair said neutrally. "Mrs. Chandler and her son are both wolves."

"If Russell Chandler is aware of his mother's dealings, it's recent. Otherwise, he wouldn't have provided me all her records—especially the medical ones."

"And Hanscombe?" Sinclair asked, his gaze unwavering.

"Hanscombe's death was another misdirection—that's her MO. Just like the shifter attacks on me. I was on alert and carrying a weapon, so she changed tactics. Discrediting me, my business, all the while undoubtedly watching for an opportunity to eliminate me. Guess she felt that was safer."

"She also didn't want to involve me."

"Yeah, that'd be a pain," I grunted, getting a slightly vexed look from Sinclair. "Sorry. I'm surprised she didn't try to arrange an accident."

Sinclair shook his head. "Wouldn't have mattered and she knew it. When I informed Mrs. Chandler that Kansas City was shutting down the investigation and why, I told her I'd be keeping an eye on you. Believing you were the primary target in KC, I assumed there would probably be more attacks and the killer was bound to make a mistake, sooner or later."

That answered why he was keeping tabs on me. "Then Donald Hanscombe obligingly came to town," I said, feeling vexed myself.

"Yes. She must have called him, set up the meeting, and then asked him to use that fake name to 'protect' her privacy. It explains his 'jaunty' attitude. He was expecting a wild sex-run with a beautiful woman. The frame was a pretty good one," Sinclair added, "considering its short notice."

Nate leaned forward. "You need to be cautious, Curt. She's got to be getting frustrated. Hanscombe's killing didn't work as expected. That reporter—Thompson? That's not gone her way either. He's even had a 'clarification' printed in yesterday's Sunday edition."

My jaw dropped slightly.

Nate grinned. "First one in the paper's history, I believe." The smile vanished. "You are a big, annoying thorn in Mrs. Chandler's paw. How much do you know? Do you have any physical evidence? If she knew this existed," he tapped the Delmarra report, "she'd blow up this apartment—maybe the whole building to destroy you and it.

"No, do not discount that," he added when I started to protest. "The woman is a paranoid narcissist with an obsessive streak a mile wide. She will do whatever she has to do to protect herself and her status. That's a professional diagnosis."

"And my professional opinion," Sinclair added. "PI license or not, she realizes you aren't going to stop. She'll plan something. Speaking of which, how do we prove this?" He waved a hand at the paperwork spread across the table. "All we have is evidence of pre-marital infidelity. And no one—*no one*—will believe the rest without a neck-high stack of very hard evidence. Which we don't have."

"True," Nate said, his expression grim. "Filicide—killing one's own child—strikes at the very heart of our culture and instincts. Strangers will risk their lives to save a child, any child. If what you're saying is true…" his voice trailed off and his eyes lost focus for a moment, then both sharpened. "I believe Mrs. Chandler never bonded with her daughter. I believe she always saw Tabitha as a threat, even before it became a proven fact. That's why she had her DNA confirmed as early as she did, using Gen-testing as the excuse. Their relationship was in name and address only—and that's sad."

"Then even that ended, followed by a decade of estrangement." My heart twisted.

"Given Dr. Gordon's analysis, I'm surprised Tabitha Chandler made it to adulthood," the lieutenant said curtly. "The child should have had an unfortunate accident."

Why didn't she? Was it possible her mother hadn't been that hardened yet? Had Mrs. Chandler's natural inclination been restrained by Steven Chandler's love for Tabitha?

"So, what do we do?" Nate asked. "Do we release the Delmarra report? Mrs. Chandler will fight it in court, assuming it even makes it that far. She'll claim the report is erroneous, that the lab either messed up by mixing samples or filed the results wrong." He grimaced. "Which has happened and there's no way to retest. It's also kind of moot now with her husband dead. Most people would only roll their eyes or snicker."

"The lawyers overseeing Tabitha's will and assets won't consider it moot," Sinclair said. "They could lay claim to half of Mrs. Chandler's share of her husband's estate."

"What about her son?" I asked, trying to remember the exact wording of Chandler's fidelity clause in their marriage contract. Was there a way to get a copy of it?

"Russell Chandler was legally adopted. Unless he was named in the fidelity clause, which I doubt, he'll inherit the other half. I'm sure he'd keep his mother provided for in the manner she prefers." Sinclair tapped the table, thinking. "I'm no lawyer, but since his sister had no heirs, I'd say the lawyers for her various foundations and the will dispensations would fight for it."

I kept my face blank and sipped my coffee. The conversation was veering close to things I did not want to discuss.

"Something else to keep in mind." Sinclair's voice was as hard as his expression. "If you do release it, regardless of how it plays out, Mrs. Chandler will want revenge. She'll destroy you in every manner she can: financially, legally, and however many more 'lys' she can manage."

"Mission accomplished," I said, bitterness creeping out.

Sinclair shook his head. "Believe it or not, there's a lot more ways she can pound you into the ground. You can still recover from what's happened so far.”

“Yeah? Have you found out how Hanscombe was killed with my gun?”

“No.”

His grumpy response didn’t help my mood. That black cloud would hang over my reputation until resolved. And solved completely or there’d always be whispers. Doubts.

“Could it have been a different gun?” Nate asked, his face crinkled in thought. “Could she have fired one of Curt’s bullets with another gun? I mean, his office *was* ransacked and bullets were taken.”

We were both shaking our heads. “Nate, those were all unfired cartridges. A bullet gets its identifying striation when it’s fired. Nor does my Ruger have a swappable barrel, which I did contemplate in a moment’s insanity.” Sinclair’s expression caught my attention. “What?”

He stopped studying the ceiling. “There are several oddities that have never been explained. In light of this new information, maybe I can figure a reason for them.”

“What do we do now?” Nate asked.

“Nothing,” Sinclair said. “There is no way I can take this to my superiors, much less the DA. We have circumstantial evidence only for the old bombing cases. There’s not a single shred of evidence linking the more recent events to them, especially multiple murders. Her lawyers will posit coincidence for some and you being the target for others. What we need is evidence tying her *solidly* to any *one* of those events. If we can do that, then the others will become more credible. If you or any of your contacts come up with something, bring it to me.”

His brows drew together and his gaze drilled into mine. “I repeat…Bring. It. To. *Me*. Let me do my job. If this isn’t done right, if the evidence isn’t one hundred and ten percent *legally* accountable, the case and us will both be shredded by her lawyers. Until then, D’Accio, you need to lie low and stay out of her sight.”

Sullen, I held his gaze for another moment before breaking it. Not what I wanted to hear. “I’m already playing down my character. Pretending to be beat down.”

"Leaving town on a fishing trip to Missouri will reinforce that," Nate said, firing a triumphant look in my direction.

"Perfect," Sinclair said. "There's several avenues I'm going to check while you're gone. Maybe I'll find an intersection."

***

Late that night I stared up at the darkened ceiling above my bed. Absolutely no answers there. There had to be something somewhere for at least one of her crimes. Some tangible proof Cynthia Chandler had missed and was unaware it existed. We had to find it before she did and methodically removed it as she had everything else.

Chapter 38

I moped for the rest of the week. At home, at the office, at *Riley's*, at the *Depot*. Getting Marge's tape recorder back and profuse thanks from the Blakely's did provide a one-hour reprieve. I verified the Delmarra report was missing from my office files and wondered if Dr. Farr's old files still had it. Probably not; she'd have found some way to get it. I got both a pep talk and disapproving silence from Diane. When Angie bought me a glass of my expensive scotch Thursday night, I realized I wasn't playacting anymore. I really was beat down.

No, not beaten, but definitely swamp mucking.

Maybe getting out of town for the weekend was for the best.

Friday morning, I pulled my suitcase out of the closet and started packing. Nate was picking me up around noon. I'd debated taking just a backpack since we'd only be gone for the weekend, but Missouri weather this time of year could be fickle. Let's see… A couple of t-shirts, a flannel shirt, jeans, and underwear. I half-folded the items as they went in. Fish wouldn't care about wrinkles. I pulled open one of the side-pockets to throw in socks and spotted a comb.

I pulled it out.

Socks fell from my hand.

I collapsed on the bed, staring at the comb. Staring at the long hairs caught in the teeth. Tabitha's hairs. I'd combed her hair there in the hotel suite before—*Hot concrete. Wet blood. Remember me.* Shudders yanked me back to the present. I sucked in a sharp breath and willed my pounding pulse to steady.

Slowly, carefully, I walked into the kitchen and placed the comb in a baggie. Mrs. Chandler and her lawyers could refute the Delmarra report all they wanted. These hairs would speak the truth.

***

The weekend was uneventful. Nate and I pretended to fish and talked about nothing in particular. We both spent a lot of time staring off into space. Or out at the woods. Or down into our cups. I had a feeling Nate was needing this away time more than me. Was he regretting going back into the ER? I didn't tell him about my find. Soon, yes. For now, I hugged that last piece of Tabitha to myself.

Dawn was lighting our way as we headed into Kansas City Monday morning. Nate didn't have to report to the ER until that night so we stopped for breakfast. I took Nate up on his offer to go by KC Marina, but not the hotel. I could handle paying homage to the first, but no way was I going to the second.

Dropped off at my apartment, I found a brief message from Lieutenant Sinclair on my answering machine. In his usual brusque manner, he said *"Press conference at noon, Monday. Watch it."* I checked my watch: 12: 07. I scrambled for the television.

...results from several Omaha Police Department investigations, along with new information obtained from various sources.

Police Chief Constantine was speaking. One of those grouped behind him was Lieutenant Sinclair. I also recognized Lieutenant Vollmer, head of the OPD Arson Division.

Miss Margret Lockewild's death has been reclassified as a homicide and her case reopened. Miss Lockewild was investigating a series of bombings that occurred thirty years ago and apparently found a link to a more recent string of arsons in Nassau.

I threw my hands up in the air. *YES!*

I listened as Chief Constantine briefly summarized both old and new events and then tied in Mrs. Calvert's homicide, which was being taken over by OPD. He ended it by requesting anyone with any knowledge pertaining to either of the two women or the old bombing case contact either Lt. Vollmer or Lt. Sinclair. I owed Sinclair a beer. He had to have pushed hard to get the don't-make-waves police chief to agree, although the old coot didn't mind taking the limelight for it.

It was a first step. If new evidence could be found, if someone came forward… I was grinning broadly, my thoughts whirling at all the possibilities when I realized the group had shuffled positions. Lieutenant Sinclair now stood in front of the podium.

A second case has also been under heavy review, Sinclair said, his gaze roaming over the reporters in front of him. *The evidence in the case of Donald Hanscombe's murder has, up until now, presented conflicting data.* I leaned forward. *The Ruger .357 owned by Curt D'Accio and previously thought to be the murder weapon is, in fact, not. It has now been determined that an unknown weapon of a size comparable to Mr. D'Accio's committed the actual murder and a bullet substitution was made in an attempt to frame him.*

The breath I was unconsciously holding released in a *whoosh*. The reporters were clamoring, wanting to know all the hows. Yes, yes, answer them.

By re-examining both the murder scene and the bullet recovered from said scene. The killer's bullet ricocheted off a brick wall and embedded itself into a plaster wall. A section of the wall surrounding the bullet's final position was removed and taken to a forensic lab for in-depth analysis.

I snickered. Bet the building's owner appreciated that.

The bullet that was recovered held more than expected blood trace, no sign of brick abrasion, and bore damage inconsistent with striking at an angle. Metallic scrapings from the ricochet point did not match the bullet casing. Finally, detailed analysis showed that the bullet in evidence did not fully match the plaster's indention. Therefore, the killer dug out the real bullet and inserted one of Mr. D'Accio's after dragging it through the blood pool. The expended bullet had undoubtedly been picked up from the shooting range Mr. D'Accio frequents.

The reporters threw more questions but Sinclair ignored them and stepped back. Chief Constantine took his place.

The Omaha Police Department will be working diligently to solve both cases mentioned here today. The OPD also wishes to stress that Mr. Curt D'Accio is no longer a suspect in the murder of Donald Hanscombe and regrets any unfortunate impacts the previous publicity may have had.

I snorted. Right. He wanted to head off any lawsuits. And I owed Sinclair a whole pitcher of beer. My phone rang. It was Nate, having caught the conference's tail-end by the time he got home and found his own message from Sinclair. I filled him in on the whole broadcast.

"This had better make a difference about your license," Nate said. "In fact, they ought to just cancel next week's review and re-instate your license."

"You'd think so," I said. "But whoever pushed for censoring me in the first place has to save face. Especially if he was being influenced. Not that he'll admit to it."

"Yeah, well, this calls for a celebration. I'll meet you at *Riley's*—not tonight. I'm working. Tomorrow night, then."

I called Diana and gave her the news. "They'll probably replay it on tonight's newscast," I told her, after she expressed disappointment at missing it.

"I know you'll going to rewatch it," she said. "You're welcome to come watch it with me. I'll even have a large bag of popcorn ready."

I laughed and declined. I hung up the phone, feeling better than I had in a long time. The black cloud was gone. My reputation was restored and so would be my livelihood.

The rest of the afternoon was a busy one. I fielded several more phone calls, including a congratulatory one from Angie and a request from Lt. Sinclair to pick up my gun. Didn't sleep on that one, getting to his office as fast as a shower and traffic would allow.

Release papers signed, Ruger snuggled comfortably into its holster, I settled back in the chair across from Sinclair. "What's our next step?" I asked.

"I continue my job. You go back to yours."

"Don't give me that. You have to have a plan in mind."

He studied me for a moment. "I will be investigating Miss Lockewild's murder. Lt. Vollmer will be looking into those old bombings here and coordinating with Inspector Balcer on his case. Since all her investigative notes are missing, they are having to start from scratch. Individually, or together, we're hoping information will be obtained that points to whatever ties them together that Miss Lockewild found."

"We know what ties them. But," I scowled and ran a hand through my hair, "I understand. You need to follow the legal steps to get that irrefutable evidence. Which means you can't use my notes. I take it you haven't informed them of our theory."

"I haven't. That could be construed later as bias. Both these cases are now high-profile." Sinclair leaned back. "Sources who haven't come forward before, for whatever reason, may do so now. And if an innocuous comment forms a suspicion that leads to a link…" he shrugged.

I grinned. "I'm sure that's exactly what's currently worrying Mrs. Chandler."

"More than worried," he said, giving me an unreadable look. "She has to be rattled."

"You really think so? I mean, she's been an ice-cold precision killer for years."

"Which is exactly why she will be rattled now. She was hit—publicly—with several things she thought were safely done with. She knows how she messed up with Hanscombe's murder, but not with Marge Lockewild's. How did we conclude it, or tie it to the bombings and Mrs. Calvert? What did she miss? What else has she missed?"

I nodded, following his logic. "It probably wouldn't take much to push her into doing something stupid." Between his blank look and silence, a sudden suspicion hit me. "Are you counting on her doing exactly that?"

"Desperation often causes thought processes to misfire. Your murder would be highly inconvenient now, but she might risk it if she believes you're our main source and it would dead-end our cases."

"And to think I was beginning to like you. I'm bait."

The lieutenant flashed me an unexpected grin. "Which you'd already set yourself up as. If and when she moves against you, I'm counting on her failing. As a trained PI and a Zero-Plus, you're more than capable of self-protection. Something her other victims have not been."

"Who told you about me?"

"Thompson—provided by an anonymous source we can assume was Mrs. Chandler. An attack on you would open a lot of investigative avenues, including Tabitha Chandler's murder."

He was right on all counts. Very sneakily so. "What if I can come up with something that'll cause that push?" I asked. About to tell him about Tabitha's hair, he stopped me with a raised hand.

"If you do, I advise extreme caution. She's proven herself very adept in numerous skills. I also don't want to know about it as she could claim entrapment later. Why don't we wait and see what today's announcements shake loose?"

I agreed and invited him to *Riley's* tomorrow night. He declined, saying he needed to keep an impartial distance. I wandered back out to my car and sat behind the steering wheel. Thinking.

Hoping someone came forward.

Wondering if I would need to plot what could be my own death.

Chapter 39

A week passed. Two weeks. Then a month. Life moved along smoothly and, mostly, uneventfully. At least, on the surface.

My PI license was re-instated, albeit ungracefully and with a warning. My lawyer, who I had wisely taken with me, demanded to know on what grounds and used words like 'harassment' and 'bias.' The one that set their jaws was 'lawsuit.' Mr. Jetter was worth his hourly fees.

Merle Smith ambushed me a couple of times. She wasn't getting far in the old bombing cases. I'm pretty sure she sensed I wasn't telling her everything and hoped an unexpected barrage of questions would let something slip. Maybe one day I would tell her. Too much hinged on secrecy right now. But another piece had fallen into place when I'd contacted the Greenbaums.

Mr. Greenbaum had been on lab duty, monitoring students and their work the night the University lab was bombed. That explained why the fire alarm had been pulled, clearing the building in time. Whether in memory of happier days or a still felt sense of obligation, she'd spared him.

Inspector Balcer closed his case after arresting Joel Higgians. He and his brother, James, had been hired by someone from the States to take out several medical labs. They'd assumed revenge or a competitor. Joel swore James had been the go-between and hadn't shared a name or even which state with him. And whoever it was, he'd murdered James when their final payment packet exploded when he opened it.

With Cynthia Chandler's leave-no-loose-ends policy, Joel was lucky he was still breathing. A badly decomposed body had been dredged from the

Missouri River. Forensics identified him as one Odell Nightengale, a Second-Gen panther with a bullet hole in his head and a damaged larynx.

No one had come forth with any significant information on either Sinclair's or Vollmer's cases. No new clues had been independently unearthed or squeezed out of the atmosphere. Mrs. Chandler continued her luxuriant, haughty lifestyle. We passed once, accidently, as I was heading to interview a witness on a hit-and-run job. We exchanged looks: hers was condescending, mine was contempt.

I had worked out how to force Mrs. Chandler's hand. But with no guarantee on how, when, or where she'd attack, it'd be difficult to set a trap. At least, one that I'd survive. If I didn't, and with no witnesses, she'd slip through our fingers again. To be honest, if there was no other way and I knew my death would ensnare Mrs. Chandler once and for all, I'd gladly join in a group hug with Tabitha and Marge.

I wanted justice. For them. For everyone who'd been taken down, their families shattered, by a woman as heartless as her wolf. It ate at me.

Finally tackling Marge's estate, I'd given her car to Angie. She had a mechanic friend go over it. The tracker he found explained why my office got searched after her murder. The law office had been simply another misdirection after searching my office for anything Marge may have left.

I'd shared a beer with Nate at *Riley's* on a couple of Fridays, but mostly I found myself drawn to the *Depot* at least twice a week. Sipped on a beer for an hour or so at the bar, the somberness of the place suiting my mood. I no longer got sniffs and stares when I walked in, so I guess that made me a regular *Despo* now.

Then one melancholy-filled night, I did exactly as she'd suggested in her fake-suicide letter: I gave Sherwood a big squeeze. The missing tape from her recorder popped out of his ass. Out of a gap in his bottom stitching I hadn't noticed.

Marge's theory on why Tabitha had been murdered matched ours, and she listed many of the things we knew about. Plus one we didn't: a Loess Hills pediatrician nurse who'd attended Tabitha during and after her birth. The nurse had died in the same manner as Mrs. Calvert *and* during the same timeframe as those first bombings. Why she'd been targeted, we'd never know.

However, Marge was wrong on the implementation. Not knowing all the details we did about Mrs. Chandler and her background, Marge had believed the woman had hired others for all of it, as Nassau had been. And she hadn't known who or what Tabitha's real father was.

The tape's last entry was an apology, a plea, and a knife in the heart. She had evidently recorded it before pushing it up into Sherwood's stuffing.

Curt, I'm so sorry. I've screwed up. The attack on you at your office… Mrs. Calvert's murder…I'm responsible. I let out too much information during Mrs. Chandler's interview. I'd go to the police, but with what? Unproven, malicious insinuations against a well-regarded citizen? I have a feeling…I'm not sure what's going to happen, but I'm counting on the master de-puzzler to figure out why I took Sherwood home. Please find something to make this bitch pay. And please be very, very careful. Use all those pluses of yours. I'll give Tabitha a hug for you.

If she'd known she was talking to a killer, Marge would have been more careful. And I'd kicked myself several times over not figuring Sherwood out, despite her managing to leave a blatant clue. Not that it would have made much difference. We'd have known the motive sooner, but still been stuck with proving it. Her own foreknowledge? Well, that drove me to the bottom of a scotch bottle. Bottles.

Nate showed up somewhere between number two and three. What did my friend get for trying to help? A curse-filled rant that included his return to ER work. He should have hit me with a bottle and left me in my puke. Instead, he and Angie nursed me through the next several days and Diana rescheduled clients.

I profusely and repeatedly apologized to my friends as soon as I was able.

***

Boris didn't even raise an eyebrow when I requested a glass of water, just charged me a dollar for the ice. I slipped slowly, my system still a bit unforgiving. Which I deserved. I relaxed, drifting with the soft strains of music I could hear now. Practicing had sharpened my hearing close to First-Gen level. I glanced over as a body slid on the stool next to me.

Angie? Well, it was a Monday.

"Slow night?" I asked.

"He's in town."

That could cover a lot of people. "He who?"

Angie lowered her voice. "Her ex-lover."

I stared. There could only be one *her*, which meant—I drew in a sharp breath. "You're sure?"

She nodded. "Saw him myself."

"Do you know where he's staying?"

"No. But remember? He likes to visit old haunts."

I stared unseeing at the cracked mirror behind the bar. My thoughts raced. After a long pause, my gaze caught and held Angie's in the mirror. "Any particular night?"

Chapter 40

I let the door swing shut behind me, scanning the room while my vision adjusted. As I approached the bar, my pulse sped up. Raynor Silverstone. Had to be him. The well-dressed stranger sitting on the bar's short side and facing the door matched Angie's description. With no idea when he'd show up, or even if he would, I'd been hanging around the *Depot* every evening since Angie told me he was in town.

Guess Friday was as good a night as any to get your throat ripped out.

I took a seat two barstools away from him. Boris cocked his head at me as he dried a glass nearly hidden by a colossal pair of hands. I ordered my favorite brand of scotch. Expensive, especially here, but tonight was not a beer night. I watched the freshly polished glass fill with aged scotch and debated the best method of gaining my quarry's interest.

Nervous, Dice?

Hell, yes.

I snorted. Talking to myself was normal, but getting a reply? Maybe Nate should be questioning my sanity. I licked my lips and took a sip. It was the first I'd had since my alcoholic tantrum. Happily, my stomach didn't object.

In the cracked mirror's reflection behind the bar, I watched a guy wobble into view toward the exit. He found it, figured out how to work the doorknob and got it open before plopping ass-first on the floor. "Would someone be good enough to call…calling a cab?" he asked, before belching hard enough to knock himself over backwards. His body blurred, there were a couple of distinct snaps as bones realigned, and then a white wolf lay sprawled on the floor.

A cab? Really? The idiot was past wasted. And shifting had just earned the artic wolf a three-month ban.

Two beat-up piles of rags coming in stepped around him and continued on in. They froze when Boris pointed at them, the unconscious drunk, and the door. Grumbling and swearing, they each grabbed one half of the large wolf and complied with the unspoken order.

My amusement faded. *We'd called a cab.*

The dingy barroom disappeared as memory took over. *Pain. Blood.* My wrist pinned to the bar top yanked me back from my nightmare. I released my shaking glass; the bartender released my arm. I wiped sweaty hands on my pants. It hadn't hit me that hard in months.

"You gonna have a fit or something, go do it somewhere else."

"Your concern touches me, Boris," I replied.

He gave me another suspicious once-over before he went to slap two bottles of beer down in front of the reluctant disposal team.

"Can't blame him," Silverstone said. "He doesn't like trouble or getting involved. Medical emergencies are often both."

An opening. "How about you?" I asked, glancing over.

He was an ice-cold shot to the nervous system. About a second and a half was all he needed to flick his gaze over me and back at his drink. The feeling I'd been evaluated and dismissed was a sharp stab in my gut. As a Second Generation lynx, he'd probably be holding my throat in his hands before I knew it was missing.

"Usually," was his only comment. He tossed off the last of his drink.

Crap. Looked like he was about to leave. "Boris should be pleased that my next medical event won't be here." When one of his eyebrows cocked questioningly, I shrugged. "Wouldn't you call death a medical event?"

His shoulder twitch was probably meant to be a shrug.

"I know who and probably the how." No doubt on that. "Where and when is still up for grabs." She wouldn't want to mess up her fancy home.

Maybe it was my utter lack of sarcasm, bitterness, or give-a-damn factor, but his gaze lingered on me. This time the evaluation was more thorough, those eyes penetrating beneath my outer shell. I felt dissected, a bug under a microscope.

"Actually," I shifted on my stool to face him, "I've managed to survive several attempts since the initial attack and her murder over a year ago."

"Murder?"

My head dipped. "Yep. Tabitha Chandler. Murdered in broad daylight."

He stilled. "Of the local Chandler Import family?"

"You know them?" He sure as hell knew Cynthia Chandler.

"Know *of* them. I remember it." His index finger did a quick tap-tap. "It made newspapers around the world. They never found who did it, I believe."

"They didn't dig hard enough."

His gaze became a laser scalpel, as if seeking to pull lies and truth apart. "You found her killer?"

"Yes." Boris was busy at the other end of the counter. I dropped my voice low, not that it'd matter with shifter hearing. "I've spent the last year hunting for answers. It's cost me a lot more than I could ever have imagined," I said, not hiding my bitterness. I stared into my glass.

His finger tapped lightly against the counter. A mannerism similar to my hand flexing? I could picture the internal debate as I mentally urged him on. *Come on, come on. Be curious.* I gave a mental cheer when his head jerked sideways in the direction of the booths and said, "Let's move over there."

I studied his back as I followed behind him. My six-foot height topped his by an inch or so and, while he appeared to be in his mid-forties, I knew he was in his late fifties. His movements were precise and graceful, courtesy of his cat nature no doubt.

We settled into a booth in the back corner, Silverstone sliding into the shadowed corner seat. It left me facing the wall and a light sconce. It was annoying to know its weak light let him read my face while all I saw of his was angles and shadows. Deliberate move on his part and unsurprising considering his occupation. Just as he'd taken the seat at the end of the bar so he could watch the whole room.

"You don't seem like the type the *Depot* normally attracts," I said, trying for nonchalance while debating with myself. Continue the pretense or admit I know who he is?

"Call it a walk down memory lane, back to when this place was a bit more upbeat."

A waitress appeared, silently removing the wet dribbles from the booth's last patrons with a few deft swipes. He tapped his glass and pointed to mine, signaling for refills. She vanished while I was still reaching for my wallet.

Really?

"Although," he continued, "I have to admit the current atmosphere does seem to match its patrons."

"Name's Curt," I told him, pretense winning the argument for now.

He shrugged. "Call me Joe."

Yeah, right. "So, Joe, how often you take these walks?"

"Wouldn't once be enough?"

"I'd think so, considering how far this place has sunk from those memories of yours." *Keep it easy, Dice.* "I've been a regular for several months and this is the first time I've seen you. Yet you know Boris doesn't like trouble or involvement." The waitress deposited fresh glasses and left with our old ones. "And, by God, you're running a tab. The stingy bastard doesn't do that for just anyone."

"Maybe I'm family."

I snorted. "They'd be the *last* he'd trust with a tab."

It took a moment, but a small grin lifted the corners of his lips. "I think I like you. Boris—as you call him—has been bartending here since the original doors opened. I paid my debts then; he knows I'll pay them now."

Or was afraid to tell this man *no*?

"That long?" I leaned forward, elbows on table. "Do you know the bartender's real name?"

"Yes. You really know who killed Miss Chandler?"

His bland voice didn't tell me anything. "Yes. What's your interest?"

"Your attitude for one. Few are so…nonchalant about death."

"Maybe I'm tired of adding to my scar collection. Give me another reason."

Another shrug. "Curiosity. I've followed the Chandler family's activities, on and off, for a number of years."

"Why are you interested in the Chandlers?" As if he'd admit it.

"Did you know Miss Chandler?"

"Yes. Your interest?"

"How did you meet her?"

Silence hung between us, each waiting for the other to answer.

Screw this. I needed to reel him in before he changed his mind. "I'm a private investigator. I met her during a job for her brother, Russell Chandler."

"Your information is conclusive?"

"Yes."

"Then why haven't you gone to the police? If you could prove what you've got, you would have." He made a small dismissive gesture. "What you probably have is supposition, rumor, or gossip against someone connected politically, monetarily, or both."

"It is *not* supposition or rumor!" My fury flashed hot before I could control it. Was he deliberately pushing me? I took a deep breath, then a second one. First strike to him. I took a large swallow. "The killer is extremely efficient and careful. Meaning, I have no solid proof. Still, there's always that remote possibility that I'll find something—concrete evidence that will tip the scales. Which is why she'll eventually succeed in silencing me before I do."

Ah. The feminine pronoun definitely caught his interest.

"Then why continue? You have your answers, even if you can't do anything with them. Isn't that enough?"

My stare probably went as blank as my mind. How do you answer something like that? How could I not continue? "Did you ever have a moment where the world just seemed to stop?" I asked softly. "And when it restarts, you're not the same person you were before?"

A long pause, followed by a sharp nod.

"I didn't believe love could come that quickly. Root that deeply. Then I met a lanky, sun-streaked brunette with an attitude, a wind-burned nose, and a wonderfully warped sense of humor. And the most incredible hazel eyes." The fire in them had burned all the way to my soul. Now, they haunted me.

Laughing. Loving. Dying.

"Obsessed, everyone called me. Guess I was. Am. Finding who did it.

Making them pay." I gulped down the last of my drink. The fiery trail down my throat did little to ease the pain in my chest. "*Nothing* will ever be enough."

Joe's gaze was locked on me. Watching, weighing, as I struggled with my self-control. He held up a finger, then dipped it toward me. I couldn't see the bar as it was behind me, but Boris must have been watching him as it was just a brief flicker of finger. Interesting.

My composure was back in place by the time a fresh drink sat in front of me. I let it sit. Was he being generous or sneaky? I needed to keep my head clear. "You going to spill his real name?" I asked.

"No. Have you told anyone what you've learned?"

I shook my head. "Uh-uh. People around me tend to end up dead and I'm running short on friends." That was a bitterness I no longer felt. Glancing at Joe, I wished I could read his face, see his eyes. It was now or never.

"So, Joe, you got anything planned for the next hour or so?"

He propped an arm along the seat top, the booth giving a warning creak as his weight shifted. The new angle brought most of his face out of shadows, but the distance between us was suddenly a lot farther than the corner he'd slid into. And I recognized those hazel eyes.

"I'm not looking to take up your crusade," Joe stated.

"I'm not asking you to. Just listen. And remember."

"Why?"

"Justice," I growled, "for those who've died who shouldn't have."

"Justice," Joe carefully told his glass, "and its needs are in the mind of the beholder and for those who can afford it. It can be…" His voice trailed away, a finger tapping against the booth top. "Dangerous. Vengeful, even," he finished, watching the ice cubes bobbing in his whiskey.

"So?"

"You don't seem concerned that I might wind up dead," Joe said.

His eyes suddenly shifted upward, capturing mine with their intensity. Their icy hardness bored into mine, drilling straight down my spine with all the enthusiasm of a wildcatter hunting black gold. I swallowed the shudder with the spit. *Only a fool would cross this man and none twice.* I didn't have to pretend when I said hoarsely, "I think you can handle yourself pretty frigging well."

The power switched off, leaving his features simply cold and hard.

Leaning back, I ran a hand across my face. "Look, Joe," I told him tiredly, "all I'm asking is that you keep the information safe. For me, for the others…for the daughter of the family you still haven't said why you're interested. Until someone with bullet-proof armor *can* find that proof."

"Maybe I'm not that interested in them or being your remote possibility."

"No? Don't you want to know why she was killed?" My smile was thin and bitter, but I didn't care. "Whatever you know about the Chandlers, whatever you *think* you know, I guarantee the truth will blow your socks off." Along with his pants, most likely.

His focus shifted downward again as he went into think mode, or maybe it was a trance. Nothing about him moved. Nothing twitched, not even his pinky. It was the utter stillness of a top-line predator.

I waited silently. My gamble would either work or it wouldn't.

Minutes passed. I resisted the urge to reach across the table to see if Joe was still breathing. Dammit. This wasn't working. *Time to unsheathe my non-existent claws and go for*—the sphinx picked up his glass.

Joe swirled its contents a couple of times, then set it back down with a *thunk*. "No promises and I leave when bullshit starts."

I couldn't tell if his annoyance was with me or with himself. Didn't matter; didn't care. This was going to be my one and only shot. Taking a deep breath and a large swallow of scotch, I settled back in my seat. He wouldn't care about my troubles or be interested in a year-long saga, so I kept it to bare facts.

I started with Mrs. Chandler's expertise with explosives and firearms and a mystery relationship—didn't let on I knew who with. When I described Steven Chandler's unexpected fidelity clause, I caught a flicker of surprise in his eyes. Evidently he hadn't known the true reason she'd dumped him. Then I spoke of Tabitha's wedding-plus-nine-months birth, the Delmarra Clinic's bombshell report, and her duel-gene hemochromatosis.

His face was assassin blank.

Last, I listed all the things Mrs. Chandler had done to eliminate all traces of Tabitha's true parentage. The bombings, then and recent. Kansas City and the *Getaway*. Marge and Mrs. Calvert. His face wasn't blank now.

How long had it been since he'd been truly shocked?

"In case you think I'm completely delusional..." I pulled an envelope from my pocket and slid it across to him.

He stared for a moment, as if waiting for it to rear up and bite him. Ever so slowly, he opened it and pulled out a small plastic bag with a single hair curled inside. Looked up.

"Any credible lab will be able to verify that half its genetics is lynx," I said softly. Standing, I paused for a moment. Should I tell him—no, he already knew.

I walked out into a cold rain that was both annoying and welcome. I was soaked but clear-headed by the time I got to my car. Sliding in, I slicked back wet hair and cranked the engine. I listened to its purr and held my hand in front of a heater vent.

Would I survive the next step in my plan?

Chapter 41

Sunday morning found me driving north of Omaha, following Russell Chandler's directions. I'd called him early yesterday morning, requesting a private meeting with him and his mother. Told him I had news about Tabitha and why she was killed. He called back an hour later, sounding annoyed.

Mother plans to spend the weekend at her cabin north of here and says we can meet there on Sunday. She still asserts that you were the killer's target and refuses to ruin her weekend with what she believes is probably worthless supposition. The cabin is isolated and overlooks the Missouri River. It will be quite private.

Sounds like the perfect spot to get rid of a body, I mused. Either buried or thrown in the river. I eventually turned onto a *private drive*, according to the sign I passed. Some drive. It was a tree-lined road that meandered several miles before I finally came to the cabin. Unlike most of the fall-colored foliage I had passed, the house was fronted by a thick, green stand of pines.

Windbreaks. Concealment.

I parked next to what I assumed was Russell's Jeep and eyed the single-story structure in front of me. Their 'cabin' was five times the size of my apartment with a wrap-around porch. Russell stood on it, waiting for me. He was dressed casually in a brown flannel shirt and jeans. I climbed out of my car and up the five steps.

Russell's nostrils flexed as I joined him, undoubtedly smelling my freshly-oiled gun. I shrugged and said, "It's been that kind of year."

"So I gathered," he replied candidly. Then added, "We're around back on the patio," and led me across the porch.

The patio was on scale with the rest of the house. More pines lined the sides, but none blocked a very scenic view of the Missouri River. The stonework was excellent and beautifully cut. It ran some forty feet out to where the land began to slope down toward the river. A fire pit burned in the center of an informal sitting area. His mother was relaxing on a chaise lounge, her makeup and hair done up perfect, and wearing a long, loose, elaborately embroidered silk caftan that probably cost more than my entire wardrobe. That and the absence of jewelry told me she was prepared to go wolf.

I took a seat and held my hands to the warmth. It felt good against the October chill.

"Nice place. How much is yours?" I asked.

"About eighty acres," Mrs. Chandler replied. "It's a great place to stretch four legs. We can *hunt* in private."

Was that meant as intimidation or warning?

"We're drinking mulled cider," Russell said, giving his mother an unreadable glance. "Would you care for some?"

"Thank you, no." Didn't care to be drugged.

"Now," Mrs. Chandler drawled, "I believe you have a fanciful tale on why Tabitha was killed?"

I smiled. "Tale, indeed. One of greed, ego, and murder. Tell me, Mrs. Chandler, have you ever felt a drop of remorse?"

"We all have regrets. I'm afraid you'll have to be more specific."

"How about taking Tabitha to the Delmarra Clinic? After all, their report was the catalyst for all that came afterward."

Russell was wearing a frown, his gaze going back and forth between his mother and me. Ah, he *didn't* know. He was in for a very rude shock.

She took a sip from her cup and set it on a small side table. The better to free up her claws?

"We took Tabitha there to verify her Gen status, naturally, as most parents do. I don't see how that could be a catalyst for anything, especially since all the clinic's reports were destroyed by some deranged bomber."

She thought she was safe.

I pulled a single sheet of paper from my jacket pocket. Unfolded it. "Not all of them. For the record, I consider you a detailed-orientated, obsessive sociopathic bomber, but not deranged," I said pleasantly. "After all, your elimination of all DNA traces was very methodical."

Russell had a 'say what?' expression. I handed him the report, keeping my attention on his mother. Her attention was on the paper. "If you note, the report's summary states Tabitha had strong canid and feline genetics but was a non-shifter herself."

"Yes, I see it," Russell said impatiently, looking up. "We knew that."

"If you flip the page over, you'll see the detailed medical analysis," I said. "I've highlighted the exact parental terminology." Mrs. Chandler's body was stiff. Poised. If she attacked, I wouldn't get my gun out in time, even loose in its holster as it was.

"*Lynx*?" came Russell's shocked voice after a couple of seconds.

"Your mother had a tryst with an old lover sometime in the week before her wedding to Steven Chandler, and *before*," I stressed, "she was blindsided by his marriage contract and its very specific fidelity clause."

Shifter fast, she reached over, grabbed the report, crumpled it, and threw it into the fire. It withered into blackened ash. She settled back into her seat.

"All right, I admit it. Steven wasn't her father." She flashed a single, quick frown at her son. "There was no love between us. I wanted security for myself and Russell. Steven wanted a lovely young wife to parade around. As a matter of fact, Tabitha's birth worked out quite well, considering he couldn't get me pregnant. Same as his first wife. Seems the man had a low sperm count.

"With Tabitha's birth and adopting Russell, he was happy." She raised her chin. "I was a good and *faithful* wife while he was alive. Since Steven is deceased, her parentage is immaterial. Announcing my past indiscretion now will only cause some embarrassment and raise a bunch of manicured eyebrows."

"Then you better hope the trustees of Tabitha's estate and foundations don't think differently." That earned me a narrow-eyed glare.

Russell stirred, rubbed a hand across his forehead. "Okay. I mean, not okay. We'll deal with it. I'll contact our lawyers as soon as I get back. You also said you had information why—wait. Wait a minute." His face turned pale. He stared first at his mother, then at me.

"You're not…what you said…you're not implying…that my *mother* hired someone to, to *kill Tabitha*?"

No, she did it herself.

But as I gazed on that stricken face, I couldn't say it. I couldn't tell a thirty-eight-year-old man that his mother was the worst kind of predator. That she'd killed dozens to hide the truth. All to protect something as pathetic as her status. He'd eventually realize that on his own. So, I prevaricated.

"When your mother learned Tabitha was coming back to Omaha for treatment for her hemochromatosis, she undoubtedly panicked. There would be medical tests. Genetic tests," I said, keeping my attention focused on the most dangerous woman I knew. "That would ruin everything she'd worked for. She quickly threw together a plan to prevent it."

Russell's horrified eyes were locked on his mother. "That's why you didn't want me here," he finally managed. "Why you insisted I attend that stupid political brunch." His voice was strained almost past recognition.

"Which you should have done," she snapped. "Happy now?" She turned to me. "Do you think the police will believe you? You have no proof." She waved a hand toward the fire.

"I'm not going to the police," I said, pulling out my gun and laying it in my lap.

"You intend to shoot me?" Her voice was hard and tightly controlled.

"No. I intend to keep my throat intact." Russell made a garbled noise as I shifted the barrel toward Mrs. Chandler. Would he leap to his mother's defense? Would familial ties trump everything else?

"What do you intend to do then? Blackmail me? With what? Again, there's no proof."

She was watching me closely, her muscles coiled. A moment's distraction on my part was all she'd need.

"You've systematically eliminated all traces of Tabitha's DNA. Her boat, any lab work, and, of course, Tabitha herself. But…" I paused, smiled without humor. "There was a comb, with a longish hair, lying forgotten in a suitcase. Until recently."

Shock flashed in her eyes. Yep, hair was an excellent source of DNA. I caught a fleeting glimpse of claw tips and curled my finger around the trigger.

"You're lying, or you would have taken it to the police."

"That would only generate a long, nasty, legal battle with the most likely outcome being a simple infidelity judgement. The rest…you stand a good chance of walking away from due to legal shenanigans and because most people just aren't going to want to believe it."

"No police and no self-righteous vengeance. Why bother with this farce of a meeting then? To gloat? To show how smart you are? Are you actually planning to do anything?"

"I wanted to know if your son knew. If Russell helped you with any of it. Plainly, he didn't. As for me doing anything? Uh-uh. Not a frigging thing. But the person I gave the hair to? Your guess is as good as mine…especially after he matches half of that DNA to himself."

Mrs. Chandler went white.

"M-m-mother?" Russell's voice was a strained whisper.

I stood, keeping both attention and weapon on her. "I'll let your mother explain how her ex-lover has made his living for the past, oh, forty years or so. I'll see myself out."

I backed slowly around the corner of the house and most of the way to my car. Once inside, I locked the doors with a shaky hand and took a deep breath. That went better than I expected.

I did a quick three-point reversal and drove rapidly down their driveway, with copious glances in the rearview mirror. If Russell had been aware and willing to fight along-side his mother, I wouldn't have left there in one piece. As it was, I could still end up in pieces. A very vengeful wolf probably wouldn't stop at just ripping out my throat.

I pressed a little harder on the gas pedal.

***

I finished my current case Wednesday afternoon, did the paperwork, and plucked my jacket off the coatrack. Stopped in front of Diana's desk.

"Diana," I said tiredly, "please reschedule tomorrow's appointment for

272

some time next week. I'm going to take the rest of this week off."

She eyed me worriedly. "Should you make an appointment with Nate?"

Three days of hyper-alertness and little-to-no sleep had wreaked havoc on my appearance. "No. I just need some downtime and sleep." I was almost to the door when Diana called my name.

"Curt? Sometimes we have to accept that there are no answers," she said gently.

I nodded, gave her a small thank-you smile, and continued on out. Diana thought I was depressed over failing to find the killer. She believed it had fueled that embarrassing episode two weeks ago.

Nope. I had my answers. I was just waiting for the repercussions.

The drive to my apartment was uneventful, as was the tense walk from my parking spot to my apartment door. I put my key in the deadbolt. It wasn't locked. I slid my key into my pocket and my gun out of its holster. I threw the door open.

Blinked. Not who I expected, that's for sure.

Raynor Silverstone, sitting on my couch with my files spread in front of him.

"Standing in the doorway with a drawn weapon is bound to alarm your neighbors. Might even prompt a call to the police."

I used my foot to close the door and approached cautiously. "What are you doing here?" No sense asking how a long-time assassin got in.

"Satisfying curiosity, mostly," he said, looking back down. "I mean you no harm."

Tabitha's file lay open on his lap. Her picture from my bedroom was on the small table to his left. I hesitated, then re-holstered my gun. "Scotch?" I asked. At his nod, I retrieved two glasses and the unopened bottle from the kitchen. I'd been cutting back. Sitting across from him, I poured us both a generous amount and set the bottle and his glass on the coffee table between us. Settled back, letting him read about the daughter he'd never known. Never would.

"Cynthia Chandler has gone into seclusion and her son on an unannounced vacation," he said, without looking up.

I just bet they had. Especially Russell. How does one deal with learning your parent is so…vile?

"Have they? I haven't paid much attention to the news lately." I noted he'd laid a couple of papers beside Tabitha's picture. Craning my neck a bit, I recognized the one on top as the Delmarra report. I pointed to it.

"Are you planning on taking that? I don't have another copy." I had expected the one I'd made for Sunday's meeting to meet its demise.

He glanced over. "No, I have my own report."

From the lab he'd taken Tabitha's hair to. Had he silenced them as per Mrs. Chandler?

Silverstone read a few more pages, then closed the file. Laid it carefully on the table and picked up his glass. We sipped companionably, believe it or not, for several minutes.

He retrieved the report, giving Tabitha's picture a lingering look. Turning, he laid it down in front of me. "This is what made things clear?"

"Yes. It tied everything else we had together. But, legally, everything is circumstantial. It would be a very difficult case to win, assuming the city attorney didn't throw us out of his office for even suggesting it. Most wouldn't want to believe what has to be the worst of a person."

"That's why you approached me. You knew who I was. That's why you had the hair with you."

"Yes." I gripped my glass. "I want justice for Tabitha…for Marge…for all those that should be somewhere with their families or sharing drinks with a friend."

An eyebrow jerked upward and he took a sip. "Are we friends?"

"No."

He snorted. "Honest. I like you. Mostly because of this." Reaching over, he retrieved the other sheet and laid it on top of the report.

Our marriage certificate.

He tapped it gently. "This would have voided any existing will and entitled you to Tabitha's estate. You haven't told anyone. Why?"

I took a large swallow, the burn steadying me as I looked at her picture.

"I loved her," I said simply, staring at the carefree, happy moment in time. Her hair blowing in the wind, laughing at me as I snapped it. "Not her money, not her status or anything else. Her estate is better off as it is, helping others. I don't need it. I asked Marge not to release it after she found it."

He leaned back and propped his arm on the couch arm. I was too exhausted to squirm under his scrutiny.

Finally, he said, "You knew what coming to me could entail."

I did one of Marge's shoulder rolls. "I didn't think you'd appreciate your daughter being murdered any more than your brother."

That piece of information slid from guess to fact by the way Silverstone's eyes sharpened. Timewise, Otis Silverstone's murder happened about the same time his brother was rumored to go professional. Ray's debut was probably his brother's murderer. Maybe I shouldn't have admitted how much I knew about him. Chalk that *oops* up to tiredness and just not caring.

At least I stopped before calling him Wolfbane.

"You told me justice could be dangerous or vengeful. The dangerous part is true, as I keep expecting a reprisal. I don't care. There must be payment for all the lives she's destroyed, for all the devastated families. As there would be if we could prove it in court."

Soul-searching at the dawn of my plan had shown that I could live with what I was going to do. But this was my decision. My burden.

"I haven't told the others about this. I haven't told them about Tabitha's hair. I haven't told them that I've spoken with you or met with the Chandlers. By the way, Russell was completely unaware of his mother's doings. The guy was nearly catatonic with shock when I left them."

"An eye for an eye."

What? No. "Children should not pay for their parents' sins."

"*My* daughter did."

I stared into the pitiless eyes of a killer. Sweat beaded between my shoulder blades. "No," I said as calmly as I could, "she was killed by a woman determined to keep her secret at any cost. I want justice, not revenge."

Silence.

He drained the last of his drink and stood. "Get some sleep. You look like road kill."

Numb, I locked the door behind him. Leaving everything else, I gathered Tabitha's picture to my chest and stumbled toward my bed. Would justice triumph over revenge? Whatever the coming days brought, I'd need a clear mind to face them.

Epilogue

"Well, Tabitha, it's been another year."

I squatted, making room for the flowers I'd brought. A large arrangement covered two-thirds of her headstone. They were fresh, despite the heat of an August day. I must have just missed Ray Silverstone. I hadn't seen him since he walked out of my apartment last October, and that was perfectly fine by me.

"It went a little bit better this year," I said, gently patting the sun-warmed marble. "No Scottish holiday required to make it through the days." Although I had been aware of Diana's close scrutiny for the past week. "I still miss you, visit with you in my dreams."

I gazed around. It was a nice place. Plenty of trees, winding paths, and benches for people to sit on and reminisce. Or talk to the headstones, as I'd found myself doing lately.

"The past months have been busy. Mr. Olineo has finally gotten all the legal stuff straightened out and I received my first disbursement deposit this month."

Five months ago, an anonymous busybody—*thanks, Ray*—had mailed copies of our marriage certificate to both the Omaha-Herald and to Mr. Olineo, Tabitha's lawyer and trust executor. The resulting hoopla—not to mention the Chandler family's shock—had me hiding out in Angie's apartment for almost two weeks, as Nate and Diana were known associates. Mr. Olineo, while commending me on my 'keep everything as is' attitude, informed me, sourly, that it couldn't as it put Tabitha's estate back in probate.

After a lot of legal wrangling, we managed to keep things pretty much how Tabitha wanted it, although the legal underpinnings all had to be reworked. The two main differences were that I now received a life-long monthly stipend and owned twenty-five percent of Chandler Import. Personally, I think Mr. Olineo was happy to shove those shares and dealing with the company onto me.

"Not a whole lot of new happenings. PI business has been steady—oh! Angie is mulling over changing professions. She'll be a business owner, if she can ever decide on what line."

A shadow fell across the grave as Russell Chandler stepped up beside me. He carried a small bunch of flowers and a small book. He gave me a hello nod and added his flowers to the grouping. We stood for a time, thinking our own thoughts as the daylight began to wane.

He stirred, turned to me. "This is for you," he said, handing me the book. Not a book; a diary.

"It was Tabitha's. She started it that last year she was at home. The usual stuff: home and school and…other. She wanted to study languages," he said, eyes focused on the headstone. "She wanted to be an interpreter at the League of Nations. Mother was pressuring her to marry—which I didn't know. Two of the 'candidates' Tabitha had listed were thirty or more years her senior."

I appreciated his disgusted tone. "Where did you find it?"

"Among my mother's things."

Cynthia Chandler had died back in February when her car careened down a steep incline in the Loess Hills. Icy road and bad luck were the assumed culprits. She was thrown clear of her vehicle but died from blunt force trauma when her head hit a rock. Or vice-versa. I'm sure Russell knew as well as I did that it wasn't the freak accident everyone was touting. But we'd never spoken of it, and he had quietly buried his mother beside her first husband in the Greenbaum plot despite the Chandler family's protests.

"Tabitha doesn't say it in so many words," Russell continued, "but she was lonely, and I didn't know that either. I always thought…guess it doesn't matter now. Her last entry is a debate about which of the two colleges she's planning to apply to. It's two days before her nineteenth birthday," he added in a neutral tone.

Realization dawned. "Your mother found it, read it. That was what their big fight was about." *I expected her to behave as a Chandler and as my daughter.*

Russell nodded, turned to leave. Paused. "Board meeting is in two nights. You need to be there as changes are going to be voted in. Some restructuring, too."

"Why?"

"Come and find out."

A childish taunt deserved a childish response, so I stuck my tongue out at his receding back. His now three-fourths ownership trounced mine. Not that I gave a flying frog, but he wouldn't have mentioned it unless there was a reason. Fine. I'd go. I hadn't found a way to shoehorn those shares back under Mr. Olineo and the Trust's aegis yet.

I tucked the diary close to my chest.

Why had Tabitha never chased her dream after leaving home? Something her mother had done or threatened to do? Had her mother slipped and told Tabitha the truth during that last heated exchange? Or was it something entirely different that caused the shadows I'd seen in Tabitha's eyes? I sighed, filing those questions away in my *will never know* folder.

Which reminded me that I had another item to share.

"Marge and Mrs. Calvert's files are in the freezer, too," I said, resuming my one-sided conversation. "Lieutenant Sinclair would have preferred all your cases got resolved properly. But without solid, credible, *useable* information, the odds of that ever happening are close to nil."

Still, he wasn't too upset. I knew he considered Mrs. Chandler's death a form of karma. As did Nate and Angie. I had passed the secret of Marge's killer to her. I did not disabuse them of their belief, just smiled and nodded in agreement.

Soft lighting came on along the footpaths. Time to go.

I brushed a last caress across the marble top. "I remember you," I murmured. Turned, and walked away into the deepening twilight.

Acknowledgements

I would like to thank the following individuals whose time and/or expertise made this book the best it could be: Captain Ron Chapman (retired, Orange County Sheriff's Office, FL), Jack Gryder, and Ray Rhamey.

Titles by R. D. Chapman

Blurring Reality Series

Shattered Reality
Blurring Reality
Tangled Reality
Reality Kicked

D'Accio Investigations Series

At Any Cost

About the Author

R. D. Chapman has been an avid reader all her life. A retired empty-nester living quietly in Nebraska with her husband, she draws on a lifetime of experience ranging from cook to software developer to craft characters and stories. She writes in a blend of SF&F, urban fantasy, and mystery with a smidgen of humor and romance. When not writing, she loves spending time with the three Rs: Reading, cRocheting, and Relaxing.

* * * * *

Thank you for reading *At Any Cost*. If you have enjoyed this book, please consider leaving a review, as they are essential to expanding my sales and readership. Even a few simple lines will help. Thanks!